NOVEL

# 1

# Magic User
## Reborn in Another World as a Max Level Wizard

WRITTEN BY
**Mikawa Souhei**

ILLUSTRATED BY
**Ryota-H**

**RANK 9 SPELL**
*METEOR*

Eight bright lights cut through the blue sky, raining down upon the twisted valley filled with daemons.

Sedam picked out a location for our camp and quickly gave directions to the other party members. When playing a TTRPG, setting up camp takes little more than a word or two, but it turned out to be a lot of work.

NOVEL
# 1

# Magic User
## Reborn in Another World
## as a Max Level Wizard

WRITTEN BY
**Mikawa
Souhei**

ILLUSTRATED BY
**Ryota-H**

Seven Seas

Seven Seas Entertainment

Lake Ryuse

Lawful Way

Relis City

Lawful Way

Mt. Farsight

Eastern Ryuse Region
Sedia Continent

MAGIC USER: REBORN IN ANOTHER WORLD
AS A MAX LEVEL WIZARD VOLUME 1

MAGIC USER Vol.1
TRPG de sodateta mahotsukai wa isekai demo saikyo datta.
by MIKAWA SOUHEI / Ryota-H

Original Japanese edition published in 2017 by
GENTOSHA COMICS Inc.
English translation rights arranged worldwide with
GENTOSHA COMICS Inc. through Digital Catapult Inc., Tokyo.

Seven Seas press and purchase enquiries can be sent to
Marketing Manager Lianne Sentar at press@gomanga.com.
Information requiring the distribution and purchase of
digital editions is available from Digital Manager CK Russell
at digital@gomanga.com.

Follow Seven Seas Entertainment online at
sevenseasentertainment.com.

TRANSLATION: Jordan Rousey
ADAPTATION: J.P. Sullivan
COVER DESIGN: KC Fabellon
INTERIOR LAYOUT & DESIGN: Clay Gardner
PROOFREADER: Peter Adrian Behravesh, Stephanie Cohen
LIGHT NOVEL EDITOR: Nibedita Sen
PREPRESS TECHNICIAN: Rhiannon Rasmussen-Silverstein
PRODUCTION MANAGER: Lissa Pattillo
MANAGING EDITOR: Julie Davis
ASSOCIATE PUBLISHER: Adam Arnold
PUBLISHER: Jason DeAngelis

ISBN: 978-1-64505-180-0
Printed in Canada
First Printing: January 2020
10 9 8 7 6 5 4 3 2 1

# TABLE OF CONTENTS

# Chapter 1

**"B**E THE HERO of your own adventure!"

When I was a student, those words captured my imagination. I must have spent hours and hours playing tabletop role-playing games. Honestly, there were plenty of times when I wished more than anything for a chance to become one of the heroes laid out on my character sheets—the personas that I spent so much time role-playing.

But I never seriously thought that wish could ever come true.

Least of all at an age when both heroes and adventures had long since lost their appeal.

··✝··

I would describe myself as a forty-two-year-old bachelor, gainfully employed at a decent-sized company, a resident of a moderately sized city in one of Japan's more rural prefectures.

There's nothing particularly unique about my looks or abilities, though I think I'm at least average by most measures. Despite that, unfortunately, there was never a time when I thought marriage was anywhere on the horizon. If asked about my hobbies, I could only say I enjoyed playing TTRPGs. When I was younger, I even helped organize conventions. However, I almost never found time to play once I joined the workforce.

But that average life of mine came to an abrupt end.

The last thing I remember was finishing up some unpaid overtime, returning to my apartment, and opening the door.

After that, I found myself in an empty void. I was unable to perceive anything above or below me—not even my own body. The only thing I was aware of was my consciousness, floating in empty space.

*I thought I had at least another twenty years before my time was up...*

Though I can't explain how, I realized that I was dead.

I thought of my work colleagues and friends, my relatives and neighbors, my unfinished work, my unread novels and tabletop sourcebooks, as well as my backlog of video games, and I felt the loss of all of those things envelop me in the void.

*Well, it's not like there's anything I can do about it now.*

Looking back on my life, there wasn't really much I could boast about, but there was nothing I was particularly ashamed of, either. *All in all, it wasn't so bad*, I thought. *It's unfortunate it had to end so soon, but what's done is done.* Gradually, I accepted my condition and made peace with my passing.

After I'd already lost my sense of the passage of time, something spoke to me.

"I am one of the Watchers."

I could not see the source of that voice, nor hear it, but its words and intent were conveyed to my consciousness all the same.

"Henceforth, you will be transported to a space that exists beyond the limits of your plane of origin—what you might call a parallel world."

"I'll be...transported to another world?" I asked.

Hearing that phrase out loud felt strange, but oddly nostalgic.

"According to a search I ran on this dimension's information substrate, 'transported to another world' is indeed the most adequate phrase to describe the phenomenon."

"Well... Huh."

Confused, I wasn't able to give more than a half-hearted response, but some part of me had already accepted whatever was in store. There was no reason to be frightened. After all, I was already dead.

Not to mention, I was a big fan of otherworldly stories like *A Connecticut Yankee in King Arthur's Court* and the John Carter series, to name a couple of the classics. I remembered hearing the genre was experiencing a sort of revival recently, too.

*But those were just stories, fiction—or at least, I thought that was the case. Now the same thing seems to be happening to me.*

"Um... Once I'm transported to this other world, what exactly is going to happen to me?"

"I will provide you with a body suitable for your new life there, so, if you would, please provide me with the information required for its creation. Your destination can be described—using the terms familiar to you—as a fantasy world of the so-called 'sword and sorcery' subgenre, so it would be best if the information you provide is well-adapted to that premise."

"A new body...in a fantasy world?"

The first thing that came to mind was a character I'd made for a western tabletop RPG called *Dungeons & Braves*. I'd played that one passionately during my student days. Over seven years and across several campaign scenarios, I'd raised this character to the maximum level allowed in the game. He was the character I felt the most attached to: the great magic user, Geo Margilus.

"I have completed a search on your character. Using the information contained in the rulebooks, sourcebooks, scenario notebooks, and character sheets found in your room, I will reproduce the physical and mental abilities of 'Geo Margilus,' as well as his possessions. However, in order to prevent any dissociation, which might negatively affect your state of mind, no changes will be made to your physical appearance."

In other words, not only did this self-proclaimed Watcher read my mind, it also looked through all my notebooks filled with the delusions and fantasies of my youth.

*This is incredibly embarrassing...*

"The creation of Geo Margilus has been successfully completed," the watcher proclaimed.

While my disembodied self was writhing in shame, the Watcher finished its work. I began to regain the sense of having a physical body.

I was dressed in a black robe, a knapsack over my shoulder and a staff in one hand.

My physical appearance was the same as before. I still had the black hair, dark eyes, and plain face of an average Japanese man, so it felt like I'd simply put on a costume. However, I could sense more had changed than met the eye. *This is the physical strength and lightness of body of someone in their twenties*, I thought, but I should clarify: I felt *more* energy than I'd had in *my* twenties, as I hated sports and was an indoor-dwelling otaku.

"Are there any issues with your consciousness or memories?" the Watcher asked.

As I searched the corners of my mind, I discovered an intuitive understanding of my character Geo Margilus's magic abilities, as well as an inventory of his magic items and a grasp of how to use them. Everything I had worked out together with the game master and written down in my notebooks as background information was now ingrained in my mind as knowledge. Despite all the new information, I could still access the memories of the forty-two years of my previous life without any problems.

"Everything seems to be fine," I replied. "But you weren't kidding. I really am a character out of a TTRPG..."

My character, Geo Margilus, was a Level 36 magic user. By *Dungeons & Braves*'s Master rules, Level 36 is the highest level any character can reach. When I remembered that fact, *after becoming him*, I was assaulted by a mix of anxiety and excitement.

*Wait, is this really okay? What have I gotten myself into?*

Even among fans of the genre, *D&B* has a reputation for being a bygone relic. What most people associate with *D&B* are parties of weak characters, only 3 to 5 hit points apiece, struggling—and failing—to survive, as they explore unexciting dungeons infested with rats, bats, goblins, and hardly anything else. This may be hard for those used to contemporary TTRPGs to believe, as more emphasis is now put on colorful characters and intricate plots, but that *is* a fairly accurate description of gameplay in *D&B*.

However, that description only applies to the *Basic* ruleset. As in-game characters mature, the nature of their adventures changes dramatically.

*D&B* has four core sets of rules: Basic, Expert, Companion, and Master, with each set corresponding to a range of ascending character levels. Once *D&B*'s Master ruleset is in use, you can expect each character to be the head of a guild or the leader of a country, for adventures to lead into space or to alternate dimensions, and for fights to be historic battles with demons or gods. Depending on the circumstances, characters may go on an adventure to *become* a god.

In order to reach the level required for *D&B*'s Master rules, one must play a character through a minimum of one hundred campaign scenarios. I spent seven years raising Geo to his final state, and his abilities—powerful enough to hold sway over the fate of the world—reflected that.

"Having done all this for me, what is it you want me to do?" I asked.

"Once you are transported, we will not direct you, nor interfere with your actions."

*You're telling me that after you go out of your way to transport me to another world, I'm supposed to do whatever I want? There must be some ulterior motive at play,* I thought, trying to read between the lines of what this self-proclaimed Watcher told me.

"This isn't something, where—for instance—it's all well and good that I've become a wizard, but Geo's magic doesn't work in the other world, right?"

*In that case, this wouldn't be a portal fantasy, but a dark sci-fi comedy.*

"The magic in your character's game is fundamentally at odds with the principles of the other world, but an implementation of it is still possible within the confines of that world's natural laws. The same applies to the details of your physical strength and abilities, as well as your game-derived knowledge."

"Are you sure about this? I might throw the whole world into disarray."

"If that is your wish, we would have no objection."

*Well, I would!*

There once was a time I'd wished I could be Geo, but the idea that I, a man in his forties, should have the energy and drive to take some grand action to save or destroy the world with Geo's powers was just asking too much of me. Of course, if this had happened to me twenty years earlier, that would be a different story.

"Don't you think Geo is a little too strong? I have a feeling a Level 6 Cleric would be much more reasonable... But then again,

Geo *is* the character I'm most used to," I muttered, weighing alternatives and backpedaling.

On the other hand, I couldn't deny the rush of excitement I felt inside me over this strange turn of events. Here was a chance to be the hero of the many adventures I'd played with my friends around the table in my youth.

Normally, I wouldn't have had the time to abandon my work and go play around—let alone visit another world—but at the end of the day, I only had this chance because I was dead.

*I guess I could think of it as an early retirement?* Regardless of whether I spent however many years I had left in Japan or another world, it wasn't a bad deal, as long as I didn't have trouble feeding myself. *Though, if I got the chance, it would be nice if I could eat good food every now and then, maybe go to some hot springs, read some interesting books... If I could fit in some roleplaying, that would just be icing on the cake...*

Let's be honest. By the end of my conversation with the Watcher, I'd forgotten all the lessons I'd learned from life. I was over the moon, painting fantastic futures in my mind.

"Well then, I shall now send you to the other world. For your reference, your destination is the continent of Sedia, as it is called in the language of its people," said the Watcher, and that was the last I heard before my consciousness was cut short.

"I don't know what I was expecting, but it sure wasn't this..."

When I came to, I found myself in a square prison cell.

I sat there staring at the rust-ridden bars of an iron cell door. The other three walls were made of stone. The ceiling was high, and there was a hole about three meters from the ground to let in light. In the cell was a rag that could maybe pass for a blanket, and a hole in the ground in place of a toilet. That was the extent of my newfound world. To top it all off, my wrists were locked in wooden stocks. Beyond the bars, my cell faced a similar one, but it was empty.

"Talk about a hot start..."

"Hot start" is a term used in Japanese TTRPG scenario-writing for campaign hooks that force the players into some kind of incident to start them off *in media res*. There was no better phrase to describe the predicament I was in.

"If there's a game master behind all this, they sure are mean-spirited," I said, taking in my surroundings and putting what information I had together.

*The best candidate for game master is probably that so-called Watcher*, I thought, my elation from before gone without a trace.

The Watcher told me I was free to do as I wished, but I couldn't bring myself to take those words at face value. No one would go out of their way to do something so elaborate for no reason.

"It's around noon, I suspect..." I looked at the light streaming in from the opening in the wall above.

I used the light to inspect my person. I was wearing pants and a long-sleeved shirt. I was barefoot. My specially crafted robe, with its extraordinarily large +5 Defense bonus, was nowhere to be found, nor was my staff, nor my Infinity Bag, which contained my spellbook. All the equipment I'd obtained by the end of Geo's long adventures was gone.

"What did I do to get thrown off this metaphorical cliff? First I die, then I'm thrown into another dimension and turned into an RPG character..."

I felt exhausted. So much for feeling twenty again.

I slumped against a wall, holding my head in my hands (as well as I could). *Has anyone found my body yet?* Preparations for next week's meeting had been left unfinished. I preoccupied myself with thoughts of my previous life. Rather self-serving, if I do say so myself.

I let out a long sigh.

"I really was transported to another world, wasn't I?"

After I spent a few minutes staring off into space, the wheels in my head finally started to turn.

I took some deep breaths to calm myself. Each time I exhaled, I felt a bit of optimism return to me. Yes, I'd died, but there was nothing I could do about it now, nor was there any way I could return to Japan. I needed to accept that and focus on what lay ahead.

Fortunately, I'd come to this world as a Level 36 magic user. It would be quicker to count the few things I couldn't do, compared to all I *could* do.

"If I just use a spell or two, I... Wait! That's right! I don't have my spellbook, do I?!"

Remembering the absence of my equipment, I felt the blood drain from my face. If I didn't have my Infinity Bag, where I kept my various magic items and other treasures, that meant I didn't have my spellbook, either.

"If I don't have my spellbook... Yeah, I'm in trouble."

Let me explain. Nothing is more important to a wizard than his spellbook.

In many games, new and old, magic users have magic points, or MP, and use those points to cast magic. However, that's not the way magic works in *D&B*. In *D&B*, a magic user must read their spellbook every morning, and hold any spells they plan to use that day in their mind. This is called "charging" the spell. But once a charged spell is used, it is gone. It vanishes from the magic user's consciousness and cannot be used again. That is, not until it's charged anew during another morning's spellbook reading session.

*If I don't have any spells charged right now, and all of my magic items are gone, then I'm nothing more than another ordinary person.*

Despite having spent forty-two years as an ordinary person, I felt myself panic.

"Come on. Do I have any spells charged?"

While I had no experience actually casting spells, I tried going through the motions of remembering something like a math formula, and after some poking around my brain...

"That's it!"

It felt as if I had come across some isolated energy source in my mind. Instinctively, I understood the energy was a charged spell. The incantation method, the steps I needed to take to cast the spell—it all became clear to me. As the Watcher had suggested, the knowledge of Geo Margilus was indeed ingrained within my mind.

"What I need to do is get out of here, and, at the very least, recover my spellbook. But who put me in here in the first place?"

While escaping was important, before I made a move, I needed to get a grasp on my surroundings. There had to be someone—or something—that had stolen my equipment and imprisoned me. Odds were, they were still nearby.

"Should I at least cast a spell to break out of this cell?"

In *D&B*, the biggest headache for magic users is selecting which spells to charge each day and deciding how to use each of those limited charges. Geo was a max-level magic user (and, by extension, so was I), which meant he could charge up to eighty-one spells a day—nine for each of the nine ranks of spells. Of the spells I considered casting, the obvious choice was *Wizard Key*, which would allow me to open the lock on the cell door or free my hands from the stocks, but there were several other spells that would also be useful if I planned to escape.

"On second thought...I should prioritize my safety."

It took me a while, but I finally decided on the first spell I would cast: *Invincibility*. *Invincibility* was a Rank 9 spell, making it one of the most difficult to cast in-game. It completely nullified all weapon-based physical attacks and any magic-based attack of Rank 3 or below, for up to six hours. If things took a turn for the worse, its effect would be indispensable.

"This *is* going to work, right?"

Everything I needed to do to cast the spell was already clear in my mind. The method was something I'd come up with together with the game master, based on *D&B* rules, over twenty years ago. It was needlessly complex. *I have to hand it to the Watcher*, I thought. *I'm surprised they were able to pick up on and understand the mess of scribbles in those old notebooks.*

"Here goes nothing..."

For the first time in my life, I began to do the thing I had role-played hundreds of times before.

I began to cast a spell.

Magic User

Reborn in Another World
as a Max Level Wizard

# Chapter 2

"**O**PEN, Gate of Magic."

I took a deep breath and closed my eyes. I was about to attempt to dive deep within myself, beyond the depths of my instincts, beyond even my subconscious, into the chaotic realm where I would release the spell's energy. I regulated my breathing and focused my mind.

First, I constructed the image of an inner world within myself. It was a space shrouded in darkness, and there I was, standing inside of it.

It is a surprisingly difficult task to clearly reconstruct an image of oneself in one's mind. But in this case, it took no time at all before I was looking at a copy of myself, wizard's robe and all.

In fact, I felt that my thought processes were running abnormally quick. If I were to think of my brain as a computer, it felt like someone had upgraded my CPU and RAM. *This must be Geo Margilus's high ability scores at work*, I thought.

Carefully, I took the image of myself standing in the cell and the image I'd created of myself in the inner world and brought them together. Once the lines between them had blurred, and my physical self had melted into my imaginary self, I slowly opened my eyes.

*Darkness.*

No longer could I see the cell I was standing in. Now I was inside my inner world. I raised my right hand and formed the image of a lantern that would light the darkness in my mind. The lantern immediately formed in my hand, lighting my surroundings with a deep red tinge.

"This is amazing... It feels so real... Wh-whoa! No! Stop!"

The weight and heat of the lantern, the smell of the oil... It was just so real. It shocked me for a moment. That moment of shock—or rather, disbelief—had sent my inner world reeling. It felt as if I were being pulled hard from all sides, and it left my stomach churning.

*Deep breaths: In... Out... In... Out...*

In a flustered panic, I first focused on restoring order to my breathing. The swaying and disturbances finally gave way to calm.

"That was a close one..."

I was still only in my inner world, so even if my images of the world and self broke down, the worst that could happen was that I would make myself terribly sick. If I had let those images fail later in the process, there was a chance I could have put myself in a coma. *Who the hell came up with this, anyway?* (I did.)

"Reveal your form to me."

Both my physical self and my self-image chanted the second verse of the spell in unison. When I raised my lantern to light the way ahead, the gate appeared in front of me.

"So, this is the magic gate."

The gate was three meters tall and appeared to be made of stone. It was inscribed with countless ominous engravings, which only emphasized its magical nature. This gate connected my inner world and the chaotic realm. It served as the way in and the way out, but it also symbolized a protective barrier between myself and that plane.

What lay beyond the gate was still part of my mind, but at the same time, it was indeed another realm. If I were to explain it in psychological terms, the chaotic realm was not unlike the collective unconscious: within but beyond.

The magic gate opened without a sound, revealing stone steps that spiraled downward in a counterclockwise flow. By the lantern's light, I slowly descended the steps. Along with the magic gate itself, this staircase and adjoining structures had taken many long years of training for Geo to construct in his mind. (According to the backstory I wrote for him, anyway.)

If any part of the image of the gate, walls, or staircase in my mind was inadequate, and my conscious self-image were to touch a part of the chaotic realm directly, my consciousness would be swallowed up by its roiling disorder, and I would lose my mind.

But there seemed to be no cause for alarm. My surroundings were built by the imagination of a Level 36 magic user, after all. From the hardness and coldness and coloration of the stone walls, to the flow of air and even the smells, there was no way to distinguish this world from reality.

I wasn't counting steps, but after descending a couple flights' worth of stairs, I came upon the first landing. There was a door and a plate above it which read: "The Beginner's Spellbook Archive." *If I just wanted to practice*, I thought, *it might not be a bad idea to try casting a Rank 1 spell, but right now the spell I want to cast is farther down*. I walked past the landing and continued down the stairs, past the second landing, the fourth, the seventh, the eighth...

Finally, I reached the ninth landing: The Grand Wizard's Spellbook Archive. This was where the Rank 9 spells were stored. The chaos just beyond the walls was palpable. In a sense, this imaginary structure I inhabited was but a temporary space, forcing order upon the formless sea of energy that was the chaos. If any of these walls were to break down, that chaos would flood in, and both this space and my self would be lost to it.

Nervously, I gulped and raised my lantern to the door. It opened like the magic gate before—without a sound. Beyond the door was an archive room filled with giant bookshelves. If I had to pin it down, the floorplan of the room was similar to that of an elementary school classroom.

Upon entering the room, I saw nine elevated bookrests immediately in front of me, each of them holding a thick tome. Every book represented a charged spell. While ordinary bookrests are tilted toward the reader, these lay flat and level, like a table. This was because the bookrests served yet another important, but less obvious, purpose.

I looked at and confirmed the titles of the books: *Time Stop*, *Meteor, Create Monster: Any*, and... *Invincibility*.

I found the spell I was looking for and touched it lightly. It appeared to have over a thousand pages, but all I needed was one.

The book opened by itself, as if it were alive. It turned to the page I was looking for of its own accord.

Both my physical self and self-image chanted the remainder of the spell.

"For the next six hours, my body will be covered by an invisible barrier that will nullify all weapon-based physical attacks and any magic-based attack of Rank 3 or below."

The spell itself was more or less the same as the description of the spell in the *D&B* rulebook. In a way, it was like computer code, detailing the target and effects of the spell. After I read the spell, the book shone brightly and began to change its form, shrinking until it fit into the palm of my hand.

When the transformation was complete, I was holding two ten-sided dice—one white, one black. With the two dice, I needed to roll an activation check. Taken together, the two dice represented a number between 1 and 100. If I were to roll a 100, a result with one percent probability, my attempt to cast the spell would result in a so-called fumble, and the spell would not activate. This activation check is not required by *D&B* rules, but the game master at the time suggested we include it, in his words, "to make the game more thrilling."

"Yeah," I grumbled, "probably shouldn't have gone along with that one..."

I tossed the dice onto the bookrest.

This was why the bookrests were flat. There needed to be a place to roll any dice the spell checks required. The sound of rolling dice brought back memories. I looked to see how they landed.

The white die read 0 and the black die 9. The white represented the tens' place and the black the ones' place, so the result was 09/100. I shivered a little. I'd almost fumbled.

"*Invincibility.*"

With that final word, the spell was cast. The two dice shone bright, and then their forms stretched and shot upward, all at once turned to energy sent out into reality. The bookrest I stood at was empty. Eight unused spells remained.

I exited the Grand Wizard's Spellbook Archive and climbed up the spiral staircase. There really was no need to—after I cast the spell, all I needed to do was cut the link between my self-image and physical self—but I decided to play it safe, and waited until I had left the chaotic realm and was back in my inner world. Then I closed my eyes and severed the link.

"Phew... I made it."

When I opened my eyes, I was back inside the prison cell.

I looked at my hands, still locked in wooden stocks, and the rest of my body. I could just barely perceive something like a thin, white, misty layer around me—a barrier. I had to squint to see it myself, so I doubted anyone else would be able to notice it. To check, I tried feeling the barrier near my abdomen. It felt cool to the touch.

In short, the spell was activated.

"I really was able to cast a spell..."

*It felt like I spent an hour trying to cast that spell*, I thought, but I knew it couldn't have taken more than ten seconds. Even if I tried to rush, it would still take ten seconds. The rules were crystal clear.

*I won't argue with the fact that it makes sense in the context of a game, but the fact that casting a spell makes me completely defenseless for ten seconds means I'll have to be really careful how I use them.*

I let out a sigh of relief, feeling the pent-up stress melting out of me. I then spent another few minutes staring into space.

But this time, my peace was broken by someone else. A rabble of footsteps and conversing voices were headed my way.

"Hey, you! Get up. You're coming with us!"

"It's time for your questioning, pal! You're gonna talk!"

Three men shouted at me from the other side of the cell's bars, wearing what looked like dirty leather armor.

*Whoa... They're all white,* I thought. *Wait, that's not what's important. They're... What's the word again?*

*Bandits. That's it.*

One of the first things I noticed was that I could understand what the men were saying, even if the words weren't pleasant. Yet at the same time, I realized that it was in a language I'd never heard before. *The Watcher must have downloaded knowledge of their language into my memories.*

"I said get up!" one of the bandits shouted. "Come on out of there!"

"Hurry up, idiot!" shouted another.

"Snap out of it!" shouted the third.

The three men making a ruckus on the other side of the bars all had either blond or brown hair, and by their facial structures and general build, they seemed like they were of European descent. None of them looked like they had bathed in a while, and all three were armed, carrying a variety of axes and swords.

It wasn't as if I had seen any in real life before, but taking what I knew from games and manga, these guys were definitely bandits. If they appeared as characters in a story, one might be tempted to dismiss them as small fry, but seeing them face to face, they looked far more dangerous than any punk you might find on the streets of Japan. *If this truly is a world of swords and sorcery, these bandits have probably fought and killed before.*

I kept quiet. Up until that moment, the threat of violence had never once been a factor in my life. The bloodthirsty aura of these bandits threatened to consume me entirely. I couldn't bring myself to move.

"Can't do *anything* by yourself, can you?"

Apparently realizing I couldn't open the cell from the inside, one of the bandits unlocked the door and walked in.

"Um... I—" Before I could say anything more, the bandit punched me in the stomach. Immediately, I yelped in pain.

And through that pain, I suddenly realized my mistake. *Invincibility* was a spell that nullified damage from weapons and some forms of magic. Nowhere in the description of its effects did it offer any defense against a bare fist.

"I said come on!" the bandit growled.

As I cowered, all the air forced out of my lungs, the three bandits pulled me out of the cell. As I was dragged along a short hallway, I saw, out of the corner of my eye, a young woman locked in one of the other cells.

For an instant, our eyes met, but neither of us were in any position to speak.

"Don't worry, we'll get to you once we're finished with him!" one of the bandits crowed. "We'll have plenty of time to get to know each other then! Ha ha ha!"

I heard the woman let out a scream, but I was still in a state of panic. Forget helping her—I couldn't even help myself.

"This way!"

The bandits took me through a door at the end of the hall, which led outside into a large courtyard bounded by thick stone walls. On the other end of the courtyard stood a stone tower. As I trudged toward the center of the courtyard, I found another group of bandits already waiting there. They laughed and jeered at the sight of me.

"Hey! It's the fake sorcerer!"

"C'mon, show us a magic trick! Why don't you try and conjure up a way out?!"

"Better yet, how about you use your sorcery to dig your own grave?!"

*Fake sorcerer?* I thought. *What's that all about?* Unable to come to any sort of answer, I was forced to my knees when we reached the center of the courtyard.

Groaning, I tried to make sense of my surroundings. I knew what sort of place this was. It was some kind of fortress, or castle—the bandits' hideout, probably. It was just the kind of place you would expect to encounter in a game. Maybe I would have been able to enjoy it from a more distant perspective, but the way things were, I certainly wasn't having any fun.

"Jargle, sir!" I heard one of the bandits say.

They held me down for several minutes before a man in robes appeared from the tower, carrying a staff in either hand. He had the sunken cheeks, long moustache, and high-bridged nose of a man easily annoyed. It seemed the one in charge of this fortress was not a bandit chief, but an evil sorcerer.

"Who are you?" Jargle suddenly screeched. "Who are you, to have such an incredible staff as this?! Who did you steal this from?! How did you come across this, and those other materia?!"

Jargle rattled off his questions without leaving me space to answer. Upon closer inspection, I realized one of the staves he was holding was my own Staff of Wizardry. That staff was a powerful magic item I'd crafted in commemoration of Geo reaching Level 36. It had cost me half his fortune to make.

"I, uh... I am but a humble magician," I said, stumbling over my words. "My name is Geo Margilus. That staff is a personal possession of mine."

I almost said my real name but caught myself. *That's right*, I thought. *I'm in another world. No one here cares about my former status as a gainfully employed Japanese citizen. None of the laws or morals of that safe nation will come to my aid now.*

"Magician? Do you mean to say you're a sorcerer? Don't you try to fool me! You have no mana! There's not a drop of magic in your veins! You could never be a sorcerer."

"Huh?" I said, confused. *I have no mana? What does he mean by that?*

"Enough with your nonsense," Jargle shouted. "Tell me who you really are!"

Before I could respond, one of the bandits kicked me in the stomach. I doubled over in agony.

"Ha ha ha! What a pathetic little wimp!"

"You're gonna have to do better than that to fool us!"

My mind went blank from the pain. In all my forty-two years, I'd never been subject to this level of violence before. But even more frightening than the violence was their laughter. No one with even the slightest whisper of a conscience could laugh that way.

"While I sense no mana in this staff," Jargle said, a touch of doubt in his voice, "it is clearly materia!"

Jargle swung the staff in his left hand—my wizard's staff—and with a flash, bolts of lightning struck the ground between us, followed immediately by an explosion of thunder.

The lightning and thunder were gone as quick as they had come, but the shock wave they created was enough to throw the three bandits who had brought me there off their feet. They cried out in fear and confusion; the other bandits watching from a distance looked dumbfounded.

"What the hell was that?"

"I've never seen sorcery like that before..."

*Damn it*, I thought. *That must have been the lightning spell charged in my wizard's staff!*

In *D&B*, as long as you equip a magic item, you intuitively know how to use it, so that part didn't surprise me. *But he said he sensed no mana in the staff... What does that mean?* I tried to wrap my head around what he was saying, but my thoughts were paralyzed with pain and fear. I couldn't focus.

"How can there be materia without mana?!" Jargle shouted. "Did those fools in the Faction of the Wise develop this?! Tell me what you know!"

"I have no idea what you're—ugh!"

Before I could finish my sentence, the gang of three bandits started kicking and punching me anew. If nothing else, Jargle and these three were all on the same wavelength.

"Hmph... You underestimate *me*, the great sorcerer Jargle? Insolent fool."

"No, I just... Gurgh..."

It took all the strength I could muster just to withstand the kicking and shoving from that gang of three, but I must have struck a nerve. Jargle commanded the bandits to drag me to my feet, and as they held me still, he lifted his right hand—the one with his own staff—toward me.

"*Icia Bolza!*"

As Jargle shouted those words, something emerged from the tip of his staff and shot into my shoulder.

"G-gyaaahh!!!" I screamed.

When I looked at my shoulder, burning with pain, I saw a thick shard of ice protruding from it.

*Magic! He used magic to shoot an ice arrow at me!*

*But if he used magic, why didn't my Invincibility spell work?! It's supposed to nullify magic below Rank 3! Did he use a higher-ranked spell?!*

"How do you like the taste of real sorcery? If you don't want to be turned into an icicle, you'd better start telling the truth!"

"That's our Jargle!"

"Show him who's boss!"

I could tell Jargle and the others were still taunting me, but I couldn't understand what they were saying. The pain I felt from the ice arrow was on another level compared to the blunt force of the bandits' kicks and punches. This pain clawed its way into the depths of my consciousness. Subject to more suffering and violence than I had ever experienced, all that filled my mind was fear...and anger.

*I don't want to hurt anymore. Am I going to die? I don't want to die. Someone help me! I don't want to be here anymore. Why did this have to happen to me? I haven't done anything!*

"What's your next move?"

Suddenly a voice cut through my tangled thoughts like a knife—the familiar voice of my friend and game master.

Even if it was only for an instant, the pain and confusion ebbed enough to allow my mind to reboot.

*That's right. I've gotten out of situations like this countless times before!* Admittedly, all of those times were in the context of a game, but I pushed that snide qualification out of my mind.

From that moment on, my brain kicked into overdrive. I ignored the pain and insults and everything else that got in my way.

In response to the first-ever real threat to my life, my concentration peaked. The light, heat, sounds, smells, and other factors of my environment came into perfect clarity. My ability to concentrate so well must have been largely due to Geo Margilus natural aptitude.

In no time at all, I knew the only choice I had was to cast a spell.

I ran through the list of spells I had charged in my mind and selected one that would both completely seal Jargle's movements and threaten the bandits enough to make them hesitant to act. Most likely, Jargle had taken my spellbook, so using a spell to run away was never an option.

"What's the matter? Answer him!"

"Don't give us the silent treatment!"

One of the bandits kicked me from behind. I fell, and my face and gut both struck the earth, knocking the wind right out of me. Even so, I gritted my teeth and looked up at Jargle.

"Open, Gate of Magic..."

With a composure that surprised even me, I began to cast the spell.

I steeled myself to keep going no matter what happened during the ten seconds it would take to cast the spell, but Jargle and the bandits must have thought I had lost my mind in fear and pain. They just kept laughing and jeering at me.

"As a consequence of this spell..."

After the worst ten seconds of my life, I activated the power of a spell from the fifth level, the Enchanter's Spellbook Archive. The dice roll for the activation check wasn't a problem.

"...one target will be turned to lifeless stone. *Petrify.*"

"It looks like you need to taste a little more of my sorcery to... Huh?"

Neither Jargle nor the bandits seemed to realize what was happening, but I noticed that both of Jargle's feet began to discolor...and turn to stone.

"What's happening to my feet? I-I can't move them!"

The discoloration spread from his feet to his ankles and continued upward with merciless speed to his calves and then to the thighs beyond, his robe undergoing the same process as his flesh. Once it reached his waist, both Jargle and the bandits realized what was happening.

"It's stone... Jargle's turning to stone!"

"I-I can't move! I can't move my legs!"

Once Jargle's lower half turned to stone, the color drained from his face, and he began to scream. First the gang of three, and then the rest of the bandits in the courtyard, started to panic.

"What are you doing?! Kill him! Kill him!" Jargle screamed.

At that moment, I felt something touch my back, and I turned around.

"Wh-what is this?! What *are* you?!" One of the bandits had frozen stiff, his arm extended in a stabbing motion. Apparently, he had tried to stab me with his sword, but my *Invincibility* spell had blocked the attack.

"You damned freak!"

"Why can't I stab him?!"

The gang of three tried to attack me with their axes and swords, but with my body protected by *Invincibility*, I could hardly feel anything at all. If any one of them had tried to attack me with their bare hands, that probably would have been the end of me, but in their panic, the thought didn't occur to any of them.

"No!!! Stop! Stop it! Somebody help m—"

With his face twisted in fear, Jargle's petrification continued mercilessly. It reached his chest, then his throat, and finally his head. In less than twenty seconds since I uttered the final words of the spell, he had completely turned to stone, with that look of horror frozen on his face. According to *D&B* rules, the spell's effect was supposed to be instantaneous, but... *At least it worked. I can't expect everything to be exactly the same.* I'll admit I felt a little bad about using a spell like that on a human, but I felt no sympathy for this particular one.

Having regained some of my cool, I let out a sigh of relief, but immediately the pain in my shoulder flared back up, and I twisted my face in pain.

Everything around me was quiet. The only thing I could hear was my own heavy breathing. The silence lasted about a minute, though it may have been shorter. Then it was broken by one of the bandits, who cautiously approached Jargle.

"H-hey..."

"J-Jargle... Sir, can you hear me?"

The bandit reached up and touched Jargle—or rather, his statue—and since he had frozen in an unnatural way, the statue lost its balance and fell with a loud thunk as it hit the ground.

"He's really turned to stone..."

"W-was it that guy who did it?"

The bandits' collective gaze, which had been focused on Jargle, turned toward me. The contempt in their eyes was gone, replaced by fear and anxiety. *Serves you right!* I thought, but because of the renewed pain in my shoulder, I was more cautious than confident. I had to get rid of the bandits as soon as I could.

*In that case, I... Ugh, what do I do? I can't think through this pain.*

"What's your next move?"

Pain or no pain, I heard the voice of that same game master, my oldest RPG compatriot, challenging me.

While I frantically struggled to collect my thoughts, the bandits were starting to grasp what had happened. Starting with the gang of three, many of the bandits started inching away from me.

"That guy really turned Jargle to stone, didn't he?"

"B-but Jargle said he wasn't a sorcerer..."

"Yeah, well, look what happened to him!"

"Wh-why don't we kill him? You know, to be safe."

Nevertheless, some of the bandits still had their weapons in hand. None seemed willing to make the first move, but if I ran, or one of them grew tired of waiting, the balance that kept everyone still would collapse.

I started casting another spell. It wasn't some carefully planned decision. I simply couldn't stand the pressure of the moment. I wanted to do something—anything—to get out of it.

"As a consequence of this spell, a platoon of six ogres will be created out of nothing, and for three days will follow my command. *Create Ogre Platoon.*"

*Create Ogre Platoon* was a spell from the seventh level, the Invoker's Spellbook Archive.

Chaotic energy released by the spell warped the space around me, twisting ripples in the air.

"What is it now?!"

The bandits didn't have long to react. Soon, six humanoid monsters—ogres with brownish-red skin—began to emerge from the distorted space. They were large—about three meters in height—and dreadfully gruesome. The first thing they did was form a defensive circle around me.

"D-daemons..."

"He summoned daemons! He has daemons on his side!"

The effect on the bandits was extreme. One stifled a scream, and the others were clearly stricken with fear.

The ogres, armed with axes and clubs, were all Level 6. Given that the maximum level a monster could have in *D&B* was the same as player characters, they were not particularly strong monsters. However, each Level 6 ogre could easily take on a party of six Level 1 adventurers, with Level 1 being equivalent to the abilities of a common foot soldier.

I wasn't sure how well the strength of humans in Sedia lined up with the level system in *D&B*, but it wasn't a stretch to assume six ogres could easily slaughter ten to twenty bandits.

The bandits seemed to come to the same conclusion and quickly lost all will to fight. Who could blame them? A few of the bandits who were nearest to the gate threw open the side door and ran.

*Is "daemon" just the term people here in Sedia use for ogres?* I thought. The word the bandits used caught my attention. I thought I understood the language, but I still wasn't sure what a "daemon" was, exactly.

There was already more than one way to pronounce the word ogre in Japanese. I was more familiar with the French transliteration, and that was the style I used in my summoning spell, since that was the reading of the word used in the Japanese version of *D&B*. More modern games generally prefer to pronounce the word in the American English style. I'm not sure why *D&B* went with French, but quirks like that were pretty common in older TTRPGs.

"Hrgh... Hyaaah!"

While I was again preoccupied with the pain in my shoulder, one of the bandits (specifically, one of the gang of three) let out a cry and ran toward an ogre, swinging his axe.

If the ogre had just sat there and done nothing, the axe might have done some damage, but the ogre deftly swung its club and knocked the axe out of the bandit's hand.

"Eep!" The first bandit let out a frightened yelp.

"Wh-what are you doing? You idiot!" the second bandit exclaimed.

"Damn it! Let's do this thing!" the third bandit yelled. The balance tipped, and everything came crashing down.

Some of the bandits haphazardly faced off against the ogres, and the rest fled. The ogres kept their defensive formation, so no one attacked me, but...

"Please don't kill them! Just drive them off!" I yelled.

The ogres responded to my command with a roar. There was no reason for me to ask politely, but the etiquette ingrained in me from working at a large company for several long years wasn't easy to break.

Every time the ogres swung their axes and clubs and boulder-like fists, bandits were sent flying. With each attack, the bandits lost more of their will to fight, but none were losing their lives, so that meant the ogres were faithfully following my command. But even with the ogres holding back, the bandits barely did any harm to them at all.

The fact that Level 6 ogres had such an overwhelming advantage was probably due to the bandits' abilities being comparable to Level 1 or 2 characters at most.

"We're not even putting a scratch on these things!"

"Run! We gotta run!"

"W-wait for me!"

Those bandits who'd tried their hand at attacking the ogres were all driven back and swiftly lost their will to fight. Dragging their feet, the remaining bandits fled after the first who ran. There weren't any left too hurt to walk, so I breathed a sigh of relief.

As I watched the last of the fleeing bandits struggling to fit through the side door, I considered tying them up. If I did that, I could hand them off to the authorities, whoever they might be.

*If I wasn't trying to conserve the spells I have currently charged, I might be able to pull that off, but I still haven't found my spellbook...* When I thought of what might happen if I used up all my spells without any way to replenish them, I quickly lost any desire to mete out justice.

Either way, it wasn't long before there were no more bandits left in sight, and hardly any longer before they were out of earshot as well.

*Just minutes ago, this courtyard was like a war zone, and now it's silent*, I thought. It was hard to believe. I took a deep breath and exhaled. My next thought was to secure my own safety.

"Three of you," I directed the ogres, "please guard the perimeter and make sure none of the bandits return. Two of you, search the fort, and please remove anything you consider dangerous. As for the remaining ogre, you will guard me."

"Grrrn," the ogres grunted in response.

After listening to my commands, all but the one ogre who was to be my guard dispersed.

"Ugh... This hurts so much..." I moaned, holding my shoulder in the quiet courtyard.

The ice arrow itself was gone, but there was a large open wound in my shoulder. Thanks to the fact that it was an ice-based attack, the wound looked like frozen meat, and wasn't bleeding much.

I still wasn't any closer to finding my spellbook, but I realized that if I left my shoulder the way it was, it might lead to lasting damage. Plus, just looking at it was unnerving.

I went to the ninth-level spell archive and cast *Complete Recovery*.

According to *D&B* rules, *Complete Recovery* could immediately cure any wound or effect with the single but notable exception of death. Given that it was my fourth time casting a spell, most of my anxiety about the process was gone.

"Whoa... It really healed..."

It was a Rank 9 spell. I shouldn't have been surprised, but as I watched my shoulder heal, it was like watching a video being played in reverse. It healed completely, without even a scar to be seen. I felt I had glimpsed the true significance of the power of a Level 36 magic user.

"Well, let's get to it, then."

Feeling better, I decided to explore the rest of the fortress. First, I had my guard ogre break open the stocks on my hands.

"So, my first dungeon is an abandoned fortress, huh? Better keep an eye out to see if anything gets squished under the doors the ogres knock in..."

*D&B* was designed with four distinct character classes—warrior, cleric, rogue, and magic user—with each class holding its own advantages and disadvantages, and each performing a different role in an adventurers party.

As was made clear by my run-in with the bandits, no matter how high a magic user's level is, they are fundamentally useless when it comes to combat in close quarters.

Magic is powerful, but it is not without its shortcomings. Every spell requires one round (roughly ten seconds) to cast, and while casting spells, a magic user is left defenseless. Recovery magic is a cleric's specialty, not a wizard's, so the spell *Complete Recovery* is an exception rather than the rule. While a magic user can cast some spells that will unlock locks and disable traps, they cannot use those skills limitlessly, like rogues can.

*The more I dwell on it, the more glaring the disadvantages are. I've got to be more careful if I'm going to make it here.*

I wasn't confident everything would go smoothly, but with my guard ogre stationed in front of me, I was able to explore the fort without any issue. There weren't any traps, and whenever I encountered a locked door, I just had my ogre break the lock.

The layout of the fortress was relatively simple, consisting of a main tower, a separate building for living quarters, and an elliptical outer stone wall. There were guard towers on either side of the main gate, and at other points along the battlements. They gave me the impression that the place was built with utility over appearance in mind. The jail compound I had been in before was connected to the building that housed the living quarters. The main tower had three floors above ground and one basement floor. Generally speaking, the basement was used for storage, the first floor was mostly open space, the second floor housed an office, and the third floor contained living quarters.

I found my stolen Infinity Bag and the rest of my items in Jargle's room, up in the tower's living quarters. The first thing I did was turn the bag upside down and make sure my spellbook was there—and there it was, thicker than a phone book, with

"Geo Margilus's Spellbook" written on the cover. Once I was satisfied I'd found the real thing, I let out a huge sigh of relief.

I was also able to reclaim my robe and other equipment. Though it was the first time I was wearing them, both my robe and boots felt well worn and broken in.

Unfortunately, I'd turned my Staff of Wizardry to stone along with Jargle, who was currently collecting moss back in the courtyard. I'd have to retrieve it later.

"It looks like this is a mountain..."

When I looked out of the window in Jargle's room, I saw that the fortress was built on the side of a steep mountain peak. The fortress was surrounded by a forest, and only a small winding path provided a way down out of it. I figured that if I followed the path, it should lead to a town or village at some point.

"Wait! How could I forget?!"

After leaving the tower and walking around the courtyard, my eyes settled on the jail compound. I suddenly remembered a very important detail.

"I've got to save that young woman!"

# Chapter 3

**"I** CAN'T BELIEVE I forgot!"

With my Infinity Bag slung over my shoulder, I ran toward the jail compound.

I should have gone and rescued her first, but instead I'd wasted hours and hours exploring, leaving her to rot in her jail cell. The sun was already starting to set. *I guess I can't expect everything to play out like it does in fantasy novels*, I thought to myself.

By the time I reached the young woman's cell, I was out of breath.

"Are... Are you okay?!" I shouted, between gasps.

"Huh? Wha? No! No!" she screamed, "Get away from me!"

*Huh?* I thought, confused.

"Umm... I-It's okay! There's no reason to be afraid of me!"

"No! Don't come any closer! You monster! You daemon!"

I paused, realizing she wasn't looking at me, but *behind* me. I slowly turned around...

"Groo?" My guard ogre, who had faithfully followed me into the jail, tilted his head and looked to me for direction.

✠

"I'm...really sorry about that. Could you at least listen to what I have to say? I'm not in league with the bandits or with what you call 'daemons.' I do not want to cause you any harm."

*No response, huh?*

The young woman retreated to the far corner of the cell, where she lingered, eyeing me warily. I'd ordered the ogre away as soon as I realized the problem, but the damage was already done.

Now that I'd had a closer look at her, I decided it was more appropriate to describe her as a girl, rather than a young woman. I wasn't familiar enough with white people to be confident I could tell her age just from the way she looked, but...if I had to hazard a guess, she appeared to be in her mid-teens. She wore a simple one-piece dress, had short, chestnut-colored hair, and looked like the energetic type. *She seems ready to snap at me if I get any closer, though...* Nevertheless, I readied myself to try again.

"I'm not lying to you. That thing I just sent away is a creature I created with a spell to serve me. There's nothing to be afraid of."

"But if you created that daemon...doesn't that mean you're on their side?"

*There's that word "daemon" again*, I thought. *It must be a term unique to Sedia, or else I'd understand it. Since everyone's mistaking my ogres for daemons, they must at least look similar. But regardless, based on how this girl and the bandits reacted, daemons must have an awful reputation.*

"Like I've been trying to tell you, I'm just a simple wizard."

"Wizard? What's that supposed to mean?"

*Based on the girl's reaction and what Jargle said earlier,* I thought, *there either must not be a proper word in Sedia's language to describe my magic, or the term isn't widely known... From what I've gathered, my magic and what Jargle called "sorcery" are probably two completely different things that work in different ways. That would explain why my invincibility spell didn't protect me from Jargle's ice arrow...*

But I had to stop myself. Those investigations could wait.

"Look, if I was on the bandits' side, do you think they would have kicked me and punched me and thrown me in a cell? You saw them drag me out of that cell over there, didn't you?"

"Maybe...you got in a fight, or something?"

I tried thinking of the situation from her perspective. *I can't blame her for hesitating to believe a guy she knows nothing about suddenly claiming that he's here to save her. Hell, I'm still trying to make sense of all that's happened myself. But at least some of what I'm saying is getting through to her, I think. As long as I'm patient, I should be able to coax her out...*

I sighed. Convincing the girl turned out to be harder than I thought. *If I wasn't my old forty-two-year-old self, but fit the image of the handsome silver-haired young man Geo Margilus was supposed to be according to his character sheet, would she have believed me right away?* I paused as I stuck upon a sudden realization. *Even if she didn't, Geo Margilus had spells like* Charm *he could use. If I just cast* Charm *on her, I...*

"You damned idiot!" I shouted suddenly, smacking my head against the iron bars of the cell.

"Wh-why did you do that?!" the girl yelled out, startled.

Even if it was only for a split second, I couldn't forgive myself for genuinely entertaining the use of *Charm* as an option. I don't think it would be an exaggeration to say it was the biggest moral failing in my life up to that point. My head was throbbing, but that was nothing compared to my indignation. In fact, I thought, *I need this pain.*

The spell *Charm* does exactly what you think. It allows the caster to control another's person's mind. *It's hard to think of anything more self-serving than that,* I thought, deeply displeased with myself. *This isn't a game! Real people are involved!*

"Just because...she's not willing...to listen to you! You have no right!" I shouted, banging my head again against the bars between phrases.

At some level, I knew I'd snapped. Flying off the handle in front of a girl I hardly knew was only going to make things worse. But I was afraid—afraid that if I didn't firmly denounce such an inhumane use of my powers immediately, afraid that if gave in even *once,* I would be tempted to do it over and over again, until the accumulated indulgence in such vices led to my downfall.

"Please! Stop already! You're bleeding!" the girl cried out.

As I maybe should have expected, I'd split my forehead. Blood was starting to seep into my eye. I groaned and staggered in pain.

"What is with you?! Why did you do that all of sudden?!"

"Well, I... I'm really sorry about that. I, uh... Huh?"

After wiping my forehead on my robe, I felt a piece of cloth pressed into my hand. It was a handkerchief.

"You're bleeding all over the place! Put that over your cut and hold it down!"

"Um... Okay..."

Reflexively, I did as I was told. I held the handkerchief to my forehead. The girl had left the far corner of the cell and must have handed me the handkerchief through the bars.

"Th-thank you..."

Setting aside the fact I had potions in my Infinity Bag I could be using, I thanked the girl and knelt down on the ground.

A few moments passed in silence.

That darling girl's face was twisted into something between a grimace and a frown as she looked down at me. Not that I could blame her. Only moments ago, she had watched a grown man throw himself against the bars of her cell like a raving lunatic. But to the extent that she was now exasperated, at least her fear of me seemed to have waned. Likewise, my anger with myself had subsided. I had a second chance to make my case.

"I'm really sorry you had to see that..."

"Okay..."

"I won't ask you to believe everything right away, but could you at least listen to what I have to say?"

"Well..."

The girl's voice trailed off as she thought for a moment, before sitting down on the other side of the bars facing me. The way she was sitting, her right leg peeked out from under her dress. Once she was situated, she reached out and massaged her right ankle.

"All right. I'll hear you out," she said, finally.

So, I'd made it past the first step. Still holding the girl's handkerchief to my forehead, I straightened myself up and faced her directly.

"Thank you again for the handkerchief. I'll make sure to wash it and get it back to you."

"You don't have to worry about that…"

"Before we talk, I have something I'd like to take care of first," I said, reaching into my Infinity Bag and taking out a cup and brass bottle.

"Is that some sort of…liquor?" the girl asked.

"No, it's a healing potion. It's used to heal wounds."

More specifically, the bottle was a useful magic item called a potion server, and, despite its size, it could hold ten doses' worth of potion. It was currently stocked with a basic healing potion, not unlike the kind commonly found in any fantasy game.

"In that case, you should hurry up and drink it," the girl said.

"Hmm?" I replied, confused.

*Oh… She thinks this is for the cut on my head*, I thought, suddenly remembering my own condition.

"No, no. This is for you. I thought you might need it. Did you hurt yourself anywhere?"

"No, I'm fine, thanks," she said, shaking her head.

But I wasn't convinced; after all, she'd been rubbing her ankle just a few moments ago.

"It's not poisonous or anything. I'll go ahead and drink the first one to show you there's nothing to worry about," I said, pouring the peach-colored liquid into the cup.

The potion had a sweet aroma, and when I drank it in a single gulp, the taste reminded me of a very sweet alcoholic beverage—almost too sweet. But sure enough, I felt my stamina recovering.

"See? It's healed," I said with confidence, though I could hardly believe it myself. The cut on my forehead closed in no time at all.

"Here, you have the next cup," I said, filling the cup again with healing potion and holding it out to the girl.

"But you shouldn't use something so valuable on me...and it's just a sprained ankle," she said, resistant.

"You can think of it as an apology from me for scaring you earlier. Please, take it."

The girl hesitated. Rather than not trusting me, she seemed more concerned about accepting something she would have trouble paying back. After her confusion over the word "wizard," I was surprised she'd understood what a healing potion was so quickly. *I suppose it translates roughly to, "an expensive medicine that heals wounds."*

"You know, it's going to make it a lot harder for you to get back home if your feet are hurting," I said, making the final push. "Especially if you decide you don't need my help."

"That's...a good point. In that case, I'll take it...but I promise I'll pay you back," the girl replied, somewhat reluctantly, before drinking it down.

Over the next few seconds, the girl's face became noticeably brighter.

"It... It doesn't hurt anymore!" she happily exclaimed, moving her foot around and stretching her leg out. In her excitement, the hem of her dress rose a bit, exposing her thighs. It wasn't really my place to say, but I thought she could stand to be a bit more careful about that, considering her age.

"Huh? Oh! I'm sorry! I guess I got a little carried away." The girl noticed I was looking away and blushed, righting the hem of her dress. I had to admit, her reaction was rather cute.

"I'm glad it seems to have worked," I said.

"Thank you very much! I'm sorry for saying all those bad things about you."

"So, you believe me?"

"Well, I believe you're here to help me, at least."

*I'll take that*, I thought, with a sigh of relief. If I was meeting someone for the first time in Japan, there would already be a degree of connection for the two of us to build upon. Excluding a few odd cases, both persons could expect the other to share the same common sense, the same frame of reference. Back home, even strangers know they both live in the same society and are protected by the same rules. Here, in this other world, I couldn't rely on that sense of familiarity. The fact that I was finally able to communicate with another human being (the words I exchanged with Jargle and the bandits didn't really count) was a huge relief.

"So, would you mind getting me out of here, then? Do you have the key?"

"Oh, right. Wait just a moment."

*That's right, this is no time to be complacent*, I thought. *Now that I've committed myself to it, my first priority is to make sure this girl makes it safely home.*

I stood up and began to cast a spell.

"As a consequence of this spell, any lock I touch I will be able to freely lock and unlock. *Wizard Key.*"

After I finished casting the spell, the lock on the cell door opened of its own accord.

"Wow, that's amazing," the girl said, her eyes wide as she left the cell. She stretched, as if seeking to confirm that she was really free, before turning toward me and bowing her head.

"I am Mora, daughter of Ild, a merchant of the city of Relis. Forgive me for my earlier impoliteness. It is a pleasure to make your acquaintance."

*Some of the new recruits at our company could learn a lot from her*, I thought, as I listened to her introduction.

"I am the wizard and magic user Geo Margilus. Naturally, I am pleased to make your acquaintance."

✦

Right after we left the jail compound, I ordered the ogres to secure the perimeter, but that immediately set Mora off on me. "Other people are going to think we're in league with daemons if they see us with them! Do you want someone from a warrior clan hunting us down?!"

There were a few terms in Mora's rant that I didn't understand, but I decided it was best to do what she said.

"As a consequence of this spell, all sources of magic within a ten-foot radius will return to the void. *Dispel Magic.*"

When I used *Dispel Magic* (an essential skill when fighting against arcane enemies) to undo the effects of my *Create Ogre Platoon* spell, the six ogres faded into thin air as if they'd been nothing but a mirage.

"Y-you really did create those daemons with sorcery, didn't you?" asked Mora.

"They're called ogres...and I used wizardry, not sorcery..." I muttered.

There were still many things I had to confirm, so I decided to go with Mora into the tower, where we would be able to sit down and talk.

"Um... What is...that?"

As we made our way to the tower, Mora noticed the statue of Jargle on its side in the courtyard. Her reaction was understandable; it wasn't a very nice thing to look at.

"That's the sorcerer who was apparently the boss of the bandits."

"But...it's a statue."

"I turned him into one. With magic."

"Well...huh."

Until then, Mora had been walking right next to me, but now she slowed her pace so as to keep a few steps behind.

At least she didn't run away.

# Chapter 4

"**T**HANKS A LOT for the food. It was delicious."

"Really? I'm glad you liked it."

Mora and I were sitting at a table on the first floor of the tower. The sun had set, but a fire in the hearth kept us warm, bathing the chamber in its light. The fact that there were several tables and benches in the main room suggested the bandits had used it as both a mess hall and general gathering place.

After coming to the tower, we both realized we were hungry, and quickly decided that food was the first priority. Fortunately, we found the bandits' stores of food fully stocked, so we borrowed a little to make dinner. That said, it was Mora who grilled the dried meat and cheese, cut our slices of bread, and stewed the bean soup. I would have helped, but she went to work so quickly that I felt like I'd just get in the way.

I was so hungry that I scarfed it all down in a hurry, but it was definitely delicious.

"Well then, shall we talk?"

"Whenever you're ready."

The first thing I did was broadly explain my circumstances. While there was a lot I wanted to ask Mora about Sedia, I thought it was important to first build up some trust. *Still, that doesn't mean I can tell her everything,* I thought. *What's the best way to explain things...?*

"I come from a far-away country...probably across the sea—maybe two seas—called Getaeus."

"Okay..."

Getaeus was the name of one of the countries my friends and I had made up for our *D&B* campaigns, and it was Geo's home country, according to his backstory. So, I wasn't *technically* lying, but Mora certainly didn't seem convinced.

"To be honest, I don't exactly know why I'm here. I don't remember. What seems most likely is that I was caught up in some accident involving wizardry—which is quite similar to what you call sorcery. I was probably transported to this area because of the accident, and lost consciousness. Then I can only assume the bandits found me and brought me here."

"I see."

Mora listened through to the end but looked as if she had some doubts. *I don't blame her,* I thought. *Even I think my story sounds ridiculous, but it's still probably better than saying I hail from the country of Japan on planet Earth.*

"Because of that, I may do or say some things that seem odd compared to what you're used to in this region—or even this whole country—but I promise you I'm not like that evil sorcerer

Jargle. If you're going to believe anything I say, please believe me when I say I mean no harm to anyone."

I was a little forceful at the end, but now all my cards were on the table. All I could do was hope Mora believed in my story, or at least in my character. When I finished, I bowed my head toward her.

"All right. I'll believe you."

"Thank you. I really appreciate it."

"To be honest, I don't know what to think of the first half of your story, but I think it's safe for me to assume you aren't an evil sorcerer."

"That is all I can ask of you for now. Thank you again."

Internally, I let out a huge sigh of relief. *To think earning someone's trust would be this difficult...or this rewarding... Anyway, I had better stick to the explanation I gave her from here on out, for consistency's sake.*

"You really are a strange one, though, Mister Geo. Not only are you a sorcerer, but you even have a last name, and you're still treating me this kindly."

"Where I'm from, treating women with kindness and respect is a given, and having a last name doesn't mean you're anyone special..."

"At least around the city I'm from, Relis, only nobility have last names, and usually the only people who can become sorcerers are either from the nobility or a wealthy family."

*The Watcher did say this was a "sword-and-sorcery" world, after all,* I thought. *It's probably similar to conditions in medieval Europe, with a strong class system.*

"It appears this place is very different from my country... Oh, this is really good," I said, taking a sip of a drink Mora had poured for me called sil tea. It had a refreshing, bitter taste to it.

"Well then. Mora, could you tell me how it is you came to be caught by the bandits here?"

Mora frowned and nodded gravely.

··✟··

Mora's father, Ild, was a merchant based in the city of Relis.

Relis belonged to a confederation of city-states established on the shores of the giant Lake Ryuse, together comprising the aptly named Ryuse Alliance. Ild had managed to shore up a considerable amount of wealth, but he still often traveled in person with his caravan along the trade routes he serviced, and Mora usually traveled alongside him as his assistant.

It was on one of these caravan trips, Mora and Ild traveling together as father and daughter, that they were attacked by bandits. It happened early in the morning, the day before I arrived in Sedia.

It wasn't the first time Mora and Ild had had to deal with bandits. According to Mora, they encountered them regularly, about one out of every three trips. Usually, the bandits would only demand a third of their goods and cash on hand as a fee for traveling on the road in their territory. I thought one third sounded like an exorbitant amount, but according to Mora, it was comparable to the tolls charged by local lords on roads that were well-guarded.

Either way, the expense was something that was already factored into the rates they charged for their goods.

However, this last time, the bandits had demanded everything they had. Ild had hired mercenaries to guard their caravan against general threats, but these mercenaries were never meant to fend off an entire band of bandits, so they gave up without a fight. But the bandits didn't stop there. Not satisfied with taking everything Ild had with him, they also decided to kidnap Mora and demanded a ransom of five thousand gold coins for her safe return.

"So, after that, the bandits brought you here?" I asked.

"Yes... This is the first time anything like this has ever happened to us. I can only guess the bandits must have changed their behavior after that sorcerer became their new leader."

It seemed that in Sedia, not only were sorcerers a rare breed, they were so powerful and feared that the mere presence of one was enough to embolden (relatively) peaceful bandits into outright marauders.

According to Mora, I'd been brought in only a few hours after she was. You could say it was good timing, because it gave me the chance to save her.

"My father should have reached Yulei Village by now. There, he might submit a request to the local order of knights for my rescue, or try and gather the funds for my ransom..."

"I see... In that case, we should make plans to leave first thing tomorrow, to make it to that village as soon as possible."

"All right, let's! I can't thank you enough!"

··✟··

"What a day..." I sighed to myself.

We decided that Mora would sleep in the room on the third floor of the tower, while I took the second.

I peered out the window at the moon. It was no different from the one I was used to. I finally had time to relax, but there was so much to think about. Not to mention that after a whirlwind of events that had put me out of my element and out of my comfort zone—a huge understatement—I was exhausted through and through.

*What will I do if the bandits come back?* I thought. *How am I going to get Mora safely back home? How am I going to build a life for myself here?*

Fortunately, I had time. The night was still young. As I sipped my sil tea, I prepared myself for a long night, lost in thought...

··✟··

"Hey! How long are you going to sleep?!"

"What?!"

In the blink of an eye, the night was gone. Morning had come.

Mora was shaking me, and I realized groggily that I had fallen asleep at the desk in the second-floor office. In other words, I was completely defenseless. *What would have happened if the bandits came back?* I thought. *This is what I get for living in a peaceful country so long... I've got to be more careful next time.*

"I've already packed us lunch, so let's get going!"

After we ate breakfast, Mora was all ready to go, which was fine and all, but there was something I had to address first.

"What is that bag?" I asked.

Mora, still in her one-piece dress, had a giant hemp bag slung over her shoulder. She looked like a cartoon thief, or maybe someone fleeing a natural disaster with everything they owned.

"These are all goods the bandits stole from my father. I can't take all of it with me, but I thought I should at least take some..."

I froze.

*This is the bandits' fort, after all*, I thought. *It's no surprise she was able to find her father's stolen goods, and there were probably others' as well.* I remembered finding a lot of things piled in the basement of the tower when I searched the place. *If this was really a TTRPG, I probably would have taken everything I found on the spot, including Mora's father's goods... If I did and Mora found out, I probably would have lost all of the trust she'd put in me... Yeah, dodged a bullet there.*

"Um... Could you wait just a minute? Let me take care of something first," I said.

"Take care of what?"

Mora looked ready to sprint out the front gate, but I called her back and began casting a spell.

"Huh? Wh-where did that horse come from?!"

Once I finished casting *Phantom Horse*, a Rank 3 spell, a black-haired courser materialized in the courtyard. Mora was shocked.

"I figured it would be difficult for us to walk the steep mountain trail, and the quicker we get to Yulei Village, the better, so I thought we'd take a horse. Also, there's some other luggage we have to take with us..."

The phantom steed glowed with a faint, bluish-white aura. This was no simple horse, but something much greater, able to transcend all the limits of a normal mount. The kind of terrain it could overcome depended on the level of the spellcaster. For instance, if the caster met a certain level requirement, the phantom horse could walk on water. As I was the highest level possible in *D&B*, that meant this horse could not only walk on water, but gallop into the *sky*. It could even walk through walls and take its rider along with it.

After the first spell, I looked over at the statue of Jargle, the "other luggage" I was referring to, and began casting the next.

"I-It's floating!" Mora exclaimed.

The spell I cast was *Sprite Porter*, which conjured up an invisible servant to carry luggage. As it was a Rank 1 spell, all this porter could do was lift objects and follow the caster, but the spell could handle a lot of weight. First, the invisible porter took Mora's bag, and then it hoisted up the statue of Jargle with ease. As the porter was invisible, it seemed as if both objects were floating on their own. It certainly was a little surreal.

"There were a few other spells I wanted to cast, but let's go ahead and get going," I said, mounting the phantom horse and reaching my hand out to Mora.

"O-okay!" she replied, and I took her hand and pulled her up.

Mora's hand wasn't like the dainty damsels' and maidens' hands described in fantasy novels. It was hard and calloused, presumably from housework and helping her father, but it was warm.

"I guess this would be the time to yell, 'Hi-yo, Silver!' huh?"

Mora looked up at me, puzzled.

The last time I'd ridden a horse was decades ago at a ranch in Hokkaido, but I was still able to get on the phantom horse and get a good hold on the reins. According to *D&B*'s Basic rules, every character is equipped with the basic skills required to ride a horse. So, assuming the Watcher faithfully reproduced that rule, my ability to do so probably had more to do with that than my own experiences. Then again, as the phantom horse was a monster I created with a spell, rather than an actual horse, it would do its best to listen to my commands regardless of my talents as a rider.

Mora rode sidesaddle behind me. She looked nervous. Being careful not to do anything that would cause her to fall, I took the phantom horse into a canter. When I looked back at Jargle and Mora's bag floating along behind us, I was once again struck by the thought that it looked eerily unnatural, but at least we were on our way. We passed under the arch of the gate and out of the fortress.

The gate opened to the south, with very little level footing. Beyond, the ground sloped down into one narrow path winding its way to the base of the mountain. The west side of the fortress was up against a cliff, and there were steep drops in the other two directions. *Anyone wanting to storm this fortress with an army would have a hell of a time trying,* I thought. *Honestly, I'm impressed anyone was able to build one in a place like this to begin with...*

"We need to hurry and get to town to let my father know I'm all right, and then we should hurry back... I'm worried about leaving all of our goods here," said Mora, a serious look on her face.

"You're right. There's no telling when those bandits might come back. Let's take some proper precautions."

"Precautions? Like what?"

I looked up at the high defensive walls of the fortress and began to cast my next spell.

"*Structural Renovation!*"

"Wh-what is it this time?!"

The earth—or more specifically, the earth directly under the fortress—began to shake and rumble.

"The f-fort! It's rising?!"

*Structural Renovation* is a spell that allows the caster to move and remake the structure of a plot of ground or earth at will. With a great rumble, the ground the fortress stood on stretched out vertically. The whole thing was lifted upward. Once the building had risen about twenty meters, I fixed it in place.

After I was finished, all we could see of the fortress was the face of the cliff it now stood on.

"That should keep anyone from breaking in, at least until we get back," I said.

Mora was quiet. When I looked, she was staring up at the fortress, eyes and mouth opened wide. While she was occupied, I went ahead and cast a few spells on myself, just to be safe. There was no telling who or what might attack us on the road.

"Sorry to keep you waiting. Let's get going, then, shall we?" I said, finally.

"Um... O-okay!"

I lightly kicked my heels, but that was mostly for show. The phantom horse was already obeying my commands telepathically, and it galloped off...into the sky.

"Wow!" I opened my mouth, unable to speak for a moment. "We're really flying!"

Mora screamed.

A few minutes later, the phantom horse was calmly trotting along the mountain path, both of us on its back.

I held my hand to my mouth, gagging as I tried to keep from vomiting.

"Please, won't you stop and *think* the next time you get the idea to do something like that? Remember, I don't know what to expect from your sorcery—or your wizardry? Is that what you called your magic? Anyway, what were you going to do if we fell off?"

"Point taken... I'm sorry... Ugh..."

The experience of riding a horse into the sky, a bundle of firsts all in one, was absolutely fantastic...for the first few seconds, anyway.

But then came the problems. First, Mora immediately fell into a panic. Second, it didn't take long for me to grow sick to my stomach. While it might not be immediately obvious, flying on horseback involves a lot of sudden ups and downs. Third, if

Mora's father was already on his way back to the fortress with ransom in hand, we might miss each other. The mountain path wound its way through a forest, and it wasn't easy to see from the air above. For all of these reasons, we decided to return to the road, even if it meant taking more time to get to Yulei Village.

Fortunately, I found that as long as the phantom horse's hooves were on the ground, it was a relatively smooth ride. That was impressive, given that the winding path through the forest didn't exactly provide ideal footing.

That aside, according to Mora, we would reach the main thoroughfare in a half-day's journey. From there, if we headed west, the road would take us to Relis City; if we headed east, it would take us to Yulei Village.

After riding together for about two hours, I was just about to suggest we take a lunch break when Mora suddenly spoke up.

"You really aren't like normal sorcerers, are you, Mister Geo?"

"You think so?" I asked. "Have you met other sorcerers and seen them perform sorcery before?"

"Well, there *is* a sorcerer's guild in Relis, and while working with my father, I once traveled with a sorceress who'd been part of an adventuring party. She's a good person, but very different from you..."

*So, there is a sorcerers' guild, huh?* I thought. *And adventurers, too...what else will I find in Sedia?*

✛

As Mora and I rode the phantom horse away from the fortress and down the mountain path, we agreed that we might not be the only ones on the mountain.

We weren't wrong.

Halfway up the mountain, dark happenings were afoot. Unbeknownst to us, in between the fortress and the main road, swarms of black creatures screeched and screamed, clambering on all fours up the tree-dotted slope.

"Gree! Gi-gree!"

The creatures—humanoid, if barely—had twisted arms and legs, pitch-black skin, and golden eyes that gleamed with evil intent. They had short horns, large ears, and cries that sounded like metal claws scraping into metal skin. Mixed in with those cries was the clicking and clacking of their many teeth, knives that struck against one other every time they opened their mouths. The creatures held simple axes and spears and clubs in their hands, and though they were not very large—one and a half meters if they stood on their hind legs—they seethed with hatred and loathing. And most of all, they loathed their mortal enemy: humans.

*These* were what the people of Sedia called daemons.

Ahead of the swarms of daemons ran their prey. A group of six men and women—a party of adventurers.

"I never thought we'd run into a swarm this big!" shouted Sedam, the leader of the group.

Sedam was a ranger who belonged to the Relis Adventurers' Guild. At thirty-two years old, he was a veteran of the guild, and the party he led was known as one of the finest in Relis. He was tall and slender, bedecked with leather armor and long boots clearly designed with mobility in mind. From his belt hung a dagger, short sword, and satchel of herbs; slung over his shoulder was a bow, quiver of arrows, and backpack. His utilitarian style, typical of veterans, was complemented by facial features that bespoke keen intelligence.

On their way back from another adventure, Sedam and his party ran into the merchant Ild in Yulei Village. As one who dealt with weapons and armor forged by dwarves, Ild was well acquainted with adventurers, and he and Sedam knew each other well.

In Yulei, Ild had approached Sedam's party about rescuing his daughter from the bandits who had kidnapped her. After some discussion, Sedam's party accepted Ild's request. While Sedam had information that suggested the bandits' leader had recently been replaced by a sorcerer, Sedam decided Ild's offer of three thousand gold coins for his daughter's return was well worth the risk. The decision had been made the previous night.

The next morning, before daybreak, Sedam's party left Yulei and headed toward the bandits' fortress in the mountains. In order to keep themselves hidden, they'd decided to stay off the main path and go through the woods.

It would have been a good idea, if it were not for an unfortunate, unexpected encounter.

"Gree! Gi-gree!"

Being chased by daemons is a completely different experience from being assaulted by an army or simple bandits. Groups of humans are always influenced by several factors: a plan of action, a leader's directions, and surges of anger, fear, anxiety, excitement, and other human emotions. But a swarm of daemons are not influenced by any of these things. They are driven only by a pure and overwhelmingly evil desire:

To slay humans and revel in their death.

The adventurers might as well have been running from a black tide of murder.

The swarm of daemons was mostly comprised of the smallest of their ilk—monsters known as imps, generally slower on their feet than humans. Yet all the same, every imp scrambled after the adventurers, rushing madly...and slowly, inevitably, they were beginning to catch up.

"Three-second counter! Now!" Sedam yelled. The nearest imps had gotten so close he could see their tongues hanging from their mouths.

"Understood!"

"Got it!"

"Yessir!"

The first to stop and turn around were two warrior-class fighters in the rear. They both wore armor reinforced with chain mail, and were equipped with round shields and one-handed swords. Of the two, the bearded, middle-aged man was named Djirk; the younger fellow, still green, was named Ted. Not a second later, a warrior-priest named Torrad joined them to form a defensive line.

"Take that!" Ted yelled.

"Gi-grah?! Gree!"

One of the imps raised its ax to strike, but Ted's boot crunched hard against its jaw. The creature went flying. Yet not a moment after it landed, it spun around on all fours and sprung back toward him.

"Damn it, Ted! Kill 'em in one blow! Or else it's *us* you're gonna get killed!"

"S-sorry!"

The imp clutched at Ted's leg, spreading its broken jaw wide open. Before it could bite down, Djirk plunged his sword down into its neck.

"Gree?!" a second imp screeched in confusion as a dagger sunk into its chest.

Fijika, the scout who'd lobbed the dagger, looked on wordlessly at the advancing horde. She narrowed her eyes and readied a second dagger for her next target. The redheaded young woman was lightly equipped, wearing little more than her traveling clothes for armor.

"Clara, prepare to slow their advance," Sedam said to the sorceress standing beside him, as he shot arrow after arrow into the swarm.

In the time he spent directing Clara, Sedam shot one imp through the skull and another in the neck—the two closest daemons of the greater swarm, still weaving through the trees after the adventurers. Sedam's speed and accuracy with the bow were exceptional.

"Griiihk!"

"Geeeya!"

But even when the imps fell with mortal wounds, they still struggled on, undaunted in their lust for mortal flesh and blood. One blindly attacked the trunk of a tree, thinking it human. Their abnormal resilience and single-minded determination were two of the reasons the daemons were despised and feared by all mankind.

In those few seconds of counterattack, Djirk had killed one, Fijika two, and Sedam four of the attacking imps.

With the closest of the imps repelled, the overall swarm's advance slowed, if only a little.

"That's enough! Run!" Sedam yelled.

"Got it!" the rest of the party responded in unison.

Djirk, Ted, and Torrad—the three forming the defensive line—were the first to turn their backs on the daemons and run. Fijika and Sedam both held ranged weapons, and they continued to strike for a precious second longer before they turned to follow their three compatriots.

In that order—first the three slowest on their feet due to their heavy equipment, then the two with lighter gear—they all ran past the final member of the party, who had taken a position above the others on the slope.

"Vile daemons!" she shouted at the horde.

The sorceress, Clara, was a beautiful young woman with wavy golden hair and clear blue eyes. She wore a cloak over clothes designed with mobility in mind.

One second passed. Then two. The daemons fixated on her, standing seemingly defenseless, all alone.

They rushed toward her in a mindless frenzy.

"*Falbolza: Chain!*"

Clara's voice, the catalyst for her sorcery, cut through the swarm like a knife. She focused her mana into the tip of her upraised staff, until that mana burst outward into eight fragments, transforming into arrows of fire in the air.

"Gree?!"

"Gheee!"

Eight fiery arrows sped ferociously into eight daemons. None missed their mark. They encased black bodies in shimmering flame. Even the daemons' tenacity was no match for sorcerous fire. They thrashed and screamed as they rolled on the ground, making it difficult for the daemons behind them to proceed.

"How do you like that? Ha!"

After taking the time to taunt the flailing daemons (not at all the kind of attitude one would expect from a woman so refined in appearance and behavior), Clara ran after the rest of her party. As her equipment was the lightest of the group, it took no time at all for her to catch up.

With their combined counterattack, the adventurers had put some distance between themselves and the daemons. With only a few directions from Sedam, each member of the party had fulfilled their different roles and complemented each other in their actions. This was the advantage humans with experience had over daemons, which functioned only according to their bloodlust.

In this way, humans and daemons were irreconcilably different.

"Incoming," warned Fijika.

Seconds later, the characteristic screech of daemons could be heard not only from behind, but from the side.

"Gree!"

"Giyah! Grrr!"

Black shadows came springing out of the undergrowth at the party's flank, joining the swarms from behind in their pursuit of the adventurers.

Sedam clicked his tongue in frustration and signaled the others with hand signs. They were changing course. It was worth risking running into the bandits if they could make it to the path that wound up the mountain. If they could make it to the road, they'd have a better chance to counterattack, and could maybe avoid being surrounded.

"I've got some bad news!" Djirk shouted, his face contorting. "There's a fiend!"

The other party members gulped as a giant shadow came bursting through the undergrowth alongside them.

The fiend, another form of daemon, was roughly twice the size of an imp. Standing three meters tall, with thick twisted horns on its head, it made Sedam look like a child in comparison. Though the fiend shared the same pitch-black hide as the imps, it was almost comically muscular, wielding a tree it had yanked out of the ground as a giant club.

"Gruuooo!" it roared—and it felt like the whole mountain shook.

"Damn, it's fast!"

With its giant body, the fiend could cover several times more ground than an imp with every step. Driven by a bottomless well of energy and madness, it hurtled toward the adventurers, instantly closing the distance they'd put between themselves and the horde.

The fiend first aimed its giant club at Djirk, who was guarding the rear. Djirk barely managed to raise his shield in time, but the shield itself couldn't withstand the kinetic energy of the swing. Djirk was thrown off his feet.

"Djirk!" Ted exclaimed, running to Djirk's aid and grabbing him by the arm.

Torrad turned as well, interposing himself between Ted and Djirk and the fiend. Even with three men, against the fiend and that giant club, the odds did not look good. If this had been an average party of adventurers, they might have given up right there.

"Clara, keep going. Secure your position. Fijika, guard her. Everyone else, get away from that thing!"

Sedam gave his orders as he nocked his bow and loosed an arrow into the fiend's shoulder. Clara and Fijika went on ahead. Sedam's arrow didn't seem to deal any damage, but it did distract the fiend long enough for Ted and Torrad to lift Djirk to his feet.

"Grrruuu... Grrahh?!"

But the fiend wasn't about to allow the three humans in front of it to escape. It lifted its club and swung, but before it could make contact, Sedam's second arrow pierced its right eye.

"Gi-gaahhh?!"

"You never know 'til you try!" said Sedam, a smirk papering over his nervous sigh of relief.

The fiend, roaring in pain, had missed its mark. Against all odds, Sedam had made his. The fiend's club tore a chunk out of the ground at Djirk's feet just as Ted and Torrad pulled him away.

"Now, hurry up!" Sedam added, as the other three hobbled from behind.

"We're going as fast as we can!" replied Ted.

But the danger was far from gone. The one-eyed fiend showed no sign of giving up on its prey.

"*Falga Wilm!*"

Once again, the sorceress's voice struck the swarms of daemons, and a whip of fiery tendrils extended from her staff. Unbound by the laws of gravity, the whip shot through the air and tangled itself around the fiend.

"Gi-graah?!"

The crimson whip tightened; the fiend's body burned and sizzled. The tendrils wound around it with such unstoppable force that it couldn't take a single step forward. Within moments, the beast had become a flaming torch.

"Gree?!"

"Grrruu!"

With the fiend still tightly bound, the outermost tendrils of the whip extended farther, wrapping around two large trees and forming a fence in the path of the daemons. Undaunted by the flames, the imps tried to break through—but the whip would not allow it. Every creature that touched it burned in unnatural fire.

"Huff... Huff..."

"Clara, you're amazing!"

Panting, drenched in sweat from both running and fighting non-stop, the others finally caught up with Clara. Though they were all exhausted, seeing the daemons stopped, if only temporarily, gave them hope—and a chance to regain their strength.

"This is only...a temporary reprieve," said Clara.

While Clara's mana reserves were undetectable by the others, as a trained sorceress, she had a clear grasp of how much remained. The amount available to her had fallen considerably from its maximum to a mere twenty-five units. Two more castings of *Falbolza*, and her power would run dry.

"You said it," remarked Sedam. "But if we just make it a little farther..."

"Grruo!"

A hint of panic flashed across Sedam's face. Two more fiends leaped out of the same undergrowth as the first.

"Are you serious? Three fiends? Three?!" yelled Ted.

The other, more experienced adventurers were at a loss for words.

"Well, I suggest we run," said Sedam, a touch dry.

"This isn't the end, not for me!" said Clara.

At the very least, Sedam and Clara hadn't given up yet.

They both knew the fire whip barricade would only last another few seconds before either the fiends burst through it or the other daemons found a way around. Every second it held was an opportunity to put a few more steps between them and the daemons. They did their best to rally the rest of the party.

"I refuse to die here," Clara whispered, a glint in her blue eyes, when suddenly a giant explosion enveloped the daemons.

··✟··

"Eee..."

"Gree...ee..."

"What is that sound?" I wondered aloud.

As Mora and I rode on the phantom horse down the mountain path at a gentle pace, I heard what sounded like the call of some strange animal. *Is that a screeching monkey?* I thought. *It sounds...somehow* evil, *though, and not like it's coming from just one or two animals, but a whole pack of them...*

It seemed to be coming from farther down the path.

"Mora, do you know what that is?" I said, turning to ask Mora's opinion.

But instead of responding, Mora only stifled a scream. Her face was pale, and she was shivering, clutching at my robes.

"What's the matter? Are you okay?"

"M-Mister Geo..." said Mora, with a look of horror on her face. "Th-those are daemon cries."

"Daemons?"

"L-Long ago, daemons attacked Relis...and...my mother... she..." Mora's voice trailed off.

*Daemons... Daemons,* I thought, jogging my memory. *The bandits mentioned them, too. And they're maybe something similar to ogres?*

Mora wasn't acting normal, so I decided we should stop and dismount.

"But what...what if they're attacking my father?! I must go to him!"

"Wait! Wait just a minute!"

No sooner had we dismounted than Mora made to run. I was able to reach out and grab her shoulders before she raced down the path, and I pulled her back.

"Let me go! My father might be down there!" she yelled, tears streaming down her face.

I tried to process what was going on. *Mora's father Ild might be traveling on the path toward us with her ransom. If he is, and those cries are daemons' cries...her father might be in trouble. If daemons are anything like ogres, an ordinary human wouldn't stand a chance against one. But, on the other hand, such a monster shouldn't stand a chance against a max-level magic user like me...*

As I listened, shrill screeches reached my ears, one after another. Technically, I was now supposed to be overwhelmingly strong, but that didn't change the fact that I was a normal person on the inside. Those ominous cries unsettled me.

"Let me go! If my father dies, too... I... I..." Mora stopped struggling and began to sob.

Life...and death. In Japan, I'd never had to face the line between them.

*But did I not, just yesterday, decide I would make sure this girl made it safely home? What good is that if I take her back to a home her father will never return to?*

"O-open, Gate of Magic…"

With my throat dry from nervousness, I began casting a spell.

"As a consequence of this spell, for one hour, one target will be protected by a shield of mana. *Mana Shield.*"

"M-Mister Geo?"

Even though I still had my arms around Mora, I was able to cast a Rank 1 spell. I could sense the chaotic energy forming an invisible shield around her. I didn't have time to cast dozens of spells, but I at least had to take the most basic precautions.

If things took a turn for the worse, Mora and I could always escape on the phantom horse.

"Let's go. If your father is in danger…I *will* rescue him."

Mora and I got back on the phantom horse and set it racing down the mountain path. Mora was holding on tight, her arms around my waist. To the left off the path was a cliff face, and to the right was a steep drop. All in all, the path was only about three meters wide at any given time.

Because the phantom horse took direction from my thoughts, rather than a secondary pathway like the reins, it was able to respond quickly to changes in the narrow path. Despite our overall speed, I felt I could trust the horse not to throw us off or stumble. So the thrill of the ride wasn't the reason my face was stricken with anxiety. I was worried about the daemons. Not only would this be my first real battle, it would be against an enemy I knew little to nothing about.

"Greee!"

"Grrruu…"

At that point, the growls and screeches had become a constant background noise, and I knew we would soon be upon them.

But the exact moment came long before I thought it would.

"Look! Over there!" Mora shouted, pointing to the right, down the slope.

"Greee!"

"Gigigigi!"

I ordered the phantom horse to an emergency stop and stared down below. There was a handful of men and women scrambling up the slope, and behind them were countless twisted shadows.

"So, those are the daemons..." I thought aloud.

The armored group of men and women was about twenty meters ahead of the shadows.

The shadows looked like the silhouettes of twisted, starved children. They were still a considerable distance away, but they looked very much like goblins, that low-level monster so common in fantasy role-playing games.

However, when I saw how their golden eyes flashed with hate and listened to their bloodcurdling screams as they pursued the humans, I couldn't think of them just as low-level monsters. Instead, an instinctual fear began to grip me. The sight of them reminded me of a swarm of army ants enveloping their prey.

"It's not my father... It's Sedam...and Clara!" said Mora, leaning forward and pointing at the group.

*Are these people she knows?*

"There are even fiends!" gasped Mora, horrified.

*Fiends,* I thought. *They must be those giant daemons—what Mora and the bandits mistook the ogres for...*

"Mister Geo... Please! Save those people! Slay the daemons!"

*If I'd continued to live my previous life in modern Japanese society, would I have ever heard someone make such a desperate plea?* I thought. I was shaken. It felt as if her plea came not only from her, but from every human in the world.

This wasn't the time to make excuses.

"Mora, call them here." I paused. "I'll take care of the daemons."

"Mister Geo... Thank you! I will," Mora said, before calling out to Sedam and Clara at the top of her lungs.

With my hands still on the reins, I concentrated, and called forth my inner world.

"Open, Gate of Magic. Reveal your form to me."

My imagined self walked through the Gate of Magic and down three floors to the third level: The Practitioner's Spellbook Archive. It was a much shallower dive compared to the depths of the ninth level archive, but that didn't mean it would take less time than the mandatory ten seconds to cast the spell.

"As a consequence of this spell, a fiery arrow will be launched into a target within a distance of 140 meters, creating a fireball with a radius of 8 meters. The damage dealt by the fireball will be determined by a 20d6 roll."

When I pointed to the spellbook labeled *Fireball,* the chaotic energy of the spellbook transformed into a multitude of dice in my hand. When the effect of a spell has an element of randomness, *D&B* holds that the resolution must be decided by a dice roll. And in this case, 20d6 was shorthand for twenty six-sided dice.

"All right... Come on!" I said, shaking then throwing the dice. I couldn't help but put my back into it. If I'd been handling real dice, some of them would probably have tumbled off the flat bookrest, but not these.

As the splash of dice settled, I read: 6, 3, 1, 1, 6, 2, 4... Not bad at first glance. Once I confirmed the total, 63, the fireball's damage was set, and the dice became a shining flow of energy that soared out into the outside world.

"*Fireball*!" my physical self proclaimed, completing the casting of the spell.

A bright, blazing red arrow shot out, whistling like a bottle rocket as it soared over the heads of the group of men and women. It struck one of the giant daemons like a guided missile.

And there, it exploded.

Some in the group below screamed or cried out in confusion.

*Fireball* is a simple spell, with effects that are self-explanatory, and it's the go-to spell for magic users who reach the level bracket required for the *D&B* Expert rules. As it was such a commonly used spell, I didn't think much of casting it. But when I saw its effect with my own eyes for the first time, the spell's power and intensity blew right past my expectations.

The fiend in the center of the explosion vaporized. Not a speck of it remained. All the imps within the fireball's eight-meter radius likewise turned to dust and ash.

If this were only a game, that would have been the extent of the spell's reach. Anything even one centimeter outside the fireball's radius would be completely unaffected by the spell.

Reality was a little messier. Due to the intense heat at the center of the explosion (I think), the surrounding air rapidly expanded, creating a shock wave with enough force to bend or break the nearby trees. That shock wave carried fragments of wood, dirt, and stone, and they shot into the daemons like shrapnel. In other words, it had the same effect as a conventional missile or bomb.

All in all, that single casting of *Fireball* dealt severe damage to at least half of that black wave of daemons.

The minimum level required for a magic user to cast *Fireball* is Level 5, and the damage a magic user can hope to deal with the spell at that level is about 20 damage points. Even at that low level, 20 damage points is enough to take down a warrior in one hit.

*So, this is what an explosion worth 63 damage points looks like...* I stood in a daze as the rush of hot air from the residual shock wave blew against Mora and me, all the way over at our perch on the phantom horse.

"S-Sedam," Mora muttered, flustered. "Clara..." She came out of her reverie before I did.

Her words jerked me back to reality and into a panic. Even if that group of people was twenty meters away from the center of the explosion, they were close enough to the blast to be damaged by the shock wave.

But fortunately, my fears were unfounded. It appeared that as soon as the fireball had exploded, the group had immediately hit the ground. They were covered in mud, but no one seemed harmed.

"Hey, you..."

"Are you a sorcerer? Could you help us?"

"Mora?! Is that you?"

As they came closer, I counted six people in total. From the look of their weapons and equipment, it was obvious they were adventurers.

But even as we met up, the screeches and swarming black shadows of the daemons not far below made clear that the remainder would soon be upon us.

"Sedam! Clara!"

"Mora?!" The man paused. "We'll save catching up for later."

It was a chaotic situation, but the adventurers wasted no time at all.

"Turn!" the same tall man with blond hair, Sedam, shouted. "We need to buy ourselves time."

"Understood!" replied three men without delay. All of them looked like warrior-class characters.

"You, can you use that same spell again?" Sedam called out to me, fitting an arrow to his bow.

"I-I can use *Fireball* one more time," I replied, reflexively. I had prepared two *Fireball* charges that morning.

"Good. There's still one fiend remaining. When it shows up, I want you to take it out, and wipe out as many imps as you can with it."

"O-okay."

Sedam spoke softly, but his voice was powerful and persuasive. As he appeared as though he was still in his thirties, I was surprised. *Is that gravitas of his something that comes with combat experience?* I wondered.

As someone with no *real* combat experience, I was grateful for his directions.

"Mora, come this way."

"Fijika!" Mora cried out in reply, as the woman Fijika took her into her arms, right off the back of the phantom horse.

This Fijika woman also seemed to be someone Mora knew. From the look of it, it seemed safe to leave Mora in her care.

"To think we'd run into such a great sorcerer at a time like this. I can't believe our luck."

"Thanks be to our lady, Ashginea! The goddess has not forsaken us!"

The men in front seemed very happy to have me. On the other hand...the woman with the cloak, who looked like a sorceress, was glaring at me. *Could she be mistaking me for Jargle?* I thought.

"Greeooaaaar!"

"Now!" Sedam yelled.

"Huh?!"

The remaining fiend had almost reached the top of the slope.

If I were able to cast my magic immediately on Sedam's signal, it probably would have been very effective. In so much as that, Sedam's timing was perfect. But I needed ten seconds, and those ten seconds were not factored into Sedam's signal.

Frantic, I immediately began to cast a spell, but not *Fireball*.

"Open, Gate of Magic..."

Sedam turned to look at me, confused.

"What are you doing?!" the sorceress shouted.

While I was casting my spell, the fiend made it onto the mountain path in front of us, with several imps following in its wake. Fortunately, it was still more than ten meters away, but only just.

In any case, the fact that I did not attack on cue was unexpected, and the group eyed me with suspicion before turning their attention back to the fiend.

Sedam was the first to act, with an arrow shot from his bow.

"*Falbolza*!" The sorceress was not a second behind, unleashing her own fiery arrow into the fiend.

"Greeaa!"

Both arrows struck the fiend in the face, and it shrieked in pain, but that was not enough to take it down. Blindly swinging its club, the fiend charged at us.

"*Lightning*!" I cried out, finally finishing the casting of my spell.

*Fireball*'s area of effect was too large. If I had cast it at that moment, we would have been caught in the blast. So instead, I decided to cast a spell whose effect followed a linear path, rather than one that encompassed a circular area. The spell took the direction I pointed with my finger and shot bolts of lightning that extended thirty meters forward and one meter to each side. The lightning was bright and blinding. It tore through all the daemons coming up the path.

"Gugyaah?!"

Thunder roared as the superheated air exploded with a shock wave that rocked our party. Several of the men cried out, and I heard a scream that was probably Mora.

The sorceress was pulled back by the wind in her cloak. She stumbled as the shock wave hit, so I reached out and caught her.

Once I saw she was right on her feet again, I let out a sigh of relief and looked up at what had happened. The upper half of the fiend's body was gone, and the rest of it, covered in the ash of what it once was, collapsed to the ground. The state of the imps was even worse. Mangled black body fragments littered the path.

My ears were still ringing from the thunder, and the smell of burnt flesh filled my nose. The only reason I was able to keep from throwing up was that the scene seemed so displaced from reality. My brain had trouble accepting what I saw.

"Let go of me." The sorceress turned to me and frowned.

"Oh, uh... Sorry about that." As soon as I snapped out of it, I released her quickly.

The battle was won. My first true battle as the great wizard Geo Margilus.

# Chapter 5

ONCE THE ADVENTURERS finished off all of the remaining daemons in sight, we decided to keep moving.

Clara and some of the other adventurers began to shower Mora and me with questions, but Sedam quickly put a stop to that. He gave us the pragmatic reminder that it was more important to reach someplace where we could secure our safety first. Everyone agreed, so I followed the adventurers on foot, leading Mora on the phantom horse.

"Well, this looks like it will be fine for the time being," Sedam said.

We stopped in the middle of the mountain path, just before a narrow suspension bridge that reached over a large chasm. His decision was probably based on the fact that as long as we weren't pinned from both sides, the bridge's bottleneck would make it easier for us to either run or defend our position.

"I am Sedam, an adventurer from Relis. We came here in response to a request to save that girl from bandits."

"I knew it!" Mora exclaimed.

Sedam explained his party's circumstances to me in detail. From the look of his bow, quiver, and other equipment, he appeared to be a ranger. He was calm and intelligent, and reminded me of the kind of university professor that appears in overseas nature documentaries.

Sedam's explanation matched what I expected. Mora looked ready to cry tears of joy.

"Now, with that out of the way," Sedam began.

I cut him off. "Wait... Please wait just a minute!"

In line with my first impression of him, Sedam was the most inquisitive of the group. Although he had restrained himself before, now he looked ready to pelt me with questions.

"What is it?" Sedam asked.

"My circumstances are a little complicated, so before you ask any questions, can you give me a chance to explain myself? My name is Geo Margilus, and I am a magic user—a wizard."

"A...wizard?"

I could barely get the first sentence out of my mouth, and the adventurers already viewed me with suspicion. The sorceress's gaze was particularly painful, and it didn't help that she was a fair-skinned, blond, blue-eyed beauty with a powerful presence. But I ignored their gazes and continued.

I explained that I was from the distant country of Getaeus, and that an accident involving magic had transported me into the nearby mountains. I summarized everything: I was captured by bandits, fought them off, rescued Mora, and was now on my way to deliver her to her father, who we assumed was in Yulei Village.

"If you're going to make things up, you should try a little harder," quipped the sorceress, with a look of distaste. "You're not at all convincing."

The sorceress, whose full name was Clara Andell, wore a fitted shirt and pants under her cloak. All of it looked well-made and expensive.

"Miss Clara belongs to a noble family," Mora explained in a whisper. "So it would be best not to make her angry."

*Well, I am—or was—a seasoned employee at a large company,* I thought. *I've had a few strong-willed women like her work under me over the years. Despite how beautiful she is, I should be able to keep my cool no matter what she says. Or so I told myself. But if I were truly confident, I wouldn't have had to give myself a pep talk in the first place.*

"Well, to be honest," said Sedam, "I have to consider the possibility that *you* are the sorcerer leading the bandits, and that you just took Mora and ran when you saw the swarm of daemons coming your way."

Although Sedam still seemed to doubt me, he didn't express as much hostility as Clara did.

"I understand my story is hard to believe," I said, "but I do have Mora to vouch for me..."

"He's right!" Mora piped in.

"...and as for the bandits' sorcerer," I continued, "He's right over there."

The others fell silent as I pointed to Jargle's statue, which the sprite porter still held in tow, oblivious to everything else around it.

"Yeah, I was gonna ask about that..."

"I see that it's a statue and a bag...but how are they *floating*?"

The first to speak up were the two warriors, a middle-aged man (though perhaps still younger than me) named Djirk, and a young man named Ted. They were fixated on the floating objects. In contrast, the red-haired woman, Fijika, was the least interested, keeping her attention on our surroundings.

"Well, you *did* save our skin and help us defeat the daemons," continued Sedam. "For that, I am very thankful." He bowed his head toward me.

"Th-thank you! It's only natural."

"Really, we owe you our lives."

Ted and Djirk followed suit with their own thanks.

"I suppose I have to admit, you did help us," added Clara, reluctantly.

While I wasn't sure how much of my explanation Sedam and the others believed, it at least seemed like I'd earned some of their trust.

"Well, you know... Mora asked me to, so..."

"Mister Geo is amazing! He can use magic!" Mora piped in again.

If you work almost any kind of job in Japan, you will experience others bowing their heads toward you in thanks as a custom. My experience was no exception. However, this was the first time I'd ever had anyone thank me for saving their life. (I hadn't ever saved anyone's life before, after all.) I was embarrassed! I didn't really know what to say, so I was thankful that

Mora jumped in. Unfortunately, what she said appeared to strike a nerve with Clara.

"He cannot be a sorcerer, because sorcerers without mana do not exist!" Clara shouted, as if she couldn't hold it in any longer.

*Without mana, huh?* I thought. *Jargle said almost exactly the same thing. What does that mean?*

"With respect to that, I have some questions I'd like to ask. Can the sorcerers of Sedia see mana?"

For the record, if I cast the appropriate spell, I should have been able to see mana as well, but according to *D&B* rules, mana was explicitly not required to cast a spell.

"Of course we can!" Clara replied angrily.

"But isn't sorcery what's making the statue and bag float?" said the warrior-priest, Torrad. Despite his heavy armor, shield, and mace, the young man seemed to have a very easygoing nature.

"Well..." Clara started.

"Wait," Fijika interrupted in a low voice. "More daemons have come."

"There are tons of them!"

"Imps, fiends, and even a gigant..."

We had moved to an area not far from the path, where there were fewer trees and a better view.

It felt good to be able to look out on such a clear day, all the way to the horizon, with the foothills in view and a road stretching east and west into the distance.

The problem was, the valley several tens of meters below was filled with an army of marching daemons. From behind rocks and trees, we looked down at the army below. Fortunately—if anything could be called fortunate in this situation—it did not appear that the daemons were looking for us.

The most common daemons in the army below were imps, and for about every twenty of them, there was a fiend. Furthermore, there was a third kind, one that stood out the most: a giant swaying daemon the size of an elephant. This was a gigant. It had short, thick legs, an overweight body, and long arms, with a nose and tusks like a boar. The closest monster it could be compared to in D&B terms was a troll.

As far as I could see, there was only one gigant. But it was so large it nearly filled the valley below, and it carried a club made of several logs tied together. One was more than enough.

The valley was forested, so it was hard to see the full scale of the army, but they most likely numbered in the hundreds in total.

"But really, these things make goblins, ogres, and trolls look cute in comparison..." I looked through my Telescope Lens, a magic item that, as its name suggested, worked just like a telescope. I'd already worked up a nervous sweat just looking at them.

These were daemons, not D&B monsters. While they could be described in terms of those monsters, they were fundamentally different. They especially lacked the feeling of being common, low-intelligence creatures only there for adventurers to slay.

The daemons were pitch black, as if they had bathed in tar, their features indistinct but for those glowing, hate-filled, golden eyes. As I watched them through my Telescope Lens, I could sense their seething hatred of humans, their desire to kill. I felt I finally understood why Mora and the bandits were so frightened of my ogres. These monsters were far more like the undead than living creatures.

Even so, it was clearly an army, not just a swarm this time. There was order in the ranks. They were marching in formation. *As long as they don't have a human in their sights to drive them crazy, it seems they are capable of organizing,* I thought, eyeing a fiend carried by imps on a pallet in the center of the march, who I suspected was their commander.

"If they continue their march through the valley, they'll break out of the forest somewhere," muttered Djirk. "Are they planning to attack Yulei?"

Mora looked frightened.

"If we hurry, we may be able to get to Yulei before them," said Sedam. "At least we can sound the alarm."

"But even if we get there in time to warn them, there won't be enough time to evacuate," responded Torrad. "Wouldn't it be better to go the Castle of the White Blade to call for reinforcements?"

*Even if we're able to do either of those things, who could win against an army like that?* I thought, listening to Sedam and Torrad's discussion.

"Once we leave the forest, we should split into two groups. Whatever we do, we need to hurry."

"Uh... Umm..." *Is it okay for me to stand here idly like this?* I thought.

Over the past two days, I had experienced combat, at least in some form, but I'd never really planned anything out. I was just acting on impulse. However, this time I had a distinct choice. I had to decide whether or not I would fight.

It wasn't a question of whether I *could* do something. The question was more along the lines of, "Is it all right for me to do this?" I was confident I could wipe the entire army out on my own, but it felt like cheating, and that wasn't the only problem. I still didn't know why the Watcher had brought me to Sedia. If I wiped out the daemon army, it was possible doing so would lead to an even greater tragedy. Was I about to pull the trigger of some metaphorical gun? What if it turned out that in Sedia, daemons, not humans, were the right and proper inheritors of the land? That was a common plot in fantasy settings.

Even if none of the above posed a problem, it was very likely that performing such a grand act would irrevocably alter my status in Sedia. Even if the result was me getting held up as a hero, that was nothing I wanted, and my potential change in status was just as likely to be negative as positive. I could be accused of performing a forbidden art or painted a heretic. All were very likely scenarios.

Was this army really going to attack Yulei? There was no proof. *Shouldn't we first try to reason with the daemons, instead of exterminating them?* (I'll admit that by the end of my stream of thoughts, I was reaching into the absurd.)

I was afraid of what the uncertain future might bring. *This is not a game. I am not Geo Margilus. Geo Margilus might be a grand magic user who has saved the world several times over, but I am a forty-two-year-old ordinary human being, used to a peaceful country where we talk things out, not engage in battles.*

A human like me needed a compelling reason to act.

"Umm... What casualties do you expect?" I asked.

"Hmm?"

"If these daemons attack that village, what kind of damage or casualties do you think there will be?"

"Did you see how many are down there?!" Ted couldn't hold back his anger. "There's even a gigant! If they reach the village, everyone will die!"

"No..." Mora looked from one adventurer to the next, pleading for someone to argue back, but they only averted their eyes.

"Mister Geo... My father's in Yulei..." Mora anxiously tugged at my sleeve.

*Earlier today,* I thought, *I fought just because Mora asked me to, but this time, I have to take ownership of this decision, and responsibility for it, no matter how much I might regret it later.*

"Don't worry," I said quickly. "I'll do something." I didn't want to wait for her to ask me to save her father. I didn't want to give myself the opportunity to use her plea as an excuse. This time, I was acting on my own.

"You'll do something? What did you have in mind?"

"After those powerful incantations you used, isn't your mana all used up?"

Both Sedam and Clara eyed me with suspicion, but readying myself for what I was about to do, I didn't have the capacity to answer them.

"All right, let's do this!" I said, slapping both hands against my face. I turned my attention to the invisible force field surrounding me. That force field was the product of one of the spells I'd cast as Mora and I were leaving the bandits' fortress: *Fly*.

With the support of that force field, my body began to float.

"What?! He... He's flying?! He's flying!" I heard the adventurers cry from below.

At first, I felt a little ill, remembering the stomach-twisting nausea from my flight on the phantom horse, but I forced it out of my mind. I didn't have time to be airsick.

I looked down and shivered. It was my first time flying without any kind of support, and it was far more frightening than being on the phantom horse. It seemed that the force field was protecting me from the wind and changes in air pressure, but having nothing under my feet was a definite psychological strain.

"This is going to be dangerous, so please evacuate this area and take cover. I will take the daemons down."

"Hey! What are you... Wait!"

"Mister Geo!"

Still nervous, I flew after the daemon army. The maximum flight speed allowed by *Fly* was fifty kilometers per hour, so it only took me a minute or two to reach the front of the march.

"As a consequence of this spell, a stone wall five meters high, fifteen meters wide, and thirty centimeters thick will be created in a location in my line of sight. *Wall of Stone*."

"Gree?!"

"Gyaiie?!"

The spell caused a giant stone wall to materialize in the valley.

I picked the spot where the valley was narrowest, so the wall was able to completely block the daemons' advance.

I then flew down and landed on top of the wall.

I wanted to look at the daemons up close before I set out to exterminate them. I could cast the spells from far away and out of sight, but I still had qualms about destroying such a great number of living things without any interaction with them, and—however unlikely—there was a small chance we might understand each other.

From the daemons' perspective, a giant stone wall had suddenly appeared out of the middle of nowhere. Of course, they were startled and confused. However, once they saw me, a human, standing on top of the wall...nothing else mattered to them. The daemons in the valley erupted into screeches and screams.

"Kshaaaa!"

"Gya, gya-ga!"

"Gruooo! Gu-gaa!"

The imps and fiends spewed foam from their mouths, fangs clacking. Their murky golden eyes glittered at me, full of hatred.

"Yeah... I don't think negotiations are going anywhere."

It took me long enough, but finally I had to admit that these daemons were mortal enemies of humanity. There was no way we could reconcile.

"Gyah! Gyaah!"

From farther back in the ranks, something came flying at me. It was a rain of countless arrows from imp archers, loosed on the orders of the commanding fiend. Though their rage appeared to make them insane, they were still functioning as an army—and that only made them all the more frightening. However, before any of the thick black arrows reached me, they were all deflected and sent flying away. I owed that to the second of the precautionary spells I'd cast earlier: *Protection from Arrows*.

"Gyarrr!"

"Gishaah!"

Once the commanding fiend realized projectiles had no effect on me, he swung his arm, and the imps in the valley all immediately charged against the wall. They pushed, they shoved, clambering over each other with swords and axes in hand, each wanting to be first to land a blow. At the rate they were going, it wouldn't take a minute for them to scale the wall—but, of course, I was under no obligation to wait.

"Gyaw?!"

I leaped from the stone wall, back into the sky. The imps shot more arrows and threw hand axes, but these were ineffective.

"Well... I suppose I'm relieved, in a sense," I muttered to myself.

Sure, I didn't feel great being subject to such an intense level of hatred. My throat was parched and I had broken into a cold sweat. But now, at least, I had no qualms whatsoever about what I was about to do.

"Open, Gate of Magic. Reveal your form to me."

Once my physical self rose high into the sky, to a point where I could see the entirety of the army, I held my position in mid-air. Then, my imagined self stole through the magic gate and down the spiral staircase. I wanted to completely destroy the hundreds of daemons that filled that valley, and I wanted it done quickly—I didn't want to give a single one of them any chance to escape.

*In that case, what spell should I use?*

In *D&B*, there are actually very few pure attack spells. Starting from the most basic spell to the highest rank, they are: *Mana Bolt* (Rank 1), *Fireball* (Rank 3), *Lightning* (Rank 3), *Ice Storm* (Rank 4), and *Meteor* (Rank 9). Of course, taking a broader sense of the word, many other spells could be used to attack. In the past, I'd even come up with a few original spells together with my game master based on manga and anime. However, we had one unwritten rule.

Only one particular spell could be the strongest.

"As a consequence of this spell, eight meteors will be summoned from the heavens to rain down upon my enemies. The damage of the collision will be determined by a 20d6 roll, and the additional damage from the ensuing explosion will be determined by a second 20d6 roll."

In the spellbook archive, I threw an absurd amount of six-sided dice upon the elevated bookrest, and once the damage had been set, a surge of chaotic energy far exceeding that generated when I'd cast *Fireball* rushed out into the world.

"Rank 9 spell: *Meteor!*"

Eight bright lights cut through the blue sky, raining down upon the twisted valley filled with daemons.

On impact, the daemons in the direct path of any of the shining meteors were sent flying, torn apart like the shreds of a popped balloon. The ensuing explosions filled the valley completely. They burned flesh to the bone. With nowhere to go but up, the shock waves sent pieces of flesh and splintered bone flying into the sky. Even after the initial wave, long after anything was left alive, bursts of energy continued to rock the valley; the land itself surged up like a tidal wave.

"Wh-wha?! Whoa!"

First, the shock wave hit hard against me, and then the sound of the blast rocked my insides. Even though I was protected by *Fly*'s force field, and was far away from the blast, I felt like a leaf in the wind. If the daemons made any sound, I couldn't hear it over the blast.

"What the hell?!"

It reminded me of the documentary footage of nuclear weapons testing I saw once on TV.

Shielding my face with both hands, I tried to get a look at what was happening in the valley. It was hard to tell from all the smoke and flames and upended earth, but I could say for certain that none of the imps or fiends or the gigant retained any form other than amorphous clumps of flesh and ash. The land itself had changed.

In the context of a game, I had used *Meteor* to destroy castles and groups of monsters before, but until I saw it with my own eyes, I didn't fully comprehend how powerful it was.

I floated there, shivering. *In Sedia, the power I have as a Level 36 magic user may be on the same scale as holding nuclear weapons.*

# Chapter 6

SOON AFTER, I managed to meet back up with Sedam's group and Mora, and close the chapter on the daemon threat.

The thunderous sound and shock waves from the blast had reached all the way to where the group had taken cover. Both Sedam and Fijika were positioned to witness the impact, so everyone readily accepted my account of events—namely, that I'd defeated the daemon army with a meteor shower.

"Well, I don't think anyone here can argue now that you're not a powerful sorcerer—or wizard, as you say, Mister Margilus... or should I call you 'Lord'?"

After everyone had settled down around a fire, and Mora had served me a cup of sil tea, Sedam formally addressed me. The tone of his voice was calm and quiet, but I could tell his expression was stiff. Looking around, I saw that Ted and Djirk looked frightened, Torrad and Fijika were anxious, and Clara was clearly on edge, viewing me with caution. Mora, on the other hand, looked as if she was worried *for* me.

"No, you don't have to do that. I'm not from a noble family. I'm not anyone important—just your average citizen. I'd prefer it if you didn't treat me as special, just...normal."

Back home, being addressed formally by door-to-door salesmen was enough to make me feel uncomfortable. I wasn't about to let anyone address me like some great and powerful lord. But in some corner of my mind I knew that after doing what I'd just done...there was no way I was going to pass as an average citizen.

"But Lord Margilus! How can I not show proper respect to you, the man who wiped out all those daemons?!"

"Lord Margilus, you're a hero!"

Not unexpectedly, Djirk and Ted were the first to protest and put me up on the pedestal I was trying to step down from. In their case, they were probably acting more out of fear than respect, but considering the circumstances, I couldn't fault them for it.

"To be clear, I am of course thankful for your actions," continued Sedam. "If we had let an army of daemons of that size attack a village, it would have been a massacre—but that is why I am concerned. If you, who can single-handedly wipe out a force of daemons on that large scale, chose for some reason to call meteors down upon *our* heads, we would have a very serious problem on our hands. I hope you understand."

*Well...yeah.* I took a deep breath and tried to reassure everyone.

"As I told you before, I am Geo Margilus, a magic user from Getaeus. I still do not know much about Sedia or its ways. But I swear to you I have no intention of using my magic for evil purposes, and I will never use it to bring harm to you or this land."

"Hmm..."

"O-of course!"

"We believe you, Lord Margilus!"

Fijika, Ted, and Djirk appeared to relax somewhat.

"You...swear? In whose name? Is there a god whose faith you adhere to?" Torrad cut back with a very warrior-priest-like response. *Hmm...* I wondered. *How should I answer this?*

"I do not know whether the gods we follow differ, but... I swear in the name of the Watcher."

"Interesting..." Sedam responded. Apparently, my answer caught his attention.

Of the god-like candidates I listed in my head, the Watcher seemed to be the most appropriate choice. After all, the Watcher had sent me to Sedia, and it may have been its intention to have me fight the daemons all along.

Torrad crossed his arms. *I might be in trouble if his god has something against heretic*s, I thought, but I couldn't take back what I'd said.

"That is not one I've heard of before...but surely your god must be a force for good, as it counts among its believers one who would use his powers to defeat daemons," Torrad said, with a smile.

"Mister Geo is an incredible person, but he's actually very kind...and, umm... He's very kind!" Mora said, springing again to my defense.

*Too bad I have to depend so much on a girl I only met yesterday to vouch for me...* I thought, half-jokingly. *But circumstances aside, she really has a knack for jumping in at the right time.*

"Well... It wouldn't be right not to give a hero who just saved an entire village the benefit of the doubt," said Sedam, wearing something between a smirk and a smile.

While I appreciated the sentiment, I really wished he would drop the whole "hero" bit. I wasn't ready to fit that mold.

"It could be that this Watcher of yours meant for you to come here. I'll be counting on you," said Sedam, patting me on the shoulder.

*Between the two of us, I'd sooner put my trust in you, not me.*

After our break, we continued down the path and out onto the main thoroughfare, heading east toward Yulei Village. Sedam and Fijika continued to stay on the lookout for daemons, but no more appeared.

The high road ran east to west over an open plain and was paved with stone. Its quality hinted that civilization had already reached a high level in Sedia. I was told we would camp on the road that night and be in Yulei by morning.

I looked back to the south down the path we'd come from, up at the mountain and its forests, and then I turned to Sedam.

"As I mentioned earlier, I really don't know anything about this place. Could you tell me more about Sedia? I don't mind if you keep it simple."

I wanted to have at least a basic understanding of Sedia before I encountered more people when we got to the village, and I also just wanted to know what I was in for, given that I'd be here a while. I was particularly interested in knowledge related to daemons and magic, but it was best to start with the basics.

"That's a very open-ended question. What exactly do know what to know, Lord Margilus?"

*Lord seems to have stuck*, I thought. *At least Sedam is more direct with me, compared to the others like Djirk and Ted...*

"Well, I suppose... I'd appreciate it if you would talk about Sedia's countries and their history."

"History, you say?" Sedam said with a smile. "It would take more than a day or two to cover that. If you'd like, once we've set camp, I can go over some of the greatest chapters in detail..."

"Really, I'd appreciate if you'd go over just the outline. Let's keep it simple."

"Well... I suppose that's fine as well."

To Sedam's credit, as excited as he was to talk about it, his explanations were very easy to understand. *He must be a scholar of some sort*, I thought.

First, I learned the name of the region we were currently in: Ryuse. At the center of this region, itself near the center of the Sedia continent, was Lake Ryuse. Around this large lake lay a collection of city-states joined together in a confederation known as the Ryuse Alliance, and through this confederation they wielded a great deal of political power.

Yulei Village, farther east along the road, belonged to one of the member states of the Ryuse Alliance, the Order of the Calbanera Knights.

In the opposite direction, the road led to Relis, on the shores of Lake Ryuse. Relis was a fortified city that both Mora and the adventurers called home, and it was the second most prosperous member state of the Ryuse Alliance.

East of Yulei was a dangerous wasteland, but on the far side lay a prosperous foreign country, leading many reckless merchants and adventurers to cross it.

Although distant, another foreign country lay to the north of Lake Ryuse's northern shores: the Kingdom of Shrendal, the continent's largest country. To the south stood yet another large foreign country, but it was in the midst of a civil war.

"That's *very* interesting."

I thought back to the many times I'd started a new tabletop campaign, when the game master would explain what kind of world the campaign was set in. This world was similar to campaign settings I'd played based on medieval Europe. *Not that "medieval" is a very narrow definition,* I thought.

"Now... Could you tell me more about daemons? What are they?"

"That's...not an easy question to answer." Sedam wasn't as excited to talk about them as he was other subjects, but he did give me a good run-down.

First, Sedam explained that "daemon" was a general term for a category of creatures that included the imps, fiends, and gigant we'd seen so far, and more besides. Those creatures formed groups with each other and shared two main characteristics: an explosive reproductive rate and a destructive impulse directed toward all other intelligent life. Most countries and regions in Sedia considered daemons an existential threat to humankind, and it was tacitly understood that their extermination took priority over any and all disputes between nations.

Strangely, no place of origin or habitat had been identified for daemons. The scenario was always the same: First, daemons would suddenly appear. Then, they would make a nest and quickly multiply. Once a nest was made, it would continue to issue forth new daemons until it was destroyed. Therefore, if a nest was ever discovered, destroying it was of utmost priority. Depending on the country, the responsibility of destroying a nest fell to either nobility or knights.

"After all, there was a time in the past when daemons almost wiped out all of humanity," Sedam said quietly.

When an especially large number of daemons gathered together, it was referred to as a legion, and whenever a giant nest capable of breeding multiple legions was created, it was referred as a brood event.

Fortunately, the overall number of daemons in Sedia was lower than it had been in the past. The last time an outbreak of daemons large enough to form a legion had occurred was ten years prior. Since then, Sedam said, his party and other groups of adventurers only encountered a few daemons at a time—that is, until the events of today.

"And what about what happened today?" I asked. "Is that number of daemons large enough to be called a legion?"

"Probably so... They had a gigant, and there were far too many for it to be a splinter group," said Sedam, frowning.

"In that case... Do you think there is a nest nearby?" I paused a moment. "Isn't that a problem?"

"Definitely. If something isn't done about it, another legion may appear and attack villages."

I groaned.

I definitely wasn't gung-ho about showing off my powers and getting into another fight, but I knew I couldn't just let them be, especially after facing them earlier that day. *When Sedam said he would be counting on me, that must have been what he meant,* I thought. *If the daemons' nest is nearby, someone is going to have to do something about it—that someone being me.*

Sedam knew a lot about the geography and history of Sedia, but he didn't have many opportunities to share his knowledge with others. After I asked questions on a few different topics, he mentioned how happy he was to be having a conversation about such things with me.

We talked for several hours as we walked, and before I knew it, it was sundown. We'd come a long way, but it looked as though we wouldn't reach Yulei until afternoon the next day.

Sedam picked out a location for our camp and quickly gave directions to the other party members. When playing a TTRPG, setting up camp takes little more than a word or two, but it turned out to be a lot of work. That said, when I tried to help out, Djirk and Ted quickly ran to stop me with a chorus of complaints. "Lord Margilus, we can't possibly ask you to do that!" Even Sedam told me I should take it easy, as I was a guest.

Mora and Fijika set to work making a stew of meat and

beans with spices, and its wonderful smell quickly made me hungry.

There was still time to wait, so I tried starting up a conversation with Clara. I wanted to understand the differences between my magic and the sorcery of Sedia.

"That is not something I can talk with you about here," said Clara, blunt as you please, while she continued to run a comb through her wavy hair.

*If it's work-related, that's one thing,* I thought, *but trying to carry on a conversation with a younger woman always tires me out...*

"Well, in that case... Uh..."

As I was looking for more words to say, Clara gave me a sharp glare. "After we arrive in the village, do you mind giving me some of your time? I'd like to talk to you alone."

"Well aren't you popular, Lord Margilus?" Ted laughed, but I couldn't see any way the meeting would go well.

"Depending on what you say, the Sorcerers' Guild might be blown away."

*See?*

✢

*Two nights ago, I slept in my bed. Last night, I slept in an evil sorcerer's tower. Tonight, I'm in a tent in an adventurers camp...*

As a guest, I did not have to participate in the night watches, so, there in my borrowed tent, I took the opportunity to go right to sleep and get as much rest as I could.

*Morning.*

"Sorry! Can I have five more minutes, please?!"

"Well, I mean... We don't mind waiting," Sedam replied.

The adventurers woke at sunrise, quickly finished breakfast, and packed up camp. By the time they were finished, I was still frantically skimming through my spellbook.

In *D&B*, a magic user must recharge any spent spells every morning if they want to use those spells again that day.

While my physical self was reading the spells from the spellbook in my lap, my imagined self was writing the spells in blank spellbooks in my inner world. Given how much magic I'd cast the previous day, I really wanted to recharge all my empty spell slots and get back to having my full complement of eighty-one spells. However, since I was in a hurry, I only took the time to recharge the one I needed.

"All right, I'm done! *Sprite Porter!*"

In a rush, as soon as I finished charging the spell, I immediately began to cast it. I didn't know what I would do—maybe find a hole to bury myself in—if I failed the activation throw, but luckily the dice gave me no trouble.

"They're floating..."

"They really are floating again, huh?"

The two objects I made the sprite porter carry were the same as yesterday: Mora's bag and Jargle's statue. The spell from yesterday had long expired, so that's why I was in such a rush to recast it. If I'd asked, Djirk or Ted might have been able to carry them for me, but they were heavy, after all. *A novel would probably abridge minor issues like this, but reality isn't so kind.*

"I still can't detect any mana being put to work... It is safe to say your magic and our sorcery are completely different things." Clara was grumbling to herself, but it was loud enough that I'm pretty sure she meant for me to hear.

If I said anything to her about it, I knew it would only lead to more trouble down the road, so I kept my thoughts to myself. *The Watcher did say something similar, after all... Her deduction is probably right on target.*

Magic User
Reborn in Another World
as a Max Level Wizard

# Chapter 7

THE REST OF OUR JOURNEY to Yulei Village passed without incident.

If I had to guess the season, it was probably the beginning of summer. The temperatures was a little warm, but the wind was cool, and it was good weather to be walking along the plain. As the hours passed, the tiny shadows on the horizon grew to be a village surrounded by farmers' fields. Slightly to the north of the village loomed a large white structure.

"There it is! That's Yulei Village!" said Mora. "See that over there? That's the Castle of the White Blade, home to the Calbanera Knights."

"It looks like we'll be able to have lunch at the inn," remarked Sedam. "I always did like the Knight of the Iron Skillet."

As Mora and the others grew used to my ignorance, they got in the habit of explaining things before I even asked. *But really... Knight of the Iron Skillet? What a name for an inn...*

Yulei Village was a lot larger than I'd expected. Most of the buildings were concentrated around the main road, and there was a wooden defensive barrier around the perimeter. There were even a few watchtowers at various points along the wall.

However, the gate to the village had been left wide open, and there wasn't much of a defensive presence in terms of guards. However, since we figured a floating bag and statue would attract unwanted attention, we hid Jargle's statue and Mora's bag in some bushes outside of the village.

As we headed through the gate, the watchman called out to us.

"Sedam! Is that Miss Mora with you? So, you were able to rescue her from the bandits?"

"No, the one who rescued Mora was this here grand wizard!" Sedam replied.

"That's right!" Mora joined in.

"Hey, wait a—"

"Wizard? Well, anyway, that's great! Thanks!"

"Um... Uh... You're welcome..."

*Really?* I thought. *Don't you want to keep a suspicious guy like me a secret?*

"Ild should still be at the Knight of the Iron Skillet inn," said Sedam, walking ahead.

The main street through the village was paved with stone like the main road outside it, and I could spot horse carts and those who looked like traveling merchants. A few such merchants in particular caught my eye. They had stout figures, long beards, and only came up to my chest in height. There was no mistaking them. *Dwarves,* I thought. The dwarves were talking with other merchants, moving goods here and there, and completely blended in with the other people in the town.

"This village is the easternmost member of the Ryuse Alliance, so it has become an important center of trade between us and the dwarves," Sedam explained.

"My father has all kinds of trade agreements with dwarves," Mora added.

"I see... By the way, I would appreciate it if you didn't make such a big deal out of me..." I said, turning to Sedam.

I'd met Mora only through sheer coincidence, and I'd only saved her through the power of my spells. I'd hardly gone through any trouble to save her. Just then, I felt like I didn't really deserve any praise. And aside from all that, it was kind of...embarrassing.

"Really? I'm sorry about that," said Sedam, "But..."

"But it won't be long before everyone finds out about the amazing deeds of the great Lord Margilus!" piped Ted.

"You say that," I protested, "but even so, I—"

"Give it a rest!" spat Clara. "You're getting on my nerves! Come over here and listen!"

"Wh-what are you...?!"

Clara dragged me into the shadow of one of the buildings and pulled my face close to hers.

"Quit acting so timid! That 'wizardry' or whatever it is you call your magic? It's powerful. *Incredibly* powerful. That's been made plenty clear. So act the part! The way you're acting right now is just going to make people even more nervous! Do you understand what I'm saying here?"

"Sh-she's right! You're amazing, okay, Mister Geo? So you've got to act like you're amazing!"

For some reason, Mora had followed us, and now she was lecturing me, too, physically wedging herself between me and Clara. Djirk and Ted looked on anxiously, but it seemed that they weren't willing to interfere with Clara.

"You know, if you don't let him go, he's not going to be able to do what you're asking." Torrad came calmly to my rescue, pulling Clara and Mora away from me. Not a moment too soon, either; the two of them seemed about ready to go off on each other.

*He's really got that calm, mediator-like aspect of the warrior-priest character down,* I thought, with a sigh of relief, but Torrad wasn't done.

"Lord Margilus, you said you were not anyone important. However, you understand you cannot pass as an unimportant person here in our land, don't you? As Clara said, if a hero does not act as one, he worries those around him. Furthermore—though I wish not to say this—if you are thought of as a weak person, there may be some people who will try to take advantage of you."

Torrad's priestly sincerity gave his words a lot of weight.

*Hmm...*

"In other words, you're saying that a great and powerful hero will put people at ease, but a weak and timid person with an incredible amount of power will do the opposite?"

"That's right!"

"Exactly!"

"Correct."

*Damn it. They do have a point...*

Soon, we arrived at the Knight of the Iron Skillet inn. There were several round tables in a dimly lit hall just past the entrance, in what seemed a cross between a bar and a mess hall. There were several men of different shapes and sizes at the bar, and the busy woman behind the counter appeared to be the owner.

"Father!"

"Mora?!"

Mora, who had been at my side, suddenly ran over to a man in the hall.

"Father! Father!!!"

"Mora! I'm so glad you're all right! I'm so glad!"

The man had brown hair and a face that resembled Mora's. Clearly, he was Mora's father. He appeared younger than I expected but had the air of a successful and accomplished merchant. All of that quickly fell away as he embraced his daughter with tears of joy in his eyes.

"I'm not hurt or anything! Not even a scratch, I promise! I was saved before anything happened to me!"

"Sedam! Thank you. Thank you! I can't thank you enough!" Ild turned to Sedam and bowed his head several times.

"Well, actually... A lot's happened. Let me explain," said Sedam.

From Ild's reaction, it was clear that he was very worried about his daughter. *He has to be at least ten years younger than me,* I thought. *I wonder. If I'd had children, would I have been able to become a father who cares this much about his daughter?*

"Come now, how about you all take a seat and relax?"

The owner spotted us, and, at her suggestion, we all took seats around a table.

••✟••

"...and that's the gist of it," Sedam said, tying up his explanation of events to Ild, who sat beside Mora.

"So, you are the one who saved Mora?" Ild turned to me, with tears in his eyes. "Thank you, sorcerer—I mean—thank you, great and powerful magician!"

Even though Sedam did not go into great detail, it should have been clear that my magic went against the common understanding people in Sedia had of sorcery. Nevertheless, Ild believed Sedam without question. I expected that Sedam must have built up a lot of trust over the years as an adventurer.

"D-don't mention it. I only did what any other wizard would..." My voice trailed off as I got an evil eye from Clara. I was still hesitant to accept such a powerful display of thanks, but considering our most recent conversation, I tried to project a more heroic image.

"Anyway," I said, projecting a little more force and authority into my voice. "I'm just glad to see justice was served!" For me, talking like that wasn't easy.

I glanced at Clara. She didn't exactly look satisfied, but her overall expression suggested I at least got a pass.

Afterward, it came time to dole out the reward for the adventurers' work. Sedam respectfully declined (though he did say he would be keeping the down payment). He instead suggested that the reward should go to me. I tried to refuse as well, but Ild repeatedly pleaded that I take it, so in the end I accepted his three thousand gold coins.

"By the way, how much exactly is three thousand gold coins worth around here?"

"Well, in general terms, one gold coin is enough to feed a family of four the best food in town for a day," replied Sedam.

"Three thousand gold coins is enough to buy a house in Relis, you know?" Mora added, "A large house, big enough for two people to live comfortably! Maybe I could have my father make some introductions for you."

"Interesting..."

From the input I got from them and from a few other people, I determined that one gold coin was approximately equal to ten thousand Japanese yen, or maybe ninety US dollars. However, in a medieval world like Sedia, where currency was not used throughout the entire economy, the comparison was a bit like apples and oranges. From what I gathered, farmers and hunters largely lived without using any currency at all.

*Still, with those caveats, my payment roughly translates to thirty million yen.*

"Damn, that's a lot!"

*Thirty million yen...hundreds of thousands of dollars... That's more than all my savings back home!*

"You think so? It certainly is above average, but it isn't abnormally high. We risk our lives for this work," said Sedam.

"Hmm..."

*When you put it that way... I thought. Three thousand gold coins split five ways is six hundred apiece. If you consider it payment for life-threatening work, it's hard to argue it's too high. It's probably wrong to view the amount in the context of a game, or modern Japan.*

"That said," continued Ild, "I don't have the payment on my person, so could you come pick it up in Relis at a later date? Naturally, I'll prepare you a promissory note for the full amount, but please take this in the meantime."

Ild took out a leather bag filled with one hundred gold coins to give to me. I wasn't in want for money; in line with Geo's character sheet, I'd received more than three million gold coins along with the rest of my inventory. However, refusing would only serve to sour our relationship, so I accepted it with thanks.

Just to be safe, I took out one of the gold Getaeus coins I had from my robe and showed it to Ild. The design was different from his, but because the composition of precious metals was the same, he said I should have no problem using the coins in Sedia, though some vendors might take time to appraise them.

After we all finished our discussion, we relaxed, sipping the sil tea the owner had brought us.

It wasn't long before Mora broke the silence. "Mister Geo, I want to ask you something!"

Thereafter, she reminded me of her father's goods left at the bandits' fortress and requested my help to retrieve them. I had raised the fortress up on a cliff, after all, so they wouldn't be able to get up to it without my help.

"Come now, Mora, we can't trouble Lord Margilus anymore than we have already," said Ild.

"B-but," said Mora, crestfallen.

"We have a saying in my home country," I said, interrupting. "'Once on a ship, you must see it to shore.' I will help you, once everything is done here."

"Are you sure?" asked Ild, hesitantly.

"Thank you, Mister Geo!" said Mora, brightly.

I looked at both of them and nodded resolutely. "Yes, I'm sure," I said, replying to Ild. "But, as I said, there are a few things I have to take care of first."

"We have something we'd like Lord Margilus to help us with as well," said Sedam.

We still had the daemons' nest to destroy. That was an even bigger ship I had to see to shore.

"I don't mind waiting, but don't forget about us! We'll be in trouble if we don't get those goods back!"

Though I'd obliterated their vanguard, it was still very likely that the daemons would regroup and launch another attack. Sedam and the others met privately with the village leader to warn him of the threat. Sedam and the mayor had a strong relationship built on years of trust, and the mayor promised to prepare for an evacuation if needed.

Plans were also made for Djirk, Ted, Fijika, and Torrad to accompany Ild and Mora back to Relis to ensure their safety.

*Well, it looks like I've accomplished my first goal*, I thought, with a sigh of relief.

"Now then, can we carry on with our previous discussion?" asked Sedam.

"Um... Yeah, I guess... I mean, uh... Proceed." I fumbled my words pretty badly, trying to project something like gravitas. Sedam, Clara, and I had moved to another room to discuss our next move.

"Our number one priority to is to find and destroy the daemons' nest," Sedam declared, looking from me to Clara. We both nodded.

"Glad to see we're on the same page." Sedam turned to address me directly. "I understand there is a lot you might not know, so I'll explain my thoughts and rationale. If you have any questions, do not hesitate to ask."

"Understood. Thank you."

I was again impressed by how well-spoken Sedam was. *The president of my old company could take a few lessons from him,* I thought.

"When adventurers encounter daemons or discover a daemon nest, they are required to report the incident to the Calbanera Knights or the Relis City Council. Given the location of the daemons we encountered, normally we would file a report with the knights."

I nodded. *So, first, people file a report, and then they let the authorities take care of it. That sounds like a reasonable system.*

"However, there are some problems. As I mentioned before, it has been over ten years since the last legion or nest appeared in this area. Many in the council and knightly order do not view their responsibility to exterminate daemons as a serious obligation."

"Are you saying we may not be able to enlist their help? We saw it ourselves," I protested. "A whole legion of daemons has appeared."

"It depends in part on whether they believe us," said Sedam grimly.

Clara nodded with a similar expression on her face.

"Huh? But why wouldn't they...?"

"We found a legion of daemons, but a wizard—a magician whose like has never been seen before—just happened to be nearby and exterminate them, with a shower of *meteors*. Do you think anyone would readily believe that story?"

"Ah... Yeah, I see what you're saying." *I really need to get it through my head: This isn't Japan. This isn't even Earth. We can't assume the police are coming to help us.*

*From the perspective of the council or the knights, the appearance of daemons is unconfirmed information, attested by only one source. While evidence of the legion and the methods by which they were destroyed do exist, they exist only out in the field. The daemons didn't actually butcher a village, and none of the knights saw any daemons themselves.*

"I'm not saying that the knights and the council completely distrust us, but I suspect that they won't believe our story. Even if they do believe it, they probably won't take the threat seriously. There's a good chance they'll delay taking action."

*Hmm... I've heard similar stories of inaction many times before, even in Japan.*

"If we were willing to take our time and show them the destruction in the valley, or wait until the daemons reappeared, eventually they would have to believe us, but that really isn't an option," continued Sedam.

"If we did that, there would only be more unnecessary casualties," said Clara.

*Oh, but in that case,* I thought, before speaking aloud. "What if I just show them that I *am* a magic user capable of destroying a legion of daemons? Do you think they would believe us then?"

"It's not an option I would like to choose, but I think they would," Clara replied.

"To be honest, that's the only option we have. What you did defies common sense," said Sedam.

*I see...*

In other words, whether the authorities believed our story or not depended heavily on them accepting that I was who I said I was, a common-sense-defying magic user. However, I ran the risk of being thought of as an even more dangerous threat than the daemons themselves through my simple show of force. I was beginning to realize there was a deeper meaning in Sedam and Clara's push for me to act the role of hero.

"Hmm..."

I understood what they were trying to say. I hadn't adequately thought things through. I simply thought I would accompany them and the knights and prepare a few spells to cast just in case.

I'd worked as a professional for about twenty years in Japan and dealt with all the discord that occurred naturally in that environment. Comparing this to my prior experiences, I realized this was a persona problem. There was a right way to act in certain situations, and it was necessary to adapt to whatever role you served in, even if that meant donning a mask.

*Until just a few days ago, I wore the mask of a twenty-year veteran of the corporate workforce in public, and in private, I donned the persona of a cordial, middle-aged man who liked games. An important part of surviving in the workforce is knowing which mask to don at what time. This is no different.*

I looked up and muttered toward the ceiling. "So, that's why I've felt this strange sense of insecurity ever since I arrived..."

*Ever since I woke up in that jail cell, I've been myself, not wearing any persona. But having no persona at all means having no foundation to stand on.*

*What aspect should a person like me, transported to another world with unbelievable powers at my disposal, decide to assume?*

I brought my gaze back down and looked at Sedam and Clara.

I had the option of simply acting like a foreign wanderer who'd lost his memory, but...I could do better.

"I understand now."

"Good," replied Sedam.

Clara narrowed her eyes. "Are you sure you truly understand?"

"At least for the time being, I'll play the role of a great and powerful wizard. It feels odd to say so out loud, but—it's true, after all."

*It was never my intention to end up this way*, I thought, *but I did choose Geo Margilus as my character before the Watcher, so I have to take responsibility for that decision. At least until the dae-mons' nest is found and destroyed, I'll wear this mask.*

"Good," said Sedam. "Keep that up—at least for the time being."

"Well... I agree," said Clara. "That'll be good enough for now."

··✝··

I was busy preparing to go to the Castle of the White Blade, headquarters of the Order of the Calbanera Knights, when there was a knock on my inn room door.

"Can you spare some of your time?" It was Clara.

"Certainly. Please, come in. Make yourself at home."

*She's probably come to talk about the differences between magic and sorcery with me—the talk she said might end up shaking the whole Sorcerers' Guild...*

"Could you be a little less polite? Your true colors are showing, Mister 'Great and Powerful Wizard.'"

It *was* solid advice, so I tried again. "I suppose I can spare a few minutes."

"Not bad," she replied, with the hint of a smile. It may have been the first time I saw her smile naturally.

I took another look at her. She was young, and really quite beautiful. Her beauty, along with her blue eyes and blond hair (a rare sight back home), sparked a reflexive defensiveness in me toward her...but that was slowly beginning to weaken.

"What did you want to ask about?" I said.

"There are many things I would like to ask, but as we're in a hurry, there's just one I want you to answer now." As Clara spoke, she looked straight into my eyes.

"Our history as sorcerers extends uninterrupted from the time the first institutions were established to study the art, over two hundred years ago. Since then, sorcery has been continually passed on and developed. I myself put forth effort for long years and months to get to where I am today. However, if the entire Sorcerers' Guild were to combine their powers, it would not come close to your magic. What I want to ask is this: Is your magic a power you alone possess? Or..."

Clara's voice trailed off, and she continued in little over a whisper, like a child sharing a rumor she herself was scared of.

"Is it something anyone can learn if they study it?"

I obviously couldn't tell her the truth—that I was a character originally meant for a game, and the background for my magic was something my friend and I had come up with.

Seconds passed.

Clara stared at me, her blue eyes watery, waiting for me to answer. It would probably look romantic to someone who didn't know the circumstances.

*What is she really asking?* I thought. *If my magic were a technique like sorcery, something which could be attained through study, what would that mean to her? Is she asking me whether all her effort to learn sorcery becomes worthless in the face of wizardry?*

*I see. That certainly* would *be enough to put the Sorcerers' Guild in turmoil. If I disrupted their whole way of life, I'd feel so bad I'd want to beg their forgiveness.*

*Hmm... I really don't know.*

Geo's magic was nothing but a fantasy I'd created with the help of the game master, and yet, in this world of Sedia, that fantasy had come to life. The Watcher based my magic on my notes, which detailed all of the things a person had to do to acquire the abilities of a Level 1 magic user, so it wasn't unthinkable that if someone else in Sedia followed those guidelines, they, too, would be able to use magic. However, it was equally plausible that magic was a skill the Watcher had only given me, and that no one else in Sedia could use it. *If that's my answer, would that put Clara at ease?* I thought.

But even after all that thought, I knew it was presumptuous of me to assume I could accurately guess the workings of a woman's mind. It was better to play it safe.

"Are you...anxious about something?" I asked, cautiously.

"Anxious? I suppose I am. You risk uprooting an entire world I've believed in."

"I see."

It seemed I was on point. However, that didn't change the fact that I didn't know the answer. *But then*, I thought, *why don't I just tell her that?*

"While there are learnable techniques associated with a wizard's magic, I am not sure whether someone else will be able to use that magic just by studying them. I simply don't know. But Clara, I want you to know I understand your anxiety. I am anxious myself."

"You are?" Clara blinked. She seemed at least partly relieved at hearing my inconclusive answer, but she was still interested in the rest of what I had to say.

"You mentioned that the world you've believed in could come crumbling down. From my perspective, your sorcery is just as bewildering to me. A sorcerer named Jargle almost killed me with it, too..."

The second half of my statement was my honest impression, not something I said to placate Clara. However, I must admit the first half was a little more underhanded. I was following the playbook of experience I'd built up in the workforce: When approached by someone you cannot give an answer to, first sympathize with them so that you do not lose their trust.

"You have a point. This isn't a conversation if it consists of me only asking you one-sided questions," said Clara, with the hint of a smile.

*Now is the time*, I thought, and decided to go for it. I asked her a question I'd been wondering about sorcery for some time.

"Sorcery is the technique of utilizing hidden power in nature by controlling the mana cycling through your own body," Clara replied, with more than a hint of pride. "About one in ten people are born with mana and can sense it flowing through their bodies. Those without this ability cannot become sorcerers."

"I see. So those with mana can see the mana in others as well."

"That is correct. That's why I can tell that you have no mana at all, with just one look at you."

*Disregarding that last bit,* I thought, *she said sorcery uses a power hidden in nature. My magic calls forth the power of chaos from outside the bounds of nature in order to alter reality, so the very root of it is different.*

"But does that mean that anyone born with mana can perform sorcery?"

"No, even if you are born with mana, if you cannot sense your sorcery frame, you cannot become a proper sorcerer."

*Sorcery frame?* I thought. Apparently, it was something only sorcerers could detect, but while it took a lot of back and forth, she explained it the best she could until I understood.

Our conversation can be summarized thusly:

A sorcerer's apprentice, with training to enhance their mana sensitivity and control, can see a frame of light, not unlike a window frame made up of various symbols. The frame itself is called a sorcery frame (though it has a much longer official name), and the symbols are called sorcery code.

A sorcerer becomes able to use sorcery by deciphering the code in their frame and rearranging that code to form a spell. Of those born with mana, only about one in ten are able to envision their sorcery frames, so there are few people who are even able to become sorcerers. According to Clara, there were only twenty sorcerers in all of Relis City.

"For instance, in my sorcery frame, there is a number representing the amount of mana I have available, and code with the associated meanings: fire, wind, whip, and arrow. If I were to combine fire and whip, reading the code aloud as *Falga Wilm*, my sorcery would initiate."

"I see... Interesting..."

It was much more systematic than I was expecting. It was extremely...game-like. (The irony wasn't lost on me.)

"Oh, I just remembered something Jargle, that sorcerer, said. Do you know what the Faction of the Wise is?"

"That...is one of the factions of sorcerers."

"Sorcerer factions, is it?"

It turned out the sorcerers of Sedia had split into factions based on differences in their approaches to sorcery. The Faction of the Wise viewed it the duty of its members to engage in research to further investigate and understand sorcery, and they were most well known for their production of strange materia. Incidentally, Clara belonged to the Faction of Conquerors, whose members viewed sorcery primarily as a means to fight against daemons.

"I am guessing that Jargle was a renegade sorcerer, despised by all the factions," I said, with a graceful shrug.

*Be it sorcery or anything else, the more I learn about this world, the more questions I have. Well, I should just accept that as part of learning all there is to know.*

# Chapter 8

**S**EDAM, CLARA, AND I reached the Castle of the White Blade about an hour after our departure, without incident.

The castle was built atop one of the gentle hills scattered throughout the plains. It boasted a large gate and walls about fifteen meters high, interspersed with many fortified towers. Looking at it from afar, I could see how it had gotten its name, with the castle walls and towers stained stark white. It lay on the border of two distinct landscapes, flanked on the west by green plains and to the east by a charred red wasteland.

It stood as if it was proclaiming to the world, "Here marks the boundary between the land of humans and the land of monsters."

The Calbanera Knights traced their ancestry to the knights of Shrendal who'd fought over a hundred years prior in the great war between humans and daemons. Whenever monsters threatened Yulei Village or its surroundings, it was the duty of the Calbanera Knights to protect the villagers.

The Calbanera Knights were long known for their skills protecting the peace of the borderland. However, according to

Sedam, with the decrease in sightings of daemons over the past ten years, the knights' morale had hit a low point.

It wasn't long before I shared Sedam's worries.

When Sedam, Clara, and I arrived, we asked for an audience with the captain of the knights and were soon led through the double gate and delivered to what looked like a conference room. However, even though we were received as guests, the man waiting for us in the conference room was not the captain. Instead, we found a middle-aged man named Espine, who introduced himself as a strategist.

"As you are a renowned adventurer, I trust you are not lying to me. However..." Espine's voice came out in a disinterested drone. There was no doubt he believed we were lying. "I have reservations."

"I could understand your hesitation if it was only Sedam who approached you with this story, but are you suggesting that I, fifth seat of the Relis Sorcerers' Guild, would be party to a falsehood?" Clara placed her hands on her hips as she glared at the strategist.

Under attack from the triple combo of Clara's beauty, nobility, and status as sorceress, Espine had to wipe a cold sweat off his brow. "C-certainly not. Only...upon hearing you say that this man here turned a sorcerer to stone and made meteors fall from the sky... You can't possibly expect me to think it anything but absurd."

"I'm sorry, but is there any way we can talk directly with the captain of the knights?" Sedam went on. "If not, could we have an audience with the commander of the first company?"

"Captain Amrand Gal Sardish has been having health issues and is currently resting, and Commander Alnogia is currently out on patrol..."

Sedam and Clara both tried to explain my magic and the appearance of the legion to Espine, but he appeared to have no interest in taking their claims seriously.

*I didn't think we would be rejected this resolutely... What are we going to do?* I glanced at Sedam.

"In that case, we'll just have to wait until Alnogia returns," Sedam declared.

"I'm sorry, but we cannot have you stay at the castle without the permission of one of the commanding officers," replied Espine.

"Tch."

*Did Sedam just click his tongue?!*

*I see. Sedam isn't one who can easily deal with hard-headed types like this,* I thought. *In that case, I'll have to rely on...*

"Why don't we just barge into the captain's room?"

*...apparently not Clara.*

*Should I step in? I don't mind going in for some persistent, long-winded negotiations,* I thought, *but Clara and Sedam seem likely to blow a fuse before anything is settled.*

"Excuse me, but I suggest you take another look at that man's credentials."

"Are you suggesting that this man is a swindler? Are you suggesting that I would be so easily deceived?!"

*This is going nowhere,* I thought with a sigh, when one of the doors opened suddenly with a slam.

A gigantic man walked in. The most appropriate description I could think of was that he was like a sumo wrestler. He looked like he weighed two hundred kilograms or more. It was a miracle he fit into his armor. By his features, he looked like he was in his late teens or early twenties.

"What are you all doing, making a ruckus in *my* castle?"

*That's the first thing out of his mouth? Please let this not be the captain.*

"Sir Gillion. The castle is owned by the order, not a single person," said Espine.

I wasn't surprised that Sedam and Clara's gazes immediately dropped below freezing, but I was surprised at how coldly the strategist Espine treated him as well. Apparently, he wasn't the captain, but his arrogance didn't let that show.

"What did you say? I'm a direct descendant of the founder of these knights, Gilzar Gal Calbanera! What is the name of this order of knights? The Calbanera Knights! So clearly, it's mine!"

"There is no such stipulation in our charter. Sir Gillion, you are nothing more than a company commander."

Hmm. He didn't seem to be doing it on purpose, but I appreciated the explanation. *I've seen types like this every now and then in the corporate world*, I thought. *If you take a swing at their pride, they tend to be rather easy to manipulate.*

"Brother! What are you doing, in front of visitors?!"

As I was occupied with my petty thoughts, another person

came bursting in, pushing Gillion out of the way. She was a knight with wild red hair. Her armor was simpler, so I assumed she was of a lower rank than Gillion or Espine.

*Wait. Did she say, "Brother"?*

"Sedam, Clara. I apologize on my brother's behalf."

"It's all right," replied Clara.

"Leo, perfect timing. Please listen to me. Daemons have appeared. We expect they came from a large nest."

Sedam and Clara appeared to know the knight. *Leo. Is that her name?*

"What?!"

"Are you serious?!"

Both the female knight and Gillion reacted immediately.

"Daemons. Daemons! And you say there's a nest?! All right! Yes! Where is it? The Calbanera Knights and I will crush it!" yelled Gillion.

"Sedam. Is this true? If it's as you say, we must do something about it..."

"Sir Gillion, Lady Leoria, you mustn't believe them. Their story is absurd!"

Silence.

Faced with three radically different reactions from all three knights, Sedam and Clara were at a loss for words. Gillion and Leoria were clearly interested in hearing more about the daemons, but Espine, the one with the most authority, was bent on driving us away.

*I guess I have no choice*, I thought. As much as I would have preferred to avoid it, it was time to don the persona of a great and powerful magic user.

"Greetings, Sir Gillion, Lady Leoria."

I slowly rose to my feet, put my hand over my heart, and took a bow, praying I looked more confident than I felt.

"Who the hell are you? Are you one of Sedam's new recruits? Though, 'new' might be a stretch at your age, Pops," said Gillian.

"Based on your appearance, I assume you are a sorcerer, good sir, but what brings you here?" asked Leoria.

"I am sorry, but you are mistaken. I am the wizard and magic user, Geo Margilus."

Gillion and Leoria looked at each other. *If they really are brother and sister, they're probably on better terms with each other than their fighting suggests*, I thought.

"Yes," Sedam explained. "With his magic, he defeated the sorcerer leading a group of bandits in the mountains, and exterminated an army of daemons before they could attack the village."

"Say what?"

"I'm beginning to understand why someone might call your story absurd," said Leoria.

"If my abilities are in question, there is no need to argue. Let my power speak for itself," I replied, and with an exaggerated flourish, extended my arm so that I pointed to a spot on the floor.

As the Calbanera siblings and Espine stared on dubiously, I kept myself from reacting to them and began casting a spell.

"As a consequence of this spell, I summon the statue in my possession. *Apport.*"

The space just above the location I pointed to on the floor warped, and what had first been a gray smear materialized into the statue of Jargle. With *Apport,* I summoned the statue of Jargle we'd hidden in the bushes outside Yulei Village. As always, the statue showed Jargle's face twisted in fear.

"What?!" Espine was aghast.

"He... But..." Gillian was shocked.

Leoria leaped with a high-pitched scream.

*It looks like my "Grand Wizard Demonstration: Part 1" was a success.*

"This knave," I explained, "is the leader of a local band of bandits who attacked the caravan of a Relis City merchant named Ild and kidnapped his daughter. I will hand him over to you, so that he may be dealt with according to your laws."

To be honest, I did not know whether the order of knights had the authority to judge crimes or mete out punishment. I'd gotten a little carried away.

"However, left in his current state, I imagine it would be difficult to interrogate him, or have him answer for his crimes. Let me take care of that for you. As a consequence of this spell, all mana within a three-meter radius will return to the void. *Dispel Magic.*"

For my next act, I cast a second spell to dispel the effects of *Petrify* on Jargle. A bright light enveloped the statue before vanishing just as quickly as it had come. What remained was a lethargic shamble of a man, collapsed on the floor.

"Rgh... Ahh... Augh," he groaned unintelligibly.

It seemed as though turning the statue back into a human being had a much greater effect on the audience than summoning the object out of thin air. The three knights stared, with their mouths hanging open, as Jargle simply lay there, unable to talk, let alone stand and react to his new surroundings.

Though less extreme in their expressions, Sedam and Clara looked shocked as well. *Magic can do more than destroy things, you know.*

"Th-the statue...turned into a human..."

"But it... You... How...?"

"A-amazing..."

I slowly walked in front of the three, who were still dumbfounded, and approached Jargle. *No rush. Just take it slow.*

I felt a small pang of guilt upon seeing Jargle's empty, unfocused eyes, but I swept it aside, reaching down to pull my Staff of Wizardry out of his hands.

"This one belongs to me."

"Wh-what are you?" Gillion stammered, a cold sweat running down his face.

Upon closer inspection, I saw that he had stepped in front of the red-haired knight, as if to protect her from me. *Hmm, he might not be so bad after all*, I thought.

"At the risk of repeating myself," I began, "I am the wizard and magic user Geo Margilus. I request an audience with the captain of the acclaimed Calbanera Knights, or other suitable representatives of the order, to discuss the threat of daemons currently facing these lands. If necessary, I am prepared to wait here until such time as my request is properly addressed."

I spoke in a slow, deliberate fashion, with as much gravity as I could put on each phrase. When I spoke the final word, I struck the bottom of my staff against the floor.

"I trust you will secure whatever permissions are necessary."

All three knights quickly nodded their heads.

Alnogia, son of the knight captain, was not due to return until the next day. We ended up staying the night at the Castle of the White Blade.

Night came early in Sedia. Oil for lamps was a precious resource, so most people slept soon after sunset. Espine led us to a guest room and provided a partition so that Clara would have some privacy.

Unable to sleep, I asked Sedam for more information about the Calbanera Knights, and he responded excitedly, like he'd just been waiting for me to ask. We sat in chairs by the glowing hearth, and the way the fire lit his face made him look like a natural-born storyteller.

"The charred area to the east of the Castle of the White Blade is now known as the Twilight Wastelands, but it used to be called the Daybreak Plains. The story of how this new name came to be will make clear to you the history behind the Calbanera Knights."

The founder and first captain of the Calbanera Knights was a man by the name of Gilzar Gal Calbanera.

One hundred and fifty years ago, when the second great daemon outbreak threatened to overtake the world, Gilzar Gal Calbanera and the Shrendal Knights faced off against countless legions and emerged victorious.

In Shrendal, Gilzar was received as a hero, and in accordance with popular demand, the kingdom permitted him to form an independent order of knights to protect the borderlands. They bestowed upon him the great Rastland Fortress, which stood in the center of the Daybreak Plains.

However, thirty years later followed the event that came to be known as the Storm of the Dead. Swarms of unliving beings swept the Daybreak Plains for reasons still unknown, and Rastland Fortress succumbed to the onslaught. Some say Gilzar died protecting the fortress; others say he was turned, and still wanders the land with the other undead.

The rest of the knightly order fled with the people of the plains out to the west, where they built a new fortress, the Castle of the White Blade. They vowed to protect the land from undead and daemons alike. While they have upheld that vow, the abandoned Rastland Fortress is still haunted by the undead to this day—at least, so they say.

"And it was then that the Daybreak Plains came to be known as the Twilight Wastelands," said Sedam, finishing the story.

"So, there are undead in this world as well," I murmured aloud, before catching myself and getting back on topic.

"What you're saying," I continued, "is that two hundred years ago, an outbreak of undead drove the Calbanera Knights from their rightful land, and the first captain died. Is that why the knights are no longer led by a Calbanera? Was the family driven out of power as a way of taking responsibility for the failure of the first captain?"

"No, there's a different reason for that," answered Sedam. "Fifteen years ago, I think, the captain at the time attempted to retake Rastland from the undead. Despite opposition, he forced his plan through..."

"Ah... I see."

"It was a complete and utter disaster," said Clara, joining our conversation. "To top it all off, the casualties they incurred were a major reason the knights couldn't mount an effective resistance when the last daemons' nest was found five years later."

"Yes, and that captain was Gillion's father," Sedam explained. "Driven from his post, they say he is now hardly even a shadow of the man he used to be."

*It's not unlike the stories you hear sometimes in the corporate world of a manager betting the fate of his organization on a giant project destined to fail, I thought. That explains the behavior of those loud siblings. They're both members of a once-proud family, trying to reclaim power within the organization once rightfully their own. And it was their own father who ruined their futures, no less. I suspect it must be difficult for them. Chances are good they've earned the ire of the other knights... That may be exactly why Gillion feels the need to act so overbearing.*

"Oh, to be young," I muttered. I didn't really mean it in a mocking way. I felt sorry for them, yes, but I also felt a little envious of them.

Sedam and Clara did not share my nostalgic feelings, especially not for Gillion.

"While I do feel sorry for Leoria, Gillion deserves any hatred he gets," said Clara.

"Maybe...but kids can't choose their parents," I said.

"Then we'll agree to disagree. Nothing justifies that behavior of his," said Clara, raising an eyebrow at me for continuing to sympathize with him.

"By the way, Sir Sardish, the current captain of the knights? He was the former vice-captain," said Sedam, changing the subject.

"He is a very wise individual," said Clara, "and although his son, Sir Alnogia, does not have as much of a strong presence as his father, he is still a splendid knight. I am sure he will direct his knights to take care of the problem."

The power structure of the Calbanera Knights began at the top with the captain, followed by his cabinet of advisors, and then the four commanders of each company, ranked one to four. The commander of the first company was the captain's son Alnogia, and the commander of the second company was Gillion.

Captain Sardish was advanced in his years and was expected to retire from his post soon, but his successor was not yet decided. The two major candidates were Alnogia and Gillion.

"You say Gillion is a candidate... Is he actually popular?" I asked, in disbelief.

"Well, he is descended directly from the founder," replied Sedam, "and in the eyes of some, his skill with the sword is considered best of all the knights."

"I *think* Leoria has him beat, even if she won't admit it, but both of them certainly have more power than Alnogia. It's no contest," said Clara, elaborating.

It seemed raw power was highly valued in Sedia.

"That female knight...was her name Leoria...or Leo? Tell me more about her."

"Leoria Calbanera is Gillion's younger half-sister," Sedam explained. "They have different mothers. I'm shocked they share even one parent though, to be honest."

"Unlike her brother, Leoria is a proper knight. She's the lieutenant commander of the second company. Her experience *is* rather lacking, though..."

*Everyone sure loves to hate on Gillion,* I thought, when someone knocked on the door.

"Forgive me. Lord Sedam, Lady Clara. Master Wizard. Are you still awake?" It was Leoria at the door.

I expected Sedam to answer, but when I looked at him, he just stared back at me.

"Yes, I am up. Is there... Aherm. Is there something you want?"

I tried to sound grandiose, but I stumbled over my words, voice cracking. Clara's mouth was twitching as she tried not to laugh.

*Hey, I'm trying, okay?*

"Thank goodness. Would you open the door? I am sorry for coming so late, but dinner has been prepared, and we'd appreciate it if you were to join us," said Leoria.

*Dinner...*

I hadn't expected to be invited for a meal, and had already eaten for the night. *But refusing to go would be rude, wouldn't it?*

"I am not very hungry, but I appreciate your hospitality. I will attend."

I ended up deciding without consulting Sedam, and when I looked his way, he responded with a smirk before going to open the door. Once he opened it, Leoria appeared with a candlestick in her hand, the dim light of the fire coloring her face. *She's quite beautiful, with those fierce eyes of hers*, I thought, having a second look at her. Unfortunately, however, her expression was stiff, and she was clearly very nervous.

"It appears Lord Margilus will be happy to join. Are we invited as well?" Sedam asked, helping her along.

"Thank you. My brother will be most pleased," Leoria said, and then turned to Sedam. "And yes, you are invited as well."

*"My brother will be happy"? Don't tell me the one hosting this dinner is...*

✦

"Heya, Lord Wizard! Eat as much as you'd like! Y'know, I picked out the castle chef personally. Guy's got real talent, don'tcha think?!"

"Uh-huh..."

Unfortunately, my prediction was spot-on. Gillion was the one waiting for us at the table when we entered the dining hall.

That massive table was laden with steaming plates of food; hardly any space was left between them. It was a fitting sight for the giant knight. I was made to sit at his end of the table and endure his idea of wining and dining. I felt certain Gillion's notions of hospitality didn't extend far beyond feeding his guests good food. Admittedly, everything *was* delicious, but still.

"This chicken is marinated in kumis overnight before it's roasted. Isn't the meat tender? Melts in your mouth!"

"Yes... It's very delicious... Ngh..."

As I bit into the chicken thigh, I was impressed by its juiciness and flavor, a subtle mix of sweet and sour, but I was already over my limit...

"Brother, don't force the food on him. It's bad manners. Can't you see he doesn't want any more?"

"Shut yer yap! We're having a real important conversation over here!"

*What part of anything you've said counts as important?*

*But, looking at it another way, these knights are our sponsors right now—and wasn't I commiserating over their misfortunes mere moments ago? Just hold it in. In fact, this might be a good time to catch their attention with a magic trick or two...*

*...or perhaps not.*

As I was falling back a little *too* hard on my corporate dinner survival instincts, I noticed Sedam and Clara signaling me with their eyes. It was time to wrap this up.

"That was very, very delicious, but I couldn't possibly eat any more," I said, washing away the last bit of meat I could fit down my throat with wine.

"Gillion, could you hurry up and tell us what you have to say? Lord Margilus is getting bored," said Sedam.

"We can't have you waste Lord Margilus's precious time with your small talk," said Clara.

Sedam and Clara dogpiled on Gillion, supposedly on my behalf, but they were clearly just using that premise as an excuse to blow off some steam.

"Quiet! A pair of damned *adventurers* don't get to talk to me like that," yelled Gillion, slamming his fists on the table and gritting his teeth.

"Brother! That's enough!" Leoria shouted and, without any further warning, smacked Gillion in the face with her fist so hard you could hear the clatter of his bones—a perfect boxer's straight right punch.

*What kind of relationship do these siblings have?! Sedam and Clara aren't reacting at all...is this normal?*

"Please forgive him, Lord Margilus," said Leoria, standing with her hand over her heart as she bowed toward me. "Would you not please stay and listen to what my brother has to say?"

"Hmph!" Gillion grunted, the side of his face already bruising, before downing his glass of wine as if nothing had happened.

"Very well," I replied. "I will listen, if he begins without delay."

Part of me wanted to lecture Gillion about making his sister apologize for him, or at least yell at him to make eye contact, but Leoria's solemn entreaty was the greater of the two forces.

Once Gillion had drained his glass he finally turned toward me.

"It's simple, Lord Wizard. I've decided to allow you to become one of my subordinates!"

*Ah, he would be one to say something ridiculous like that, wouldn't he?*

I was too stunned to speak right away. Without turning my head, I looked over at Sedam and Clara. Sedam clicked his tongue in frustration, while Clara had a large vein pulsing on her forehead and a violent smile pasted on her face.

"Sorry, I'll pass." In the moment, I let the act slip some, but who could blame me?

"What?! Are you saying that you would reject the invitation of the heir of the Calbanera family?!" Gillion swept his log-like arms across the table, sending plates clattering.

"At this time, I have no intention of serving under *any* master."

If I had been yelled at like this back in Japan, I probably wouldn't have been able to stay calm—I'd probably fare worse than a deer in headlights. That's pretty much what had happened with the bandits, after all. But even if it was only my third day in Sedia, it seemed I'd already begun to grow thicker skin.

"What did you say?! I'm a Calbanera!" said Gillion, raising a clenched fist.

"Brother!" Leoria was quick.

"Wha?! Ah! Ow! S-stop!"

She promptly grabbed his arm, twisted it behind his back, and began dragging him out of the room as he flailed in pain.

"Ow, ow, ow! Leo! Sis, you can't just—oww!!!"

"I'm sorry, Master Wizard! Sedam, Clara, I had no idea this was what he was up to... I'll apologize properly later!" Leoria paused to bow her head several times, while Gillion cursed and fought fruitlessly.

Then she dragged him off.

"I knew it was going to be something stupid," muttered Sedam, taking the chance to have another glass of fine wine before we left.

# Chapter 9

THE NEXT MORNING, we were informed that an emergency meeting was to be held. We all hurried to get ready.

"It's about time we got going," said Clara, by the door.

*As high and mighty as Clara tends to act, she is really good at keeping tabs on everyone*, I thought, dusting off my robe and combing back my hair.

I'd decked myself out in rare magic items. From my robe to my boots, I looked every inch the wizard, with rings and amulets to spare. If a *D&B* aficionado saw what I had equipped, they would appreciate the dizzying exquisiteness of it all, but apparently Sedia's sorcerers couldn't detect the value in my equipment.

"Looks forbidding enough, don't you think?" I said, quoting the great magician from the classic fantasy film *Dragonslayer* and striking a pose.

"Uh...yeah," said Sedam.

"Absolutely...terrifying," said Clara.

*Then why are you both looking away?*

The meeting was held in the castle's great hall.

I straightened myself up, shoulders back, like I was giving a presentation to a board of directors. I went over the outline of our "presentation" with Sedam, and we decided together how to proceed. Our goal was to convince the order to deploy at least one company's worth of knights for the extermination of the daemons' nest.

To be honest, if the goal were just to destroy the nest and another legion or two, I could make do all by myself, if I were liberal with my spell use.

The problem was, if we let some daemons slip past us, they might build another nest before we could catch them, or even multiple nests. In order to prevent that, we needed enough people with us to surround the area and make sure no daemons got away—so said Sedam. The best-case scenario would be if we could get all of the knights to cooperate with us, but a company would provide enough units to meet the bare minimum—again, according to Sedam.

It was convenient for the purposes of our presentation that the great hall was on the top floor; it had a wide balcony looking out to the east past the castle and the lands beyond.

"Lord Adventurer Sedam, Lady Sorceress Clara Andell and Lord...Wiz...Wizard? Geo Margilus have arrived," said a servant, announcing our entrance before opening the large doors and showing us in.

The room was filled with a majesty that reflected the Calbanera Knights' storied history of over one hundred years. The floor was covered with an embroidered carpet, paintings of scenes from the order's past hung from the walls, and from the ceiling hung a chandelier and flags with the order's crest.

On the far side of the hall, an elderly knight sat on an ornate chair. He, I suspected, was Captain Amrand Gal Sardish. We were told the day before he could not meet with us due to his poor health, but it seemed he'd made the effort to join the meeting after all. On his right was a young knight I did not know, and to his left stood Gillion, with another knight I did not recognize. The knight standing beside Gillion was the commander of the third company. The commander of the fourth was absent, as he was out on patrol.

The other knight, the young one on the opposite side, was the captain's son and commander of the first company, Alnogia Gil Sardish. He was attractive, slender, with blond hair and delicate features. He struck a stark contrast with Gillion.

Apart from the three clustered around Captain Sardish, there was a group of five knights of commanding rank who formed the captain's cabinet of advisors, and a group of several other knights standing at attention. I spotted Leoria among the latter group.

"I am Amrand Gal Sardish, captain of the Calbanera Knights. Adventurers and Great Wizard Margilus, I appreciate your contribution of valuable information to us."

A sickly pallor touched the captain's face, lightening the naturally dark skin behind his white hair and beard. However, his voice was strong and firm, and there was no hint of weakness to be found in his seated posture or his piercing gaze. His eyes had a light that shone stronger than the luster of his silver armor, a light only those who have seen countless battles earn.

"I only did what is required of me, captain," said Sedam, with a simple bow. Though his show of reverence was slight, it was clear he had more respect for the captain than any other knight.

"It is an honor," said Clara, with an elegant bow.

"There is no need to thank us. Daemons are equally a threat to us all. I come to you with the assumption that the Calbanera Knights will be able to deal with this threat accordingly," I said, offering a brief bow of my own.

Under normal circumstances, I would have preferred to show Captain Sardish the utmost respect, but I was warned by Sedam and Clara that if I did not act as if I were on equal footing with him, I risked the other knights looking down on me. But frankly, it was stressful for me to act that way. I'd been nothing more than a desk jockey for all my life, but he was a veteran, one who'd commanded men and knights for long, hard years. I could feel sweat dampen my palms as I gripped my Staff of Wizardry.

"Now, let us hear the details from Sedam, an adventurer from the Relis City Adventurers' Guild," said Espine, in a restrained, formal tone.

When Sedam finished with his explanation, it would be time to move to phase two of our presentation. Would everything continue to proceed as planned? I didn't know. Instead of worrying, I furtively eyed each of the cabinet officers while Sedam talked, in an attempt to glean as much information from them as I could.

"We were on our way to the fortress to rescue Ild's daughter when we met Lord Margilus, the great magician. He'd already saved the girl, captured the enemy sorcerer, and turned him to stone..."

As Sedam carried on with his explanation, I looked around the room. The strategist Espine appeared to be deliberately avoiding my gaze. Leoria and Gillion's expressions were stiff. The other cabinet officers—the heads of finance, intelligence, internal affairs, and the chief secretary—were all looking my way, faces marked by an anxious suspicion.

*Stay calm*, I told myself.

"Finally, Lord Margilus caused meteors to rain down from the sky upon the daemons with his magic. Thanks to him, we were saved."

When Sedam got to the part where I used magic to defeat the daemon army, all the knights reacted with incredulity.

Even Espine and the Calbanera siblings—knights who had seen my magic before—showed clear disbelief. Only the old captain seemed unmoved. Alnogia, on the other hand, showed more fear than doubt, as the color drained from his face.

"And with that, we were able to destroy the daemon army before it could threaten Yulei Village. However, our work is not done. There is no way a force of so many daemons could coalesce unless they spawned from a single nest nearby. If we search the valley, we should be able to find it, but we need to act quickly."

Sedam went seamlessly from the end of his report into a clear warning, an appeal to act.

"Thank you, Sedam," said the old captain. "Is there anyone here who wishes to share their views on this matter?"

A heavy silence fell upon the room.

"I believe we have a serious situation on our hands," said one of the knights, breaking the silence with a deep and heavy voice. "First, I would suggest sending out a reconnaissance team to assess the situation."

The knight was the commander of the third company, a man whose name I later learned was Ord. His build was muscular, and he had a grim face framed with short hair. Clearly, this commander had worked his way up the ranks, as opposed to the others who benefited from their family names.

"A reconnaissance team? That's all well and good, but what will we do if there really is a nest?" Espine objected, his tone constrained. Murmurs swept through the lower ranks standing at attention.

"If there's a nest, we'll just crush it!" yelled Gillion, spit flying.

"Precisely," added Ord with a nod.

"A reconnaissance team is definitely doable, but if it comes down to us destroying a nest..."

"Is there some sort of problem, Sir Igould?" Alnogia addressed the treasurer, a middle-aged, slightly overweight man.

"If we undertake a special operation, we must provide the knights and other troops with supplementary pay, medical supplies, bedding, maintenance for weapons and armor, fuel, and feed for horses. Any casualties will entail additional medical expenses, and any deaths will require compensation payments for the families of the deceased...and that's not all. While the operation is in progress, we must increase patrols and buttress the village's defenses, which will require more work hours and overtime pay. If I'm to be frank. We just don't have it in our budget."

By the end of this exposition, Sir Igould looked emotionally exhausted. I did not doubt his assessment—but it was depressing that even in a so-called world of swords and sorcery, lack of proper funding was still an organization's greatest weakness.

If it really was a problem, I didn't mind pitching in with my own funds, but I didn't know how or where to jump in to make the offer.

"But...do we really have a choice? Can't we scrape the funds together somehow?" Alnogia asked, almost pleading.

"He's right! If we, the Calbanera Knights, refuse to fight daemons for lack of funds, we might as well not be here at all," Gillion shouted.

Even Ord silently nodded his head in agreement, while the lower ranks observed the argument nervously.

"Are we even sure that any daemons actually appeared? I haven't heard any such thing from my subordinates," said another officer in a raspy voice.

The voice belonged to a small, elderly woman with a sharp gaze, who stood out in comparison to the other officers. She was the head of intelligence.

"The daemons' appearance is certain truth, Lady Ireza," Sedam cut back sharply. "Did my report leave any room for doubt?"

"Are you sane, Sedam? Or is this latest fantasy the product of a bad mushroom gone to your brain?!"

"I must admit," added another officer, Sir Logick, head of internal affairs, "I find it difficult to believe this magic user—this wizard, or whatever you call him—exterminated an entire legion on his own."

*Here it comes*, I thought. *Well, it's a logical conclusion. In this world, what I can do defies all common sense.*

"No matter how powerful sorcerers can be, there's no way one can take out a gigant in one blow. That's crazy..."

"I knew their story sounded too good to be true..."

The lower ranks began to mutter among themselves, all voicing a similar refrain. It was time for me to act.

"Interesting," I said, taking a step forward. "You suggest I am a fraud?"

*Good*, I thought. I was able to say my lines without stumbling over them. Everything so far had played out as we expected. It was time for part two of our presentation: my magical demonstration.

"O-of course not, Lord Margilus! No one is suggesting anything of the sort!" The color drained from Espine's face as he hurriedly tried to appease me.

I ignored him.

"I do not fault you for struggling to understand the art, for the workings of my magic are foreign to this land of Sedia. So, let me afford you this opportunity! Behold the power of my spells!"

An uncomfortable shiver of embarrassment ran down my spine. When I was young and first started playing TTRPGs, showy in-character roleplaying wasn't really a thing like it is now, and, needless to say, I didn't exactly start declaiming my lines when I went back to play as an adult.

"Open, Gate of Magic. Invite me into your depths."

It helped that Alnogia, the officers, and most of the other knights stared right at me and gulped nervously. If anyone had chuckled, or even smiled, I might have lost all faith in myself to carry on with my performance.

"As a consequence of this spell, eight meteors will be summoned from the heavens to rain down upon my enemies."

I pointed my Staff of Wizardry toward the balcony, aiming at a spot in the charred wasteland east of the castle. Long before the meeting, we'd ensured that no one would be there.

My imagined self threw the massive pool of dice as it had before. Not that it really mattered this time.

"*Meteor.*"

The moment I finished my spell, the air was filled with a whistling. It grew steadily louder, a strengthening drone, like the sound of falling bombs. Suddenly, eight meteors could be seen shooting through the sky out beyond the balcony, hurtling down toward the wasteland.

The explosion was massive.

The blinding light and thunderous sound from the explosion filled the hall, and the shock wave rocked the walls and ceiling.

"Is that fire from the sky?!"

"What's going on?!"

"I-Incredible..."

"Did you see that explosion?!"

Some yelled, some screamed. Some fell to the ground and covered their heads. Some were shocked and confused, and others simply looked on in awe.

*It worked.*

The cabinet officers in particular all stood frozen, eyes wide and mouths open as if they were in a daze.

"Damn, that's so cool!!!" Gillion was a bit of an exception.

But so was Captain Sardish. The act had not moved him. He had not so much as twitched. The same could not be said of the captain's son, Alnogia, who was struggling to maintain an outward appearance of calm.

"It's all the more incredible, seeing it up close like this..."

"So, this is the true power of magic..."

Not even Sedam or Clara—both of their eyes opened wide— were exempt from the awe and wonder that gripped the room.

*Well,* I thought, Meteor *is orders of magnitude more powerful than other attack spells they've seen, like* Fireball. *I can't blame them.*

"I apologize for riddling your training grounds with craters. If it is a problem, you may bill me for the damages."

I was glad I'd confirmed beforehand that the land was only used for training purposes. *Even so,* I thought, *I did just put eight giant holes in the ground. Hopefully it isn't too much of a nuisance for them.* I glanced at the treasurer. *That bill for damages might really come.*

"But... But how...?"

"H-how is this even possible?"

"That's no charlatan's magic trick... And certainly it's no sorcery..."

"A wizard's magic...is real..."

"There are giant holes in the ground...huge craters!"

The knights were still mumbling to themselves. Some had raced over to the balcony to look outside and confirm the truth of what they'd seen from the marks my magic had left behind.

I took a deep breath and then exhaled. My pulse had quickened with a sense of excitement, both from following through the act and wielding such a great power—but as I breathed out, I reminded myself: *You didn't earn this. The Watcher gave this to you. Letting yourself indulge in a high over this kind of display? You should be ashamed of yourself.*

"Your point has been made."

Just as the commotion was starting to get out of hand, the deep and heavy voice of Captain Sardish echoed through the hall.

"I apologize on behalf of all of us for offending you, Lord Margilus. You have made it very clear to us how incredible your powers are."

*If he's shaken by this, he isn't showing it*, I thought, impressed.

"I do not mind, Captain Sardish, and I, in turn, acknowledge my reaction was unduly rash." I nodded magnanimously.

By the time we came to this exchange, the captain and I had established eye contact. He was attempting to reel in the unease in the hall and steady the ground on which his order stood. If I had not understood his intent so clearly, I doubt I would have been able to answer him with as much confidence as I did. When the other knights saw that he and I were engaging in a calm conversation, they gradually quieted down, and order was restored to the hall.

"I suppose you understand now the information we—erhem— the great wizard Lord Margilus provided is credible," said Sedam.

The knights nodded slowly, as if coming out of a trance.

"In that case, let us return to the matter at hand," I said. "I have full confidence that the Calbanera Knights will be able to deal with the daemon threat accordingly... However, if you require my assistance, I will gladly offer it."

"Your help will surely rival an army one million strong. From this day forth, great wizard Lord Margilus, you are our order's strongest ally," declared Captain Sardish.

"Rejoice, ladies and sirs of the order, for the great magician is our ally!" Alnogia declared, with impeccable timing, unsheathing his sword and pointing it skyward. "Victory to the white blade! Death to the daemons!"

"Victory to the white blade!"

"Death to the daemons!"

The other knights joined in unison, almost reflexively.

*Alnogia does have some things going for him*, I thought. *He has the potential to become a charismatic leader.* A similar thought must have run through Gillion's head, because while he seemed bothered that he'd missed the chance to start the rallying cry, he joined in after Alnogia nonetheless.

However...his potential was just that, nothing more, and I knew it—for I did not miss that the captain, Alnogia's father, had pinched the back of his hand to prod him into making his charismatic gesture.

# Chapter 10

**O**UR PRESENTATION was successful.

The Calbanera Knights decided they would dedicate their entire force to finding and destroying the daemon nest. No one mentioned anything about the budget any longer. The treasurer looked as if he might faint after the decision, but most of the knights in the order were gunning to fight.

Once the decision had been made, the knights quickly set to work planning the details of the operation, and by the end of the day, only a few specifics were left undecided. Incidentally, Sedam received a formal request from the order to participate in the operation, and Clara also agreed to come along, as a representative of the Relis Sorcerers' Guild.

"Not that it's a problem, but they've formally designated you as their 'ally' now. That captain really is a sly one," Sedam remarked to me privately, after the day's meetings were over.

"Ah..." I had not thought much of it at the time, but Sedam was right. As allies, we would be expected to help each other out. While I had gained the help and support of the Calbanera

Knights, I now had a responsibility to support them as well. *If Amrand had this all thought out before he spoke to me, he is certainly worthy of his title*, I thought.

"Be careful not to create too many alliances, or you won't be able to do anything," Clara added, with a hint of snark.

*Definitely something to keep in mind...*

"Ugh," I grumbled to myself, savoring a few more lingering seconds of rest. But soon I left the grandiose room I had been re-assigned to and made my way out into the courtyard.

I was tired, but Alnogia had called for me, and I knew I couldn't refuse.

"I apologize for calling you so late, Lord Wizard," said Alnogia. For some reason, he was in full armor, and his company of knights, twenty in number, stood behind him.

"I do not mind, but...what is it you want with me?"

"I wanted to see if you could help with our training."

"Your training?"

"I heard you were able to create monsters akin to daemons..."

*He must be talking about* Create Ogre Platoon, I thought. *That was not a spell I showed them, but I imagine Mora told Sedam, and Alnogia heard it from him.*

Nevertheless, this was an opportunity for me to measure the ability of the knights and get a general grasp on the balance of power in Sedia. Based on what I'd learned from Sedam's history lesson, the order had experience fighting undead and daemons. How would they fare against six ogres?

"I myself have not fought a real daemon before," Alnogia continued. "The same is true for half the knights in the order. I've brought a good number of the men under my command, in the hope that you could provide us with an experience similar to the fight we will face against the daemons. In this way, we hope that we may grow more prepared."

Alnogia's request was more well thought out than I'd first assumed. *It really is easy to like him, for how earnest he is... The twinkle in his eyes is far too pure and bright to suit a cynical adult like myself...*

"I will not ask you to do it for free!" Alnogia said, bowing his head and taking out a leather bag of gold coins, which he reverently presented before me.

"No, no... You don't have to do that. I couldn't possibly take anything for such a simple request. Use that money to the benefit of the order."

"Th-thank you!" said Alnogia, bowing his head again, and all of the knights in his company followed suit. Alnogia was visibly relieved.

*I've already heard from Igould how tight you all are on money. Don't be so quick to spend that...*

⋅⋅✟⋅⋅

"As a consequence of this spell, a platoon of six ogres will be created out of nothing, and for three days will act on my command. *Create Ogre Platoon.*"

"Grrr!!!"

"Whoa…"

"He really summoned daemons…"

"But the color's different."

"He can even do stuff like this?"

Murmurs ran through the ranks of Alnogia's company, and even his own face was pale.

My spell created six large, red-skinned ogres in the courtyard. As this was only for training, I didn't have the ogres equipped with any weapons. However, any of those three-meter giants' rock-hard fists could easily kill a human. Based on my impressions of both, ogres were roughly equivalent to the second type of daemon, the fiend.

Admittedly, a fiend's skin was pitch black, while an ogre's was brownish red, and the ogres lacked the searing hatred of a daemon. While I noticed a few of the knights in the company pointing the differences out, most were overreacting.

"W-well then," said Alnogia, "I think we should split up into two groups." He turned to me. "Is it okay for us to fell them?"

"Sure," I replied. "Have at it."

"Wait! Wait one goddamned minute!" It was Gillion, leaping and hollering, with Leoria and the rest of his company in tow.

"Al! What are you doing, trying to get a leg up on me?!" he yelled.

"P-please stop, Gillion," said Alnogia.

"Brother, give it a rest! You're being rude!" said Leoria, catching up.

It was clear Gillion hadn't a shred of respect for Alnogia, menacing him with his girth, despite Leoria's protests. Alnogia kept a strained smile on his face, but the ranks of both companies glared at each other with blatant animosity. Even so, as I looked around at how others in the courtyard reacted to the confrontation, it was clear that the only ones on Gillion's side in this were the knights of his own company.

"Lord Wizard! Let me fight those monsters first! I deserve to go first!"

"B-but I *asked* first..."

Alnogia clearly didn't like dealing with Gillion (admittedly, it would be strange if he did), and it didn't help that Alnogia seemed weak-willed in general. Although the fact he did not give in right away was proof that he wasn't completely overpowered by Gillion.

"Gillion." I said.

"Yes, Lord Wizard."

Back when I was in Japan, I didn't like dealing with people like Gillion either, and if I'd had a subordinate like Alnogia, I'd probably be annoyed by him, too. However, with a change in status comes a change in perspective. As I looked at these immature, boisterous youngsters, I took a liking to them both.

"Alnogia beat you to the punch this time, but there's no need to worry. I can make more ogres, if need be. Can I get you to wait until Alnogia has had his turn?"

"F...fine," Gillion grunted.

"I am so sorry to have troubled you, my lord! Thank you for your kindness and consideration!" added Leoria, her eyes sparkling.

After witnessing my *Meteor* spell, even Gillion now seemed inclined to hold his tongue. In fact, he seemed caught between mixed feelings of fear and awe. Leoria, on the other hand, appeared to view me as some sort of embodiment of justice, worthy of her complete trust—which I was definitely not, unfortunately. Sorry.

"Well then, my good knights. Take your positions," I said, eager to change the subject, raising my staff into the air.

"Understood." Alnogia nodded.

"Everyone! Prepare for battle! Platoons one and two, form a defensive line! Platoon three, prepare to flank the enemy! Platoon four, stand by in reserve!"

"Yes, sir!"

Alnogia's voice was unexpectedly sharp and clear while giving orders, and his twenty knights quickly got into formation. Ten knights formed a line in the front, five clustered on the right end of the line, and five took positions in the rear, Alnogia among them.

"Ogres, attack the knights. However, you must not, under any circumstances, kill them," I commanded, surprising myself by how in-character the tone of my voice was. (Not that it mattered. The ogres would obey me whether I was convincing or not.)

"Gruooow!"

"Graah!"

The ogres rushed headlong into the knights' defensive line.

"Ready your shields!"

At Alnogia's command, the front line raised up their shields, each one emblazoned with the order's insignia. Every shield was raised level with their faces. Alnogia's knights were well-disciplined. They acted in chorus, a synchronized machine that formed an impenetrable iron wall...or so it seemed.

"Grrooo!"

With the very first swing of the ogres' fists, the knights' wall of flesh, armor, and shields nearly faltered. No one was sent flying or anything, but several stumbled and were forced to step back. The line was losing its order.

"Don't give up," yelled one of the knights from the center of the line. "Stand your ground!"

"Grroow! Graah!"

But under the force of the six ogres' fists, the line seemed ready to break at any moment.

Alnogia opened his mouth as if to order another command, but he must have been at a loss, for nothing came.

"Grraah!!!"

But the ogres would not wait. A few seconds later, the first knight was sent flying—then the second, and the third. None could withstand the force of the constant barrage, and those who were not sent flying fell to their knees.

"Platoon four, forward! Platoon three, flank them now!" Alnogia finally found his voice. Though he was struggling, he had not given up yet.

"Gyah!!!"

"Uwah?!"

But despite their best efforts, the ogres' strength was too much for the knights to handle. Even as the fourth platoon rushed to fill the gaps in the front line, another hole was made in the wall.

"Take that!"

"Graahhh!"

The flanking platoon attacked, slicing their swords into the sides and backs of the ogres. Though they were finally able to deal damage to the ogres, they could not withstand the monsters' retaliatory punches.

"Regroup! Form a circle! Victory to the white blade!" Alnogia cried, gathering the remaining able knights together, in an outward-facing ring.

"Oh, look at them go," I said, impressed.

"Al! Don't you give up! Aim for the eyes!" Leoria yelled, cheering them on.

"What the hell is he doing? If it were me..." Gillion, on the other hand, seemed incapable of showing others support.

Still, even Gillion's reaction was better than the rest of the staring onlookers, silent and frozen.

*Well, I suppose I can't blame them. The ogres are stand-ins for daemons, after all...* I thought, then paused as I realized the more obvious problem. *What's going to happen when they have to fight the real thing?*

"That's enough!" I yelled.

Alnogia fought well, and dodged the ogres' fists several times, but his sword was knocked away by one of the ogre's muscular arms. I commanded them to stop just as that ogre was about to make contact with Alnogia's head.

The obedient ogres immediately froze.

That did not stop Alnogia from whimpering, his face

ashen white, but it also didn't take long for him to regain his composure.

"Everyone, you did well!" he declared. "Please rest for the remainder of the day. We still have time to rework our strategies before the operation commences. Remember, this is only training. You will have plenty of opportunities to show your strength and bravery when the real battle comes!"

I was impressed at Alnogia's quick rebound and his dedication to his company. I watched him go around, helping other knights to their feet. It was especially impressive, because I knew from the look on his face that he did not believe his own words. He knew how important it was to act the part of a strong leader.

"F-forgive us for our failings..."

"Next time will be different..."

Even as the individual knights fought against shame and despair, their respect for Alnogia held them all together.

"I can't believe you all!" Gillion spat. "I'll show you how it's done!"

Gillion, tactless as ever, invited a volley of cold glares upon himself.

*They say Gillion and Alnogia are both candidates to be the next captain, but is it really a contest at all? In terms of popularity at least, there's no way Gillion could beat Alnogia.*

✠

"Take that! And that! Now how about this?!"

The fighting style of Gillion's company was the absolute opposite of Alnogia's. As soon as the training began, Gillion rushed forward and abandoned his knights without any orders.

As it turned out, Gillion's confidence was not for nothing. He fought well, receiving the ogres' blows with his shield and pushing them back, hitting weak points accurately with his sword on the return. Despite his enormous size, he was very agile, and on close examination it was clear his agility was the product of carefully calculated actions, rather than quick reaction times.

"Hiyah! Yah!"

Leoria was fighting in a circle around Gillion, and she raced back and forth so fast it was as if she wasn't wearing armor at all. With her speed, she was able to confuse the ogres with feints, and she used the openings she created to target the ogres' legs.

"Yeah!"

A cheer swept through the crowd of onlookers. One of the ogres Leoria attacked had fallen to its knees. After seeing the performance of the knights in the previous matchup, it was hard to believe Leoria was human. *If she were matched against an ogre, one on one*, I thought, *I would be hard pressed to say who was stronger.*

*So, this is the true face of Sedia*, I thought. *In this world, humans with different aptitudes and experiences can exhibit such a broad range of skills and abilities, so much so that I'm made to question whether they're really 'human' anymore. This truly is a fantasy world of swords and sorcery—a world of heroes.*

"Good going, Leo! Hrrngh?!"

"Hey! Let me go!!!"

However, unfortunately, these two heroes hit their ceiling.

Gillion was kicked by an ogre approaching from behind, and Leoria, out of breath, was grabbed by another and dropped her sword. Maybe this goes without saying, but I should also point out that the rest of the second company had already been defeated.

"Stop! That's it!" I said, hurriedly commanding the ogres to stop.

"Damn it!" Gillion cursed from the ground, covered in sand. "Let me have one more go at it, Lord Wizard!"

"You...you brute! Let go!" said Leoria, as she continued to struggle, punching the ogre that still had her arm with her other fist.

I was impressed with both of them, though for very different reasons than I had been impressed with Alnogia. However...

"What are you doing, ruining morale before the operation even starts?!" Clara said, incredulously. I hadn't noticed, but apparently, she had come to watch.

*Can't you spin that a little better*? I silently protested. *At least now I have a better idea of what they're capable of... As an ally, it's my responsibility to know these things.* I nodded, hoping to convince myself this wasn't a disaster.

✦

Back in the guest room...

"No, I agree. That was completely your fault."

Sedam took Clara's side.

"I can't believe you disgraced Alnogia in front of all those people," Clara charged.

"But you told me that fighting daemons was this order's main objective, so I thought—"

Sedam clenched a fist. "If your plan was to simulate real combat, you should have paired two against twenty, not six!"

*Hmm...* I thought. *So that's the power dynamic between humans and daemons in Sedia.* Between what he'd said and what I'd seen with my own eyes, I pegged the equivalent *D&B* character of an average knight at Level 3, give or take.

"If you matched six knights against twenty imps," Sedam continued, "those knights would probably emerge victorious. However, that's not how this is done. The extermination of daemons should be done with strength in numbers. Daemon hunts demand the coordination of a full-scale army, not the strength of a few heroic individuals!"

In fact, the two companies being deployed for the current threat numbered over four hundred knights in total.

"I...I hear you." I rubbed at my temples. "But while we're on this topic, what would you say is the average strength of adventurers like yourselves? Is your party stronger than average?"

"Our strength..." Sedam paused, a troubled expression on his face. "If we include Clara in our party, we are probably one of the strongest bands in all Ryuse. However, without her, we are only average, I would say."

"I *can* use high-ranked sorcery, after all," Clara said with pride, thrusting out her chest.

*So, sorcerers do play an important role in the power dynamics in Sedia.* It didn't surprise me one bit.

"However," Sedam continued, "there are not many adventuring parties out there that can take on a fiend. There are probably only three in Relis that can manage that feat, and that's including ours."

Among all known daemons, weighing their aptitude for battle against their rarity, fiends reigned as the most threatening. While imps were common, individually, they could not overwhelm a common soldier. In other words, a swarm of them was manageable as long as you had the advantage in numbers. Of course, "manageable" here meant just that. An advantage in numbers didn't guarantee that you wouldn't suffer massive casualties, especially with the wrong kind of luck.

However, if a swarm of imps had even one fiend among them, you could expect your casualties to skyrocket. According to Sedam, a group of twenty heavily armed soldiers was required to take down a single fiend, and even with that, if you were unlucky, your entire team could be wiped out.

"However," Sedam said stubbornly, "I think it important to add that an adventurer's worth is measured by far more than his strength at arms alone."

Unlike an army, a party of adventurers could specialize in several fields, including tracking, defense, and battle. It would be wrong to focus only on a party's strength in battle. Sedam's complaint was absolutely a valid one.

However, that did not change the simple fact that humans in Sedia had a clear disadvantage when it came to fighting daemons.

"What about those you might call heroes?" I asked.

"If you mean heroes involved in the extermination of daemons, there's a warrior known as Lade the Daemon Killer. He could probably take down five or six fiends, and maybe even a gigant, on his own," said Sedam.

"Among sorcerers," added Clara, "the first seat of the Ryushuk Guild, Pelishra, can face a gigant alone. Rumor has it he is able to use one of the highest ranked incantations, *Icia Hels*.

"In addition to him, the strongest party in Sedia is led by a sorcerer known as 'Hellfire' Calbaran. Someone like him could probably take on several gigants at once.

"However, they are based in the capital of the Shrendal Kingdom, so we cannot count on them for help this time," said Clara.

*Daemon Killer, the first seat of the Sorcerers' Guild, and Hellfire, huh?* I thought. *If this were an RPG and they were NPCs, I could expect to run into them later in the campaign...*

I paused, slapped both my cheeks, and drove that inane thought away. *These are real people, not characters in some game.*

"Well, you look like you're raring to go," quipped Sedam. "Ready to join the ranks of our heroes?"

"No, that's not what I... Practical issues aside, I'm not suited to filling that kind of role." *There's a huge difference between fighting and wanting to fight.*

Both Sedam and Clara just shrugged their shoulders at me.

"Damn you! Take this!"

"Brother! Behind you!"

We could still hear the shouts of the two Calbanera siblings—
they'd asked for overtime—training in the courtyard.

✠

"Take that!"

"Ga-gyaah!"

Astonishingly, after two days of relentless practice, Leoria managed to take down an ogre, largely by herself. She did have Gillion
and her knights assisting her, and the ogres were weaponless besides, but that didn't make her fast improvement any less amazing.

"Thank you, Lord Magician! This is all thanks to you! Thank
you so much!" Leoria was covered with dirt and blood from the
ogre, but seeing her pure smile, I couldn't help but think she was
beautiful.

"Damn it, Leo! Don't get too full of yourself, you hear? I'll
surpass you soon enough!"

Alnogia stood by, long-suffering. "Sir Gillion, you should
probably focus more on giving orders to the knights under your
command..."

Gillion had certainly improved, and Alnogia didn't hesitate
as often in giving directions to his knights, either. All of them had
what it took to one day be heroes.

*I really don't want to see any of these young people die before
their time.*

✠

The first and second companies of the Calbanera Knights assembled at the Castle of the White Blade for departure, a combined force of 430 knights and twenty attendants.

The captain saw us off, alongside the residents of Yulei, who'd come out en masse after hearing rumors of our expedition.

"I pray for your success," Amrand cried. "Victory to the white blade! Death to the daemons!"

"Victory to the white blade! Death to the daemons!"

"Good luck!"

Though we departed with much fanfare, we did not set out directly for the daemons' nest. We didn't even know where it was located. Therefore, our first destination was Jargle's fortress in the mountains. We planned to use it as a base of operations as we set up our defensive line. We'd encircle the daemons and make sure none escaped after we destroyed their nest.

We made our way up the narrow, winding mountain path with our forces in tow. For better or worse, we didn't encounter any daemons or bandits along the way. When the fortress finally came into view, I was overcome with nostalgia. It was my starting point in this world, after all.

"What the hell?"

"That cliff wasn't here before!"

"How is there a fortress up there?"

Of course, that nostalgia was quickly pushed aside by the commotion from the knights when they saw what I had done to the fortress with my *Structural Renovation* spell.

After I returned the fortress to its original position, the knights began hauling in supplies. With nearly five hundred people in our ranks, not everyone could stay inside, but the knights set up camps around the fortress yard.

It bears mentioning that I'd separated Ild's goods from the rest of what the bandits had stolen. I let the knights confiscate the remainder. I figured they would take and use what they could, as a way of softening the effect of the operation on the order's finances. I shed a mental tear for the treasurer.

"Now, let us confirm the details of the operation," said the strategist, Espine.

All vital personnel and ranking officers gathered in the commander's office in the tower.

"The first company will head out east, and the second company south, to form a defensive line. The current plan is to hold this line for a period of three days, after which the operation will conclude. However, please keep in mind this duration is tentative and may be revised if the operation is extended. Remember, there are villages to the west of our line and the Lawful Way to the north. Do not, under *any* circumstances, let the daemons break through. Once our defensive lines have been established, Sedam, Clara, and Lord Margilus will accompany an elite force to the valley where the legion was last sighted. There, they will identify and eradicate the daemons' nest. After the nest is destroyed, this elite force will rejoin our defensive forces to assist in the extermination of any remaining daemons."

In short, the success of the operation depended one hundred percent on Sedam's tracking abilities and my magical power.

At the first meeting, when the operation was still coming together, I'd planned only to provide support. However, after seeing how the knights performed in training, I'd forced the decision makers to give me a more active role. At first, Alnogia and Gillion protested, but by reminding them of how they'd fared against the ogres, I was able to shut them up.

Maybe I was acting a little overprotective, but who could blame me? I felt bad for damaging their pride, and was anxious for my own sake, but I was ready to shoulder more responsibility if it meant saving lives.

"Now, allow me to share some lesser-known details about the daemon nest we seek to destroy," said Gunnar, a middle-aged knight who was the lieutenant commander of the first company. He had participated in the extermination of a daemon nest ten years earlier.

"A daemon nest is unlike the nest of any other creature or monster. What we call a 'nest' colloquially often takes on the appearance of a black sphere, but not always. It can change. Indeed, it is thought to have no set shape or form."

*Hmm...* While it had been hinted at during previous meetings, Gunnar made it clear that a daemon nest was far more than a nest in the traditional sense of the word.

"The nest I encountered ten years ago was roughly the size of a bull, and I witnessed daemons being spawned, dripping, from its core."

*The more I hear about them, the more disgusting they turn out to be.* The daemons of Sedia were completely different from the monsters I was familiar with in novels and games.

"Just to confirm," I began. "You were able to destroy this nest with swords or sorcery?"

"Correct, Lord Wizard."

*Well, if it can be destroyed through spells and physical trauma, I should have no problem destroying it with my magic,* I thought.

"You said we will accompany an elite team... Is that team not just the three of us?" Sedam asked, suddenly.

"Please take me with you!"

"Don't be stupid! I'm the one that should go with them!"

"I want to go, too!"

Alnogia, Gillion, and Leoria all immediately spoke up. *I knew this would happen,* I thought. *If we only knew where the nest was, I would have asked to go alone.*

Alnogia and Gillion were *so* enthusiastic to join that it struck me as suspicious. I wondered if they were doing it to score points with the other knights in the order. They were both vying to be successors of the captain, after all.

"Leoria aside, you two are commanders! Think about your duties!" barked Gunnar. His reprimand seemed pretty effective to me; it didn't hurt that he had a scar across his face. But the protests continued.

"B-but... We can't just let Lord Margilus do all the work," Alnogia insisted.

"No! Do not speak to *me* of duty! I'm a Calbanera! My duty is to be the one who slays the daemons!"

"Shut up, brother! I'm a Calbanera, too!"

One look at their earnest faces and my suspicions about ulterior motives faded. For better or worse, they were driven by a sense of mission, not political calculus.

*Regardless of their motives,* I thought, *it would make no sense to have both of your candidates for the next captain participate in the most dangerous part of the mission.* But I kept my opinion to myself, not wanting to get involved in the order's politics.

"In my opinion," said Espine, "I think it best if Gillion, Leoria, and Gunnar accompany Lord Margilus, Sedam, and Clara to the nest. I will take command of the second company."

"Oh! You do have some good ideas after all, strategist!" said Gillion.

"Thank you!" said Leoria.

The Calbanera siblings were ecstatic, and Alnogia bit his lip in silence. *Is he trying to get these two killed so they'll be out of the way?* I thought, exasperated. *Well, at least they're happy, I guess.*

"Well then. May our efforts bring us total victory."

"All right! Leave it to me, Lord Wizard! We'll get this done!"

"I swear this: I shall protect you!"

*Thanks for your enthusiasm,* I thought, *but if all goes as planned, there may not be much for you to do...*

# Chapter 11

THE NEXT DAY, our "elite team" stood alone in the middle of a valley filled with charred daemon remains. From there, we were to make our way up the valley and in search of the nest.

"We don't know when we might be ambushed by daemons. Everyone, be on your guard," said Sedam.

"Understood."

Sedam and Gunnar proceeded to consult one another over what might be the best formation to take as we trekked up the valley. Meanwhile, I selected what spells I thought might be useful, and cast them.

"As a consequence of this spell, all allies within a three-meter radius of me will be transported to the outer plane. *Move Outer Plane.*"

By the power of the spell, all six of us were moved into a space dimensionally removed from—but parallel to—normal space.

From our new perspective, our surroundings were gently warped, bluish and swaying, as if we were looking from within an aquarium to the outside. From anyone else's perspective, we would have appeared to vanish into thin air.

In the outer plane, we would be safe from daemons or anything else that meant to cause us harm. In fact, we were undetectable by any conventional means. The only major downside was that while within the outer plane, we could not affect or influence anything in the material realm. However, this worked both ways. For example, by moving to the outer plane, we could walk right through any physical barrier. That was one of the biggest advantages the spell had to offer. Furthermore, as long as the spell remained active, we could freely move back and forth between the outer plane and normal space.

However, as suggested by the warping and discoloration, what we could sense of the real world from the outer plane was limited. Sounds and smells were particularly hard to perceive.

"Anything goes with you, huh?" muttered Sedam, sardonically.

Clara said nothing, but looked angry as she examined the outer plane.

"Whoa..." Gillion stood in naked amazement.

"L-Lord Magician..." Gunnar's face grew pale. "Are you a god?"

Leoria turned her eyes up toward me. "My lord, are you not an angel of the winter protector, Ashginea?"

*Leoria, please don't get down on your knees like that.* "Wh-what are you talking about? I-I am certainly not a god."

Being treated like a god was *definitely* more than I'd asked for. While, strictly speaking, Geo's level was high enough to attempt the kind of quests in *D&B* that led to your character becoming a god, you must remember, on the inside, I was still just an ordinary human being.

"My dealings with the immortals are few and far between. If my magic looks like the power of a god to you...perhaps your faith is a little too strong," I said, in a flustered panic. I hardly knew what I was saying. It was a saving grace that behind the other three stricken with awe, Sedam and Clara were rolling their eyes at me.

To reiterate, my powers were far from the omnipotence of the divine. While my spells were powerful, as a magic user, I had tons of weaknesses. One was the upper limit on the number of spells I could charge each day. For example, here is a breakdown of the Rank 9 spells I had charged that day.

### RANK 9 SPELLS

| SPELL NAME | REMAINING USES / TOTAL CHARGED |
|---|---|
| Meteor | 2 / 2 |
| Complete Recovery | 1 / 1 |
| Time Stop | 1 / 1 |
| Create Monster: Any | 1 / 1 |
| Word of Death | 1 / 1 |
| Chaotic Wall | 1 / 1 |
| Move Outer Plane | 0 / 1 |
| Invincibility | 0 / 1 |

The maximum number of spells a magic user can have charged per rank increases as a magic user levels up. In my case, I had nine charges per rank. The spells that had zero remaining charges for the day could no longer be used. (I cast *Invincibility* on myself before we set out.) Of course, I had nine spells charged for all of the other ranks, one to eight, but I'll hold off on listing them out in exhaustive detail.

If I had extra charge slots available, I would have charged another *Complete Recovery,* and also *Shapeshift*, a spell that has many uses, but as I have said many times before, a restricted arsenal is one of the many limits of a *D&B* magic user.

"Well then. Shall we?" I said, urging the group on.

After all, *Move Outer Plane* did not have an infinite duration.

✦ † ✦

Sedam took the lead as we continued up the valley.

The valley was unexpectedly complex, winding its way deep into a maze of many passages. Every time we came to a fork, Sedam investigated the surroundings; he was soon able to find traces left by the legion as they'd marched through the valley. Despite the dulling of all our senses in the outer plane, Sedam was still able to quickly pick out footprints and hairs left behind. I couldn't help but be impressed by his tracking skills.

Thanks to Sedam, we found the daemons' base only two hours after we set out.

"There's a gigant..."

We stood at the deepest part of the valley, an area about the size of a baseball field, surrounded by cliffs. Nearby loomed an elephant-sized gigant, about four meters tall and five meters long, surrounded by dozens of imps.

It looked like the imps were feeding the gigant. Some of them held up what looked like a boar. Fortunately, as we were safely within the outer plane, none of the daemons noticed our presence.

The gigant sloppily grabbed the boar from the imps and bit into its head. Behind it was a giant stone door, which looked almost like a lid set upon the deepest part of the valley. The space sealed by that door was so large even the gigant could have easily fit through it.

"The nest has got to be behind that door," said Sedam.

"Almost certainly," replied Gunnar.

The door itself was simple, but it was covered with unsettling symbols that looked like the work of some avant-garde abstract artist.

"So, I take it the plan is to kill the gigant and then charge through the door?" said Gillion.

"That's the plan, but I think you should let me handle it," I replied.

"You're right."

*Oh?* I'd thought Gillion would want to charge right in, but it seemed he had already started to show some growth.

"Before we do anything else, let's first investigate what's behind that door," I said, taking a scroll out of my bag. Clara gazed intently at it and then turned to me with a puzzled look on her face.

"It's...blank, isn't it?"

"Well, it is right now, but... Well, just watch."

I placed the blank scroll on the ground and spread it out.

"Oh? I see something!" said Gillion.

"Is this...a map?" asked Gunnar.

Gunnar was right. The scroll was a magic item, a Mapping Scroll. Normally it remains blank, but when spread out, it automatically creates a map of any dungeon in the vicinity. If we were playing a TTRPG, it would be enough to just map out the dungeon on graph paper as we explored it, but this wasn't the time for the traditional method.

"As I suspected," said Sedam. "There's a path behind that door leading underground." He stood analyzing the map as its details slowly, automatically revealed themselves.

"This nest is producing gigants, so as long as we follow whatever path is wide enough for a gigant to pass through, we should be able to find the nest...here," he said, pointing to a corner of the map. It depicted a large chamber located deep underground. As he predicted, a wide path led from it all the way to the door.

"It looks like there are other branching paths and smaller rooms," said Clara. "I wonder if there are any other paths leading out..."

"All of them are narrow, it seems. So narrow, even a fiend would have trouble getting through, let alone a gigant," remarked Sedam.

*So, we're lucky*, I thought. If there were many large branching paths, we would have to make sure all of them were blocked.

"I suggest we enter here," I said.

Even though we could use the outer plane to slip through physical barriers, that didn't mean we could just ignore the layout of the dungeon. Deep in the earth without a clear line of sight, it would be very easy for us to lose track of each other, or our place on the map. There was no point walking through walls if we weren't able to get to our destination.

"In order for me to cast another spell, we must first exit the outer plane," I said. "While we are back outside, I'll need you to protect me."

"All right! Leave it to me, Lord Margilus!"

"I'll protect you!"

The Calbanera siblings excitedly moved in front of me, while Sedam and the others took defensive positions behind.

"I have a defensive incantation, *Ludora Ward*, which should at least temporarily be able to fend off an attack from that gigant," said Clara, holding her staff ready. Her blue eyes sparkled; I could feel her excitement.

Not for the first time, I thought about how both Clara and Leoria were capable of so much energy at such grim and dangerous times. *These two women are so bright and brimming with life it's almost too much for an older guy like me to handle...*

"Well then, let us return to the material plane."

We weren't in the middle of the clearing, but in the shadow of a boulder near the entrance. As soon as we left the outer plane, the terrible stench of the daemons, which the spell had shut out, assaulted our noses.

"Open, Gate of Magic!"

While my physical self endured the awful smell, my imagined self descended to the sixth level.

"As a consequence of this spell, I shall bring death upon the living in my sights, within an area of eighty-one square meters, up to a cumulative level of thirty-two. *Death Gaze!*"

All was silent.

Even after I had finished casting the spell, no immediate change in the gigant or the surrounding imps could be seen. It still had its hands around the boar shoved in its mouth. I could feel the nervous tension of the knights, but I could also perceive the chaotic energy unleashed upon the world, the power of death itself, wrapping the gigant and imps in a cold embrace.

One second passed.

Then things began to change.

"Gi...?"

The body of the gigant went limp. It dropped the boar, and with its tongue still hanging out, the gigant fell to the ground. It seemed as if it all was happening in slow motion. If you looked closely, you could see that several of the imps had fallen as well.

"Gweh?!"

"Gyaahh!"

"Grrr! Gyu!"

The gigant, lying face down on the ground, did not move or twitch at all. *Death Gaze* is a spell that can kill any number of monsters in a given area up to a cumulative level. According to the rules of the *D&B* game system, all targets have a chance to make a saving throw—if they roll successfully, the spell has absolutely no effect on them at all. I'd worried about that technicality maybe posing a problem, but it looked as though the spell worked just fine.

"Did... Did it die?"

"All you did was stare at it..."

That wasn't exactly what had happened, but now was not the time to correct anyone. The remaining imps, very much still alive, had noticed our position.

"Gigyah! Gaah!"

"Gyaar!!!"

"Open, Gate of Magic!"

The imps brandished their primitive axes and spears—and charged. Their cold hatred sent a shiver down my spine. Their hate-filled eyes glimmered with gruesome malice. As I began casting my next spell, I heard Sedam loose an arrow from behind me.

"Gyah?!"

The imp in the front of the charge took an arrow to the chest and flipped backward.

"*Falbolza Chain*!"

Clara shot ten fiery arrows from her staff, engulfing imps in flame, one after another. As I watched them burn, I was reminded of the first time I saw Jargle use his ice arrows on me. Sorcery's strength is that its incantations take very little time to complete. If a magic user had to fight a sorcerer without any preparation, there is no way they could win.

"All right," Gillion bellowed, "Come at me!"

"I won't let you lay one finger on Lord Margilus!" yelled Leoria.

The Calbanera siblings and Gunnar took up their shields and formed a defensive line in front of me, but before the imps could reach them, I finished casting my spell.

"As a consequence of this spell, I will bring under my control the dead in my presence as zombies, up to a cumulative level of thirty-six. *Control Undead.*"

I think you get the picture: *Control Undead* was classic necromancy.

A false life blew into the gigant and several dead imps, raising them from the ground as zombies.

"Grooo..."

As *Death Gaze* leaves no visible wounds on the target, the undead gigant and imps looked no different from before. However, as the gigant swung its giant arms and legs, it targeted the living imps, not us.

"Gyah! Gu-gyah!"

"Groooo!"

The zombified gigant and imps fought the living imp survivors in a scene right out of hell.

Apparently, the desire to kill humans took precedence over any concern for themselves or the crazed zombies. The living imps ignored the assault of my risen undead. They kept right on charging at us. However, the gigant sent most of them flying, and Sedam sniped those few that slipped past our gigant guard with his arrows.

"This is crazy. It's like a nightmare."

I shared Gillion's sentiment.

In only a few short minutes, all of the sane daemons (if indeed any daemons were sane) had died. All of the zombie imps had fallen in the process, but the gigant zombie still stood strong. *Now that the guards are gone, let's charge right in.*

"As a consequence of this spell, one target will be obliterated. *Destruction!*"

"What now?!"

"The gate!"

The giant stone door crumbled to dust.

*Destruction* works on organic and inorganic objects alike, breaking them down at the molecular level. Once the dust had settled, the mouth of a cave lay exposed. The darkness of its lower reaches awaited us beyond.

With *Move Outer Plane*, getting inside wouldn't pose a problem, but now that we had a gigant zombie, I wanted to put it to good use.

"Go. Kill all the daemons inside," I ordered.

"Guuu."

On my orders, the gigant zombie headed down into the cave, sluggishly stomping over the destroyed gate. The knights looked on, their mouths hanging open.

*Wait a minute.*

*Couldn't I have just had our zombie open the gate instead of destroying it?*

"Errm... Eherm," I cleared my throat. I could feel Sedam and Clara staring at me, and it stung.

"Well then, shall we?" I hoped I sounded at least ten times more confident than I was.

"Wait a min—Margilus!"

*So, my sorry excuse for an act can't fool seasoned adventurers,* I thought, as Clara grabbed my robe as I moved to leave.

"I thought it better if we left the door as it was," said Sedam, with the hint of a sarcastic smile. "Couldn't we have just slipped through the door using the outer plane? Or am I missing something?"

*No...you're right on point...*

We could already hear the gigant zombie wreaking havoc down below. However, with the door gone, it was much more likely that a fiend or another gigant would get out.

"I'm sorry," I said, turning to apologize. "I wasn't thinking. I got carried away,"

"Sedam, what are you doing?" Gillion hissed before eyeing me nervously.

"L-Lord Margilus..." Leoria looked nervous as well.

*Are they worried I'm angry?* I thought. *Sedam's point was more than valid. I had genuinely made a mistake. Why should I be mad?*

"You didn't do anything you need to apologize for," said Sedam.

"More importantly, what are we going to do about that hole?" said Clara. "I could collapse the ceiling with my sorcery to seal it off, but..."

Sedam and Clara quickly moved on and went about finding a solution. While Clara could make do with her sorcery, it would end up costing her a significant amount of her mana reserves.

"I'll seal it," I said.

With a rumble, the earth shook, and a gray wall rose from the ground to block the entrance. This stone wall, created by the aptly-named *Wall of Stone*, made a near-perfect seal over the entrance to the cave. While it wasn't airtight, or even water-tight, the wall was certainly good enough to keep any daemons from breaking free, as long as it held. And naturally, we would have no problem passing through it with *Move Outer Plane*.

"You really can do anything with magic," said Sedam. "However, that's not without concern..."

"He's right, Margilus," said Clara. "We're relying on you to destroy the daemons' nest. It doesn't make sense for you to waste your mana reserves when we have other options."

While I appreciated Sedam and Clara's concern, the system of magic I used didn't rely on mana reserves or anything like that. "I still have many spells I can use. Using a few like this won't pose a problem when it's time to destroy the nest," I said.

"If you say so, I won't doubt you," said Sedam.

"It's hard for me to believe, personally..." said Clara. "However, even if that is the case, please don't waste your magic unnecessarily."

··✟··

With the problem of the open cave solved, we returned to the outer plane, walked through the stone wall, and continued down the path leading underground.

Normally, it would be pitch black and impossible to see, but as we were in the outer plane, the inside of the cave seemed lit as if by a dim blue light. However, to make our surroundings even easier to see, I cast *Light* on my Staff of Wizardry.

"The gigant's still fighting!" Gillion exclaimed.

Underground, the zombie gigant and several other daemons were still locked in the heat of deadly battle. Several fiends had leaped onto the gigant's back, plunging their swords into its un-living flesh. Countless imps swarmed around its feet.

"Grooo!"

"Gyaaw!"

The gigant zombie reached up and grabbed at a fiend cling-ing to the back of its neck. With a mighty fling, it slammed the fiend into the wall, where it nearly exploded, its death announced by a gruesome splat. New fiends leaped upon the gigant to take the other's place; they continued to rain blows upon it with their swords and clubs.

"Grrrooo..."

Gigants are not especially agile to begin with, and its zombi-fication made it even less so. While the imps were no match for it, the repeated attacks from the fiends were clearly beginning to wear it down. It would have been nice if the gigant was able to exterminate all the daemons for us, but the world does not make things so easy.

The very creature they had planned to use as the core of their next assault now came barreling down upon them. The gate to their cave had been destroyed and replaced by a stone wall. Even the daemons, no matter how single-minded they seemed to be, were thrown into a panic, fiends and imps alike. We saw them up close as we passed, but out of their reach in the outer plane.

"So...the daemons seem to have some culture after all," Clara whispered.

As we trekked through the daemons' base, we came across strange paintings on the walls. They looked like little more than colorful swirls to me, but it could pass as art, I suppose. There were also some objects on the ground that looked like board games.

"Well...if you could call it that," replied Sedam, pointing to a spot where it seemed the game pieces were made...right beside a pile of human remains.

Someone gagged. Gillion cursed, and Gunnar invoked the name of the creator-god Rimeydal in a prayer for the deceased.

That was not the last we saw of the daemons' artwork or toys. Among all of the "source material" for these things, I couldn't shake the feeling that I recognized something, until I realized that this is what had become of the bandits under Jargle's command.

*One reason the bandits suddenly began to demand more from people passing through their territory may have been because they realized daemons were gathering... Perhaps they planned to take all they could and then flee.*

Now it was my turn to gag. I could feel the cold hatred of the daemons as a palpable knot within my stomach, and I had to fight the urge to vomit. *Even if my body's inherited the Strength and Constitution of my D&B character, none of that has helped to strengthen my soul. Any mental and spiritual toughness I might have been born with almost certainly atrophied over the long course of a comfortable life...*

"You damned daemons," I heard Gillion mutter under his breath. "I'll make sure you regret ever underestimating us humans. I'll make sure you pay."

I could feel the burning fire of anger in his voice, and the heat of it helped thaw my frozen soul. I couldn't let my spirits shatter, not here.

"We take a right here," said Sedam, suddenly.

"Thank you," I nearly exhaled. "I almost missed that."

Although we were taking the widest path from the entrance to the depths of the daemon's base, just like the Mapping Scroll had shown, the journey took us through several turns and down several flights of stairs.

Even though we knew exactly which way to go, plus the general structure of the base and our destination, the base itself was dimly lit. Little more than a stray torch or two at junctions drove off the gloom. On top of the ominous paintings and human remains, the air was thick with the sense of daemons and their malice. If it weren't for Sedam reminding me to stay on the path, I would have easily lost my way.

I remembered I'd considered coming here alone, ostensibly to minimize casualties. But now I wondered: *Would I have even been able to make it this far?*

"Our destination lies ahead," said Sedam, stopping ahead of the path's end, where we could see the daemons' lair open up into a vast chamber with a domed roof.

I soon realized that the room took the shape of a flat-bottomed sphere. The entrance was not level with its floor, but rather the center of the sphere, and stairs of giant stone led from the floor up to the opening in the wall.

"So, we finally made it," I said. "Wait, is that...?!"

Although I knew we were safe inside the outer plane, I was stunned silent when I saw the daemon's nest.

"How horrifying..."

"What *is* that thing?"

The nest itself was a series of jet-black, spherical masses—or at least that's the best way I can describe it. There were five clumps, each one the size of a gigant, about five meters in diameter. Their shapes stretched past and overlapped each other. Based on the explanations I had heard thus far, I imagined the nest was more of a living, breathing thing, but seeing it with my own eyes, it looked surprisingly inorganic.

Around it, I could see the shadows of dozens of daemons.

"Is that...something coming out of it?" I asked.

Down where it touched the ground, part of the mass swelled up—and then a piece of it jutted out. At first, I thought it was a pole of some sort, but then the end of it split into five fingers, and I knew I was looking at a hand. The shoulder, twisted head, and thick torso were next to emerge. It was like looking at a sadistic take on a cheap game show routine, a contestant trying to break through a thin rubber sheet. Finally, the fingers tore through, and with a slimy, oily glooping sound, a gigant tumbled out of the nest. The ruptured film was swiftly absorbed back into the mass.

Even Sedam's voice was shaking. "So, *this*...is a daemon's nest..."

Magic User
Reborn in Another World
as a Max Level Wizard

# Chapter 12

THE ONE TARGET we absolutely *had* to destroy was that nest. However, there were many other daemons nearby that we had to deal with. First, there was the gigant the nest just spawned. Then there were scytherns—daemons with long, slender limbs like scythes—and other strange, unidentified daemons lurking in the shadows.

Without leaving the outer plane, we all sat down and began to discuss strategy.

"The nest I saw ten years ago was only about the size of one of those spheres," said Gunnar, a grim look on his face.

Sedam's expression was nearly the same. "I suspect the reason this nest was not found before is because the daemons were intentionally hiding it from us, down here, underground—until they could amass a force strong enough to be unstoppable."

"Are you suggesting that the daemons planned this out?" said Clara.

"Well, daemons have been known to act in an organized way

and use tactics in battle under the direction of a few leaders," said Gunnar.

As I listened to the adventurers and knights carry on their discussion, I considered the best way to destroy the nest. In this situation, the one and only choice was *Meteor*. Although the spell is generally used to summon meteors from the sky, it is possible to summon the meteors inside an enclosed space. Given how large the room was, casting the spell would not pose a problem.

However, in order to cast the spell, I would have to leave the outer plane and return to normal space. It would be convenient if the nest did not react, but if it was able to attack in some way, simply casting the spell without any other precautions would be too dangerous. I floated the idea all the same.

"Absolutely not," said Clara.

"If you die, we won't be able to return from the outer plane, will we? Did you think about that?" said Sedam.

"Don't even joke about doing that!" said Gillion.

"If something happens, I'll be your shield!" said Leoria.

"If we become a burden to you, I will not begrudge you for abandoning us. Do as you will," said Gunnar.

Everyone was against my idea of going out alone.

*While I appreciate the sentiment*, I thought, *I'm not doing this because I'm overconfident. I'm just afraid of hurting you all if I make a mistake.*

"I, for one, am sick and tired of you underestimating us," said Clara.

"Clara, I..."

"Do you think we're all dolls or something? Look again. These are warriors who have fought in numerous battles, he is a skilled adventurer, and *I* am a sorceress!"

Clara spoke with even more pride in her expression than usual. I did as she said, and took another look at the knights and adventurers who had come with me. I saw fear and anxiety, but also a strong will in each of their eyes that overpowered everything else.

*These people have seen the horrors of the daemons and have not shrunk back. They have seen the power of my magic and yet do not cling to it*, I thought. *They deserve my respect. As much power as I have, compared to them, I am but a novice.*

"All right."

*That is why I need the help of people like them.*

I thought over the spellbooks I had ready in my archives and the magic items I had on hand, and considered a number of scenarios: What if that nest thing somehow charges at us? What if we're attacked from behind?

"I want you all to lend me your help."

Finally, I decided on a basic strategy to discuss with the rest of my team.

"In order for me to cast *Meteor*, we need to get inside that dome."

*While I should have no problem casting* Meteor *inside this dungeon...if I try to cast it from the hallway, it will probably explode against the walls of the dome before it gets anywhere near the target.*

"So, once we get down to the bottom of the dome, we return to...normal space, correct?" said Clara.

"That's the first hurdle. Next, I want to avoid the door. Instead, let's move through the walls so we can get behind the nest, and then go down into the room."

"Why don't we walk down the steps?" said Gillion. "They can't see us while we're in the outer plane, right?"

Gillion was correct, but I still shook my head.

"I want to be extra careful. We haven't run into any problems so far, but I don't want to take any chances with that nest."

"Hmm... Well, as long as I get a good grasp on the distance and concentrate, I don't think I should have a problem leading us there," said Sedam, volunteering.

"Then, once we're back in normal space, I'll need to be protected from the daemons and the nest."

"From the looks of it, there are imps, gigants, scytherns, and other types of daemons as well. I'm not sure I can guarantee your safety. We're a little short-handed for that," said Sedam.

"Margilus, can't you summon servants with your magic?" Clara asked.

"I can, indeed..."

At Clara's suggestion, I decided to summon ogres to act as decoys and attack the nest head-on.

"Still, the gigant and even the nest itself may attack us. Regardless, I will need you to protect me for at least ten seconds, no matter what the cost."

There was silence.

I, myself, had come to terms with the fact I could be stabbed or blown away by some incredible force. *But as long as I keep as much of my concentration as I did when I petrified Jargle,* I thought, *I should still be able to cast the spell.*

"Lord Margilus. Are you sure ten seconds is all you'll need?"

"Yes. After that, you can leave the attacking to me."

"You're absolutely sure that you'll destroy the nest after that?"

"Absolutely."

Gillion was persistent. While it was hard to say such an attitude was admirable, I could tell from the tone of his voice that he was serious, so I nodded with conviction. Seeing that, he smiled.

"Understood! If that's the case, then I won't charge in and leave you behind. I'll stay by your side and protect you!"

"Uh, thanks."

*You were planning on charging in?!*

*Well,* I thought, *better to have a little too much determination than none at all. Especially after setting eyes on that monstrous thing, and—if he's suppressing his instinctive will to fight in order to protect me...that's admirable in its own right.*

"Brother... I will do the same!" said Leoria.

"I, too, will follow Sir Gillion's fine example of courage," added Gunnar.

Leoria and Gunnar, who knew Gillion far better and far longer than me, understood the weight behind his decision to concede the attack to another.

"Well...I may have to re-evaluate my opinion of you, Gillion," said Clara.

"Agreed," said Sedam, both of them smiling.

"Well, it took you long enough to see my greatness! I'm a Calbanera! Don't you forget it!"

"Before we go in, allow me to cast some spells to strengthen your bodies and your weapons."

"You're going to use enchantments? Without tools or a proper workshop? Just how ridiculous are your powers, really?"

"Calm down. You can have that discussion later," Sedam said to Clara, who looked exasperated.

"B-besides," said Clara, pointing her finger at me, "when you summon meteors into that room, won't we be blown away by the blast?"

That was a valid question. Without the proper preparations, we would, as Clara so delicately put it, absolutely be blown away by the blast.

"I have a special spell for that. You see..."

••✝••

A few minutes later...

"Guraahh!"

"Gaaah!!!"

A dozen giant red ogres came barreling out of the hall and into the domed room. I had specifically charged two *Create Ogre Platoon* spells that day and I used both of them to form a team of decoys.

"Graah!"

The ogres lumbered down the stone steps and then scattered, some attacking the nest, some the newborn gigant, and the rest charging the other daemons in the room. When I created the ogres, I also cast *Wall of Iron* to seal the passage behind us and make sure other no daemons would come to join the fight.

Not for a moment did I believe the ogres had a chance at destroying the nest for us. I knew they could only serve as a diversion.

"Grroo?"

The gigant was slow to react to the ogres' surprise attack and was dealt several blows, but none appeared to be lethal—and even though its reactions were slow, some of the ogres were thrown back when it swung its giant arm.

"Hyeee!"

There came a bird-like screech, one I had not heard from a daemon before. It was one of the scytherns. It used its avian limbs to spring into the air and slice into one of the ogres. Like its name suggested, the scythern had sharp appendages like scythes for its arms. It seemed to have missed its mark, but only just—while its first blow was not lethal, the ogre nonetheless sprayed blood from its wounds.

"Arroo!"

Flaming arrows came flying from a group of daemons clustered around the nest and struck into the ogres.

"Gwah?!"

These arrows of fire were far stronger than Jargle's ice arrows. One ogre that was hit in the chest by one of those flames was instantly enveloped in fire. It burned like a torch.

"Those are mystils," Gunnar explained. "They're rare. The last confirmed sighting was ten years ago, and even then, there was only one."

The mystils were taller than imps, and each held a staff. *So, these are the sorcerer-type daemons*, I thought. *In that case, I expect there are other kinds to mirror warriors and priests. At this rate, it's only a matter of time before the ogres are all wiped out.*

*But I have more than just ogres.*

"Ghraaaa!"

*It's time for reinforcements.*

A massive red creature with folded wings crept out from the tunnel beyond the chamber's entrance. I had conjured it with the spell *Create Monster: Any*. It was a small red dragon. The beast measured six meters long, with a wingspan twice that length... small, by dragon standards, perhaps. Even so, this was a Level 12 monster, twice the strength of the ogres.

"Gyaoh!"

"Gii?!"

The red dragon flew straight at the gigant and sunk its sharp claws into its flesh. The mystils focused their attacks on the dragon, but their flame seemed hardly even to touch its hide.

"Amazing..." said Gunnar. "If it continues like this, that thing may take care of the daemons for us..."

"I doubt it," I cautioned. "Remember, the purpose of these monsters is only to create a diversion."

The nest itself had yet to make a move, but as an experienced gamer, my intuition told me that *thing* had something in store for us. Every gamer in every format knows: The last boss never goes down without a fight. I wanted to finish it off before it had a chance to show us what it could do. The fact that it wasn't reacting to the ogres or the dragon only made my hunch more insistent.

"So far, all has gone according to plan. I'm counting on you to see this through."

"Just who do you think you're talking to?" said Clara, sarcastically.

"Yeah! Just you leave it to me!" Gillion replied.

Gillion and Clara were both energetic in their own way, but I could detect a hint of nervousness in them, as I could from the others, who nodded silently.

"W-we made it!"

"I told you we would."

While the dragon and ogres continued their death match with the daemons, we were able to circle around inside the walls and come out on the other side of the domed room. It was all thanks to *Move Outer Plane* and Sedam's ability to guide us through the earth accurately with nothing but his excellent sense of direction.

"Shaaa!"

"Grooo!"

The red dragon leaped onto the back of the gigant. The wyrm's claws dug in, and it forced the daemon to the ground—and then showered it with plumes of fiery breath. As the two thrashed about, the dragon struck other daemons—scytherns and mystils—with its tail, turning its head to rain scorching fire on them as well.

And even then, the nest lay silent.

"All right," I shouted, "Let's go!"

*It is time,* I thought. *No matter what happens next, concentrate on casting the spell.*

We left the outer plane and returned to normal space.

"Gu-gyaah!"

"Gruooh!"

I raised my Staff of Wizardry high, its magical *Light* driving back the dungeon's natural darkness. The screeches, screams, and howls of the monsters now filled our ears unimpeded, and their awful stench made it difficult to breathe—but I couldn't let those things trouble me now.

"It's time to show you what the Calbaneras are made of!"

"We're counting on you, Lord Wizard!"

Gillion, Leoria, and Gunnar stood in front of me with their shields raised, while Sedam and Clara stood on either side of me. I had already cast *Physical Boost* on their bodies and *Enchant* on their weapons. Both spells had short durations, but their offensive and defensive abilities should have been significantly enhanced.

"Open, Gate of Magic. Reveal your form to me."

The clock had started. Ten seconds to cast the spell. Ten seconds to slay the daemons. In my inner world, the black doors of the Gate of Magic appeared.

"Hii!"

"Arrooo!"

A few of the mystils and scytherns had already noticed our presence. *Damn, they're quick,* I thought. The mystils aimed their staves at us, and the scytherns leaped ahead, blade-arms glistening.

"You think you can handle me?"

"You'll have to try harder than that!"

The knights deflected the mystils' fiery arrows with their shields and parried the scytherns' arms with their swords.

*Eight seconds remaining.*

I heard the twang of a bow string, and two of the scytherns charging at us were struck dead between the eyes, stumbling face forward into the ground.

*Seven seconds.*

My imagined self trod through the Gate of Magic, into the chaotic realm, and down the dark stone steps of the spiral staircase.

It was then that I suddenly froze.

The nest opened its eye and looked at me.

The nest was made of several spheres piled atop one another. The eye appeared at the very top. It was not an organic, living eye. In fact, it might be more accurate to describe it as an eye-shaped symbol rather than a true eye. However, when those white lines appeared on the black surface of the sphere, I instinctively knew without a doubt that it was looking at me.

*Six seconds.*

A gruesome tearing rent the air, and the torso of the red dragon split open as it fell to the ground.

It was the work of a single tentacle ripping through the air— and anything else in its way—at high speed. That dark appendage was about as thick as a human torso, extending out from the surface of one of the spheres, and now it turned—slower after killing the dragon, but still fast—sweeping toward us.

*"Ludora Ward!"*

As Clara cried out the name of her incantation, a wall of gale-force winds howled between us and the nest; sand kicked up from the ground in a screen around us.

The wind wall stopped the advance of the tentacle...but only for an instant. The wind buckled, and then dispersed entirely. The Calbanera siblings raised their shields together.

"Don't you underestimate us!"

"Yeah!"

The tentacle struck the siblings' shields.

*Five seconds.*

"Haah!" Gillion and Leoria cried out in unison, and with a perfectly synchronized motion, they redirected the force of tentacle upward with their shields and over their heads.

With their doubled strength from *Physical Boost* and the added magical defense of their shields from *Enchant*, they were both able to withstand the force of that blow, deflecting it just high enough that it passed over all of our heads—though if it weren't for Clara's incantation deadening a significant portion of the strike, the siblings' efforts may well have failed.

As the tentacle swung over us, the sudden change in air pressure fell heavy on our shoulders, alongside a loud rush of wind.

*Four seconds.*

Back in the chaotic realm, I touched the spellbook I had chosen on its rest and released its chaotic energy. It swirled in a flash of light and then converged in my hand.

Gillion and Leoria's knees buckled. They both fell to the ground, rolling from the residual force of the strike they'd endured. Gunnar leaped forward to grab them before they left the safe zone I'd specified before we left the outer plane.

*Three seconds.*

The nest's giant eye blinked, and its tentacle accelerated as it spun back around.

The shining chaotic energy folded into a small triangular pyramid: a single four-sided die. As a player of old TTRPGs, its form was very nostalgic to me, but I did not savor it.

*Two seconds.*

*"Ludora Ward!"* Clara shouted, but this time, the wall of wind did not materialize.

"Come on!" I shouted, rolling the die.

*One second.*

The numbers of the four-sided die were labeled at the base of the triangle. After a few short hops, the die landed on 1.

*"Time Stop,"* I cried, and everything froze.

"Phew..." I let out a sigh.

The Rank 9 spell *Time Stop* froze the flow of time for everyone but me. The shouts and screams and yells had ceased, and no one else moved: not the knights, not the adventurers, not the daemons, not even their nest.

The rules were ironclad: a die roll of 1 gave me twenty seconds before everything was set back in motion. With those twenty seconds, I cast two spells.

Time resumed—and the two spells I cast simultaneously went into effect.

The first spell I cast during *Time Stop* was *Wall of Force*, which created an impenetrable and transparent spherical force field encompassing the six members of our team.

The second spell I cast was *Meteor*, but this time I used a different variant, which summoned one giant meteor to strike one target, rather than eight smaller meteors to strike an area.

The sound that followed was more like a short whistle than a scream. The giant meteor I summoned to the ceiling of the dome collided with the nest with such force and speed that the path it took was nearly imperceptible.

What *could* be seen was the aftermath. The nest's original shape and form was instantaneously destroyed. What was left of it sprayed out in all directions. It was like someone had popped a balloon full of mud. The outward spray of the nest's remains was soon followed by a blinding white flash of flames, their searing roar accompanied by an intense shock wave.

I felt as if someone was screaming, but I couldn't hear or see a thing. It might have been me.

In terms of physical sturdiness, *Wall of Force* is the strongest barrier that can be created in *D&B*. The rulebook states that it cannot be destroyed by any physical means. As such, it completely shielded us from the force of the blast from the meteor's impact.

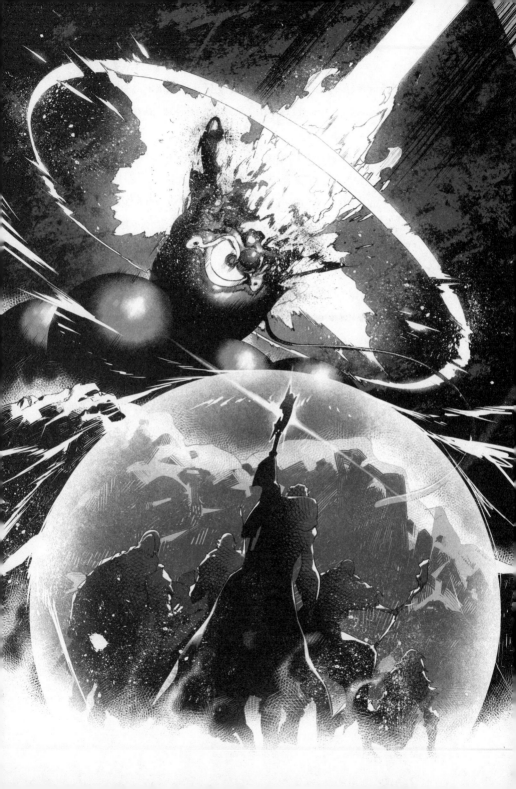

However, the barrier *was* permeable to light and sound, and the strain these two effects put on us caused everyone to fall to their knees.

I felt something soft on my back and neck and realized that Clara was clinging to me from behind. Dazed, I looked around—everyone had made it. Gillion's left arm was unnaturally twisted. It must have broken when he redirected the tentacle attack.

"Damn, this hurts."

"Brother!" Leoria ran over to Gillion.

"We did it, didn't we, wizard?" Sedam sat on the ground beside me, an exhausted smile on his face.

I couldn't answer.

I was still trying to process what I'd just seen. *The very instant the nest was destroyed...inside it, there was...*

In the center of the explosion, as the outer layers of the nest were blown away, I'd seen a closed set of pitch-black doors.

*I've seen doors like that before... That thing has the same essence... as the Gate of Magic!*

# Chapter 13

OUR ESCAPE AFTERWARD was uneventful.

Although we'd destroyed the nest, it wasn't as if all the remaining daemons suddenly turned to ash—though that would have been convenient. What did happen was that explosions and shocks from below threw all the remaining daemons in the floors above into a panic.

However, we returned to the outer plane and did not leave it until we were safely above ground. We didn't have to worry about being seen. Once everyone was safe, I cast *Meteor* again to destroy the underground passage along with the daemons left inside, and healed Gillion's wounds with *Complete Recovery*.

I seemed to be the only one who'd noticed the doors appear. I knew it wasn't my imagination—black doors, so similar to my Gate of Magic, looming there just as the nest was destroyed. The memory of that moment remained, an ominous black thorn wedged deep within my chest.

We were able to return to the fortress without any trouble.

We reported what happened, and the Calbanera Knights responded with excitement. Under Alnogia's command, the defensive lines turned on the offense, moving to surround the cave where the nest had been found and picking off any surviving daemons left in the field.

While this final clean-up operation took five more days, the knights were able to clear the mountain and surrounding forests of daemons. However, as we could not be one hundred percent sure no daemons had escaped, we planned to station some knights at the fortress so that they could respond quickly if any daemons were spotted.

Alnogia declared, "As it is the duty of the Calbanera Knights to eliminate this threat, we will see the operation through, even if we must continue to fund it with the Sardish family's personal wealth."

Still, I did not feel that all the weight had been lifted from my shoulders. *What are daemons, after all?* I thought. *What is a daemon's nest, really? If another nest appears...will the people of Sedia be able to deal with it on their own?*

*What if the daemons are somehow tied to the Gate of Magic? Could the Watcher be tied to the daemons' existence? Either way,* I thought, *I can no longer treat the daemons as an unrelated problem. Do I, personally, have to do something about humanity's mortal enemy?*

I had to wonder whether my fate was now tied to the daemons' existence. Our connection could not be denied. I *wanted* to deny it—such a fate was too much for an insignificant person like myself to handle. *But,* I thought. *But I've already gotten involved, and this mask of a grand magic user that I now wear would not forgive even the notion of pushing this role on someone else.*

••✝••

Seven days after the nest was destroyed, we stopped in Yulei on our way back to the Castle of the White Blade. The main force of the Calbanera Knights came along, while Gunnar stayed to command those knights that remained at the fortress.

By the time we arrived, news of the Calbanera Knights' efforts and the destruction of the daemons' nest had already reached Yulei, where a large celebration was being held.

A large bonfire had been erected in the center of the village square, and the village leader opened up his stores to donate food and drink. The knights, dwarves, and men of the town drank heavily together while the women dressed up and danced. The villagers sung pastoral folk songs, the dwarves their hymns of smithing and of war, and the youngest sang light-hearted melodies of love.

I, however, shut myself off from all the buoyant cheer. I brooded alone, in my room at the Knight of the Iron Skillet.

The room itself was lavish, but it enjoyed nothing of the positive atmosphere that ruled the village out the window. The villagers were well informed of my deeds, such as destroying the nest with a meteor and controlling a dragon...but I wished they hadn't known.

I had been showered with thanks and praise, far more than after I'd saved Mora, but the villagers did not look at me the same. When a child bumped into me in the square, the color drained from their parent's face and they immediately beat them, forcing them to grovel and beg forgiveness. When a barmaid spilled some wine on my robe, she broke into tears and wouldn't stop telling me how sorry she was. I tried to make it clear that I wasn't angry in both situations, but that did not change the way they looked at me—their fearful expressions were engraved upon my mind.

While I most certainly had secured my status as a great and powerful magic user, that meant being feared. While I understood that accepting that status was part of taking responsibility for my actions, it did not make it any easier for me, just a normal person inside, to bear.

While I was agonizing over it all, sprawled on the bed with my head in my hands, Sedam and Clara came to visit.

Sedam smirked. "Aren't you a little old to be holed up sulking in your room?"

"You really are a handful," said Clara. "I bet you haven't eaten, have you?"

I have to admit, Sedam and Clara's sarcasm was much more comforting than the sound of the cheers outside. When I sat up, I saw they had brought some kebabs and wine.

"It's the job of the young ones to take care of the old and weary," I said, with a laugh. It was hard to hide how happy I was they had come.

Afterward, we had our own three-person celebration...at least until Leoria and Gillion barged in on us, but at least this time, I was thankful for their company.

·····

The next day, we returned to the Castle of the White Blade, and over the rest of the week there were various ceremonies, awards of honor, feasts, and other celebrations before things finally wound down.

"What should I do next?" I wondered aloud with a sigh. I was back in my guest room at the castle.

"What do you mean by that?" asked Sedam. Both Sedam and Clara were with me (as usual) though Sedam had said he planned to return to Relis City soon.

"Well, *I* would like to turn you in to the—I mean, have you visit our Sorcerers' Guild in Relis," said Clara.

Clara certainly didn't waste any time. *That's right*, I remembered. *She did say one of her reasons for hanging around me was basically to monitor my activities...*

"May I ask why?" I said, after a short pause.

"One reason is that any sorcerer, our guild's members included, would be interested in learning more about your magic—to determine whether it is a more advanced form of sorcery, an irregularity, a subdivision, the source of it, or whether it is something else entirely..." Clara said, trailing off at the end.

While I had already explained my magic, in part, to Clara...I could understand the Sorcerers' Guild not wanting to leave me be without further investigation.

"All right. I'll make plans to visit. I, too, want to know more about sorcery, and if possible, I would like to build a cooperative relationship with your guild against the daemons."

"A cooperative...relationship?"

Having experienced the horrors of the daemons firsthand, I felt there was a need to take action. I was not sure what I myself could do, but I knew that if I was to continue to be involved in matters of daemon extermination, I needed more information, and to form alliances with others in positions of power who could help me.

From what I had heard, sorcerers' guilds were important players in the fight against daemons. If possible, I wanted to be on friendly terms with Clara's, but her reaction was strangely opaque, even though she nodded.

Another reason I had for going to Relis City was that I needed to have copies made of my spellbook. The one spellbook I had was carefully stowed away in my Infinity Bag, but I did not want to risk losing it again. I had heard there were guilds of book copiers in Sedia, and I planned on enlisting their aid. Additionally, even though it was lower on my list of priorities, I also wanted to secure a residence where I could one day retire in peace.

"Retire?" asked Clara incredulously. "Do you think anyone would just let you disappear after knowing what you can do?"

*She makes a good point...*

Our discussion was interrupted by a messenger who stated that the captain requested an audience with me, so I headed to his private room, which was lavishly decorated.

"Allow me to thank you again for your concerted efforts," said Captain Amrand Gal Sardish.

"As a wizard and as your ally, I only did what was to be expected of me," I replied, taking a sip of the sil tea he had poured for me.

"I hear Gillion and Leoria pulled their weight as well. Gillion, in particular, seems to have changed after participating in the operation with you. Don't you agree?"

"He has changed some, to be sure..."

If I were to be honest, I would have told the captain that Gillion's bravery and the strength of his rage at the daemons saved me more than any way I could have influenced him...but perhaps it was not my place to say that to a man who most likely wanted to choose his own son as his successor over someone like Gillion.

"By the way..." The captain set his cup on the table.

*So, it's time to cut to the chase*, I thought.

"I wanted to ask if you might do something for me. It has to do with that fortress."

"Hmm?"

"The fortress, which you seem well acquainted with now, has been a den of bandits the last few years, but ten years ago it was a holdfast the order used as a lookout for various threats."

Captain Sardish explained that due to the decline in appearances of daemons and a reduction in size of the order itself, the fortress had been abandoned. Though Gunnar was currently stationed at the fortress, keeping a force there was not economically feasible for the order in the long run.

*What is he trying to say?*

"Of course, I am not suggesting you take any action until we have confirmed there are no surviving daemons in the area, but I would like to offer you the fortress with the recommendation that you take it as your permanent residence. Will you accept?"

It was only fifteen days ago that I woke for the first time in Sedia, in the jail of that fortress. I'd spent time there with Mora after I'd driven away the bandits and time with the knights and adventurers after I'd destroyed the daemons' nest. It wasn't a stretch to say that no place was more familiar to me in all of Sedia. I already knew the place like the back of my hand.

*He's offering that place to me? To live there?* I thought. Back in Japan, I used to live in a thirty-year-old apartment building and always dreamed of one day being able to buy a house...

"I'm sorry, but...I am having trouble understanding what it is you want me to do."

"This is embarrassing to admit, but..." The captain gave a wry smile. "The bandits who made that fortress their base were the relatively docile sort. I hear their behavior changed once a sorcerer was installed as their leader, but before that, the worst they did was extort tolerable fees from merchants and travelers."

According to the captain, rather than driving out the bandits and risk the vacuum being filled by a more malicious group, the order had turned a blind eye to their activities. *I suppose it's embarrassing, but the world is full of issues that aren't cut and dry. It's hard to make it if you're not willing to compromise on some of your ideals.*

"In other words, you believe if I take up residence in the fortress, there won't be as much crime in the area?"

"I believe more than that. Order will be restored. I doubt there is anyone willing to risk doing any evil on the doorstep of a great and powerful magician like yourself."

*Well, that's a very grandiose way of putting it, but put simply, you want to use me like a guard dog. It's the order's job to keep the peace, not mine.*

"Forgive me, but I struggle to see how exactly I benefit from this arrangement."

"I'm not saying you have to *live* there. Your ownership of the fortress would serve as enough of a deterrent."

*But owning the fortress makes me responsible for it, I thought. I'll still have to keep the peace whether I live there or not... However, I suppose I don't mind helping to make sure bandits don't run rampant...*

"Forgive me if I'm wrong," said the captain, changing his tone, "but I assumed that great wizards...like sorcerers...prefer to live in lofty, isolated places like that fortress."

*Hmm... He has a point, I thought. Great magic users and philosophers almost never live among common people in fantasy novels. Given how the people of Yulei have come to treat me, I'm starting to understand why.*

"I thought it would be a nice, quiet place you could go to whenever you don't want to be bothered," said the captain.

*As he says, it could function as a nice hideaway. Compared to the stock ideal of a house with a garden, he's offering me a whole fortress with a forest around it to boot. I was surprised at how quiet and peaceful it was the first night I stayed there, and the view of the stars was amazing...*

"According to reports," the captain added, "there is hardly any part of it that needs repair, and it has everything anyone might need."

I thought back over the few days I'd stayed there with the knights. There was nothing inconvenient about staying there at all. I remembered taking a hot bath in a barrel on the top floor of the tower and looking out at the view of the forest and mountains... It was beautiful. The more I thought about living there, the more it made sense to me. I could properly store the treasures I had in my Infinity Bag, and I could set up a workshop so I could craft more magic items.

"While giving you the fortress is not enough to pay you back for your help in exterminating the daemons, it would help us save face if you accepted it."

"Well...when you put it that way," I said, "I can't say no, can I?"

*Honestly, how could I refuse?*

❖

"You're an idiot, aren't you?"

After I returned to my guest room and reported my decision, Clara blinked a few times before raining on my parade. *Rude.*

My bruised ego aside, I knew Clara wasn't being malicious. I preferred her regular jabs to the general affirmation of a yes-man.

"I only came to my decision after a good deal of thought. It's quiet, it's safe, and I won't be bothered by many visitors..."

"That's not what I'm talking about! Weren't you supposed to come with me to the Relis Sorcerers' Guild?!" Clara stood with raised eyebrows, hands on her hips.

"Well, I need a quiet environment where I can work in peace. I haven't forgotten about visiting the Sorcerers' Guild. Could you just wait a little longer for me?"

I hadn't lost focus of the other things I needed to do just because of this new prospect of a secret hideaway. The first item on my list of priorities was gathering more information about the daemons. Next was creating a backup copy of my spellbook.

If I was going to spend the rest of my life in Sedia, I couldn't expect to carry a tome around with me twenty-four seven. The first precaution I needed to take was to secure a place I could safely store my spellbook when I wasn't carrying it with me, and the second precaution was to make copies in case my spellbook was ever stolen or damaged. Even if I had the Copiers' Guild make blank copies of the book for me, transcribing all the spells from the original into the copies would take a considerable amount of time. Strictly speaking, gathering information on the daemons was higher on my priority list, but until I made copies of my spellbook, I felt limited in what I could do. Therefore, realistically, it made more sense to accept the fortress as a step toward completing priority number two before going to Relis in pursuit of priority number one.

"Fine..."

After I carefully explained my reasons, Clara reluctantly accepted my argument.

"In that case, when will you set out toward Relis?"

"First, I have to wait until the detached force declares the area free of daemons... I expect to be officially handed the deed in three or four days. Then I'll have to drop a few things off at the fortress, and then..."

"I will wait seven days for you, and no more! After that, you're coming to Relis, got it?!"

"You in that big of a hurry to drag Geo off to your new lovers' nest somewhere?" Sedam smirked. "There's no need to rush. Take your time."

It was the first time I'd heard Sedam make a joke like that. *Not a great habit to have*, I thought. *Where I worked, you'd be accused of sexual harassment...*

"You can only crack jokes like that because you're not a sorcerer," said Clara, brushing him off. "You have no idea how bothersome—I mean, threatening—his existence is to us."

"I wasn't lying about wanting to know more about sorcery myself. I won't make you wait any longer than a week."

I knew I probably couldn't have copies made of my spellbook the same day, but I had to go to Relis City to gather supplies either way.

"All right. In that case, I'll be going with you to the fortress," said Clara.

"Huh?"

My dreams of having the fortress all to myself in perfect solitude suddenly came crashing down.

"What's with that look on your face?! Stop being so disrespectful!" Clara yelled, stomping a foot on the ground like an incensed child.

··✟··

I stayed the next few days at the Castle of the White Blade. During that time, I took walks around Yulei, borrowed from the castle's library, helped the Calbanera siblings with their training, and otherwise took it easy.

As I spent more time in the area, I saw that both the knights of the order and the people of Yulei lived simple, laid-back lives. However, the looks I got from the villagers were still ones filled with fear. I wasn't hated or anything, but that didn't change the fact that it was uncomfortable for me to be around others in the village, no matter how much they respected me. *He was right*, I thought, remembering what the captain had said. *There really is no place for a "great and powerful magician" in a village like this.*

On the third day, Sedam left the Castle of the White Blade to return to Relis City.

"I won't be able to get out of delivering a report to the Adventurers' Guild about you," said Sedam, "but I'll put in a good word and say you're a great hero."

"Please don't overdo it," I replied, shaking his hand.

*No, really, I'm begging you—please.*

On the fourth day, Gunnar and his group of knights returned to the castle. They reported that, after going on several patrols, they were able to confirm that no daemons were left alive in the area. Clara and I decided to make the trip to the fortress the very same day. Before we left, I asked the knights to deliver Ild's goods, so he would have them before we arrived a few days later.

Satisfied that everything needing doing at the castle was done, and overall in high spirits, I summoned my phantom steed and mounted it.

"We're only staying two nights at the fortress, okay?!" Clara held up two fingers. "After those two nights, you're coming to Relis with me!"

"You don't have to yell. I heard you the first time," I muttered, rubbing my ears. Clara did not have her own horse, so she was riding in the saddle behind me.

"Now that the daemons and bandits are gone, it's quite pleasant to ride like this through the countryside," I said, thinking aloud.

Though the sun was a little on the bright side, there was a gentle breeze, and the lovely green of the trees was easy on the eyes. Despite the fact that she was annoying at times, I was also sharing my ride with a beautiful young woman. A few short weeks ago, when I was still in Japan, if I were shown a picture of me now, I guarantee you I would have been thrown into a fit of jealousy—especially if I didn't know that this world harbored daemons.

"Oh? There it is! My own Castle Getaeus."

I'd decided to name the fortress after Geo's (fictional) home country. It might have been a bit of a stretch to call the small fortress a castle, but these kinds of naming conventions are more about feeling than following strict definitions. Before the knights left the fortress to me, they'd cleaned it and performed needed maintenance. Seeing it now, it looked both more lavish and sturdier than I remembered.

I dreamed of the days ahead: *During the day, I might search for mushrooms and wild vegetables in the pristine forest surrounding my castle. I could go fishing in the stream and set traps for animals. There is more land than I could ever have hoped for—tilling a plot for a vegetable garden might be a fun project as well.*

*If it rains, I could read books in the top floor of the tower. Ah, the mark of a stress-free life is to only work when conditions are best for the mind and body. At night, I can enjoy the stillness, far from the hustle and bustle of towns. For dinner, I can whip something up from what I've gathered during the day. I'm not really that confident in my cooking ability, but it's not as if I have to impress anyone. I can make do with the basics...*

*And the stars! Every night I could soak in the bath and look up at the starry night sky—a real one, the kind you just can't see in modern Japan. Sure, the only bath I have now is a makeshift barrel tub, but I could probably dig up a natural hot spring in the mountains...*

"Ah..." I sighed, a smile on my face, my head filled with the kind of leisurely activities all middle-aged men dream of. *Easy street, here I come!*

Of course, I still had plans to create copies of my spellbook and gather information on the daemons, and I wouldn't stay idle if another daemons' nest appeared... *But no one can fault a man for taking time to enjoy the little things in life, right?*

Although I was under the impression we had kept to a stately pace, we arrived at the fortress just as the sun was beginning to set—despite having left the Castle of the White Blade early in the morning that same day. Normally, the distance required a traveler to camp one night out on the road. Again, I was impressed by the excellence of my phantom steed.

It wasn't long before I began to feel like it was high time for some dinner. I left Clara in the large room on the first floor of the tower and headed toward the kitchen, which directly adjoined the living quarters. I did have some magic items that gave me some limited options for conjuring up a meal from nothing, but using them when I had a perfectly good kitchen in front of me felt like cheating.

"All right. First, I should light a fire in the stove."

I took some flint stones out of my Infinity Bag.

"Hmm... I just hit these things together, right?"

I had used flint as an item countless times in TTRPGs, but I had never actually used real flint stones to create fire before. *How hard can it be?* I thought. I'd watched the adventurers create a fire when we camped on the road, and it didn't look terribly difficult.

*One, two...*

"Ow!!!"

On my first try, I hit the fingernail of my thumb dead on.

"Damn, that hurt... Ow!"

As I held my thumb, the pain helped bring me back down to reality. I looked around the kitchen and noted the absence of a refrigerator, gas stove, and rice cooker—the foundation of every kitchen in Japan.

"This may be more of a problem than I thought."

I kept striking the flint stones against one another, growing more panicked every second. Although I was able to make some sparks fly, I couldn't get a fire started.

"Wait, that's right. I can't start a log fire with just sparks. I need some kindling...something that will burn easily, like newspaper...is there any newspaper I can—"

*Of course there isn't any newspaper, you dimwit!* I found what looked like a box of kindling with some shreds of wood, but as you might have guessed, I had no luck with that either.

"I guess life here isn't going to be as convenient as life in Japan..."

I had lived on my own for decades—in Japan. I could handle basic chores and simple cooking—in Japan. My mistake was assuming that those skills would carry over into this world. I thought back over all the previous nights I'd stayed at the fortress. Either Mora or servants of the order of knights had cooked for me, made my bath, and laundered my clothes. There was no supermarket or convenience store in Sedia where I could get fresh vegetables and meat... Even if Sedia did have something similar, it wouldn't be nearby. The area around Castle Getaeus was uninhabited.

I couldn't believe I'd gotten so carried away with my dreams of the easy life that I had forgotten something so simple.

In an effort to calm myself down and ground my thoughts, I made a list of the fortress's facilities:

Main Tower

Basement: Storage Rooms (used for general goods, weapons, and wine)

First Floor: Main Hall (used for assemblies and dining)

Second Floor: Commander's Office, Archive, Guest Room

Third Floor: Bedroom, Study, Treasure Room

Roof: Lookout

Living Quarters (two stories plus basement)

Knights' Quarters (five individual rooms)

Attendants' Quarters (two small rooms)

Soldiers' Quarters (two large rooms)

Servants' Quarters (three rooms)

Kitchen

Mess Hall

Food and General Storage (basement)

Linen and Bedding Storage

Jail Compound (attached building)

Courtyard

Horse and Livestock Stables

Chicken Coop

Wells (including for laundry)

Designated Work Area

Main Gate and Defensive Towers

During the operation to destroy the daemons' nest, the fortress was operating over capacity, but even so, it was built to house about fifty knights, soldiers, and servants. *Can one person really clean and maintain this fortress all by himself?* I thought. *It's...too early to say. If I spent some time crafting servants with my magic, I could still make this work.* I wasn't ready to give up just yet.

Still, I thought it strange. As Captain Sardish had said, great philosophers and wizards and the like had a reputation for living in solitude...but was that really complete solitude? I couldn't imagine someone like that doing all the cleaning themselves. Needless to say, it was far too late, but I was beginning to regret having agreed to take the fortress so quickly.

"Regardless, I still need to do something about dinner..."

Although I reflected on my mistakes, none of that changed the immediate problem. All that reflection only made my current outlook even more bleak (though of course this was all in my head).

As described on Geo's character sheet, I found rations, dried fruit and meats, beans, bread and other food items in my Infinity Bag. Without a specific goal in mind, I laid all of these things out on the table and stared.

"What am I supposed to do with this?" I wondered aloud.

The only thing I could think of was cutting up some of the dried meat and cooking it, but I couldn't even get a fire started. Sure, I could make a fireball with my magic, but doing that would just blow up the kitchen. My spellbook didn't have any spells that I could use to simply light a fire.

*I guess it doesn't have to be cooked. It's dried meat, after all. I can just cut it into smaller pieces...*

*What is this feeling?* I stared dumbly at the dried meat. *After all that's happened since I arrived in Sedia, is this what defeats me? Am I doomed to be vanquished by a kitchen?*

"I knew it," said Clara, dry as anything.

I deserved that stare, big time. "Ha, ha... It seems I was a bit unprepared to face the challenges of having a secret hideaway all to myself..."

"Secret hideaway? Forget that! I *knew* you didn't have the first clue about cooking. And boy, was I right."

"As embarrassing as it is to admit, you're not wrong. Fortunately, though, you're here."

"Hmm? What do you mean?"

"Well, you know, women are much more dependable when it comes to this sort of thing. I hate to ask, but you see how things stand. Could you whip something up for us?"

"You wanna try that again?"

"Please?"

✢

In the end, I decided to make do with a magic item for our dinner that night.

Clara and I returned to the main hall, back in the main tower, and spread a tablecloth over one of the tables—a *magic* tablecloth, called a Dinner Cloth. Then I issued a command: "Dinner for two—something warm," and the Dinner Cloth responded.

First, the table was set for two, with plates, bowls, glasses, knives, forks, and spoons. The dinner appeared soon after, with a faint billow of steam. The Dinner Cloth served us steak paired with wine, soup, and a side salad.

Clara shot a small fire arrow into the hearth, and the room was filled with a warm glow.

"Is this wizardry, too?" she asked. "You conjured this food and wine out of nowhere... How does something like that work?"

"I wouldn't think too hard about it..."

The Dinner Cloth could make meals for up to four people, three times a day. I really didn't want to rely on it—at least not right away, but hunger easily won over my desire to do things right.

"This...tastes better than I expected, coming from materia," said Clara, cutting into her steak with her knife and fork in an exemplary demonstration of proper etiquette.

"Thanks—glad you like it," I replied, taking it more or less as a compliment.

*Materia must be what Sedia's sorcerers call magic items,* I mused, but most of my attention was not on Clara's words, but her hands. *If I remember correctly, forks weren't in wide use in medieval Europe...though I guess I shouldn't be surprised a fantasy world is ahead of the times, so to speak.*

Clara seemed to tell I wasn't paying much attention and raised her eyebrows at me, perturbed.

"I do not *particularly* mind, but you should pay more attention to your manners," she said, then paused. "If you had materia like this with you, why didn't you use it in the first place?"

*Yeah, yeah... I know*, I thought, and sighed. "Men sometimes like to do things just for the heck of it, even if they know it's a waste of time."

"Well, I won't dispute that. What we're doing right now is a complete waste of time."

"Point taken... I really do need to hurry up and get back to investigating what the daemons are all about."

*If it were up to Clara, we would have gone straight to Relis. She has every right to voice a few complaints, given that I'm forcing her to delay her plans*, I thought, but what Clara said next surprised me.

"Though I have to say, I'm relieved, seeing that you're like this."

"Relieved?"

Clara drank the remainder of the wine in her glass and then smiled kindly at me.

"I know I was one of the people who told you to act more like a hero, but taking everything into account...in a way, you've acted too much like one."

"What do you mean?"

"I mean it in the sense that, like a hero, it seemed like you weighed all your choices with a mind to whether or not those actions were morally just. There is such a thing as being a little *too* obsessed with justice. Follow that road and you're bound to end up hurting yourself...and others."

*Daemons are powerful enough to be a threat to humanity, and I was equipped with the power to fight against them. I only did what I thought was right, given those two facts... Is that really something to be concerned about?*

"So, like I said before," Clara continued, "what we're doing right now *is* a complete waste of time, but in Sedia, we call pointless ventures like this part of being human."

*Did I just get schooled in life by a woman twenty years younger than me? That almost brings tears to my eyes.*

"Both as a sorceress and a daughter of nobility, let me give you some advice," said Clara. "A castle of this size needs at least three full-time caretakers and a steward to make it livable. Might I suggest you look to hire some while you are in Relis?"

*First lessons in life, and now practical advice on living arrangements? What did I do to deserve such tutelage?*

"But that can wait until *after* we visit the Sorcerers' Guild. Are we clear?"

"Uh, yes, ma'am."

# Chapter 14

THE NEXT DAY, after I raised the castle back upon a cliff with *Structural Renovation*, Clara and I set out for Relis City. (After all was said and done, I really didn't feel like spending another night at the castle in its current state.)

The road that connected Yulei to Relis and stretched northward to the distant Shrendal Kingdom was called the Lawful Way. I learned from Sedam that the road was one of many paved throughout the kingdom at the height of its prominence, two to three hundred years prior.

In the chaos that followed a large outbreak of daemons, the kingdom declined and was divided into separate states and unions, like the Ryuse Alliance that controlled this region—et cetera, et cetera. Upon hearing that, my first thought was, *So, Shrendal is this world's stereotypical ancient advanced civilization, huh*? However, my assumption was somewhat incorrect. The Shrendal Kingdom continued to exist, and was no different from any other country with a storied past.

Even though it had lost much of its territory, the Shrendal Kingdom continued to wield power and influence befitting of its status as the oldest civilized country in Sedia. As evidence of that fact, the Calbanera Knights still pledged allegiance to Shrendal's royal family (though they paid them no taxes), and Clara boasted that the Andell family line traced its origins back to the Shrendal Kingdom.

Clara complained that the phantom horse would make us stand out in a bad way if we continued to ride it along the more heavily trafficked Lawful Way, so we decided to dismount and continue on foot.

While there were some dips and rises in the road, it was relatively level, and thus made for easy walking. We occasionally passed shepherds herding livestock, merchants with their caravans of carts, and simple travelers. It was very peaceful—so much so, I was beginning to wonder where all the bands of bandits were, whom I had heard so much about, but one of the merchants we camped with along the way was only too happy to explain. "Recently, a great and powerful magic user moved into the area, and all the evildoers turned tail and left!"

The news had traveled a lot faster than I'd thought! Although, once I reasoned it out, I assumed much of that speed was due to Captain Sardish purposefully spreading rumors about me.

I wondered when the last time was that I'd been able to simply walk, carefree like this, for hours on end. It had to have been decades...or, I thought, *This might be the first time I've experienced something like this at all. Looking over a medieval-ish countryside, traveling with a beautiful (but loud) woman...* It was probably the first time since I'd arrived in Sedia that I felt thankful for being sent, though I would probably be uncomfortable admitting that to my old friends, my co-workers, and the workplace I'd left behind.

··✝··

Three days after we left Castle Getaeus, no matter how fun and peaceful the road was, I began to get bored of the never-ending sameness of our journey. *People these days, bored after only three days?* I thought, shaking a metaphorical cane at myself from my metaphorical porch—but then relief came.

"Once we get to the top of that hill, we should be able to see Lake Ryuse and Relis City," Clara said.

"Really?" I asked, delighted as a child, before quickening my pace up the slope toward the peak. *Now that she mentions it, I feel a bit more moisture on the wind*, I thought. When I reached the top, I was awestruck.

If I had not known ahead of time that it was a lake, I might have mistaken it for the ocean. The blue of the water's surface stretched as far as the eye could see, off into a misty horizon, with no hint of an opposite shore. I thought back to when I'd looked out over Lake Biwa in Japan, from an observation deck—this lake was certainly larger than that.

*So, this is Lake Ryuse*, I thought, but my attention was soon stolen by the city on its shores.

"Wow! It's a real fortified city!"

Lo and behold, there was Relis City, spread out along the shores of Lake Ryuse. Two rings of fortified stone walls encircled the city, though the outermost wall partly gave way at the shore to a port, where I could see large sailing ships docked. Most of the buildings in the city appeared to be made of stone, and their colored roofs delighted me.

I'd been impressed when I first saw the Castle of the White Blade, but this city was on an entirely different level.

"Wait up! You're going too fast!" It was Clara.

I glanced back at her. She was sweating and struggling to keep up, but I paid her no mind—at least at first. I would be lying if I said I didn't feel at least a small pang of guilt.

"Sorry about that... I just really wanted to see the city."

"That's all well and good, but...how do you have so much stamina at your age?"

"Well, listen to you! 'At your age,' indeed. Entirely uncalled for."

To answer her question (though I didn't tell her): The boots I was wearing were magical traveling boots. If I wanted to, I could walk at the same pace as a horse for an extended amount of time and not feel any exhaustion. Although, now that I thought of it, cutting corners like that probably wouldn't be good for my overall health.

Relis City took advantage of its access to water by having a moat dug around the outer wall. A drawbridge spanned the gap, congested with the traffic of merchants, peasants, and cargo-laden carts.

"But the city really does look amazing," I said. "It makes Yulei seem very rural in comparison."

"Relis City is the largest city in the Ryuse Alliance. It vies for first or second place among all the cities on the continent—not just in scale, but in terms of its history and culture as well." Clara stuck out her chest with pride.

The Lawful Way not only spanned eastward to Yulei, but extended northward as well. The city appeared to be a major hub, and the number of travelers gathered outside the gate were the most I had seen in one place since I arrived in Sedia.

The gate on the other end of the drawbridge was wide open, but it was flanked with guards, who were conducting inspections of people and goods as they waited to enter the city. The guards wore matching helmets and chain mail, and were equipped with short swords and spears. It was as you would expect in any medieval fantasy setting, but I noted that they were energetic as they went about their work. *Morale must be high*, I thought.

After about twenty minutes of waiting, Clara and I made it to the front of the line, where we stood in front of the guards. Beyond the gate, I could see a stone-paved square complete with a fountain, around which bard-like men and women were performing music.

"Pay attention," said Clara, elbowing me in the side. "Here— write your name, status, and where you'll be staying."

After Clara pulled my attention back from the square, a guard with a bit of a forced smile handed me a travelers' registration application (a blank wooden writing board to be exact) and something to write with. Clara, meanwhile, had an official-looking pass, which she presented to the guard.

"Oh, I'm sorry about that. My name is Geo Margilus," I said as I spelled it out. "Status? Will 'commoner' do? As for where I'll be staying..."

"You don't have to think too hard about it. 'The Sorcerer's Guild' will do," Clara said. I wasn't sure if she was trying to spell or just make a point, but she put a lot of stress on those words.

"A-all right, I'll go with that then..."

"Wait a second! Did you say you were Geo Margilus?!" the guard exclaimed, stunned.

"That is correct... Is there a problem?"

*That's right*, I thought, remembering how fast the rumors of me had spread. *I have a bad feeling about this...*

"So, you're that great magician, right?! The one who helped the Calbanera Knights destroy the daemons' nest?!"

"What?!"

"The great wizard is here?!"

"It's Lord Geo Margilus! The hero!"

"It's the lord wizard!"

Not only the guards at the gate, but the people waiting in line behind us quickly caught on. I felt my face turning red.

For a second, I was worried I might be mobbed by the crowd, with everyone trying to get a better look at me—but the opposite happened. Soon, a ring formed around Clara and me (and the guard inspecting us) as everyone took a step back to stare. I saw a variety of emotions on all of their faces: respect and excitement from some, but anxiousness and worry from others.

I remembered the reaction I got at Yulei and felt my mood sink.

"He looks a bit more normal than I thought..."

"Kind of...plain?"

"Well, I hear he comes from a country beyond the sea..."

"Is that the staff he used to summon meteors?"

"Hey, don't push! If we make him mad, he'll turn us to stone!"

The people began to murmur, but otherwise, no one moved.

"We're not going to get through unless you say something to them," said Clara, with a sigh. She seemed surprisingly calm.

*There's no telling what rumors will be spun from whatever I say here*, I thought, but it didn't seem like I had any other choice. *I might as well kiss any possibility of living a commoner's life goodbye...*

"I apologize for the disturbance, good travelers and citizens of Relis." I stood my Staff of Wizardry upright on the ground and slowly turned to look at everyone watching me.

"I am indeed the wizard, Geo Margilus," I continued, raising my voice so all would hear. "I am pleased to make your acquaintances. I find it an honor to visit the beautiful city of Relis." I paused for a few seconds and then turned to the guard. "If that is all, I don't suppose you would mind letting me through, would you?"

"F-forgive me! Yes, please, head on through. Welcome to Relis!"

The exact wording aside, as a (former) Japanese corporate employee, I was used to the practice of addressing others in formal style, so I wasn't entirely out of my element here. The guard didn't need much convincing, and in a show of respect, all the other guards struck the ends of their spears on the pavement. *Man, that's cool*, I thought.

"In that case, my friends, if you would excuse me..."

Acknowledging who I was seemed to help allay the fears of those in the crowd: Many of them called out to welcome me, or bowed their heads as they cleared the way for me to enter the city, but no one reached out to me for a handshake—everyone kept their distance.

"All right, then. Let's go," said Clara, paying the crowd no mind.

I remembered that she had only accompanied me thus far to take me to the Relis Sorcerers' Guild. *We should probably get going, then, before I waste any more of her time*, I thought, but someone suddenly stood in the way.

"Hey! Mister Geo! Mister Geo!"

*Umph.* A little person came flying out of the crowd and tackled me with a hug, nearly knocking the wind out of me.

"Mister Geo!"

I looked down and saw a teary-eyed girl with chestnut-colored hair looking back at me. It was Mora.

"Mister Geo!" Mora said, hugging me tighter.

"H-hey, Mora. It's been a while. I never thought I'd run into you so soon after I arrived."

If I had been twenty years younger, maybe even just fifteen years younger, it would have probably made me happy to have a sun-kissed young girl like this be so clingy with me, but I was over forty years old, both inside and out—her fondness for me was no different than a child excited to see a visiting relative. I was taken by surprise and still had some of the grandiose tone in my voice from my acting before, so I worried Mora might take offense, or think strangely of me, but I needn't have worried. Once I regained my composure, I patted her on the head and gently pulled her off of me.

"But Mister Geo! I waited for you, but you never came! Even after you destroyed the daemons' nest! Then the knights came to deliver my father's goods, but you weren't there... I thought that you were avoiding me!"

"Of course I wasn't avoiding you. How could I, after all you've done for me? I still have business with your father as well."

"But...I hardly did anything at all... You're the one who helped me."

*Mora's view may be correct, objectively speaking,* I thought, *but she is the first person I met in Sedia, and I'll never forget how I felt when I first gained her trust.* (For those taking notes: Yes, I may have "met" Jargle and the bandits first, but I don't think you can blame me for choosing not to count them.)

"Great wizard... I cannot thank you enough for what you have done..."

"Our young lady has been passing by the gate every time we go out, waiting for your return."

A kind-looking, middle-aged man and woman stood behind Mora. I guessed they were servants assigned to look after her. Both bowed their heads toward me in thanks.

"It wasn't much trouble for me. Please, don't mention it."

"We live on Commerce Street. I know my father will be pleased to see you again. Let's get going!" Mora tugged on my arm, but Clara stood in her way.

"Mora? I'm sorry, but we have some business to attend to," said Clara.

"Really? Then I guess I'll see you later," replied Mora. "This way, Mister Geo."

"I said *we*!" Clara exclaimed, grabbing my other arm and pulling me in the opposite direction.

*What's going on here?* I thought. *Are these two beautiful young women fighting over me?*

*There's no reason to panic. Think about this rationally. I'm not well versed in child psychology, but Mora's fixation on me can't be anything more than what a child feels for a teacher or a relative, or something similar. Clara, on the other hand, is just determined— out of a sense of duty—to make sure I get to the Sorcerers' Guild. Well, if I'm a bit more optimistic, she might think of me as a comrade in arms, after what we've been through together...*

*I've known many a poor creature (middle-aged men) to mistake such a tug-of-war for being "popular with the ladies," but I will make no such mistake.*

"Um... Uh, Mora? I'm sorry, but I've really kept the Sorcerers' Guild waiting for a long time. In this kind of situation, it's always better to get the worst things over with first. Is it all right if I visit later?"

I had to keep my priorities straight.

"I-I'm sorry," said Mora. "You must have some difficult job to do, right?"

"Something like that. Once it is over with, I'll be sure to stop by, so please tell your father I'm coming, all right?"

"Okay!" Mora said, brightening up. "We live in the biggest shop on Commerce Street, so it should be easy to find. I'll be waiting for you!"

Mora bowed and then skipped off with a smile on her face. The two servants also bowed and followed after her.

By then, most of the onlookers had already dispersed, and one of the guards helped break up the crowd of those left. However, before the guard returned to his post, he couldn't resist telling me one more thing. "The bards have already begun to sing of your heroic deeds, Great Magician!" That was more information than I cared to know...

"I'd rather not stand out even more than I do already..." I grumbled. "Still, I didn't think I'd meet Mora again so soon."

"How nice for you..." growled Clara, a vein pulsing at her temple.

"I'm sorry about that. Anyway, let's get going. To the Sorcerers' Guild!" I said, realizing Clara was near her limit.

"Yes, let's get that...what did you call it? *Worst thing* over and done with, shall we? My *lord* wizard."

"I said I'm sorry."

The streets of Relis, or at least the stone-paved main roads, were clean and pleasant to walk on. Some of them even had mosaic designs in their pavement. Most of the buildings were constructed from wood and stone, reaching three stories high or more. Given that walled cities could not branch out laterally, once their concentration hit a certain point, the only way to go was up. Especially in this aspect, the city itself was very much in line with the descriptions of medieval cities in the game materials I read up on when I was an active TTRPG player. The passersby on the street were dressed in bright colors, and none of them were barefoot. Though the designs of their clothes were for the most part simple, the wealthier accessorized with hats, shawls, capes, and skirts worn over their clothes.

None of the people we passed realized who I was, but many waved or gave short bows to Clara. *She really is famous, isn't she?* I thought. *Come to think of it, she did say she was the daughter of some noble.*

*Wait...* I thought with a shiver.

I had been lost in thought for the past few minutes, paying only enough attention to not lose track of Clara as I followed her—but after remembering a troubling bit of trivia, I refocused my attention to the upper windows and roofs of tall buildings.

I did not say anything, but I must have been acting strange, because Clara turned around.

"What are you doing?" she asked.

"It's nothing, just...from what I've heard, in large cities like this, people dispose of their excrement by throwing it out of windows..."

"What?!"

Thankfully, as Clara later explained, sewers were installed in cities that reached a certain size, and Relis City was no exception. In fact, there was even proper plumbing installed in parts of the city, made possible by Relis's access to fresh water.

"Is this city aiming to be this world's Rome or something?" I muttered.

*Well, I suppose I should not be surprised that there are differences between medieval Europe and Sedia—it would be strange if there weren't. The Watcher did paint a picture of a more light-novel-themed other world, after all...*

"While we're on that topic," I wondered, "how large is the city, population-wise?"

"If I remember correctly, when I looked up the records from a few years ago, about twenty-five thousand citizens were registered...if you include those without citizenship, I would guess the city's population was between thirty and forty thousand."

*Forty thousand! I thought. Relis is definitely a big city, then! If there are even a handful of other cities this size, it would be safe to say Sedia is farther along the path to civilization than medieval Europe. When I think that the daemons' nest was only a few days' walk from this city... We really were on the verge of a catastrophe.*

# Chapter 15

"**F**INALLY, WE'RE HERE," said Clara.

Clara stopped in front of a large building on a street a short distance away from the central square. My first impression of the building was that it was a structure standing in obstinate disregard for all the buildings or people around it. It was something of a mix between a mansion and a miniature castle, surrounded by a high fence. A crest made of four staves adorned the gate.

"Sorcerers' Guild: Relis Branch," a nearby sign read.

"It is I, Clara Andell, fifth seat of the branch," said Clara.

"Yes, ma'am," responded a guard. "We have been waiting for you." He opened the gate. He was dressed in a different uniform than the ones we saw at the entrance to the city.

Clara and I were led into a waiting room and given the VIP treatment. From the way the guard and the servants acted toward me, I assumed that they had already been informed of who I was.

After waiting about ten minutes, a servant came to lead us to a room where we would meet the officers of the guild.

"This way," she said.

We entered a large oval-shaped hall on the top floor of the building. It was about the size of a school gymnasium. The inside of the room matched the style of the exterior, mostly black colors, which only added to the overpowering aura of the chamber. The domed ceiling was fitted with stained glass windows (probably one of the most valuable items in the room), and tapestries hung from the walls, each decorated with designs that resembled sorcery code.

There were three sorcerers seated at a round table. The middle one stood up to greet us.

"Welcome to the Sorcerers' Guild. I am Heridol Sylem, president and first seat of the Relis Branch."

Heridol Sylem appeared to be in his mid-thirties, and he wore a heavily decorated robe with his blond hair combed back—very handsome overall. In his hand, he held a staff engraved with the crest of the guild, and brimmed with sociable confidence in both his expression and attitude. To use an example from my previous life—he carried himself like the young president of a venture capital firm at its initial public offering. He thought he was better than everyone else, and was not afraid to let it show.

"I am the magic user, Geo Margilus, from Castle Getaeus. It is an honor to be invited to your establishment."

I introduced myself with a well-worn set phrase and took a simple bow. It was a considerable relief to me that I could add "from Castle Getaeus" to my introduction—having a fixed address, in and of itself, is a wonderful thing.

"Oh, no, the honor is ours," said the man to Heridol's right, standing.

"Likewise—it is a pleasure to make your acquaintance," said a woman to his left, following suit.

The man and woman introduced themselves as Yahman, the vice president and second seat of the guild's branch, and Nasaria, the third seat, respectively.

"Well then, please take a seat."

I sat down at the table across from the other three. Clara wordlessly moved to the other end and sat down next to Nasaria.

As I slowly lowered myself into the ornately engraved wooden chair, I took the time to furtively examine the others. The only person in the room who was clearly relaxed was the president. Yahman's and Nasaria's faces were steely with nervousness, and Clara remained expressionless.

"I heard you have come from a very distant land. Do you find Relis to your liking?" Heridol asked.

"From what I have seen so far, the architecture is splendid and the people lively—a good city in my opinion."

*Starting out with small talk, huh? So, he's not one of those types only concerned with his own research,* I thought.

"Well, I hope you fully enjoy the sight of Relis's famous network of canals and sluice gates, and take an opportunity to watch one of the city's boat dances."

"I see... Thank you for your recommendation."

*Boat dances? That sounds entertaining.*

"President, I believe we should move on," Yahman whispered to Heridol.

"Yes, I suppose you're right," Heridol replied.

After a few minutes of inconsequential chatter, Yahman stepped in to rain on our parade. *So, he's that number-two type that serves to keep the president on task—or rather, serves as the president's excuse to stay on task,* I thought. *But given how important a guest I am (or am supposed to be), that's not a very good move. This guild has a lot to learn, from an organizational standpoint.*

"Lord Margilus, let me be frank with you," said Heridol. "As of now, all we can confirm with our own eyes about you is that you have no mana reserves. Yet reports from the Calbanera Knights, the Relis Adventurers' Guild, and Clara suggest you used a grand form of sorcery capable of destroying an entire legion of daemons..."

*Alnogia did say something about meeting with the city council, and Sedam told me outright he would be delivering a report to the Adventurers' Guild. If Heridol knows the contents of those reports,* I thought, *there must be some degree of information sharing within the city...*

"The mere suggestion," Heridol continued, with a hint of irritation in his voice, "that there exists another form of sorcery, which follows a different set of rules than the ones we know, is astonishing to us."

"I could say the same. From my perspective, my magic is the norm, and sorcery is the astonishingly foreign technique," I said.

"So, you feel the same?"

"Of course," I said. "In fact, I would love to learn more about sorcery, and, in exchange, I plan to offer as much information as I can about a wizard's magic."

Heridol and the others were clearly suspicious of me, so I did my best to appear cooperative and allay their fears. I desperately hoped it was working.

"We would very much appreciate that. However..."

I cut him off. "You would like me to show you some magic first. Is that right?"

*In the end, wizardry is no more than nonsense to them right now. The only reason they are listening to me at all is that I have several people to back up my story—but that can only get me so far.*

"Is it true...that you can turn people to stone and summon meteors from the sky?" Nasaria asked, hesitantly. Her wording was polite, but the doubt was clear on her face.

"Well, as it is with such things... I hope you understand our desire to see what you can do with our own eyes..." Yahman, the eldest of the three, quickly added.

*I get it. Don't worry, I get it...* I thought. *But still—I'm starting to get tired of having to summon meteor showers everywhere I go.*

"While I have no problem showing you my magic, I think it may be best to use a spell other than *Meteor* for an example."

"Y-yes, I agree," stuttered Yahman, and Nasaria nodded.

"All right, but be sure to show us something that clearly cannot be mistaken for sorcery, okay?" Heridol said, scoffing.

*Does he think I'm trying to worm my way out of doing a real demonstration?* I wondered. I looked over at Clara. She was giving him an ice-cold stare in response to his comment, and it made me more than a little happy that she was standing up for me.

"Oh, I know. According to Clara, you are able to create dragons and daemons out of nothing. I would love to see that," said Heridol.

"Hmm... Very well."

"In that case, you would not mind if we recorded our observations, would you?" asked Yahman, standing from his seat and approaching me.

"Of course—I do not mind," I replied.

"Thank you for your cooperation. In that case..." He trailed off and turned to Heridol, who replied with an affirmative gesture.

On Heridol's signal, Yahman took a crystalline medallion out of his pocket and showed it to me.

"Th-this is a device that is sensitive to even the smallest amounts of mana. I promise you it is not something that could harm you."

"I see. Well then, I shall begin."

I purposefully left my staff of wizardry at the table and stood up, making sure I secured enough space for the spell.

"Open, Gate of Magic. Reveal your form to me."

"Hmm?"

I had hardly begun casting my spell before the sorcerers began to murmur in surprise. Unlike magic, sorcery only required the user to utter a single phrase—the name of the incantation, so I must have appeared very strange to them.

My imagined self went through the magic gate I summoned to my inner world and proceeded down the stairs into the chaotic realm. In the outside world, Yahman continued to hold the crystalline medallion out in front him, but nothing changed. With the exception of Clara, the sorcerers looked on with a mix of suspicion, interest, and scorn on their faces, but remained silent.

My imagined self reached the ninth-level archive. I reached for the spellbook I was looking for and touched it, releasing its chaotic energy.

"As a consequence of this spell, I will create one baby red dragon in this space under my command for a duration of thirty minutes. *Create Monster: Any.*"

Fortunately, I did not fumble my dice roll. *Well, there is only a one percent chance of the spell failing, after all*, I thought, as the chaotic energy became a crimson flow, spiraling in the center of the hall.

"Whoa..."

"What is that?"

As the sorcerers focused with amazement on the red spiral, the monster began to take form.

Crimson scales covered the dragon's body, from its head and long neck to its lengthy tail. Each of its short limbs were armed with curved claws, and its reptilian head housed sinister, snake-like eyes and murderous crocodilian teeth. It was a hatchling, only about the size of a bull, but anything larger would not have been appropriate for the space and location.

"Gyahr!" the dragon roared.

In response, I heard the sorcerers cry out in fear and awe with stifled screams and muted gasps.

But after roaring, the dragon laid itself down on the floor in a show of submission to me and was quiet.

Heridol had half-risen from his chair, his staff in hand and ready to fire; Yahman, the closest to the dragon, had fallen backward in fear. I looked for Nasaria, and it was a few seconds before I realized she had fallen backward out of her chair, toppling it over.

"Yahman!" Heridol barked. "What does the sensor say?!"

"It isn't detecting any mana at all!"

"How...How can that be?" asked Heridol, his voice shaking as he trailed off into silence.

*They hardly lasted a minute*, I thought.

The only sound that could be heard was the calm dragon's breathing, seemingly amplified by the silence of the room.

That uncomfortable silence continued until even I reached my limit.

"Th-this is wonderful!" Heridol said, the first to break the silence. "You're the real deal. To think that you could make something like this without any mana..." However, his voice sounded artificial, his face was tense, and he sweated visibly.

"S-still..." Heridol continued. "Can that dragon...do anything? If it's just an illusion or a fake, then..."

*What's that now?* I thought. *This isn't good enough for you? Is it really that hard for you to accept that another kind of technique for this sort of supernatural phenomenon exists?* I will admit I was irritated, but I was not about to hold such a minor thing against them. My goal was to form a cooperative relationship with the guild.

"Oh, don't worry," I said. "It's real. See?"

"Gyaaahr!"

"What is it doing?!" Heridol cried out.

Nasaria screamed.

As with any creature created with a spell, I could control the dragon with my thoughts, as long as it was within a certain range.

The dragon spread its wings wide and opened its mouth, spewing forth red, fiery breath. The hall was filled with a reddish glow, and a wave of heat instantly began to beat against us. Of course, I took care not to burn anyone or anything, but the sorcerers still screamed.

Even so, the heat was enough to startle even me. When I'd sent my telepathic command to the dragon, I'd specifically imagined a small flame—apparently, my idea and the dragon's idea of a small flame were a little different.

*I, uh...didn't overdo it...right?*

"Oh, calm down! You're all a disgrace!" barked Clara.

Clara had been sitting quietly at the table throughout the ordeal, but after Yahman fell to the floor with his hands on his head and Nasaria hid under the table, she had apparently had enough.

"Y-you don't have to show us any more," stammered Heridol. "That's enough! You've convinced us your magic is real..."

"P-p-please, just g-get rid of that thing!" said Yahman.

"My apologies..." I replied, as calmly as I could, and cast *Dispel Magic*.

The red dragon melted away into empty space, and once it was gone, the sorcerers gave an audible sigh of relief.

··✝··

It took a while for the sorcerers to calm down. Though they went about righting fallen chairs and nervously sipping at their tea, their expressions were far graver than when I'd first entered the room—or at least, Heridol's was. There was not even a trace of his earlier confident smile. Yahman and Nasaria's expressions were more frightened than they were grave. Clara was the only one in the room who appeared fine.

*I overdid it, didn't I?* I thought.

"I apologize for startling you. Are you convinced now that wizardry exists?" I asked.

I kept a calm persona, but on the inside, I was still holding my head in my hands.

"Y-yes... I must admit, it truly is an awe-inspiring art," said Heridol, after a long, hesitant pause. "We were rude to be so dismissive. Will you accept our apologies?"

"Absolutely. In fact, I should thank you for believing me, in the end." I saw a wave of relief wash over them.

*Good. I might still be able to recover from this*, I thought.

··✝··

Ten minutes later...

"Interesting... What an astonishing hidden art."

"So, you don't use a sorcery frame, or even sorcery code..."

I finished briefly explaining the magic system—or at least the in-game explanation for it, as written by me with input from the game master. (I couldn't believe how complicated I had made the system, but I had no one to blame but myself.) However, as a precaution, I left out important details, such as: how to train yourself to construct the inner world in your imagination, everything about the Gate of Magic, and the fact that spells needed to be charged before they could be used.

Even without explaining everything to the sorcerers, what I said was enough to deliver a heavy blow of culture shock. To be honest, I felt a little bad. Sorcery was a real technique, which these sorcerers had perfected through years of effort. My magic was no more than a byproduct of a game I'd played years ago.

"The mana we use in our sorcery exists prior to us using it, in people and in nature, but the mana used in Lord Margilus's magic is something that is drawn out of chaos and channeled through his spirit," said Clara, summarizing.

Clara was quick to catch on, but she had heard most of this explanation once before. *It's confusing to use the same word to refer to two different things, though*, I thought.

"In that case, let us use 'magical power' instead of 'mana' to describe what I use," I said.

"I see... That makes sense. Magical power, huh? It would be wonderful if we could find a way to use that power, too..." said Heridol.

"However," Yahman said, "it appears to require many years of training..."

"Do you think it would be possible to use both at once?" muttered Nasaria.

The sorcerers were already starting to get lost in their own discussions, so I deemed it was about time to leave.

"Branch President Sylem, I hope to forge and maintain a cooperative relationship with your guild—one with us both on equal terms," I said.

"I-I appreciate the offer. However..." He averted his eyes.

I could not tell exactly what Heridol was thinking, but it was obvious that he was reluctant to team up with me. *Trying to force him into an agreement is only going to make matters worse*, I thought.

"That said, I do not need an answer now," I said, before Heridol could finish his sentence.

He glanced back up at me, puzzled.

"I am sure that my magic is like a bolt out of the blue to sorcerers like you. I think it best if you took time to discuss my offer among yourselves. In the meantime, if you have any questions, feel free to summon me so that I may answer."

*I just called everything they knew about the world as sorcerers into question*, I thought. *They need some time to collect themselves. I'll pull back for now, and return once everyone has had a chance to cool their heads. This was never something that could be resolved in a single meeting.*

"Branch President, I agree," said Clara. "I think it best to take some time to process this information and discuss it with the other officers."

Heridol finally righted himself and faced me directly.

"Yes... I am sorry, Lord Margilus; please allow us more time to consider your proposal."

As I left the hall, I heard one of the sorcerers ask, "What is a 'bolt out of the blue'?" and another reply, "I don't know. Maybe it's just a phrase that wizards use..."

"It looks like I won't be lodging at the sorcerers' guild after all," I said, a little frustrated.

"Well, it would have been hard to get them to lodge you after all of that." Clara helpfully supplied the obvious.

"I just hope I don't negatively affect your standing in the guild," I said. "If there's anything I can do to help, just tell me."

"In that case, it would be very helpful if you went back in there and said that magic is fake and you're a fraud," Clara spat, her eyebrows raised.

I knew Clara's kindness and heroism well enough by then to know she was only half-serious, and I appreciated her lightening the mood.

"Well then, if it's in order to protect your status, I may just have to do it."

"Oh, you tease," she said, and we both laughed a little.

*I'm really starting to get along with her*, I thought. *There's probably a lot we could accomplish together.*

"I do understand what Heridol is going through, though,"

Clara said quietly, gently setting our joking mood aside. "Many people in my family died fighting daemons ten years ago," she continued, crossing her arms over her chest. She narrowed her eyes, as if looking back on her memories. "The reason I became a sorceress was so that I would have the power to protect this city against them."

"Heridol's motivation and mine are similar, but not the same. Both of us use sorcery as a way to fight daemons more effectively, but he specifically worked so hard all these years to use his sorcery to become a hero—a protector of the people." Clara's fingers tightened around her arms. "What I am afraid of is having all of the hard work I put in being overwritten by your magic. What Heridol fears is having the position he has built for himself taken away by you."

*Damn you, Watcher! What have you done?!* I tried shouting and shaking my fist (all in my head)...but that farce wasn't terribly effective at anything other than offering a small distraction from the silence that followed.

*To think something my game master and I made up would end up causing trouble for so many people!* Although Clara and Heridol's concerns might have seemed outlandish because of words like "sorcery" and "heroes," the problems they faced were not unlike what many faced in Japan.

"If you ask me," I said slowly, "I don't think that your effort and what you have achieved can be overwritten by anyone. If you ask all the people you've saved with your sorcery, I don't think anything I could do would change how they feel about you."

"But that's..."

*When trying to comfort someone who is intelligent...it helps to give concrete examples*, I thought. *I'm not sure if that will work here, but it's worked for me before...*

"For example..." I continued, "when we were fighting the nest, you protected me with your wind sorcery. For a task like that, wizardry is absolute garbage."

The Calbanera siblings were the ones who'd made the final deflection, but if Clara's sorcery hadn't taken the brunt of the nest's tentacle attack, they would not have been able to do so. Without Clara's sorcery, we would all have been done for—so I reminded her of that.

Faced with my pathetic attempt at comforting her, Clara just stared at me, dumbfounded. Then, she suddenly turned her head away. *Did I mess up?* I wondered. *I guess what works sometimes doesn't work always... I don't have much experience in this area, after all...*

"I... I'll let you comfort me this time, okay? But don't get used to it!" Clara said, still looking away.

"Used to... Huh?"

"Mora's waiting for you, remember?" Clara scowled. "So hurry up and get going! Off with you! Go! Shoo!"

*Well... I guess it worked? I think? I don't know*, I thought, trying to piece together Clara's reaction. *Either way, I think this is it for today.* I turned to leave, and then remembered something important.

"Yeah, about that..." I turned back around. "I'd love to get going, but I, uh...don't know the way."

"What?!"

*Mora said she lives on Commerce Street...* I thought, trying to remember, but I had already forgotten the way we had come and wasn't really sure exactly where I was. Under normal circumstances, it would be hard for a grown man like me to admit he was so lost, but who could blame me? Life hadn't exactly afforded me a lot of opportunities to go wandering around medieval cities.

"Well, I'll probably be fine, as long as I ask a few people out on the street where to go..." I muttered, feeling the weight of shame.

"I cannot *believe* you sometimes!" Clara exclaimed before walking off—but a few strides later, she stopped and turned back toward me. "What are you doing?! Once the sun sets, they'll close the gates to each district, and we won't be able to pass through. So hurry up!"

Apparently, Clara was offering to guide me.

As I followed after Clara (who was still fuming), I took time to study the people of Relis as they passed by on the street.

We went by a market lined with carts, where merchants heatedly negotiated the prices of their wares, and soon passed storefronts, where master artisans were harshly coaching their apprentices. We passed children and young people stuffing their faces with fruit and candy and kebabs, but we also passed humble beggars reaching up from the ground, and heard the sounds of ruffians shouting and fighting among themselves. As we passed through the streets, I saw the city's network of canals, filled with colorful boats carrying people and cargo. Its waterways were punctuated by arched stone bridges.

We'd spent a long time talking at the Sorcerers' Guild, and night was starting to fall. I didn't know if it was for a special occasion or if it was part of a daily routine, but the streets and bridges were lit with countless lanterns, dappling the city streets with a dreamlike atmosphere.

"Is that the boat dance Heridol was talking about?" I asked Clara.

"Hmm? Oh. Yes, it is," she replied.

As we continued to walk along one of the many canals—which I had begun to think of as the arteries of this vast city—I noticed a line of decorated boats. It stood out from the others I had seen so far. It was like a parade, but on water. There were crowds of spectators, both on either side of the canal and on the bridges. When I looked more closely, I saw a stage on one of the boat decks, which is what all the crowds were watching.

The stage was lit with finely decorated lanterns, which resembled the paper lanterns common in Japan. Upon it moved dancers draped in flowing clothes of red and white silk. Some of the boats in the parade carried musicians playing music. While the melodies they played at first seemed light and playful, I felt a sorrowful tone underlying it. When the dancers turned in unison, it was like watching fireworks from a distance.

"It's beautiful...but it seems a little subdued to be part of a festival," I thought aloud.

Clara turned to me with a bit of a pained smile.

"Their performance today is a dance of requiem—for all those killed by daemons," she said quietly.

"I see..."

I had no other words to say.

*This isn't a game. This is a world where people live and die*, I reminded myself, yet again, and thought back to when Clara and I traveled along the Lawful Way to Relis, immersed in nature, dwelling among other travelers. That was another time I'd felt this way.

"Ten years ago, daemons invaded this city, after all," Clara said, pointing to a stone memorial on a corner of the street, carved in the shape of a soldier with a spear. People had lain flowers and wine beside it.

I read the inscription. "Here, the Relis City Guard's twenty-third regiment fought and died to impede the daemons' advance. May the winter goddess offer them peace."

"Hmm? What are you doing?" Clara asked.

"It's nothing. Don't worry about it."

I had reflexively brought my hands together, the way one might do by a grave in Japan. It might have seemed a foreign thing to do in Sedia, but whatever our difference in customs, I thought it right to show my respect for the fallen.

After we crossed several more stone bridges, we returned to a street situated near the front gate, where several shops with elaborate signs stood. *So, this is Commerce Street*, I thought.

"Mora's house is right over there," said Clara. "You don't need my help finding the front door, do you?"

Clara was ready to head back, and I didn't have any reason to stop her. This was her home turf, and it would be a little much to ask for any more of her time.

"Thank you, Clara," I said, with a bow.

Clara turned away from me, playing absentmindedly with her wavy hair. On our walk, Clara had shared something personal about herself, and while I did want to make up for making her talk about it, I realized I had never properly thanked her for all her help, so I felt I had to be especially insistent.

"What's this all about?" she said. "All I did was show you the way back to Mora's."

"It's not only that. You've done a lot for me over the past few days, and I realized I haven't thanked you yet. Thank you again."

"All I did was my duty," Clara said, after a pause.

"Even so, thank you for everything. I owe you a lot."

"So, the great magic user owes *me*? Well, I suppose I should consider myself lucky. I'm sure that's worth a ton." Clara spoke sarcastically, one eyebrow raised.

*At least she's back to her normal self*, I thought. *I guess my "comforting" helped a little, then.*

"Uh, well..."

As much as I felt I had gotten used to wearing the mask of a great magic user, it didn't take much for the façade to fall away. *At the end of the day, I'm just not suited for this role*, I thought, for the umpteenth time.

"I'm only joking," said Clara. "I know you're just a normal, kind person on the inside."

If I were back in Japan, and Clara was a young woman on the street or in a bar, I would have automatically translated that line into "I'm not interested in you," but her face looked too serious for me to dismiss her comment entirely.

"It's just..." Clara paused, then continued. "In this world, you never know when daemons might come and kill you or your family. If there's a real hero out there somewhere who could change that, I..." She trailed off, her blue eyes turning to me as if clinging to some unsteady hope. "I don't know where your path will take you, but I am confident that whatever you choose to do, it will be something that is *right*... Whether or not what you choose is something I'll be able to help you with," she said, finally.

Clara waited a few moments for an answer that did not come. As I struggled to find something to say, she closed her eyes once, and when they opened again, all the emotion they held was gone—compartmentalized.

"Good night," she said, and then she was gone.

# Chapter 16

"**T**HANK YOU AGAIN for coming!" said Ild.

"Mister Geo," called Mora, "eat as much as you want, okay?!"

I'd made it safely to Mora's house. The first floor was used for Ild's business dealings, but the upper stories were their residence. Despite this dual use, their home had a gate and a garden and reflected Ild's well-to-do social standing. When I arrived, it seemed that they'd pulled out all the stops to welcome me.

First Ild, then Mora and their many servants, thanked me many times. Extravagant plates were laid out upon an exquisite table. Mora had helped make many of the dishes, so I knew I had to at least try some of everything.

"I'm just glad that both of you made it back safely," I said.

"It's all thanks to you!" replied Ild.

I thankfully partook of the food, and Ild and I brought ourselves up to speed on current events as we poured each other wine.

First, Ild's goods, as I mentioned earlier, had been safely delivered by the Calbanera Knights. That apparently did not sit well with Mora, who interjected, "I was supposed to go with Mister Geo to get them!"

Ild had prepared the three thousand gold coins to exchange for the promissory note he'd left with me, and would not listen to me when I tried to refuse, but after a few back-and-forths, I came up with a compromise.

"If you really must have me accept something, could I ask you to do something for me instead of paying me the gold coins?" I asked.

"So, you want me to do a job worth three thousand gold coins for you? In that case, I'll do anything, but what is it you had in mind?"

"I was given ownership of that fortress in the mountains by the Calbanera Knights, but it's inconvenient for me to take care of the place all by myself. I would like to find a number of servants I can trust, as well as someone to oversee their work," I explained.

The was the business I had with Ild that I'd mentioned to Mora earlier. Ild slapped his leg and nodded.

"Understood. I take it that I may pull from the three thousand coins to pay expenses related to hiring them?" he asked.

"Yes. Of course."

"Do you have any specific requests in regards to the kind of servants you want working for you?"

"As long as they are trustworthy, I will have no complaints. Given that there is a possibility they may encounter dangerous circumstances because of me, I would prefer people who are able to protect themselves and who are not held back by allegiances to other groups or special interests."

"Understood. I will find you the best people I can."

··╈··

"Lord Margilus! That's why I told 'em, if ya ain't gonna splurge for the boat dance now, then when *are* ya?! Right?!"

One hour later, the sincere, intelligent merchant I knew as Ild was gone, and replaced by a drunk with the same name. That was the only reasonable explanation. *These two cannot possibly be the same person...*

"Then that district head—you know what he said to me?!"

Apparently, the boat dance was supported by separate districts, each donating funds, boats, and performers. Ild wanted to offer more funds than was previously customary, but donations were capped by the head of fundraising for the district. I was relatively sure of the gist of the story, as it was the tenth time I was hearing it from him.

I was partly at fault. After Ild told me about Mora's mother being killed ten years ago, and how he struggled to raise her as best he could, I couldn't help myself from repeatedly pouring him more wine.

"I-I'm sorry, Mister Geo. It does not take much to put my father over his limit... Usually he doesn't drink that much, but this time..." Mora looked mortified.

"I don't mind. There isn't a man out there who doesn't want to get drunk and let loose every now and then," I said.

"Really?"

"Stop right there! Don't you flirt right in front of me! I'm Mora's father, y'know—and she's only fourteen, okay?!"

"Father, stop it!"

"Ha ha ha, Ild. I don't think you've had enough to drink yet."

"That's what I like to hear! Bring it on! The night is young!"

Ild took his mug and started chugging his wine. *When it gets this bad, the best thing to do is let the drunk drink 'til he drops,* I thought. Though, naturally, I made sure to pull the cup away at times to make sure he didn't get all the way to the point of alcohol poisoning.

Sure enough, within a half-hour or so, Ild was out cold. I could hear him snoring as the servants carried him to his bedroom. *Finally,* I thought, with a sigh of relief.

"I'm so sorry, Mister Geo," said Mora, pouring me some water. "My father kept talking about how he wanted to thank you and pay you back, and I suppose when you finally visited, he must have gotten carried away..."

"Appreciated," I said, taking the cup. "I've already said this a few times, but there's really no need to thank me for what I did."

"But we want to!" said Mora, almost angry. "First you saved me from the bandits, and then you exterminated all of those daemons, and destroyed the nest... You've done so many amazing things!"

"Well...I suppose so..."

From the perspective of a former Japanese bachelor like me, Ild—who owned a successful business and was raising his daughter all on his own—seemed far more amazing than I could ever hope to be.

"It was because of you that me and everyone else were saved," said Mora.

"Because of me, huh?"

*If you look at everything that happened objectively, yeah.*

Mora eyed me. "Mister Geo, is the reason you look so stressed because you're really just a normal person inside?"

*Is it that obvious I'm not who I say I am?*

It was still hard for me to wear the mask of a great and powerful magic user. The role and the responsibilities that came with it were too great for me to handle. *But wait*, I thought, *Mora saw me before I ever put on that mask, so of course someone as smart as her would be able to see right through me.*

"Um, I... There's a lot I don't understand, but even if you are a normal person inside, that doesn't make you any less amazing, or any less kind. Even if you're normal, there are a lot of people who need help that you can save!" Mora spoke quickly, her face bright red as she talked.

"Okay, um... Thank you?" I was a little exhausted, from the dinner and the drinking and everything else.

Mora must have noticed, for she energetically bowed her head.

"G-good night!" she said, her face still red.

"Good night, Mora." I said—and with that, she darted out of the room.

The room was quiet.

*This power*, I thought, *is really not my own. It would be stupid of me to think I was great or strong because of it. Ever since I arrived in Sedia, many people have heaped praise on me. It never felt bad, per se, but the guilt I feel for it being undeserved will probably never go away. If I'm going to keep wearing this mask, I'll probably have to deal with this feeling for the rest of my life.*

*But even if this power is something I never deserved, does that really mean I shouldn't use it if and when I can?*

*Mora said that even a person like me can save people who need help.*

••✝••

I was the only one left in the dining hall. After the hustle and bustle of the dinner party, it was a comfortable loneliness. I drank some of the water Mora had poured me. It had a refreshing tartness to it, as if it was flavored with a bit of fruit juice.

"Even with everything I've had to deal with since coming here, it really is a nice place," I said quietly.

I thought back over everything I had experienced since being transported to Sedia (or reincarnated in Sedia? I did die, after all...). I had seen so much, and met so many different people.

I had been in Sedia for less than a month, but I was already starting to feel an attachment to it. It was less convenient and more violent than Japan—there were evil people like Jargle, and monsters like the daemons, but, like Japan, it was full of wonderful people and rich in culture. All in all, Sedia was a wonderful world.

"Changing my entire way of life at my age sure is rough," I grumbled.

*"I'm going to protect this world" sounds great on paper, but it's tough for a guy like me to commit to it. I'm used to an unchanging, mediocre life.*

"But if I'm serious about exterminating all daemons, I need to bring together enough people to make an organized effort. If possible, I would like to track down the source of the daemons and end it there, so they'll be gone for good..."

*The people of Sedia have fought daemons for hundreds of years but were unable to get rid of them,* I thought. *But what if an ordinary guy from another world with the powers of a great magic user joins forces with everyone else to defeat them?*

"Well, I guess it's worth a shot... I mean, uh—" I stopped to clear my throat. "Bring it on."

*I guess it means postponing my retirement...but let's give it a try. I'll become a great magic user—for real.*

··✟··

When I got up the next morning, I expected to be hit with a hangover, but to my surprise, I felt perfectly refreshed. Thankfully, it seemed, I had underestimated the effect Geo's ability scores had on my body. Particularly, his (my) Constitution score of 16 was nothing to shake a stick at. Incidentally, if I were to rate the Constitution score of my previous body, that of an otaku in his forties, it would likely be somewhere in the neighborhood of 9.

"Mora, this is delicious. You really are a great cook."

"Eheheh... You really think so?"

As I ate the breakfast Mora served me, I felt a sort of energy well up inside. It was a feeling I had not felt in a while, and I suspected it was because I now had a clear goal to work toward.

Although Mora was with me at the table, Ild was out on business. As a merchant in charge of many itinerant caravans, he had a lot to do, and usually started work early in the morning. *After all he drank last night, he sure has energy, to get up so bright and early…*

"But it's not just that," Mora said, a suspicious look on her face. "A lot of people came to visit this morning…"

Whatever the case, I thought the relative calm was a good opportunity to organize my thoughts.

The previous night, I'd settled on a single goal I wished to pursue: protecting the people of Sedia from the threat of daemons. I did so after considering the various problems the people of Sedia faced, such as war and poverty—I was not so deluded as to think I could solve everyone's problems all at once, so after some deliberation, I decided my focus should be the extermination of daemons.

*Daemons*, I thought. *They're a menace that just cannot be left alone.* After seeing them, after fighting them, I knew in my bones that they were an unnatural abomination, one that must be exterminated at any cost.

*But then, how will I do it?*

It was difficult to plan against creatures that seemed to appear without warning, out of nowhere. It would cost too much to keep a force ready for them all the time. It would be impossible to maintain. I'd seen a glimpse of that truth when I saw, firsthand, how the Calbanera Knights struggled with funding.

I could see two ways around this problem. One was to get every country to cooperatively share its information on daemons and form an alliance. Every country's military would assist in the effort to eradicate the daemons whenever there was an outbreak. Another way was to build up an independent force, distinct from any country's military, whose sole purpose was to exterminate daemons, regardless of where they appeared.

*Along the same lines*, I thought, *I should help with the extermination of daemons in other countries as well.*

*If I join forces with a larger group and fight on the ground, I do not think there is a daemon I cannot defeat—but I also cannot be in multiple places at once. Because of that, it is more important that I use my magic and skills to help train other forces, so that they do not have to rely on me alone...*

In the back of my mind, I jotted down those two broad ways to bring about the extermination of daemons: form a military alliance between nations to fight daemons, and build up an independent anti-daemon force. There was no reason I couldn't pursue both, as long as they remained viable.

Under those two broad goals, I listed the steps necessary to make them a reality: First, I needed to raise my status to a level where I could negotiate with other countries, gather staff, and so on and so forth. *This is going to be a lot of work*, I groaned.

"I also have to get to a place where I can develop new magic items," I mumbled, thinking aloud.

Mora smiled. "Mister Geo, do you feel better today?"

*What a nice girl she is*, I thought.

"Yes, thanks to you," I said.

"Thank goodness!" said Mora, with a little hop.

*If all daughters are as cute as she is, maybe I should have tried to find someone to settle down with, so I could have one of my own,* I thought.

After breakfast, just as I thought I might take a walk around town, Ild returned.

"Lord Wizard, I apologize for my behavior last night. Were you planning on going somewhere?"

Ild's face showed no signs of a hangover. His drunkenness from the night before was gone without a trace.

"Actually, I thought of something else I wanted to ask you to do...in addition to what I asked last night—if you're willing," I said.

Ild replied immediately and without hesitation. "Ask away. I'll do anything."

"Could you arrange a meeting between me and your best contact closest to the city council?" I asked.

"Perhaps...but for what reason?" Ild said, looking somewhat confused.

*Maybe I should have worded it differently?* I thought.

"I want to hear what measures Relis is taking to protect itself against daemons. I would like to offer the city my support, if possible."

I thought I might startle Ild if I told him something like, "I want to save the world from daemons," and I was not yet confident

I would be able to achieve so grand a goal. So I started off with a smaller scope. After I explained what it was I was trying to do, in simple terms, Ild's face lit up.

"So that's what you meant! That won't be a problem. You see, people have been sending messengers here all morning."

"Messengers?"

"Yes. It seems word has gotten out that you stayed the night here with us. The messengers were from various guilds, plus the church and nobles. Everyone has been asking for me to introduce you to them."

*Ah, so that was why he was so busy this morning... I feel a little bad about that, but all the attention is definitely convenient.*

"I'm sorry to cause so much trouble," I said. "Is there anyone close to the council who sent a messenger?"

"No need to worry. The first person who sent a messenger was the head of the Merchants' Guild, Zatow Brauze, who also happens to be the current chairman of the Relis City Council. I'll set right to work arranging a time for you to meet him."

"Really? Well in that case...thank you. I appreciate it."

"Don't mention it! I'd do anything to help out the one who saved my daughter, and after hearing your intentions, as a resident of Relis, it's surely my duty to assist you."

I was momentarily overwhelmed by Ild's sincerity. If I were still just an ordinary employee of a Japanese company, I wouldn't be able to bear the weight of Ild's expectations...

"I will work hard to live up to your regard," I said.

But now, I was a grand magic user.

⸱⸱✝⸱⸱

After my conversation with an unexpectedly cooperative Ild, both Ild and Mora saw me off, and I set out to walk around town.

It seemed that rumors of me had spread since the day before. I noticed people staring at me, the mysterious and great magician, from a distance. A mix of fear and awe was etched in their faces. But I noticed less fear in their eyes compared to when I was in Yulei.

"All right, let's do this."

The first thing I needed to do was learn more about daemons, so I headed for the Relis Public Library. While I admit it did take me long enough, I realized for the first time, when I subconsciously read the inscription on the memorial the day before, that *I could read*. Knowledge of the written language of Sedia was already imprinted in my mind, just as the spoken language was. That was how I knew the script.

Ordinarily, the library was only open to citizens who paid high taxes for the privilege, but when I gave my name at the reception desk, I was given access with the utmost courtesy. I figured it only proper to at least show some token appreciation, so I donated a few gold coins.

The chief librarian offered to help me personally, so I asked them to bring me books and other resources with "daemon" in the title.

Several hours later, still immersed in a pile of books...

"Oww..." I moaned, my lower back gone stiff.

As I mentioned earlier, I had the benefit of Geo's Constitution score, so I didn't expect any serious issues...but for my back to hurt like it did, I must have hit the books a little too hard.

"However, if this is all they have, I've hardly learned anything new about the daemons at all..."

There were many books, documents, and articles about daemons, but most investigations only covered what I already knew, or ended simply in "X about daemons remains unknown." Daemons did not form countries or societies. Once a nest appeared, the daemons that emerged from it would attack humans until they were killed. They did not seem to understand language, and all attempts to communicate with them were unsuccessful. The more I read, the more daemons reminded me of the monsters you find in science fiction stories rather than in fantasy.

Though disappointed by the lack of new information, my investigations weren't all for naught. I found several references to the term "brood," which Sedam had used for a massive daemon outbreak. A brood was described as a continental-scale disaster. During one, you could expect multiple nations to collapse.

According to what I'd read, Sedia had experienced two brood events.

According to the Shrendal Calendar, which began the year the kingdom was founded, the first brood event occurred in the year 815. I learned that the current year was 1300, so it had happened approximately 500 years ago. The nest that had appeared during the first brood event was located in a place called the Valley of Earthen Disaster. According to records, nearly half of the cities on the continent had been destroyed. However, it was unclear exactly what ended the first brood event. There was mention of a hero who'd brought together the surviving forces at the time, but no specifics. *A hero, huh?*

The second brood event occurred in year 1134 of the Shrendal Calendar. Records confirmed what I had heard before, that the Calbanera Knights' founding coincided with this event. The attack launched by the daemons of the second brood event had originated in a cave known as the Earthen Jaw and was reportedly less than half the scale of the first brood event. However, that had not stopped the daemons from destroying several cities at the center of the continent and triggering the fracture of the Shrendal Kingdom.

In response to the second brood, a coalition of humans, elves, and dwarves were able to defeat the legion at the Battle of the Daybreak Plains (now the Twilight Wastelands), after which a party of skilled adventurers traveled to the Earthen Jaw and destroyed the daemons' nest.

Unlike the first brood event, records of which were scarce, the second was covered in great detail. In other words, the first was more of a legend, while the second was part of established military history.

After the second brood event, daemons' nests continued to appear, one every few years. However, the last ten years had been exceptionally peaceful.

"If you include the legendary history, a coalition was formed twice before in response to daemonic threats," I thought aloud as I stretched.

*It's good to know it's been done before.*

••✦••

"Thank you, Mister Geo!" Mora beamed in delight.

I had bought sweets from a cart on my way back from the library, which Mora was delighted to see. They appeared to be some sort of cookie baked with bits of fruit, and went well with Mora's sil tea.

"Lord Margilus, about your meeting with the city council chairman—would tomorrow morning be all right with you? Brauze is very much looking forward to meeting you," said Ild, reaching for a cookie.

"Of course, and send my regards. Thank you."

"Understood, I will let him know. I will also arrange a carriage to take you to him. It is wrong to ask a great magician like yourself to go anywhere on foot—I apologize for not arranging a carriage for your errands today."

"I-It's fine. You're doing enough already..."

"Thank you. As for hiring servants for your castle, I am currently in negotiations with several candidates... I will need a little more time."

*What a guy,* I thought. *It's no wonder he's a successful merchant.*

*He really knows how to get to work fast. I expected this would take more time...*

"Don't worry, I'm in no rush," I said.

"With those matters out of the way, I..." Ild hesitated. "I have something I would like you to be aware of."

*Something he would like me to be aware of? I feel like I've become some company president. This kind of respectful treatment is really hard to get used to*, I thought.

"It seems there are some people in the city, and not the nicest sort, sniffing around, trying to find out more about you. No one has disturbed the shop or tried to enter our home, but I have noticed others attempting to eavesdrop on conversations about you, or glean information in other ways..."

"I-Interesting..."

"Who do you think is trying to investigate Mister Geo, Father?"

"I cannot say for certain. Almost everyone who holds power in Relis has taken an interest in you, Lord Margilus."

*So, everyone in the city is a suspect, huh? I thought. I don't fault anyone for being interested in me, and if general information is all they are after, I suppose it's nothing to worry about, but still...*

I couldn't shake the feeling that this was an omen of some sort. Anxiety filled me, an entirely different kind than what I'd felt before I faced the daemons.

"Do you know if you were followed today?" Ild asked.

"If I was...I did not notice."

I thought back over the events of the day. I couldn't remember anything suspicious, but I had not cast any spells to help me detect that sort of thing, so the fact that I hadn't noticed was no guarantee I hadn't been followed. Cloak and dagger skills, along with detecting them? That was the specialty of the rogue class, not magic users.

"I see. With all that is scheduled for tomorrow, would you like me to arrange guards to accompany you?" Ild asked.

*This guy never ceases to amaze me*, I thought. *How incredibly talented and considerate can you be? Is this the norm among merchants in Sedia? Well, he does seem to have a significant amount of influence within the Merchants' Guild, so he is probably above average, ability-wise. If I had someone like him working under me back at the company, my life would have been so much easier... Although, it is possible someone as capable as him might have quickly gotten tired of dealing with me...*

"No... I think it's better not to provoke them or anyone else," I said. "I consider myself a friend to the city, and I will make that clear when I meet with the city council chairman tomorrow. Once I do that, there should be nothing to worry about."

*If whoever it is continues to stalk me after that, it'll be clear they're an enemy of some sort*, I thought. *An enemy, huh... And a human one at that...*

"Mister Geo, are you alright?"

"You don't have to worry about me," I said. "To be honest, I'm more worried about you two. It would make me feel better to know you're taking precautions, just in case."

"We absolutely will," said Ild.

*There is a real possibility Ild and Mora could be put in danger... I may have to take some precautions of my own for them.*

..✟..

As Mora served me breakfast the next morning (a routine I was beginning to get used to), I thought about what I'd learned the day before, and considered the day ahead.

I tried to think of my advent from the perspective of the people in town: If another human being, powerful enough to eradicate a legion of daemons along with its nest, was roaming around town only days later...I would be curious, at least, about their aims—especially if I was in a position of power in the city.

Therefore, it was only natural that Ild would be swarmed with messengers requesting an audience with me, and certain that those in power would be scrambling for rumors of my activities. I had no experience of being this famous, but I was sure that trying to hide my aims or act surreptitiously would only garner unwanted suspicion.

*In that case, what is the quickest way for me to come out and show that I am not a threat to the city?*

"Anyway, those are my thoughts. What do you think?" I'd just finished explaining the results of my brainstorming to Ild.

"It is as you say," Ild agreed.

"No matter what the circumstances, it is hard to reason that there is anyone in the city who would deliberately do something that would anger you. I know I am the one who warned you, but I don't think it necessary to make a big deal out of it."

I was still no expert on what qualified as common sense in Sedia, so I put great weight behind Ild's view that I should not overreact—especially given that he was a merchant; dealing with other people was his specialty.

"But it must feel terrible, knowing there are people snooping about," Mora said with a frown.

*Well, of course,* I thought, but hearing Mora's comment immediately triggered another reflexive thought in my mind, the kind I would only normally get if I were playing a game. I didn't want to acknowledge it, but it came all the same: *This is definitely foreshadowing.*

"I'm sure everything will be fine, but it pays to take precautions. I will leave these two items with you." I handed Ild a silver ring and Mora a light green cloak, both of them magic items.

"This is so beautiful, and so light! It's...huh?"

"Mora?!"

When Mora donned the cloak, she immediately vanished into thin air. The cloak I gave her, a standard magic item in *D&B*, was an Elven Cloak, which granted invisibility.

"Don't worry. Mora is still here. The cloak makes whoever wears it invisible. You'll be back to normal as soon as you take it off," I said.

"Really? Oh, look! I'm back!" said Mora, as she removed the cloak.

"I can't believe you would give us such valuable items... We are not worthy of these," said Ild.

"You two are my friends, some of only a few people I can trust. I don't want anything to happen to either of you. Ild, the ring I gave you is a djinni ring; if you rub it, a wind spirit will appear and grant you three wishes. However, remember that it is not an omnipotent being. What it can do is mostly limited to fighting and manual labor."

"Th-this materia can control a spirit? I have only heard of such things in myths and legends. This is on the same level as a national treasure. Thank you so much for entrusting it to me," said Ild.

The djinni summoned by the ring was a Level 12 monster, and therefore rather powerful, but I was sure Ild would use it wisely. Ild bowed as he held the ring in his hands, and Mora followed suit.

"Thank you so much for your concern. We will keep these items with us until you return," said Ild.

"Thank you so much, Mister Geo!"

As an extra precaution, I cast *Invisible Demon* twice, which allowed me to assign both Ild and Mora an unseen bodyguard. Although the demons could only be assigned one command, and you had to be careful with the wording of said command, lest the demon interpret it in a way that was at odds with your intent, the spell had the benefit of lasting a very long time. I ordered the demons individually to: "restrain anyone who attempts to bring harm to Ild or Mora."

In a way, it felt over the top, like assigning a battle tank to follow someone as a measure against stalkers, but I knew it was better to be too careful than not careful enough and regret it later.

After I was finished with Ild and Mora, I cast *Invisible Demon* a third time on myself, in addition to *Detect Enemy*, and *Emergency*. I made a mental note to make sure to keep this set of three spells continuously charged and available for the time being.

# Chapter 17

A FEW HOURS LATER, I was on my way to Relis City Hall to meet Zatow Brauze, chairman of the city council. As I looked out the window of the horse-drawn carriage, peering at the hustle and bustle of the city, I mulled over what Ild had told me.

The area around Lake Ryuse was originally part of the Ryuse Kingdom, a vassal state to the Shrendal Kingdom. However, when the Ryuse Kingdom had collapsed during a period of civil unrest forty years earlier, a group of powerful merchants and nobles in Relis had come together and declared independence to form a city-state.

Relis was governed by its city council. Those who were eligible to become members of the council were the heads of each of the city's guilds—mostly wealthy merchants—as well as members of the noble families who were party to Relis's declaration of independence. (Clara's uncle, Duke Andell, was one such person.) As you might expect, the council was split into factions, which constantly vied for power.

Zatow Brauze was the head of the Merchants' Guild, and had, for many years, reigned as the top man of the mercantile faction. According to Ild, he was one of the few people with a position of power in the city who considered the interests of all of its people when he made his decisions. *Well*, I thought, *Brauze is the head of Ild's guild, so I assume his praise is somewhat biased.*

Regardless, as my primary objective was to present myself as harmless, or better yet, useful to the city and its interests, Zatow Brauze was the perfect person to speak with. *If all goes well*, I thought, *I may be able to convince him to let me be involved in the city's anti-daemon countermeasures...*

I was still lost in thought when the carriage stopped in front of the city hall. The building possessed an overpowering presence, looming out over the city's central plaza. The entrance was flanked by two statues: one of the city's guardian deity, the god of mercantilism, and the other of the winter goddess, Ashginea, who protected humans from daemons.

"So, you are the great magician, Geo Margilus. We were expecting you. Please, come in," said an attendant, who led me to a reception room.

"Welcome, Great Wizard. I am the Relis City Council Chairman, Zatow Brauze. I apologize for calling you here on such short notice."

Brauze was a middle-aged man with a magnificent beard. He bowed deeply toward me, but in his mannerisms, it was clear that the bow was out of courtesy—not in any way an admission that he stood below me.

"I am indeed the magician Geo Margilus of Castle Getaeus. It is an honor. Forgive me for not paying you a visit earlier."

I could feel my hands sweat as I gripped my Staff of Wizardry. Brauze reminded me of Captain Sardish of the Calbanera Knights, in that both had an almost overpowering presence and majesty to their character. The only difference was that Sardish's gravitas came from being a veteran of the military, and Brauze's came from being a veteran of both political and economic spheres. Brauze would easily rival any of the business elites I'd encountered working in Japan. It was difficult not to be overwhelmed, and I had to constantly remind myself of the role I played: *I am a great and powerful magic user. I am a great and powerful magic user.*

After we greeted one another, Brauze invited me to sit down at a table (in a gorgeously elaborate chair, no less). He soon followed suit.

"I have heard of your great accomplishments from Sir Alnogia and Sedam. On behalf of all the citizens of Relis, allow me to thank you for destroying the daemons' nest." Brauze motioned for a secretary, who wheeled out a small chest on a cart. The servant opened it to show me its contents. It was filled with gemstones and gold coins.

"Our gratitude is greater than what can be expressed in monetary terms," Brauze continued, "but we would appreciate it if you accepted this small token as part of our thanks."

"I only did what should be expected of any mage, but I appreciate your show of thanks and will gratefully accept."

Normally, I would not have had the courage to accept such a large amount of treasure, but Ild had cautioned me earlier not to refuse. According to Ild, exchanging gifts was a matter of course among the powerful, and my refusal would be an insult.

"That I am glad to hear," said Brauze, smiling. "Now I have one less thing to worry about."

Brauze picked up a hand bell from the table and rung it. As the secretary left the room, a young woman entered, pushing a cart with a tea set. She had chestnut colored hair tied in a bun, and wore a long black shirt and skirt, as well as a white apron and white gloves. *She looks just like a French maid*, I thought, staring.

"We have some fine canel leaf tea, if you would like—or would you rather have wine to drink?" asked Brauze, interrupting my trance.

*Sorry, guy...* I thought. *It's not that I'm not interested in having tea, this is just the first time I've ever seen a real, old-school, European-style maid...*

The graceful way the maid went about making our tea suggested a high degree of skill.

"I did hear that you were looking for servants," said Brauze. "If you would like, I could—"

"No, that's fine... I have Ild looking into that for me," I said, cutting him off.

*If I stare any more, Brauze is going to get a wrong idea about me,* I thought, trying to refocus my attention.

"Among the younger generation of our guildsmen, Ild is one of the very finest. We are most pleased to see you on good terms with him. Truly, this must be thanks to Ashginea's divine providence."

"Yes, he has been very helpful to me, and I am grateful. Unfortunately, I cannot repay the favor by helping him in his business endeavors."

"Oh, but of course. So grand a magician, working in the professions? Even wishing for such a thing would only court Ashginea's anger," Brauze replied.

While not serious on its surface, this exchange was another matter Ild had cautioned me on: "Some of the guild members likely suspect I plan to use my relationship with you to my advantage, to rise in the ranks of the guild," he said. "I am sure Chairman Brauze has similar concerns, so I would appreciate if you dispelled those suspicions."

To address those likely worries, I stated my intention was not to get involved in any business matters. From Brauze's softened expression, I seemed to have played the right move.

"I am sorry to have kept you waiting," said the maid, who proceeded to pour tea into expensive-looking cups of fine porcelain.

I had to admit the tea had a more fragrant aroma to it than the sil tea Mora usually prepared for me.

"These leaves can only be found in the Canel region of Shrendal. While you are in Relis, I hope you use the opportunity to enjoy specialties from all corners of the continent."

"Yes, I have enjoyed many such already," I said.

Brauze took a light sip, almost as if he was testing for poison. I saw no particular reason to be suspicious and so took a larger sip of the light brown liquid—and could not help but make a face.

"Does the tea not suit your tastes?" said Brauze. "Canel tea has a somewhat stronger flavor to it than sil tea, after all."

"N-no, it was just more delicious than I was expecting..."

The truth was that it wasn't as good as I expected it to be, but Brauze seemed to be enjoying it, and I didn't want to do anything offensive, or suggest I was a country bumpkin that couldn't discern good tea from bad, so I steeled myself for another sip.

Our conversation carried on like this, vital information interspersed with everyday small talk. This sort of dialogue flow was partially out of my area of expertise—less the habit of a businessman and more that of a politician. However, Brauze played along with my slightly stilted school-presentation-ish speechmaking, and I was grateful for it. The art of political speech aside, unless he was deliberately trying to deceive me, Brauze seemed very open to my plans, and I felt that I could expect others in the city to react the same.

"Therefore," I explained, "I would like to support the city and unify its people in their fight against daemons."

"I see. I think that is a wonderful plan," said Brauze.

"Daemons are the bane of all humanity. If it is to protect humans from daemons, there's nothing I won't do, and no effort I won't endure."

"Your words are most heartening; I will convey your intentions to the other guilds and council members. I imagine they will be overjoyed when they hear of your plans."

"If there is anything I can do to help concerning the city's defenses, please let me know," I said.

"Yes... Again, thank you for your offer of support. There is much that I cannot decide on my own, so as far as this matter is concerned, I will discuss things with the commander of the guard, and...then..." Brauze's face suddenly went pale, and his elbow fell against the table.

I rose from my chair. "Are you all right?"

I suddenly remembered a scene a couple years back when one of my coworkers at a restaurant started hyperventilating and fell to the ground.

"Urgh!" Brauze vomited and fell to the floor.

"Hey!" I shouted, running over to Brauze. "Can you hear me?!"

*Is it poison?!* I thought frantically. *It has to be, that's the only thing that makes sense.* I looked over my shoulder and scanned the room, but naturally, the maid was long gone.

Chairman Brauze, who had just moments before been in complete control of the conversation, was now moaning, blue in the face.

It felt like I was living a scene out of a television drama or video game. As absurd as it felt, I knew that poison was the only explanation. One of the windows in the room was wide open, where I suspected the maid had escaped.

Brauze continued to moan.

"A-are you all right?" I said, reflexively, even though I knew the question was stupid.

The first thing I did was lift Brauze's upper body and rub his back in an attempt to prevent him from suffocating on his own vomit. It was only then that I realized something odd. *I drank the same tea, didn't I?*

"Lord Margilus... A-are you...okay?"

"Yes, I seem to be fine... Does this mean my resistance to poison successfully nullified the effect?" I wondered aloud.

In *D&B*, a player character's resistance to poison grows stronger as the character's level increases. At Level 36, most poisons are nullified with a success rate close to 100%. *It's not a very flashy ability*, I thought, *but it's pretty incredible, when you think about it...*

"Chairman Brauze?!"

When I turned in the direction of the voice, I saw Brauze's secretary in the doorway, stunned.

*Hmm... Well, this doesn't look good, does it? Is this supposed to play out in such a way that I'm framed for murder?*

I surprised myself by how calm I was about the whole thing, but part of that was because I knew exactly what I needed to do if there was poison involved.

"D-don't make a fuss!" Brauze yelled to his secretary, heaving. "Don't let anyone come close!" He turned to me. "L-Lord Margilus... Th-there must be a plot against us..."

"Don't worry, I know. Now let me heal you."

"Th-this is not the will of the people! Th-they would never seek to poison you..." said Brauze, as he moaned in pain. "Wait... Did you say...heal?"

It was clear that Brauze's primary concern was protecting the people of Relis (from my wrath, it seemed) and not himself...but he stopped, mouth gaping, as he realized I did not seem to be angry, or worried at all about his condition.

I reached inside my Infinity Bag and took out a silver ring. I then touched it to his body and uttered an activation command.

"Dispel all poisons from this man's body."

"Urgh... Oh?"

The ring was a magic item called a Medical Ring. It allowed the user to cast a maximum of three cleric spells a day. Once I cast *Dispel Poison*, the color quickly began to return to Brauze's face. Brauze's secretary, who had been frozen stiff, came running to his side.

"Chairman! A-are you okay?!"

"Y-yes, I'm fine... It's like nothing ever happened... Lord Margilus, are you also a priest?"

"Unfortunately, no. I was only able to heal you because I happened to have this magic item with me."

For good measure, I activated the Medical Ring once again to use another spell to restore Brauze's stamina.

"Wh-what incredible materia..." Brauze stared in amazement as I wiped his mouth clean.

His health returned, Brauze suddenly looked up, as if remembering something, and yelled at his secretary.

"What are you doing?! Someone just attempted to poison Lord Margilus and me! It was that maid! Don't let her get away!"

"Y-yes, sir!" The secretary hurried out of the room, giving orders to the guards and nearby staff.

I paused a moment before I spoke. "Well, nobody got hurt, so..."

"My apologies, Lord Margilus! We will catch the criminal, no matter what!" Brauze prostrated himself on the ground before me, yelling his apologies. "Please contain your anger!"

It appeared Brauze was still genuinely afraid I might obliterate Relis with a meteor shower in retaliation. *Well*, I thought, *he doesn't know me that well, so I can't blame him for being overly cautious.* However, although his pleading made me feel uncomfortable, I couldn't help but feel a bit of respect for the man. After all, despite having maintained a sense of unyielding strength throughout our talks, he was willing to throw away his pride for the sake the city. *This is a man who truly cares about his city and its people*, I thought.

It took me a while to get Brauze to stop apologizing.

I told him several times that I was not angry and had no intention of doing anything to the city before he finally listened to me and was visibly relieved.

Once Brauze was back to normal, I was able to discuss plans for moving forward. First came the issue of the maid: The city guards initiated a search but were unable to find any trace of her. What they were able to find was the original maid, who had been locked in a closet. It appeared that the assassin had assaulted the maid as she was on her way to bring us tea and switched places with her. Although it appeared that the assassin had escaped through an open window, there were no witnesses who saw her escape. The maid's uniform, stolen by the assassin, was found discarded in an alley adjacent to the city hall.

The assassin had been able to thwart the guards and escape unseen by any member of the public in broad daylight. *This is no amateur*, I thought, and that was not the only problem. *She didn't even trigger my Detect Enemy spell. What could this mean?*

"Who does she think she is, Fujiko Mine?"

Not only was she undeniably skilled, she was attractive, even wearing that plain and modest maid uniform. She seemed just like the heroine of a certain famous animated series about a renowned thief.

"I have already ordered all of the guards to commence inspections at all of the gates and internal checkpoints in the city. We will not let her get away."

"Uh... Yeah, sounds good. Yes, please do that."

"It would be one thing if they were only targeting me, but for the assassin to make an attempt on *your* life as well... That is unforgivable."

"So, you think that the aim of whoever's behind this was to kill me?"

"To be honest... I am not certain," Brauze said, shaking his head.

The fact that Brauze and I had scheduled a meeting that day was easily discernable upon investigation of the city council or city hall. Given how skilled that fake maid assassin was, it was no surprise that someone might order her to kill two targets instead of one. *However, it's definitely harder to target two people at once, so there must be a reason,* I thought.

"The deeper I read into it, the more I think whoever is behind this wanted to put a rift between you and me."

"I see. The best-case scenario for them would be if both of us were killed, but even if both of us survived, there would be ill will between us."

"Yes, I believe that was their aim."

"Do you have any idea as to who might be responsible?"

"I do know of someone who would wish to assassinate me... However, I do not have enough evidence to merit a formal accusation."

"Hmm..."

I already knew, from what Ild had told me, about the rival factions of merchants and nobles on the city council. If this incident was only part of a power struggle between the two factions, I didn't want to get involved. *However*, I thought, *the fact that the attempted assassination occurred in my presence suggests I am also a target, and if I am, then Ild and Mora may be in danger.* I was not about to take a chance on Ild and Mora's lives.

I wanted to find the assassin—this fake maid—as soon as possible. However, I had charged my spells for the day with a defensive outlook in mind. I hadn't prepared anything that would be useful for tracking down an assassin.

I had no choice but to depend on Brauze for the time being.

"I will leave the investigating to you, but I want you to let me know if you find anything," I said.

"Understood. You will be the first to know."

For the first time that day, I felt that I was the one in control of the situation. The possibility that Ild and Mora were in danger drove me to take charge more than I usually would.

"Forgive me, but I believe I should get going," I said.

"I understand. Again, I am terribly sorry about what happened today,"

Brauze looked as if he wanted to continue discussing countermeasures with me, but I couldn't stay there all day. Even if it was unlikely that Ild and Mora were in danger, I had to take proper precautions.

"Oh...before I go—and I must stress to you that this is for the purposes of investigation—could I borrow that maid outfit the assassin used?"

Brauze said nothing but put the clothes into a box and handed it to me. His expression did not change in the slightest. *No less than a professional could manage that*, I thought.

··✝··

After I left the city hall, I clambered into the carriage that was waiting for me and cast two spells: *Fly* and *Move Outer Plane*. After a word to the driver, I phased into the outer plane and flew out of the carriage, up into the sky.

The combination of flight, coupled with the freedom to ignore obstacles in the outer plane, meant that I could travel very fast.

My first stop was the Sorcerers' Guild. The only people— rather, the only *person* I could think of who might wish to bring me harm—was he whose authority was threatened by my very existence: Heridol Sylem, president of the Relis Sorcerers' Guild.

I did not know if the guild office had any sort of security system based on sorcery, but in the outer plane, there was nothing that could stand in my way. I was definitely trespassing, but if Heridol was the mastermind behind all this, I knew it would be useless to try to arrange a formal meeting.

I was able to enter Heridol's office without being noticed. Heridol sat at his desk working on paperwork with a frown on his face. *This isn't the time to care about being impolite*, I thought and returned to normal space, appearing right in front of him.

"Lord Heridol, I'd like to have a word with you."

"Excuse me but I'm—wait, what?!"

As I expected, I took Heridol by surprise. He immediately leaped from his chair and grabbed his staff.

"M-Margilus?! How did you... What are you doing here?!"

"My apologies, Lord Heridol, but not long ago, someone tried to assassinate me with poison."

"Assassinate? What are you talking about?!"

In my hand, hidden in the sleeve of my robe, I gripped a magic item and stared directly into Heridol's eyes. The magic item carried the effect of *Detect Enemy*; anyone who harbored hatred or a desire to kill me would appear to give off light... Heridol seemed greatly perturbed, but the magic item did not change his appearance.

"So, you were unaware? I just assumed any person who wished to kill me might also have attacked the guild, as we are on such good terms with one another."

"Unaware?! What does any of this have to do with me?!" *What is he on about?! Is he trying to lay blame on me for something to show that he's better than me?!*

*Well, my ESP Medal seems to be working without any issues. Heridol doesn't seem to have any resistance to it.* I listened to his thoughts echoing within my mind. *So, he really does know nothing about it...*

"I see. Then I apologize for interrupting you. While I'm here, though, do you have any idea who might wish me such harm?"

"Lord Margilus... You are a hero who defeated a legion of daemons. I seriously doubt there is anyone who hates you..." *Me! Right here! I hate you! Stop getting in the way of my dream of becoming the leader of the anti-daemon resistance! Not only are you a threat to my dreams, your so-called magic makes a mockery of all sorcerers and their arts!*

"I see... So that's how it is."

*So, Clara was right about him,* I thought. *At least Heridol's hatred of me is not strong enough to trigger* Detect Enemy... Although Heridol hated me for something I had no control over, as someone who hadn't uttered the word "dream" in decades, I could not simply dismiss his hatred as petty. The strength of his hatred only emphasized the years of his hard work I was endangering with my magic.

*Now that I know he does not mean me, Ild, or Mora any harm,* I thought, *I should prepare myself to talk things out with him later and address his concerns. It's best for everyone if we reconcile...but for now, I have other problems to deal with.*

"I'm sorry to press the matter, but could you please try and search your mind a little bit deeper? You know far more about this city than I do. I'm not asking out of concern for myself; what happens to me is beside the point. My greatest worry is that harm is coming to those who are close to me." I bowed my head.

Heridol gave a deep sigh and then brought his hand to his chin as he began to think seriously about my question.

"Rumors of you have flooded the city. Anyone who believes even ten percent of what they hear would be crazy to pick a fight with you. It would have to be either someone who firmly does not believe in your powers, or..." Heridol furrowed his brow. "You defeated a legion of daemons... So, if anyone hates you, it's the daemons...and the daemonists..." *Could it be? Are there still daemonists around, and in Relis?* I saw Heridol shudder. *If there are... they may be after me as well...*

As I held my ESP Medal and felt Heridol's fear rise within him, I, too, was thrown into a dark mood.

Although Heridol grew paler with each passing minute, he explained the daemonists to me.

"As the name suggests, daemonists are a cult of fanatics who worship daemons. They see the destruction of the world by daemons as salvation. Their activities include offering sacrifices to daemons and other rituals in which they seek to become more like daemons themselves. It is said there are daemonists in all social classes: from the slums to nobility, even in the clergy...

"I hear they still have a presence to the north in Shrendal," continued Heridol, half talking to himself, "and to the east in the newer kingdom of Ferde, but...the daemonists in Relis should have been wiped out in the war we had ten years ago..."

As Heridol was of the Faction of Conquerors, the group that viewed sorcery primarily as a means by which to defeat daemons, it was no wonder he was so disturbed by the daemonists.

"But if there really are daemonists in Relis..." I began.

"Then they would certainly hate you, and far more than I do..." Heridol spoke confidently, his mixed feelings evident upon his face.

Although it was an unenviable position to be in, hated by a cult of fanatic daemonists, it was still a position I had stolen from him, so I could empathize a little bit...but only a little.

"Thank you for that information, Lord Heridol. Again, let me apologize for intruding. I promise never to do so again."

"Yes... Please don't."

My reconciliation with this man, a youth overflowing with hopes and dreams (or so it seemed to me), could wait for another time. I'd save making reparations for my intrusion until then.

If there really was a cult of daemonists in Relis, it made sense that they would want to get rid of me, one way or another. *And if they're so deranged as to worship daemons*, I thought, *there's no telling what they might do.* My concerns about Ild and Mora suddenly seemed to carry a lot more weight.

*I have to go. Now.*

⋯✟⋯

I left the guild and started to make my way back to Ild and Mora's home.

*In games and novels, it's a common motif to see a heroine or friend kidnapped or killed while something else has the protagonist's attention,* I thought. *I may be overthinking this, but if I'm not...* Call me a worrywart if you would like, but I was overcome with a desire to confirm that Ild and Mora were okay.

Using the outer plane, I made a beeline for Ild and Mora's home.

*Commerce Street is, as its name suggests, a street lined with shops and full of people, so it should be relatively safe...* I assumed all the witnesses would be a problem for a theoretical attacker, but when I got to Commerce Street, I could sense that something was wrong. There were very few people outside, and when I arrived at Ild and Mora's home, it was dead quiet. The few people I saw looked anxious, and the outer walls and windows were damaged.

Was I too late?

"Mora! Ild!" I shouted as I ran inside.

"Mister Geo!"

"Mora!"

Mora leaped into my arms with a force that could be mistaken for a tackle. When I reflexively hugged her back, I noticed she was shivering.

"Are you all right? Where is Ild?" I asked.

"Lord Margilus!"

The moment I saw that both Ild and Mora were still in one piece, I gave a huge sigh of relief. My worst suspicions had missed their mark. We all sat down in the living room to share what had happened to each of us that day.

While I was out, not long ago, Ild explained, two women broke into their home and tried to kidnap Mora. The two entered undetected and knocked Mora unconscious, but as they were about to make their escape one of them was bound by "something invisible" (Mora's invisible demon). When that happened, the woman who was bound let out a cry, which alerted Ild and his servants. Upon seeing Ild summon his djinni, the other woman lost her will to fight and ran. The damage to the walls and windows I'd seen had been caused by the djinni as it tried to pursue her.

"So that's what happened... I am just glad you are all right," I said.

It seemed the *Invisible Demon* spells I'd cast earlier that day had paid off, as well as my decision to leave Ild with my djinni ring. I gave another sigh of relief.

"You were the one who protected me, right? Th-thank you very much!" said Mora, with tears welling up in her eyes.

"Not only once, but twice now, you've saved my daughter. You have my deepest gratitude..." said Ild, bowing his head.

"But if it weren't for me—this would have never happened to you," I said.

The fact that Ild and Mora were targeted meant that whoever was behind the assassination attempt was trying to get at me, and not just pursuing some power struggle between political factions in the city. There was not enough evidence yet to say whether daemonists were involved, but when I told Ild and Mora what Heridol told me about them, Ild agreed it was a definite possibility.

"You often hear rumors of daemonists performing sacrificial rituals deep in caves under the city," Ild explained. "But that's beside the point—"

"Yeah! It's not your fault, Mister Geo!" Mora interjected. "You did nothing wrong!"

"It is as my daughter says," Ild continued. "You have nothing you should feel bad about."

As I patted Mora's head (she was still clinging to me), I tried to collect my thoughts.

*So, this is what it means to become a great magic user—a hero,* I thought. *Whether I want to or not, I have an outsized influence on the lives of those around me. This may be one of the reasons why mages in stories always seem to live alone in high towers, away from other people.*

*Is protecting them as I pursue my goal of protecting humanity from daemons something I can truly accomplish alone?*

"I'm sorry—or rather...thank you. I will not let anyone lay a finger on you two, or anyone else in this home."

*That's right,* I thought. *Even if it's almost formulaic for the people a hero cares about most to get hurt, there's no reason I have to play nice with those rules.*

Although one of the invisible demons did bind one of the intruders, she was still able to escape. *If those two women were anything like that fake maid, I guess I shouldn't be surprised,* I thought.

*It was a mistake not to have* Psychometry *and other spells useful in gathering information charged today... Tomorrow, I'll focus my spell charges on defense, information gathering, and tracking. If it comes down to a fight, I should be able to rely on my Staff of Wizardry and other magic items...*

Then I remembered another option open to the Great Magic User Geo Margilus for adventures that took place within the confines of a city.

"There's somewhere I want you to take me tomorrow," I said, taking out a leather bag filled with gems and gold coins.

"Where?" asked Ild, with a puzzled look on his face.

"The Adventurers' Guild."

It was an option only open to high-level characters: hire an army.

·· ✟ ··

When I woke the next morning, I immediately set to work charging the spells I needed for the day and cast one of them right away: *Psychometry.*

*Psychometry* was a spell that allowed the caster to retrieve the memories of inanimate objects or places—the sort of cheat-like spell that makes game masters cry. Needless to say, the object I cast the spell on was the maid outfit the assassin had worn the day before.

The process required me to meditate while holding the object, which, for obvious reasons, is not something I would have liked to see caught on camera, but that was the least of my concerns.

The image of a woman dressing herself in a maid outfit was projected in my mind. Conveniently, I seemed to have struck on the moment the assassin was changing into her disguise. I also saw a different woman in her underwear passed out on the floor. *She must be the real maid.*

I focused on the woman who was changing, and the details slowly came into focus.

*She's rather—no, very attractive, isn't she?* I thought. Her skin was dark brown, nearly black. She had long violet hair, with thick lips the same color, and golden eyes. Of all the women I had seen since I arrived in Sedia, she was the one who looked the most like she belonged in a fantasy setting. Her ears were long and pointed, too. *There's no denying it*, I thought. *She's an elf, and a dark elf at that...*

I already knew from what Sedam told me that elves and dark elves existed in Sedia as two separate species. Just as in many fantasy settings, dark elves were ostracized as an evil species. There were even some regions that considered dark elves just another form of daemons. It was a relief for me to know, however, that Sedam did not buy into that perspective. "It's all just discrimination, really," he said. *But if I remember correctly*, I thought, *he also said they were a rare sight around Lake Ryuse...*

While I was lost in thought, the dark elf woman had finished changing and drew a complicated symbol in the air with her fingers. *It must be some form of sorcery*, I thought, and, sure enough, once the symbol flashed, a fair-skinned maid with chestnut-colored hair stood in place of the dark elf.

"So, that's how it is... Well, it's not surprising. Female assassins are often dark elves in fantasy settings. It's standard fantasy fare..." I said, thinking aloud.

As the effects of *Psychometry* wore off, I rubbed my temples and came out of my trance.

"What were you doing, hugging a thing like that, Mister Geo?"

When I opened my eyes, I saw Mora glaring at me with a frown on her face. She seemed particularly fixated on the maid uniform I was still holding.

*Speaking of standard fantasy fare, this is a scene I could do without...*

✝

After breakfast, Ild, Mora, and I got a horse-drawn carriage to take us to the Adventurers' Guild. I planned to submit job offers for the protection of Ild and Mora and for the apprehension of daemonists in the city. In other words, I was playing the part of what would normally be reserved for NPCs in an RPG.

I had already cast several spells and used numerous items on Ild and Mora's home for protection, but it would not do to keep Ild, a merchant in charge of five caravans, locked up at home all day. I wanted to get this over with before it started to affect his business.

"Before we arrive at the Adventurers' Guild, there are a few things I would like to confirm," I said, speaking to Ild.

From what Ild had told me the day before, Sedia's Adventurers' Guild was significantly different from the ones I knew from games and novels. The basic concept was the same: Individuals and groups submitted requests to the guild if they had problems they wanted adventurers to solve, and the guild itself initiated quests involving exterminating dangerous monsters and exploring dungeons. However, it was not an open organization where anyone could walk in, register as an adventurer, and then pick a request off a bulletin board to try and fulfill.

There were five ranks of adventurers in the guild: the president, advisors, leaders, members, and trainees. There were still parties made of a leader and other members, but unlike in other settings, the leader of a party had an elevated status and more responsibilities coded into their position. The relationship between a leader and a member was similar to one of a master craftsman and an apprentice. The leader of a party had final say over all decisions, and it was his or her duty to teach the other members and coach them in their techniques. Advisors were specialists, and their job was to instruct other members in their field. There was one for each area of expertise pertinent to adventuring: fighting, scouting, espionage, and so on.

The guild president presided over all requests made to the guild and decided which requests would be assigned to which leader. As for monster extermination and dungeon exploration, leaders would collect information about possible quests and present them to the guild president for approval.

In other words, the Adventurers' Guild was exactly the same as a carpenters' guild or tanners' guild or any other guild of specialists.

"All right, I think it's time we get going," I said.

"O-okay," replied Mora.

"Understood," said Ild.

After the carriage pulled out onto one of the main city roads, it was time to move on to the next phase of our plan.

The carriage was not taking us to the Adventurers' Guild. After the events of the previous day, I thought it safe to assume we were being watched. I wanted to create a diversion, so I instructed the driver to drive around aimlessly for the next few hours. Meanwhile, we would use *Move Outer Plane* to slip out of the carriage and make our way to the guild undetected.

Fortunately, it wasn't hard to find the Adventurers' Guild on our own, but compared to the Sorcerers' Guild, the building was a lot plainer. The only way to distinguish it from other guild offices was the sign above the door. We had notified the guild that we were coming, and when we arrived, an elderly man who introduced himself as the guild president led us into another room, where ten party leaders were waiting for us. Sedam was among them.

"Welcome, Lord Margilus. Once again, I am Guild President Rekt, and these are the leaders of the finest parties our guild has to offer."

I looked around the room. Before we'd left Ild and Mora's home, I cast *Sense of the Adept* on myself, which caused information about each person I looked at to be displayed over their heads. Guild President Rekt's information read: Human Male, Age 65, Level 8 Rogue.

As Sedia did not have a real level system, *Sense of Adept*'s level measurement was no more than a rough estimate of what level these people would be in a *D&B* game. The class measurement was also the result of shoehorning a person's abilities into one of the four *D&B* classes. For example, the person with the highest-level display in the room was Sedam, which *Sense of Adept* measured to be a Level 9 rogue. However, Sedam was really more a mix of ranger and archer. Of course, I did not need a level reading to know that Sedam was dependable, but it was a relief to see that several others in the room had a similarly high grade.

*The guild president should have already explained my offer to the leaders*, I thought. *Now I just have to play the part...*

"I am the wizard Geo Margilus," I said, trying to maintain the appearance of majesty. "I come to you today because I believe you are brave and passionate adventurers. Although the mission I request you fulfill is a difficult one, I ask you to lend me your strength."

"Hey, you're that guy that can send meteors flying like 'Bam!' right? You mind showing me what you've got?"

As the guild president was beginning to speak, one of the young leaders cut him off, his voice brimming with sarcasm.

The man who spoke had both of his feet up on a table and was playing with a knife in his hand. *Sense of Adept*'s measurements read: Human Male, Age 23, Level 6 Rogue. His was one of the lower levels in the room.

"Cut it out, Shaup!"

"Stop being so disrespectful!"

Some of the other adventurers barked back at him, but Shaup did not seem to care.

*In an adventurer's line of work, rebels like this Shaup are probably more the norm than the odd one out*, I thought, as I saw that some of the adventurers, rather than criticizing him, were nodding in agreement, or staring at me with suspicion.

Given that the guild president was mum on the matter, I suspected that he was fully content to let Shaup stand on the front lines, so to speak. It gave him an opportunity to judge my reaction.

When I looked at Sedam, he shot a glance toward Shaup and raised one of his eyebrows. Although the time Sedam and I had spent together thus far was short, we had both fought daemons together. I easily interpreted his signal as: "Go right ahead."

"So... You're saying you want me to cast a spell of some sort?"

"Yeah, that's what I'm saying. You hard of hearing, old man?"

*Sorry kid, but this old man isn't in the best of moods right now.* Ild and Mora were in danger because of me, and my patience had worn thin. Plus, this was a good opportunity to show everyone in the room I was serious.

"All right then... Open, Gate of Magic!" I began casting my spell.

If I fumbled, it would have been the height of embarrassment for me, and this whole effort would have backfired, but fortunately, my dice roll in the spellbook archive was successful.

"As a consequence of this spell, I change this man into an abominable pig. *Transform Other.*"

"Huh? What the hell are you on about? Hurry up and summon meteorrrrnk? Oiiinnngk? Oink! Oink?!"

*Transform Other* is a spell that allows the caster to transform someone else into an animal or monster. The chaotic energy from the spell entered normal space and enveloped Shaup. *You may be capable enough to be a party leader in Sedia,* I thought, *but if you're only Level 6 by* D&B *standards, there's no way you can resist my magic.* Shaup's form began to warp as if he was made from multi-colored clay. Some parts expanded and others contracted, until a few seconds later, a piglet stood where Shaup had sat.

"Oink! Oink!"

"I'm sorry. I didn't quite catch that. You said you wanted me to do something with meteors?"

Shaup, now an energetic little piglet, darted back and forth across the floor. The other adventurers, including the guild president, were all silent. Even Ild and Mora appeared mildly horrified.

*First the Calbanera Knights, then the Sorcerers' Guild, and now this... It feels like I'm going around threatening everyone with my magic like I'm part of a protection racket. Maybe I should re-examine my moral compass...*

"Guild President," I said.

"Y-yes, sir," he replied.

"Did you hear what Shaup was trying to tell me? I would like to oblige him, if possible."

I felt a *little* bad, but if these adventurers were going to work under me, I couldn't risk any of them underestimating me again, so I decided to give the trembling guild president a little extra push.

"P-please, forgive us!" he said, falling to his knees. Many others immediately followed suit.

"We're sorry!"

"I-I told him to stop!"

"Please don't turn us into pigs, Lord Wizard!"

There were only three exceptions, and Sedam was one of them. *Come on, Guild President,* I thought, *under normal circumstances, I should be the one showing you respect, not the other way around. Stand up, please.*

Only three, including Sedam, remained standing.

"Lord Margilus," said Sedam, with a smirk on his face as he took a politely orchestrated bow, "I did tell them about you, but it appears I did not do a very good job of conveying your greatness. I must take some responsibility for the indiscretion of my colleague. I apologize."

"We will make sure that Shaup pays for his rudeness, so could you quell your anger just this once on our behalf?"

"We are truly sorry."

I looked at the two others besides Sedam who were unmoved by Shaup's transformation. *Sense of Adept* measured each respectively as: Human Female, Age 30, Level 7 Cleric; and Human Male, Age 38, Level 8 Warrior.

"Hmm..."

With these three acting like the adults in the room, I felt a little embarrassed about my short-tempered reaction.

"He asked to see my magic, and so I showed him. That is all," I said. "Do not worry, I am not angry, and...in good time, I will return him to the handsome young man he was."

"Th-thank you very much," said the president.

"Well then, let's get down to business, shall we?"

"Y-yes, go right on ahead."

After that, no one dared to interrupt me with snark.

"And that is the situation we find ourselves in," I explained. "Therefore, I want you to, first and foremost, protect my two friends and their property, as well as determine the mastermind behind this plot."

"If I may confirm..." The guild president spoke timidly. "You want to prioritize the first item?"

Both Ild and Mora, but especially Mora, looked uncomfortable as the adventurers in the room all looked their way.

"Of course," I replied.

"However, I foresee it will be difficult to properly conduct investigative work without compromising their safety..."

"That only applies if I were to hire one party, correct? I plan to hire all of them."

"F-forgive me if I am being rude, but it would cost a considerable amount of money to hire all ten parties..."

"A considerable amount, you say? Is this enough?"

I'd thought this might happen, and had prepared my answer. I stood up and upturned my Infinity Bag.

"Mister Geo?!"

As its name suggests, the magic item Infinity Bag allows the user to fit an unlimited amount of items within it, as long as all those items are within a certain size. When I turned the bag over in front of the adventurers, a river of gold, platinum, and gems poured out and formed heaps on the floor.

As I looked at everyone's dumbfounded faces, I could not help but feel a little joy in the experience of, as we might say on Earth, "slapping them in the face with a wad of cash." Although this was more like "punching them in the face with fistfuls of gold." Sure, it felt a little wrong, but it was for a good cause.

"Mister Geo! Mister Geo!" Mora said, trying to get my attention with a loud whisper. She was making an X with her fingers as if to say, "That's enough!"

It wasn't just Mora. Ild looked a little worried, and while Sedam looked mildly amused, his look told me I should wrap it up.

"I haven't counted it, but will this do?" I asked.

The guild president vigorously nodded.

⋅⋅✟⋅⋅

"Oink! Oink!"

The piglet Shaup raced around the piles of coins. If it weren't for Mora, those piles might have grown into a whole mountain range.

I reached into my Infinity Bag and felt around. I knew I'd had over three million coins in my bag to start with, and I could hardly notice any difference in the amount. Even so, the guild president estimated there was more than one hundred thousand coins on the floor.

Ild planned to pay Sedam's party three thousand gold coins for Mora's rescue, so assuming it would normally cost about that much to hire one party, one hundred thousand was significantly more than enough to hire ten.

"Let me know if that is insufficient," I said. "However, if the payment is adequate, I would like to get right down to business and discuss strategy."

"Y-yes, sir. Understood."

The guild president joined the party leaders to discuss how they might complete my objectives. Immersed in their work, it was hard to believe these were the same people from before, but as should be expected from professionals, they immediately coalesced behind a plan. The high-level warrior and cleric from before would head a team of four parties tasked with protecting Ild and Mora; meanwhile, Sedam would direct the investigation effort with the remaining six parties.

"I'll go check first with the Rogues' Guild," Sedam said, and then turned to me. "I'd like to take Shaup with me...do you mind changing him back?"

"The spell should wear off on its own after six hours, though I *could* if you need me to."

"Oh, in that case, leave him be," he said with a chuckle. "I'll take him later, as-is. If I show him changing back to the guys at the Rogues' Guild, I'm sure they'll be more willing to talk. I'll tell 'em you'll turn 'em into pigs if they don't cooperate."

*That Sedam, dependable as ever*, I thought. *I've only been in this city a few days. If I were to try to track down the assassins and whoever's behind them on my own, I couldn't possibly pull it off. It's best to leave this to Sedam and the others.*

*Speaking of others...* "Where is Clara?" I asked Sedam.

"Clara's a sorceress—both sorcerers and priests are treated differently from other classes when it comes to their involvement in adventurers' parties."

As both priests and sorcerers had very specialized abilities, they were generally not allowed to register at multiple organizations concurrently: e.g., A sorcerer could not be part of both a sorcerers' guild and an adventurers' guild. Clara was a member of the Sorcerers' Guild, and that was where her priorities lay, so her participation in Sedam's party was irregular.

"Lord Margilus! Whether it's dark elves or daemonists behind this, we'll catch 'em!"

"Yeah! Don't you worry, just leave it to us!"

As the adventurers left the guild to start their work, they left me with words of encouragement. The investigation team would start by gathering information from the Rogues' Guild, the slums, and other locations around the city. Then, they'd conduct a sweep of the sewers and other locations that might be used as hideouts. The guard team would rotate parties to monitor Ild and Mora and their home so that they would always have guards ready to defend them.

After I signed an official contract, Ild, Mora, and I left the guild.

••✝••

On our way back from the Adventurers' Guild, we stopped by the city hall to see Zatow Brauze.

Although Brauze appeared to be in fine health, he simply would not stop apologizing for what had happened, so I told him that instead of wasting his breath, he should focus on catching the culprit.

"Indeed. On my honor as a representative of Relis City, I swear we will catch the perpetrator."

"The perpetrator is one thing, but I would like you to capture the mastermind behind her as well, especially after my friends were targeted. I don't want to leave any loose ends that will come back to bite us later."

"So...you are suggesting there is a connection between the one who poisoned us and the ones who tried to kidnap Ild's daughter?"

"Chairman Brauze, I have a favorable opinion of this city and its inhabitants. I understand those involved in this are a very small subset of the population, so stop equivocating and speak plainly to me."

"My apologies... Yes, that seems likely."

Once I was convinced Brauze and I were on the same page, I made a small "donation" to serve as encouragement for the city's efforts. There were about fifteen hundred guards employed by the city, and I expected each would be able to take home a nice bonus the next time they were paid. On the ride back to Ild and Mora's home from the city hall, I could already see the guards energetically involved in questioning people at the city's checkpoints.

··✟··

"Mister Geo, don't you think you're being wasteful with your money?"

"Um... Well..."

As soon as we returned, Mora confronted me. I should have seen it coming. As a merchant's daughter, of course she would be sensitive to the cost of things. It didn't help that even I thought my actions that day were a bit childish, so her words hit hard.

"Now Mora, Lord Margilus is doing all this to protect us, you know," said Ild.

"Well, I *know* that, it's just... I hate causing Mister Geo so much trouble..." Mora turned back to face me. "I'm sorry, Mister Geo! You have already done so much for me, and all I do is keep getting in your way and holding you back..."

*I need to be more aware of the consequences of my actions,* I thought. *All the money I spent is nothing more to me than a number on Geo's character sheet, but that's not the case for the people of this world. I should have known that shelling out all of the that money would have made a responsible person like Mora uncomfortable.* I knelt down in front of Mora, so that our eyes were level.

"I'm sorry for making you feel that way," I said, finally. "You said you were getting in my way, but that couldn't be further from the truth. It is because you choose to call me by my name—by *who* I am, instead of what I am, and treat me like a normal person— that I am able to stay grounded in this world. If, for instance, you were to cheer me on for what I did today instead of rebuke me, I shiver to think what would become of me."

"B-but..."

"That's why I feel that if it's for you or your father's sake, money should be no object. I think of you as family."

I would never have been able to utter such a cheesy-sounding line in my previous life in Japan, even if I meant it. *But*, I thought, *this world is a little simpler than Japan, and here I wear the mask of a great and powerful magic user. I should be allowed a few lines like this, right?*

••✠••

I didn't like the idea of being away from Ild and Mora for long, and didn't know the city well enough or have the right connections to investigate on my own. Aside from accompanying Ild whenever he had to leave for something work related, I spent the next three days cooped up in Ild and Mora's home.

Which is not to say that things were uneventful. In that time, Ild and Mora's home was attacked twice by rogues who were apparently hired by dark elves, and an uncharted waterway was discovered in the sewer system, to name a few things. Whatever happened, the adventurers handled everything smoothly. I didn't need to raise a finger.

There was one other thing that happened, which I was unaware of until after it was over: A group of dark elves attempted to kidnap Clara. When I learned what had happened, I realized I should have considered her as a possible target, as I was close to her. However, in my mind, Clara more closely fit the role of someone I could count on, rather than someone who needed protecting, so the thought had slipped my mind. In a way, I was right: She was able to hold off her attackers and keep them at bay with her sorcery. However, she might not have been able to escape if it were not for help from one of the investigating parties, which came to her aid at the last minute. I shuddered to think about what might have happened otherwise.

I got an earful from Clara about it later, but when I offered to assign one of the adventurer parties to guard her, she refused. "I'll show them what it means to make an enemy out of me!" she cried, and joined up with Sedam's party to help with the investigation.

Finally, on the fourth day, the efforts of the city guards and the adventurers bore fruit. The dark elves' hideout was found in an uncharted area of the sewer system. In the struggle that followed, the adventurers successfully managed to capture one of the elves alive.

"Why?" I muttered, looking down at the dark elf brought before me at the Adventurers' Guild. "Why does her outfit have to show so much skin?"

$$\cdot\cdot\dagger\cdot\cdot$$

Fifty years ago, a dark elf was born to the Haiklus tribe, and given the name Reyhanalka, meaning "beautiful shadow."

Every dark elf tribe specializes in a certain trade, with all members of the tribe expected to serve the roles assigned to them flawlessly and without complaint. Reyhanalka's tribe was no exception. Haiklus translates to "saboteur," and from birth she was trained in the ways of assassination and sabotage. Upon completing her training, she was given five assassin subordinates and the title of Rue, meaning, in their tongue, "leader of assassins."

Reyhanalka Haiklus Rue served many masters in Sedia's criminal underworld, until one day, she carelessly let one of her subordinates die. The sight of that subordinate's lifeless eyes as she lay in her arms left a splinter in her heart that would fester for years to come.

Twenty years ago, when the tribe relocated to the Shrendal Kingdom, there was a "master" who irrevocably changed Reyhanalka and her tribe's fate. As to who this master was, she could not remember. From the moment she looked into those terrifying golden eyes, all her memories were clouded and muddled.

Ever since meeting this master, Reyhanalka was trapped inside her own consciousness. The connections to her body were severed and replaced by black, fleshy, twisted ropes. They bound to her arms and legs and moved only by the will of her master. Dark tendrils bound her body and soul, extending from a giant figure that loomed behind her always.

This master commanded her to execute many horrible tasks, and even if she wanted to resist, the fleshy ropes would only tighten around her body, controlling her like a marionette.

Ten years ago, Reyhanalka was sent to serve the daemonists in Relis City. By that time, she had grown used to the things that manipulated the whole of her being.

*If my soul were free*, she thought, *I would be able to move my body tens of times more effectively, but that does not matter anymore.*

*If I leave everything to this overwhelming power that binds and controls me, I do not have to fear the consequences of my actions. I do not have to worry. I do not have to think. I need only wait until the day comes when I meet my end...*

A few days ago, Reyhanalka was vaguely aware that her body was carrying out an assassination. However, to her surprise, she was unsuccessful. The shadowy figure controlling her reacted with a panic she had never felt before, forcing her to take several countermeasures. Her four subordinates, controlled just as she was, similarly tried everything to right the wrong, but all their attempts ultimately failed.

Not only that, but it seemed that the tables had turned. Their target was closing in on *them*. Reyhanalka and her subordinates were being driven into a corner, and it felt like the city itself was bent on capturing them.

One hour ago, Reyhanalka's underground hideout had been attacked by a group of city guards and adventurers. The guards flooded the city like rats, blocking all means of escape, and adventurers came at them from all sides.

It was then that Reyhanalka first felt the figure behind her tremble with fear. The grip its fleshy tendrils held upon her body and soul loosened, ever so slightly; a cold pain shot through her body. It was that old splinter, the image of her dead subordinate's eyes looking up at her. The pain freed a portion of her soul, and for the first time in twenty-five years, she fought of her own free will, fought to let her remaining subordinates escape. In that, she was successful, but she herself was still captured and bound.

Now, she felt a colorless, formless, boundless power ripping through her consciousness.

Under the intensity of that power, the figure behind her thrashed and screamed, still connected by fleshy ropes to every inch of her body—but not for long. The figure contorted and crumbled, and so too did the powerful ropes that bound her, as if it were burned away by an intense flame. What awaited Reyhanalka was freedom from her comfortable bondage. She was awash with despair.

As her body and soul's supports gave way, she was assaulted by a fear of falling into nothingness.

"NO!" she screamed, tears flowing from her eyes.

The figure behind her was reduced to dust. Reyhanalka felt empty. There was nothing left inside of her. Her mind teetered on the edge of collapse.

But then, just as Reyhanalka felt her soul losing its form, she felt an incredible power envelope her, the same power that burned away the figure controlling her. But the power did not burn her. Instead, it gave life. It touched her face, her shoulders, her hips; Reyhanalka remembered who she was.

She was reborn.

"Ahh!" Again she cried out, but this time, with joy.

Reyhanalka was no longer a puppet, but a true dark elf again. However, she felt her title was no longer valid. No longer would she be Rue, leader of assassins, but Si, loyal servant—Reyhanalka Haiklus Si.

Behind me, Sedam, Clara, and the other party leaders stood, looking down upon the dark elf. She was covered in wounds, her arms and legs restrained, her mouth gagged. I could hear faint groans from under her gag, but she still appeared to be unconscious. I recognized her faint violet hair and striking features from my *Psychometry* spell. I was certain this was her.

*But...why?*

"Why does her outfit have to show so much skin?" I thought aloud.

She was dressed in a bodysuit, but that was typical assassin attire: no problem there. However, it was open in the back and around her thighs and chest—needlessly risqué.

"Do you need my help to look somewhere else?" Clara growled.

"I'm not looking anywhere I shouldn't," I said, sighing.

*I've got to be more careful*, I thought. *Back in Japan, I almost got in trouble for staring at one of our female employees' name tags too long because it was crooked... Anyway, this woman tried to poison the city council chairman and me, and tried to kidnap Mora and Clara. This is no time to be distracted by her outfit.*

"You want us to wake her up for interrogation, Lord Margilus? A few kicks should do the trick," said Shaup with a smirk. He was human again—at least in the sense that he was no longer a literal pig.

"She's a dark elf," said one of the other adventurers. "Interrogation won't get us anywhere."

"Then torture?" suggested another.

"Well, I suppose that's an option," offered a third.

It was clear most of the adventurers saw dark elves as subhuman. *I understand she's a criminal and all, but torture? I thought. Obviously, there's no reason to treat her like a guest of honor, but as someone who grew up in modern Japan with modern Japanese values, I cannot sanction torture. It does not matter whether she is guilty or innocent, beautiful or ugly.*

"Let me try talking to her. I'm sorry, but could everyone except Sedam please—actually, everyone except Sedam and Clara please leave the room?" I corrected myself midway through. Clara had asserted her plans to stay with a violent glare.

Once everyone was gone, only the dark elf's muffled breathing could be heard.

I had Sedam lift her upper body off the ground and remove her gag.

I knelt down and shook her shoulders. "Are you all right?"

The dark elf's eyes slowly opened.

"My name is Geo Margilus. Um... Are you feeling all right?"

She did not say anything, but lazily shook her head in response. Her golden eyes showed no sign of a conscious will.

*Could she be brainwashed or hypnotized?* I thought. All I knew about hypnosis and brainwashing was from games and novels, but it made sense. If she was being controlled somehow, that would explain why *Detect Enemy* failed to respond to her during the assassination attempt.

"Do you think it's possible that this woman is being controlled by a daemonist?" I asked.

Clara frowned. "I have heard it rumored that when someone is possessed by a daemon, their eyes turn the same golden color..."

*Bingo.*

"As a consequence of this spell, I purge from you the evil infecting your mind. *Curse Break.*"

*Curse Break* is a spell that removes curses and evil spirits from a host. When I cast the spell, a gentle white light shone from my outstretched hand onto the dark elf's face and body.

The dark elf, still held up by Sedam, began to tremble. Then she raised a bloodcurdling scream.

"NO!" Her face twisted; her back arched. Her tongue hung out as she writhed.

"What did you do?!" asked Sedam.

"What is she doing?!"

"What? Is she...? Wait! Hold on! Whoa!"

When I tried to look at her face again, the dark elf leaped forward against me. We both fell to the ground.

"Ahh!" she cried out again, and a black mist burst from her body. It vanished in seconds.

*Curse Break* had done its job, purging whatever was inside of her.

*Did it work?* I thought, a little absentmindedly, as the dark elf in my arms finally looked up at me.

"I... I-I..." she stammered.

"A-are you all right?" I asked.

The dark elf's golden eyes had turned a faint violet. It seemed that whatever it was that had possessed or brainwashed her was fully undone.

The dazed look on the dark elf's face only accentuated her allure—she was incredibly sexy. *If she's acting, I have to hand it to her, she's good,* I thought, but if I'd learned anything from all my years of life (and sexual harassment prevention seminars), it was to keep my eyes on her eyes and make sure I wasn't touching anywhere that could be construed as problematic.

"Are you the one who destroyed the daimon inside of me? Are you the master of that incredible power?"

"Yes... Probably."

"Then...then I am no longer a Rue."

I could feel strength and will returning to her body, but I did not understand what she was talking about.

"What does that mean?" I asked.

"From this point onward, I am Reyhanalka Haiklus Si. Your Si, my Olry."

*Hmm?*

The fact that *Curse Break* had an effect on her meant that her previous actions were forced, not of her own will. *Who would do that, and why?* I wondered. *It is something to look into, but at least the curse is broken now, and this Reyhanalka is back to normal.*

"Although I was under the control of a daemon, I remember acting insolently, against your will. Not even with the bite of a thousand swords piercing my flesh could I atone for my great sins against you. I beg that you punish me to your satisfaction," Reyhanalka said, bowing as she knelt before me, both her hands over her voluptuous chest.

When she threw glances at me from her bowed position, I felt a strong sense of obsession and dependence emanating from her. Frankly, it was unnerving.

*And that's not all*, I thought, noticing that she had removed the ropes binding her arms and legs, as if it was nothing to her.

"What's going on here?" I asked, to her as much as anyone else.

"Olry is a title the dark elves use to denote a master of higher status than Rue, who is, according to their legends, the leader of their species," Sedam explained. "But does it really matter what she calls you? She's saying she'll serve *you* now. Isn't that great? I'm sure it'll be useful to have your own dark elf assassin."

As always, Sedam showed he was well versed in all sorts of trivia. *Master, though?* I thought. *Where did she get that idea?*

"I don't want to be the master of anyone. Now that your curse is broken, you are free... Well, sort of. You still have to answer for the crimes you have committed..."

*If I remember correctly, Relis has a courthouse. If she wants to atone for her crimes*, I thought, *she should go through the normal legal process and serve whatever sentence is handed down to her. As long as she can prove she was being manipulated by someone else,*

*I'm sure the courts will be lenient with her sentencing—at the very least, she should be able to avoid capital punishment.*

"If that is what you desire, I will gladly follow your orders... However..." Tears welled up in Reyhanalka's eyes. "I am your Si! I would murder a babe of my own tribe if you so commanded me! If you desire influence, I can infiltrate and bend whole organizations to your will. If you command me to die, I will commit suicide before your very eyes. If you desire this filthy body of mine, I will give it to you gladly, but please...please! Do not say that you do not want to be my master—anything but that!"

"What is with those ominous and *erotic* examples?! Why are you so hellbent on becoming something like that?!"

"*Something like that?!*" Reyhanalka cried out in despair. I could see her grow visibly paler as the blood drained from her face. She fell to the ground, bereft.

"Calm yourself, Lord Margilus." Sedam slung his arm around me and led me to a corner of the room. "You don't have to be so harsh," he continued, lowering his voice to a whisper.

"But Sedam," I said, "She's acting like she wants to be a slave. I can't just—"

"You're mistaken," said Sedam, cutting me short. "A slave is owned by her master, and must serve them regardless of her own will. With that in mind, let me ask you: Is there anyone forcing her to bow down before you? She wants to serve you of her own free will. The least you can do is show respect for that desire."

"But can't we just be friends or something?" I objected. "I don't see why I have to be anyone's master..."

"What are you whispering about over there?!" snapped Clara.

"Wait, what? Ow!"

Clara grabbed my right ear and pulled hard. She looked furious. I could practically see horns on her head.

"I can't believe you! You said you were going to break a curse on her, but I bet you just added another layer of brainwashing with your magic!"

"That's not what I did!"

"I never thought you were such a dirty old man! You should be ashamed of yourself!"

"I'm telling you, this is all just a big misunderstanding!" I insisted.

"If you *didn't* brainwash her, then this act of hers must be a ploy to seduce you! Stop falling for it!"

Whether she believed me or not, Clara showed no sign of calming down. Obviously, if I had brainwashed Reyhanalka, Clara's anger would be more than justified, but I'd done no such thing.

"Please, madam, wait!" The one who came to my aid was none other than Reyhanalka herself. She came between us and knelt before Clara.

"Madam?" said Clara, confused.

"I have not been brainwashed, but even if I was, it would not matter, for I have no greater desire than to serve my Olry! So, madam, I beg of you. Please do not be angry with your husband."

"M-my what?!"

*Let's review the facts.*

*Currently, Sedam, Clara, and I are in the process of interrogating a dark elf who attempted to kill me and kidnap Mora at the order of an individual we assume is a daemonist...right? So why is this dark elf suddenly trying to be my slave, and Clara suddenly supposed to be my wife?*

"Th-that's not—I mean, I'm not... W-we're not in that kind of..." Clara stuttered.

"You do not have to hide it," said Reyhanalka. "I can say for certain that a man as powerful as my master could not possibly tolerate such verbal and physical abuse from anyone other than his wife."

*Really? That seems like quite a leap, if you ask me...*

Clara was apparently too flabbergasted by that argument to speak, her face bright red as she fiddled with her long hair. *Moments ago, she seemed ready to explode. Now she looks like she could cry at any moment.* I sighed silently. *I'm the one that's going to have to deal with her when she rants about this later...*

*I've got to put a stop to this before it gets any more out of hand.*

"No, Reyhanalka—Clara is not my wife, but a friend and trusted companion of mine, as is Sedam," I said, pointing as I introduced both.

"Y-yes! E-exactly!" said Clara.

"He is right, my good friend's Si," seconded Sedam. "Pleased to meet you."

"I apologize for jumping to conclusions," Reyhanalka replied.

Although I'd been able to successfully defuse the tension between Clara and our captive, so far, our interrogation had yet to yield anything significant. *That has to change.*

*We need to hurry up and extract any information we can from Reyhanalka and use it to catch whoever is behind this plot,* I thought. *There are other dark elves still on the loose, and the longer we wait, the more we risk letting the mastermind escape.*

"Why do you think our Margilus is your Olry?" Clara asked Reyhanalka. She spoke quietly, as if the previous outburst had exhausted her.

"For decades, my actions were ruled by the daimon lurking in my soul. I only tried to assassinate Master Margilus because I was under its control. What I find most repulsive is that, over the long years, I had grown to accept the daimon's dominion over me... However, it rules me no longer. Master Margilus just now released me from it with his awe-inspiring power."

*"Daimon" must be the word she uses for daemons...* I thought. *Does this mean daemons have infiltrated society and are plotting to overthrow it? Or was Reyhanalka being controlled by daemonists using daemonic powers? Either way, her story suggests a broader conspiracy is in play...*

"Words cannot describe the fear I felt when my daimon was extinguished, nor the intense gratification I felt when I realized I was being saved. Dark elves value the preservation of their tribe more than any individual's life, but when a dark elf owes someone a debt of gratitude that they feel eclipses even the fate of their tribe, they will call them Olry and serve them as their Si."

"Well, that makes sense, don't you think?" Sedam glanced at Clara and me.

"I suppose dark elves are entitled to their own customs..." said Clara, not entirely convinced.

*This is Sedia, not Japan,* I reminded myself. *Sedia has its own system of ethics, and I have no right to force Japanese morals on the people of Sedia. But even so, I don't know about this...*

"So," I said at last. "I take it you will cooperate with us, then, right?"

"More than that... I pledge to you my undying loyalty and—"

"Yes, yes. Can we talk about that later?" I said, cutting her short. "First, I need you to provide us with information about whoever was controlling you, so we can find out who it was that wanted me poisoned. If the other dark elves working with you are also being controlled, I would like to help them as well...but once we catch whoever is responsible, you must all stand trial before the city. Once you have paid your debt to society, if you still wish to serve me...then, and only then, do as you like."

*That should work as a compromise,* I thought. *Getting the information we need comes first. After that, the trial and sentencing should give Reyhanalka some time to think things over. I'm sure she'll change her mind about being my servant.*

"Good for you," said Sedam.

"Well...if it is your heartfelt desire to pledge your loyalty to him, I suppose I cannot stand in the way of that," Clara conceded.

"Thank you! Thank you! I promise you, I will be useful!"

In Sedia, apart from the obligations of loyalty that came with one's birth—such as to their family and their country—it was fairly typical for some people to willingly devote themselves to another person, organization, or cause. I had seen that while I was working with the Calbanera Knights, but I had yet to fully accept it.

My struggle to accept this cultural difference was one reason I could not help but have doubts about Reyhanalka's true intentions. However, there was a simple way to clear that doubt, as underhanded as the method felt to me.

✦

In the end, I decided I would use my ESP Medal to confirm Reyha's testimony. (Her name was long and hard to say, so I decided to shorten it from then on.) When I explained my ESP Medal to Sedam and Clara, they did not seem to like the idea that I could read minds, but Reyha herself enthusiastically consented to its use.

"Let's get started then," I said. "First question: Erm... Was the one responsible for brainwashing you and your companions a daemon?"

"The one who first put me in that state was a human...I think. However, behind the power that rendered me thus, and within the being I was bound to for so many long years, I sensed the presence of a daimon. I can never do enough to repay you from rescuing me, even if I serve you for the rest of my life." *How disgraceful it was for me to yield so completely to another... But being able to let go, in and of itself, offered a form of salvation to me... Right now, before me, is one whose power greatly exceeds the power of that daimon... Oh... How I wish to be dominated, bound, and forced into submission by that incredible power...*

I had to catch myself from stumbling.

"Are you all right?" Clara asked.

The dizzying kick I felt from Reyha's pure and unfiltered loyalty (was that really the right word?) was almost enough to knock me off my feet.

When I was younger, there were times I felt willing to take on more work than was reasonable, if it was for a supervisor I respected. So, on some level, I understood the desire some have to sacrifice themselves for others...but the intensity of Reyha's desires put her in a completely different dimension.

"I-I see... But you must understand: Although you say you pledge your loyalty to me, it is difficult for us to take you at your word. How do I know this is not part of an act to aid in your escape?"

"I would never do such a thing! Nothing is more natural than a Si pledging her undying loyalty to such a worthy Olry as you, my master! If you doubt my sincerity, I will tear out my heart and show you that it bleeds in the truest red you shall ever see." *Woe is me, for my Olry doubts me! The only one I have to turn to—the only one I should turn to, does not believe me... Rather than live like this, I wish he would end my sad and sorry life right this instant!*

"You...don't have to do that. I get what you mean."

As frightening as it was to admit, whatever Reyha felt, whether it be loyalty or devotion or something else entirely, she was not trying to hide it. Although her words, taken at face value, were an oversimplification of everything simmering beneath the surface, I had already witnessed more than I needed or wanted to.

While it certainly was uncomfortable experiencing others' hostility toward me, like with Heridol, Reyha's amity (there was an understatement) had gone far beyond what I was comfortable with. From my perspective, all I'd done was cast a single spell for her sake. *If that is all it takes to sow the seeds of emotions powerful enough to change the course of someone's entire life...* I shivered at the thought.

As silence fell, Clara looked at me, then Reyha, and back again, with a mixed expression on her face.

"So, how about it? The little lady means what she says, right?"

Meanwhile, Sedam was clearly having a great time at our expense.

I'll admit, despite being past my prime and less interested in the opposite sex compared to my younger years, it was not as if I was incapable of feeling attraction. It did not help that I now knew Reyha's obsession was not an act—it made it harder for me to dismiss what she was saying, and Reyha was a beautiful and enticing woman. I would be lying if I said I wasn't happy to have her interested in me.

But...you understand, right?

"I still find it hard to accept...but yes, she does," I replied, finally.

"So, you believe me?! Thank you so much!" said Reyha, her eyes sparkling as she knelt down before me.

*So, she didn't run over and hug me*, I thought. (For the record, I was glad she didn't.) It was a welcome sign that Reyha desired acceptance more than affection.

"This is fine and all," Clara drawled, "but shouldn't you ask her about who was controlling her and her companions? You know, the mastermind we are trying to catch?"

"Good point," I admitted, turning back to Reyha. "I understand your memories may not be very clear, but if there is anything you can remember that might help us, please let us know."

"Of course," Reyha replied.

I decided to return my ESP Medal to my Infinity Bag. I had already heard more than I needed from it, and if I could help it, I hoped I would not have to use it for a while—but as I turned, Clara caught my eye.

"Just so you know, if you ever use that thing on me, our relationship is over. Do you understand?!" She glared, hands on her hips, face flushed.

I have to admit, I felt a surge of relief upon hearing Clara say that. Her reaction was the most human out of anyone in the room—it helped ground me in reality, even in this fantasy world.

"Wh-what?" Clara said, when I didn't answer. "Hmph! I bet you're wishing I was like that dark elf right now, a woman who would do anything you say!"

After the weight of Reyha's dark and obsessive loyalty, Clara's harsh words were like a cool, refreshing shower.

"No," I said finally. I looked up at her. "Thank you, Clara. I hope you never stop berating me like you always do. Please, don't ever change."

"Wh-what did you just say?!"

Although the remainder of our interrogation of Reyha was not without event, it's best I simply summarize the rest. Reyha was cooperative, and provided us with all of the information she could remember.

Reyha described the one who'd controlled and commanded her to assassinate me as a thin man who appeared to be of the nobility. His home was adorned with a family crest that contained a sword and sail. As soon as Sedam heard that, he clapped his hands together and said he had it. There was someone the Adventurers' Guild had labeled a person of interest who met all the criteria.

His name was Knave Corbal, a baron who held a seat on the city council. Corbal was infamous for being a thorn in the side of the mercantile faction, from the city council chairman down to the rank-and-file members.

There had been unconfirmed reports of persons gone missing near Corbal's estate, as well as reports of suspicious figures entering and leaving. One maid testified that she witnessed a ceremony honoring daemons being held at the estate, and the list went on and on. In response to these rumors, the Adventurers' Guild had conducted its own investigation, which concluded with a high degree of confidence that the rumors had a significant element of truth to them. Reyha's testimony was just the cherry on top.

"This settles it," Sedam said. "Corbal is our daemonist."

"So, shall we get ready to storm his estate?" asked Clara.

"I'm coming with you!" chimed Reyha.

"With what warrant?" I said. "I seriously doubt the law would stand for us to conduct an extrajudicial interrogation and arrest. Even if *we're* convinced, we don't have the authority to act on our suspicions alone."

*First, we need to notify the Adventurer's Guild and city guard of our suspicions,* I thought. *Then we will ask both to take measures to locate Corbal, prevent him from leaving the city, and stake out his estate.*

After I explained my plan, Sedam, Clara, Reyha, and I headed straight to the city hall. Although I knew it was short notice, I demanded an audience with Chairman Brauze and the captain of the city guard.

When the chairman and captain arrived, looking flustered, I explained that Knave Corbal was the mastermind behind the assassination attempt and that there was a very high chance he was a daemonist. Although Corbal was a political enemy of Brauze, it still shocked both him and the captain that someone so high up in the ranks was steeped in the worst of Sedia's taboos.

"I would never have guessed it to be him...but it appears that there is little room for doubt," said Brauze.

"In addition to the testimony from the dark elf," said the captain of the guard, "there is an abundance of circumstantial evidence obtained by the Adventurers' Guild that corroborates her story. I believe we should move forward and arrest Lord Corbal on suspicion of orchestrating an attempted assassination and participating in daemon worship."

"Hm... What do you think, Lord Margilus?" Brauze asked. "Is that acceptable to you?"

Under normal circumstances, it would be absurd for someone of Brauze's stature to ask for confirmation from someone like me, but I could tell he already knew what I was thinking. Yet again, I was impressed.

"Of course, I have no problem with you arresting him," I said. "However, I fear that Corbal will use strange daemonic powers if cornered. As a countermeasure, I would like to be involved in the effort to arrest him. I also think it would be a good opportunity to show the people of Relis that I am on their side."

"Ch-chairman?" the captain stammered. "Is that okay?"

"I am overjoyed to hear you say that," said Brauze. "At the risk of being forever in your debt, by all means, lend us your aid! Captain, please do not hesitate to involve Lord Margilus in all aspects of the arrest, nor hesitate to seek his aid."

"Yes, sir."

Sedam, Clara, and Reyha stood by restlessly as the chairman, captain, and I carried on with our conversation. From the perspective of those used to taking immediate action, my groundwork must have seemed as slow as molasses to them.

However, from the perspective of one used to the Japanese legal system, events were moving at a breakneck pace: the decision to arrest Corbal was finalized in a very short time, and with no complications. It was another reminder that there was a vast difference in values between this fantasy world and modern Japan.

"Chairman," I said.

"What is it?"

"Thank you for trusting me."

"Having witnessed your actions over the past few days, it was a very easy thing to do," Brauze replied. "Anyone would, if they knew enough about you."

In other words, in a world like Sedia, where science and the law were less developed (though "less developed" is an oversimplification of the complexities of nation-states, and a phrase I prefer to avoid), the most important currency is not a physical object, but trust. You could even say that a nation's traditions and authority structure were aimed at building that essential element of trust among individuals.

As a counterexample, if the citizens of Relis thought I was one to heed the law only when it suited me, I would have very quickly lost the people's trust. Chairman Brauze understood that it was my aim to show I respected the law of the land, and agreed to help me.

"Lord Margilus, as for that dark elf..." The captain turned to me, hesitant.

"Yes, I almost forgot," I said, turning to the captain. "I will hand her over to you and the city guard. I would like for you to arrange a public trial to have her answer for her crimes."

The room fell silent.

Reyha's hands were bound, if only for appearances' sake. She had insisted that I, not Sedam, do the binding. Although Reyha clearly expressed delight at having me bind her hands, I didn't notice. Not one bit. That's my official position.

One other thing I did my best to ignore was the fact that Reyha was determined to kneel by my side whenever I was stationary, only moving when I did. However, my ignoring her did not make it any easier for the captain of the guard.

"But, Lord Margilus..." He frowned. "As far as I can tell, she appears to now be acting as if she is your servant..."

"This and that are unrelated," I said. "As unfortunate as it is, Reyhanalka has committed crimes in this city, and it is only natural that she should answer to the city's laws."

It wasn't as though I didn't feel sorry for her. Especially after having her feelings of loyalty directly conveyed to me, I felt a slight pang of guilt for handing her off to the authorities.

If I were to dismiss Reyha's crimes and claim her as my servant or Si, I was sure no one (other than Clara) would complain. However, if that happened, her debt to society would go unpaid. It was not enough for me to forgive her. *Even if she was brainwashed*, I thought, *it is likely she has killed others in the past, long before that. It is not up to me alone to decide how her debt should be paid.*

"If that is what you wish..." the captain said. "We normally hold trials at the end of the month—in ten days. Until that time, we will hold her for you."

"At the trial, she will require a lawyer and guarantor," he continued. "May I assume you will be her guarantor?"

"Hmm? Uh... Yes, absolutely."

*Guarantor*? I thought. I did not know how the legal system worked in Sedia, but I was not against aiding her case. *In fact, I would be more than happy to argue on her behalf,* I thought. *Hopefully, she won't get more than a few years of prison and hard labor...*

"Just so you know..." I said, "Reyhanalka was brainwashed by a daemonist's daemonic sorcery, during which she committed crimes against her will. She has reflected on her actions and has expressed her desire to make amends. If you could help me make sure that is considered during the trial, in regard to her sentencing, I would greatly appreciate it."

*Did I go a little too far?* I thought, immediately after I finished. *If I throw too much weight into her case, my efforts could backfire and even lead to a harsher sentencing...*

"Don't worry, we know. Rest assured and leave the matter to us," said Brauze.

"I will let all the guards know she is to be kept comfortable until her court date," the captain added.

*Comfortable?* I thought. Something about their responses seemed...off. Sedam had said nothing throughout the entire thing, but had a blatant smirk on his face that I should have noticed earlier.

Magic User
Reborn in Another World
as a Max Level Wizard

# Chapter 18

K NAVE CORBAL was not special—and, like all ordinary human beings, could never admit he was anything *but* special: *Others just can't see it*, he thought.

Ten years ago, a few months after the chaos following the outbreak of daemons subsided, a man from a village under the Corbal family's purview came bearing a strange offering. If Knave had not laid his eyes on it, he might have lived out his days unchanged, an ordinary nobleman of Relis.

"What *is* that? It looks disgusting," said Corbal, when presented with what can only be described as the skull of an imp—the black surface of it glistened, as if it had been rolled in pitch, lacquered and shined to a finish.

"I agree, sir," said Corbal's elderly butler. "To think anyone would accept this as an heirloom piece... It is preposterous."

The butler was right. Anyone with a shred of common sense would think the same. However, something about the strange object must have caught Corbal's attention. He raised it closer to his face, peering into the skull's empty eye sockets, where he saw, or thought he saw, a faint golden glint.

"If it's something no one else would accept..." said Corbal slowly, "all the more reason to keep it, I say. It has more impact as a showpiece than a sculpture, or anything anyone else has."

Once Corbal began to keep the skull in his bedroom, a small change came over him: He became able to perceive enmity in others' glances. He became able to hear the voices of those talking behind his back.

It did not take long for that small change to have a significant effect on his psyche.

By the third day, Corbal viewed humanity as nothing more than a conglomeration of malice bent on mocking him. By the seventh, he began offering the skull his own blood. By the tenth, he welcomed a daemonist bishop into his home.

"I knew you, of all people, would understand the grave importance of our cause," said the bishop.

"Yes... We must eradicate those senseless, disgusting creatures at any cost," Corbal replied. "Humanity has no place in Sedia."

The ominous bishop was the one who'd sent the daemon skull to Corbal. He was completely shaved, from head to toe, and had served as the chief of a small village on Corbal's land. By the time the skull arrived at Corbal's estate, he had converted the entire village to daemonism.

"But you must not be hasty," cautioned the bishop. "We do not yet have enough power to bring about humanity's extinction. That is why I want you to secure support for our cause in Relis."

"Consider it done. Before the truth was revealed to me, my only wish in life was to live comfortably. But no longer. I will spare no effort to drag those despicable merchants out of power."

"Then I hope you will find these women useful."

The bishop gave Corbal five dark elf assassins. He had not procured them himself, but received them from daemonists higher up in the power structure.

Corbal used the elves to expand the reach of his influence in the city, assassinating more than a dozen politicians. He was told the elves were incapable of reaching their true potential, a consequence of the method used to brainwash them, but this made no difference to Corbal. In his eyes, they were exceptional. Even the Rogues' Guild was unable to trace the assassinations back to him. However, it still took ten years before Corbal was able to rise to the top of the nobles' faction, the only other faction in the city that could stand toe to toe with the merchants. During that time, he led all of his servants, including his butler, into the arms of the daemonist cult.

As instructed by the bishop, Corbal held a daemonist ceremony every month. Without fail, countless bones from the countless humans he sacrificed filled the bottom of the underground lake beneath his estate.

Everything was going according to plan—until a few days ago.

It happened just as Corbal was making plans to finally get rid of Zatow Brauze, one of the worst thorns in his side. A man had appeared who, with some trickery he called magic, was able to easily destroy a daemon nest. It made Corbal furious. *Such a man should not be allowed to exist!* he fumed.

"We must defeat Geo Margilus at any cost," said the bishop, who had returned from his village to report on the matter.

"Yes, I know that well. Destroying those who threaten daemons is our highest calling," Corbal replied.

Corbal and the bishop hatched a plot. Their first opportunity to do away with him came when Margilus and the chairman scheduled a meeting. There was little for Corbal to gain politically from rushing an assassination without first ensuring the fallout was favorable to him, but as he reminded himself, his rise to power in Relis was only a means to an end, and not the end itself. The most favorable outcome would be for both Brauze and Margilus to die, but if only one died, the other could be framed for murder. Even if both survived somehow, the incident was likely to sow discord, which Corbal could take advantage of.

However, not only did the assassination attempt fail, when Corbal rushed to the scene to get a look at Margilus, he was shocked. This man who claimed to be a great magician wore equipment worthy of his title, but he himself did not look any different than an ordinary middle-aged man. Why was this Margilus so gifted when he was not? Corbal was furious.

With his fury fueling him, Corbal sought to trample over everything Margilus held dear. He ordered an attack on the merchant family Margilus was staying with, but that, too, ended in failure.

While Corbal was tearing his hair out over these failures, he received reports that a group of adventurers and city guards were combing Relis for information on daemonists.

In the beginning, Corbal did not let this bother him. It was not the first time he'd had to evade suspicion—he had deftly handled it many times before—but this time was different. His pursuers were more persistent than ever before. To make matters worse, he learned that the Rogues' Guild had taken to the sewers to hunt for daemonists, and he knew they would not return empty-handed.

When he decided to take action, his efforts were foiled again and again, by the adventurers, by the city guards, and by the Rogues' Guild besides.

*Relis City is supposed to be mine to rule and destroy!* he fumed. But now the city was at his heels, and he knew it was only a matter of time before his playground would become his cage.

However, it was far too late before he realized this inevitability. His most able pawns were already taken from him, and the city was overflowing with voices claiming he was a daemonist. His home was under constant surveillance; he could not take one step out of his mansion. Even people not involved in the effort had come to gawk.

As hard as it was to believe, his sources told him all of this was orchestrated by that damnable wizard, Margilus.

"Lord Corbal," said the bishop. "We have no choice. We must begin the final ceremony."

"That damn Margilus!" Corbal fumed. "Who does he think he is, coming here and spoiling everything I've worked for?!"

A crowd of people had gathered outside Corbal's mansion, cheering and jeering. Corbal was backed into a corner now, and prematurely executing the final solution he and the bishop had worked so hard for seemed to be the only option left available to them.

"If only we had five more years to perfect the curse," the bishop opined, "we could have resurrected a true djaevul…"

"How many hundreds of humans' flesh and blood do you think we've sacrificed to it? It should be complete enough to decimate them."

"Yes… Let us hope so," said the bishop, gazing longingly at the daemon skull, where it sat on an altar—it had grown to five times the size it had been when Corbal first saw it.

The bishop knelt before the altar and spoke unholy words to the skull. In response, the skull began to shake. A yellow light glimmered in its eye sockets, growing stronger with every passing second.

At that moment, the door to the room flew open. A messenger relayed to Corbal that Geo Margilus was approaching, a contingent of city guards and a party of adventurers close behind.

Knave Corbal was not difficult to find. He had not left his home, a stately mansion in an upper-class residential district overlooking the city, for days—at least not according to the adventurers' surveillance.

By the time my presence was requested, teams of adventurers, city guards, and rogues had already surrounded Corbal's mansion.

I left Reyha with the city guards and Sedam's party accompanied me to the mansion.

Like the estates of other noblemen and wealthy merchants, Corbal's mansion was surrounded by a high wall. The firmly shuttered gate was adorned with a crest displaying a sword and sail—the same one Reyha had described in her testimony. There was no sign or sound of anyone from beyond the gate—it almost seemed abandoned. In contrast, the square in front of the mansion was full of people.

"I never would have thought Lord Corbal would be in league with daemons..."

"But it does make sense, doesn't it? I don't know how we never questioned it before."

"Do you think my wife's passing had something to do with him...?"

In addition to the adventurers and guards I'd hired, many ordinary people had come to witness the confrontation.

*The fact that Corbal has not shown himself, despite the commotion on his doorstep,* I thought, *either means he has given up, he has a secret passage he is using to escape, or...he may be preparing for a final stand. My intuition tells me it's the last one... At least, that's what the villain in a fantasy setting would do. If this were a TTRPG, I could guarantee it.*

"Lord Wizard! Whenever you are ready, give the order and we'll storm the gate."

Seven city guards in full armor formed a line in front of me. Each wore full plate armor and was equipped with a pavise, flail, and crossbow.

Before we'd set out, I'd asked the captain of the guard to provide me with an elite unit of city guards to accompany me (although, ostensibly, *I* was accompanying *them*). As far as I could tell, they seemed fairly strong—at least compared to the Calbanera Knights.

"I am sorry for dragging you along with me when you've already done so much," I said, turning to Sedam.

"Considering how much you have paid us up front, don't mention it," Sedam replied with a valiant grin.

Counting the seven guards, the six members of Sedam's party, and me, our unit was fourteen people strong, not to mention the other groups positioned around the mansion to prevent anyone from escaping. *All in all, it is a rather large group for the task*, I thought, *but I would rather be over-prepared.*

"On a more serious note…" Sedam said, "If Corbal does not come willingly, I would not underestimate him."

"What makes you say that?" I asked.

"Corbal will have heard the rumors about you. Whatever his plan is, you can bet he will have methods for dealing with sorcerers."

"What kind of methods do you think he'll use?" I was a bit confused. *What does sorcery have anything to do with me, anyway?*

"The most common method to disable a sorcerer is *Sympha Myude*," Clara responded, visibly irritated. "Corbal is rumored to have dabbled in sorcery."

"*Sympha…* What?"

"It is an incantation that erases sound in a given area. Won't that cause some problems for you?"

*So, it's like* D&B's Silence *spell,* I thought.

"Yes...that would be a problem."

"I thought so," said Clara. "Other measures include using light or darkness incantations to obstruct a sorcerer's vision, and a sorcerer's mana can be drained by use of materia or certain monsters as well."

*I shouldn't be surprised,* I thought. *As powerful as sorcery is, it's no wonder that people would research ways to counteract it... This could pose a problem. It just goes to show that even a Level 36 magic user can't handle everything alone.*

"If that sound-cancelling incantation is used on us, what do we do?" I asked.

"The best course of action is to move out of the affected area. Assuming Corbal's sorcery is on par with a novice, he shouldn't be able to affect a large area. One option for a group with multiple sorcerers is to spread them out so that both cannot be affected at once."

*So, even if one person is silenced, the other can still perform incantations or cast spells...*

"In that case, Clara, can you and Torrad stay some distance away from me?" I asked.

"Why don't we just split into two groups, my party as one group, and you and the guards as another?" Sedam suggested.

"That sounds like a plan," Clara agreed.

*Even if we split up, we'll probably end up in the same place in the end,* I thought, but it wasn't a bad plan overall.

"With all the people gawking... I mean—with all of the

witnesses, I think it best that you announce your entrance before we break down the door," Clara said.

"Ugh... Yeah, I probably should..."

I knew I *should* take Clara's advice, but I really wished I could avoid it.

The square in front of Corbal's mansion was crowded with Relis citizens from all walks of life. Most had probably come to see the spectacle of me exacting revenge on Knave Corbal. Perhaps I had been a little too flagrant in the way I'd directed the investigation over the past few days; everyone in town seemed to know Corbal was a suspected daemonist. It did not help that the nature of Corbal's alleged crimes was so extreme. The first rumors begat secondary rumors, which begat tertiary rumors, and on it went.

It was not only the onlookers who were curious—the city guards and adventurers, too, looked to me with anticipation, as if to say, "What will the great magician, destroyer of daemons' nests, do here?"

"Before that, I want to say something to you two first," I said quietly.

"What is it?" Sedam asked.

I turned to Sedam and Clara, my two young friends whom I had relied on ever since I arrived in Sedia, and declared:

"I'm no hero. I'm just an ordinary human being. Despite that, I've decided to fight to protect everyone from daemons."

Both Clara and Sedam froze.

I knew what I said sounded like a line out of a terrible melodrama, and it was incredibly embarrassing to say, but I did not regret it. Instead of waiting to see whether they would laugh or just act exasperated, I quickly turned to the crowd.

"Beloved people of Relis! I am the wizard and magic user Geo Margilus." I spoke in a loud voice, addressing the populace as cordially as I could. The crowd fell quiet. *Compared to what I said before*, I thought, *this is a piece of cake.*

"I apologize for making such a scene. As you all probably well know. I am here to accompany the city guard in its attempt to seek an audience with Baron Corbal, whom we have reason to believe is a daemonist."

"It *is* true!"

"Do you think he's going to get mad and cast meteors down on us?!"

"It's the baron's fault for being so aggressive... Now he's really gone and done it..."

When I said the word "daemonist," you could see the shiver sweep through the crowd. Every face was stricken with fear—and I knew a significant portion of that fear was directed at me. It reminded me of what had happened in Yulei, and I couldn't help but feel a little depressed.

"Do not be afraid! As of now, Baron Corbal is merely *suspected* of being a daemonist. Once we have a proper word with him, it may turn out that we are mistaken. However, if Baron Corbal really *is* a daemonist..."

I had to urge myself to continue and power on through. As I paused, the crowd gulped, waiting on my next word.

"...I can promise you that we will capture him and protect you all, for I am the wizard Geo Margilus, enemy of daemons and all who align themselves with them! Uhh... Death to all daemons!"

*I almost had it!* I thought, as I had begun to get the hang of these speeches. *If I had not stumbled over the end, the delivery would have been perfect.*

"Lord Margilus!"

"We're counting on you!"

The first who responded, in shouts and cheers, were the city guards and adventurers.

"Yeah!"

"Great magician!"

"Our hero!"

"Please protect my children from the daemons!"

After the first few shouts, the rest spread like wildfire. Soon everyone was cheering. Even though I was the one that had spurred the crowd on, I still felt uncomfortable about the attention.

"You're starting to get the hang of this, Lord Magic User," said Sedam.

"Yeah! That's the spirit!" said Clara.

"Uh... Thanks."

I felt like a dimwitted child being over-enthusiastically praised by his parents—but I would be lying if I said it didn't make me feel better. *I'll have to ask them about the other thing I said later on*, I thought.

"He's coming."

Fijika's calm voice was like a bucket of ice water thrown on my face. *I'm getting flashbacks*, I thought, feeling an ominous sense of déjà vu as I looked in the direction she was pointing.

The gate, which until that moment had been firmly shut, slowly began to open.

"I-It's him!"

"It's the baron!"

"The daemonist!"

The crowd assembled in the square erupted with shouts and cries. However, to my surprise, only a few people panicked or ran. That may have been because of the presence of so many guards and adventurers (as well as me, as much as I hate to admit it) acting as an emotional safety valve. Even with that safeguard, the crowd still took a few steps back, all focused on me and the gate.

"I wasn't expecting him to come out and meet us," I said, nodding as Sedam led his party away to put distance between us, just as we had planned.

"Into formation, everyone!" shouted the leader of my guard unit, upon which all seven guards raised their shields to form a defensive line in front of me.

Although it felt a little cowardly to stand in the back, behind the line of guards, I focused my attention on whoever or whatever would come out of that gate.

"It's the baron..."

"Why is he in such a strange outfit?"

"I'm scared..."

The crowd murmured as seven shadowy figures emerged from the gate.

Of the seven, five were muscular strongmen who wore black cloth masks. They'd covered their faces completely, save for the small slits of their eyes. All of them brandished large, unsheathed swords. I suspected the man who stood in front of them, wearing a grotesque cloak decorated with skin and bones, was Corbal. Although he was probably the same age as me, he looked much older, thin as he was. Deep rings sank around his eyes. The final man was partially hidden behind the others, but he wore black robes and had a bald head.

"Welcome to my mansion, wizard Margilus and citizens of Relis!" The baron's voice carried easily, much louder and clearer than mine.

I saw the guards in front of me shiver—I was sure I did the same. Although we had never met before, Corbal looked straight at me when he spoke.

"It's nearly time for supper! I do hope they're paying you overtime," Corbal scoffed. "What business have you with Knave Corbal?"

Despite Corbal's menacing look, sunken eyes, and oddly powerful voice, there was something enticing in his tone. *So, this is what a daemonist is like*, I thought.

I saw something golden flash out of the corner of my eye. It was Clara. She was gesturing at me from about ten meters away, where Sedam's party was. I interpreted her gesture as, "Don't just stand there and take it! Say something back!"

"Lord Corbal! It is a privilege to meet you. I am indeed Geo Margilus."

"Is this the part where I say that I hope we shall get along swimmingly?" replied Corbal, his words dripping with sarcasm.

"Let us cut to the chase. Baron Corbal, we have reason to believe that you are engaged in daemon worship, and that you orchestrated an assassination attempt targeting the city council chairman and me. What say you?"

For what it was worth, I'd already received the go-ahead from the chairman and captain of the guard to detain Corbal even if he denied our allegations—but I no longer expected him to, not after he came out in that outfit and entourage. *Then what's his aim?* I wondered.

"Well done. Well done. You are correct! I am a daemonist! Now, mage, disrupter of our long-awaited third brood event, I have only one thing to say to you. Die!"

"Eh?!" I almost choked on air.

*Die.*

It was obviously not the first time I had heard the word uttered as a command, and it was not the even first time someone had told *me* to die, but it was the first time I had ever witnessed someone *mean it*. The will behind the word's malice was unlike the inorganic blaze of a daemon's hatred. No, this patently human hate was closer, more intimate, more unsettling. I felt my heart stop, and then race. I shuddered.

"I... I refuse!"

As I clutched at my heart, I forced myself to respond. My confidence was an empty bluff, and I knew it, but I chose to wear this mask. A great and powerful magic user could not falter before mere words.

"Ready!" shouted the leader of my unit, interpreting my words as an okay to attack. "Fire!"

Three of the armored guards circled behind the other four and shot their crossbows. In that time, Sedam loosed two arrows of his own.

"Kill them! Kill them! Kill them!" Corbal roared. "Kill them so they cannot speak! So they cannot see! So they can never mock me again!"

"Arrghh!" The masked men roared as the arrows met their mark.

One took two arrows to the face and fell, but the others charged despite their wounds. Two rushed toward me and the other two rushed toward Sedam's party.

"Shields up!"

At the leader's command, three of the guards raised their shields. The two masked men swung their swords, but the defensive line held.

"Take this, you daemonists!"

The three guards in the back discarded their crossbows and drew swords from their sides, stabbing through the gap between the shields. Their teamwork was excellent.

The two masked men spewed blood from their wounds, but continued to swing their swords, even as they screamed. Out of the corner of my eye I saw that the two attacking Sedam's group behaved similarly.

*Something's not right*, I thought. *I expected more.*

My suspicion did not stem from real battle experience, but from experience playing games and reading fantasy novels—it was hard to explain, but something just felt *off*. In my unease, I turned my gaze to Corbal and his bald companion. Both remained at the gate.

"Djaevul!" the bald man shrieked.

The bald man had an eerie design painted on the front of his black robe, and his bald head and hairless face made him look almost reptilian. This reptilian man raised both of his arms and screamed...before thrusting a knife into his own neck. Only then did I realize the man's eyes glowed the color of sullied gold.

At first, I did not know how to react. I was dumbfounded.

Then, with a cry that sounded like air being let of a balloon, the reptilian man fell forward in a shower of blood. Corbal stood by, unmoved.

Bam! Next came a sound like an explosion.

I turned toward the sound. It came from the square. A section of the pavement had been sent flying. Out of the hole that formed below (later I learned it was an entrance to the sewers) there extended a long, thick, black *thing*.

It looked like the leg of a giant crustacean. When I looked closer, the leg seemed to be formed out of bones.

"Kyu-gree! Kyu-gree!" A metallic screech erupted from the ground. I could not see exactly where it was coming from.

Some in the crowd began to scream.

"It's a monster!"

"A daemon!"

After about three or four meters of leg extended out of the hole, a daemonic skull appeared, golden light shining from its eye sockets. The crowd was immediately overcome with panic, and both the guards and adventurers shouted as they tried to evacuate the people in the square.

*Did the man commit suicide in order to resurrect that thing?* I thought. *He called it a djaevul... like a daemonic devil...or daemonic god?* It looked like a cross between a giant shrimp and contorted crustacean blown up to the size of a city bus.

By measure of its unnaturalness and grotesquerie, the djaevul rivaled both the legion horde and the daemons' nest. Made of countless bones, it squirmed all eight legs as it tried to rise to the surface. I was surprised by how calm I was. Although, *That may be only because I'm so frightened I cannot even register my own fear,* I thought.

"*Falga Wilm*!" Clara's voice cut like a strong wind through the rotten air of the square, followed by her whip of fire, which shot out from the tip of her staff and tangled itself around the djaevul.

"Greee!" The daemon skull rattled and shrieked from its position on the back of the creature.

Djirk, Ted, and Torrad, the advance guard of Sedam's party, were the first to rush toward the djaevul, and other groups of adventurers and guards in the square drew their weapons.

"Wh-what should we do, Lord Margilus?!" cried the leader of my guard unit.

"Hold your position and stand by for ten more seconds!"

The black masked men from before had all been defeated. I hesitated for a moment, but decided we should first deal with Corbal, as quickly as possible, and then face the monster.

I was kicking myself for my subconscious decision not to make my move as soon as Corbal showed himself earlier, but I could reflect on my mistake another day.

"Open, Gate of Mag—"

"*Sympha Myude!*"

As I began casting a spell to paralyze Corbal, he yelled out an incantation. I tried to ignore him and continue, but my imagined self evaporated, along with my inner world.

"...?! ...!"

I tried to speak, but I could hear neither myself nor any of the guards. In fact, I could not hear anything at all from my immediate surroundings.

*Silence*! I thought.

I broke into a cold sweat. *What do I do? What was I supposed to do if he cast* Silence*?!* I still could not hear anything, but I saw Clara's fire whip dissipate. Then, I suddenly remembered what she'd said: "The best course of action is to move out of the affected area."

I waved my arms so that the guards would see me, and then pointed toward Corbal and ran.

*How far away is Corbal? About ten meters away?* I ran as fast as I could. Finally, I heard a voice break the silence.

"Kill them! Kill them so they can never mock me again!"

I dug my feet in and stopped. I had made it outside the curtain of *Silence*.

"Charge! Charge!" the leader of my unit shouted.

The guards charged, the leader in front, all of them brandishing their swords and flails.

Corbal was struck down mid-laugh. A splatter of blood flew from his head. The guards moved quickly to hold him down.

Once Corbal was down, I turned my attention back to Sedam's party, which was still fighting the monster...and saw four shadows come at me from above.

Caught off guard, I stumbled.

*These must be the dark elves we were not able to capture*, I thought. *This must be Corbal's final trump card. He kept the assassins near the gate, planning to lure me within range of attack.* The dark elves all held blades, which glimmered with a dull shine.

*Did I cast* Invincibility *on myself today?* I thought. *If I did, is it still in effect?* One of the elves was bound, suddenly, and struggled as she fell to the ground. *That's my invisible demon, but there's still three more.* Their knives and my thoughts both seemed to move in slow motion.

Reflexively, I raised my Staff of Wizardry in an attempt to block the attack, but that did nothing to stop them. Their knives would soon hit their marks—my throat and other vital organs.

"Master!"

I heard a husky feminine voice. A dark-skinned beast of a woman flashed in front of my eyes. Her long arms and legs flashed like lightning, striking the dark elves in the neck or stomach. At least that is what I thought. It all happened so fast I couldn't follow everything with my eyes.

"Urgh?!"

"Guh?!"

"Oof!"

By the time she knelt in front of me, the three others lay sprawled out over the ground.

"Lord Margilus!"

"Are you alright?!"

Some of the guards who had been restraining Corbal noticed that something had happened and came running.

"Master! I went against your orders! Please punish me!"

Finally, I remembered who the lascivious woman in front of me was.

"Now's not the time for that, Reyha!"

"Gyah!"

"Uwaah!"

For the ordinary guards and other adventuring parties, the djaevul was too much to handle. Their bravery was admirable, but a single sweep of the djaevul's giant legs was enough to keep them down on the ground.

Only Sedam's party was able to keep going.

"Gyaree! Gyuree!"

"This thing's ridiculous!" shouted Ted.

"Fall back! Fall back!" yelled Djirk.

If the djaevul were to fully extend its legs, the full spread of the thing would probably be between ten and twenty meters in diameter. It was a nightmare of a creature to fight, but Sedam's party was holding its own. Even so, Sedam's arrows and Fijika's throwing daggers did not appear to be dealing any damage. Even Clara's sorcery seemed to be at its limit.

Djirk, Ted, and Torrad, under Sedam's orders, continued to change their positions on the ground and keep drawing the djaevul's attention. They raised their shields to deflect the djaevul's arms, rolled over the ground, and dodged attacks by a hair's breadth. Their tactic was working, but just watching made me break into a sweat.

"Lord Margilus! What should we do?!" cried the leader of my guard unit.

"Master. If you give the order, I will sacrifice myself to take down that monster." That was Reyha—I ignored her.

"Guard me, and make sure nothing interrupts me this time," I said.

I had already decided which spell to cast.

"Open, Gate of Magic. Reveal your form to me."

I was relieved to hear my voice follow through. *I've made it this far*, I thought. *No matter what happens to me now, I'll make sure I finish the spell.*

"Gyuree!"

"Ugh!"

"Djirk!"

The daemon skull on the back of the djaevul opened its mouth and shot out what looked like thorns. One of the thorns, about the size of a short sword, cut into Djirk's thigh. Ted raised his shield to protect Djirk, but one of the djaevul's legs struck him to the ground.

My imagined self traipsed through the Gate of Magic and down the spiral staircase to the sixth level.

"As a consequence of this spell, one target will be obliterated."

The spellbook on the bookrest transformed into one black and one white ten-sided die, both of which came to rest in my hand. *If I fumble this*, I thought, *someone may die before I can cast another spell.*

"Please..." I said, gripping the dice, and rolled.

The dice clattered across the surface of the bookrest, and the white die, which represented the tens' digit landed on 0. If the black die also landed on 0, the roll would be 100...a fumble.

The black die came to a stop.

"That was damn close, but it's a 9! *Destruction!*" My imagined and actual selves cried out in unison, and the spell was complete.

A small white ball of light formed at the tip of my staff. I glared and thrust it forward—the light shot off at the rampaging djaevul. It vanished from sight, absorbed within the monster's form.

I took a deep breath.

"Gye?!"

The giant, eight-legged creature began to break apart from the inside out.

There was no explosion, no blast of heat. It was as if someone had smashed an ice statue with a giant hammer. First, the djaevul shattered into dozens of fragments, which then split into thousands of smaller pieces, all of them ultimately dissolving away into nothingness.

"Wh-what happened?"

"The monster just..."

"I-It turned to dust..."

Everyone in the square: the people who had been fleeing, the guards, and even Sedam's party; they all stood silent, dumbfounded.

In the silent square, I clung to my Staff of Wizardry, completely worn out.

"That was exhausting..."

••✝••

By his own admission, Corbal was arrested for the crime of being a daemonist. In the aftermath of the investigation, the reptilian man and that strange creature were only partially identified. I pitied the victims of all of their evil actions, but perhaps we were able to offer some comfort to their families in that we were able to recover some of their remains. Corbal, meanwhile, continued to face a stern interrogation into the nature of his deeds.

The four dark elf assassins were all younger members of Reyha's tribe. As I suspected, they had golden eyes and vacant expressions upon their capture, so I used *Curse Break* to return them to normal. Unfortunately, like Reyha, they all designated me as their master, and pledged eternal fealty to me.

Reyha had them convinced that I was their Olry, and nothing I could say would change their minds. Despite the circumstances, I remained committed to having them all face trial before the city.

In the meantime, awaiting the dark elves' trial date, I met with the Sorcerers' Guild and Copiers' Guild to procure the materials I would need to make a copy of my spellbook. I also went about hiring staff for Castle Getaeus, so the days went by quickly. While I busied myself, dozens of other nobles and merchants were arrested in connection with Corbal's crimes. Furthermore, it came to light that an entire village had been converted to daemonism, shocking everyone involved in the investigation.

As more and more details were uncovered, it became clear that the dark elves had been used broadly and often by the daemonists to do their dirty work. In other words, as the date of the trial approached, more and more evidence mounted against Reyha and the other elves, which made my heart feel heavy.

However, when the day of the trial finally came, I learned that Sedia's justice system was completely different from what I had expected.

The trial was held in the large square in front of the city hall.

I sat facing the judge, and jurors sat on either side of him. The captain of the guard, serving as the public prosecutor, stood to my right. The five dark elf defendants and their lawyers sat to my left.

That much was ordinary, but it didn't feel at all like I was attending a trial—there was none of the grave or solemn atmosphere you would normally associate with any kind of legal proceedings. It felt more like a festival. The square was filled with spectators, and the crowd flowed over and into the streets and canals.

My role in the trial was that of a guarantor. Although the result of the trial was determined by a majority vote among the jury, I soon learned that the guarantor held the largest sway over the jury's decision—and it was less of a matter of what the guarantor said and more who he or she was. If the guarantor for a defendant was someone well respected and trusted by people (and by extension those who would make up the jury in a trial), it was understood that the defendant was also someone worthy of their trust. It was hard to call such a system fair, but for a world without scientific tests for incontrovertible evidence or universal human rights...it could be worse. As a system that utilized existing relationships of trust, it did make some sense as a method of keeping the peace and minimizing disputes.

In the end, as I was the most famous and well-trusted person in Relis at the time (at least, according to my sources), there was no question that both Reyha and the other dark elves would get off scot-free.

Neither the chairman nor the captain of the guard had any interest in holding on to a group as problematic as those five dark elves. From their perspective, the task of detaining them would be more trouble than it was worth; on the flip side, they could frame the lenience of the trial as a way of doing me a favor.

"And so," I said, wrapping up the statement I was given to read, "these dark elves were under the control of a wicked sorcery of the daemonists. I dispelled this sorcery, and guarantee that these elves will be good citizens."

"That's right!"

"Let's give it up for Margilus! Our savior Margilus!"

Every time I spoke, cheers erupted from the spectators. Fighting daemonists and a djaevul in front of a large crowd of people, it turns out, had a huge positive effect on my popularity. Although the turn of events was unexpected, *If this is the way Sedia's laws work*, I thought, *then there is not much else I can do but accept it.*

Once my part to play in the script was over, the judge cried out: "I will now announce the verdict! Due to a unanimous consensus from the jury, all of the defendants are acquitted of all charges!"

"Master!"

As soon as the judge declared the dark elves' innocence, they shed their handcuffs as if they were loose gloves and knelt before me. My original plan to give the elves time to rethink their decision to serve me had been swept away like a cloud on a windy day...

"We cannot thank you enough for advocating for us," said Reyha.

"From now on, like sister Reyhanalka, we, too, will serve you as your Si," said one of the other four.

There was much fanfare, with cheering spectators accompanied by the sounding of trumpets and throwing of confetti, but I was troubled. *What am I going to do now?* I thought, breaking out in a cold sweat. I could not deny that I liked the *idea* of several beautiful women waiting on me hand and foot, but in a practical sense, how was I going to manage the lives of five other people? *Forty-two years of single life has not prepared me to take on five dependents...*

*Well, what's done is done*, I thought. It wasn't as if I could just toss them to the winds. For the time being, at least, I would have to accept that our fates would be intertwined.

After all, I was sure there were bereaved families of the dark elves' victims still in Relis. Now that an official atonement for the elves' actions was out of the question, I had no choice but to take charge of their penance by using them to help protect the city. *If possible*, I thought, *I should find a way to pay reparations to the bereaved families through the city council. That way, I might be able to quell any soured feelings that remain over the result of this trial...*

However, the day was not over yet. Soon after the trial ended, Chairman Brauze came to me and announced I would be attending a parade in celebration of the daemonists' defeat.

"Lord Margilus!"

"Our hero, the great magician!"

"All hail Lord Margilus! Savior of Relis!"

"Sedam!"

"Clara!"

I was seated on a large riverboat decorated with dazzling flowers, flags, and lanterns. It felt like I was riding in the back of an open convertible decked out for a street parade. Both shores of the canal and the intermittent bridges were packed with spectators, who threw flowers and confetti as they cheered and drank wine.

Sedam and the four other members of his standard party stood at the front of the ship. As they were some of the finest adventurers in Relis, they, too, were popular. Their fans called out to them by name.

Reyha sat to my right and Clara to my left. I suggested to Brauze that Clara should be at the front with the rest of Sedam's party, but his response was that I would look better flanked by two beautiful women, and he would not be convinced otherwise. The other four dark elves sat in a circle around us, matter-of-factly.

At first, Clara made a fuss about sitting beside me, but as soon as we were on the ship, she was all smiles and waved to the people with the elegance you would expect from a nobleman's daughter. On the other hand, Reyha's demeanor could be accurately described as enthusiastically on high alert. Her lavender eyes bespoke a stern determination to not let anyone who might threaten me come near, but she also looked proud at the fact that her master was the subject of so much praise.

I, of course, had a strained expression on my face, because I was very uncomfortable.

"I'm really not cut out for this..." I grumbled.

"Considering what you want to do, things like this are necessary, you know?" Clara spoke with a rare tinge of concern.

"Really? This?"

"Most of the people of this city have the fear of daemons so ingrained in them that they are afraid to sleep at night. Think of this as a way of helping them sleep soundly. That *is* one part of protecting everyone from daemons, am I wrong?"

The tone of Clara's voice was gentle, but it had a backbone of steel. She was not about to let me forget that if I was going to wear this great magic user mask, keeping up the façade was an important part of the job.

"Mister Geo!"

It was Mora. I was surprised by how clearly I could pick her voice out of the crowd. When I turned toward it, I saw her leaning over the rail on a bridge, waving frantically at me.

As I waved back at Mora, I thought back to when I'd declared to myself that I would protect everyone.

*I know it is foolish to take pride in a power you did not work to obtain yourself...but does that make it wrong to use whatever powers I have, earned or not, to reach for a higher purpose?*

Though I did not have an answer to that question, I decided I would use my power.

*If I had come to this world back when I was younger and admired the idea of being a hero and going on adventures*, I thought, *I would not hesitate like this. Twenty years since that time, my life has been nothing but hesitation.*

"If you understand," said Clara, falling back on her usual high-and-mighty mode of speech as she read my facial expression, "you had better puff out your chest and show some pride. Everyone is expecting that out of you.

"Including me," she added, with a hint of embarrassment at the end.

"Well, this is a role I chose to play," I conceded. "As you say, living up to others' expectations is part of the job."

*As full of hesitation I am, with a little help from my friends, this forty-two-year-old man has made it this far,* I thought, *but if it were any easier, I might not have gained as much as I have from the journey. I expect there are some answers in this world that you cannot find without questioning yourself every step of the way.*

*In that case* I thought. *I have no choice but to continue on ahead, however hesitantly, no matter what this journey throws at me.*

I stood and raised my Staff of Wizardry high into the air.

# Dungeons & Braves

## Character
## Sheet

Geo Margilus

# Dungeons & ~~Waves~~ Character Sheet

**Player Name**

**Game Master Name**

Yagi-chan

**Character Name**

Geo Margilus

**Character Appearance**

**Class**

Magic User

| **Level** | **Hit Points** |
|---|---|
| 36 | 66 |

## Ability Scores

| Score | Ability | Bonus |
|---|---|---|
| 10 | **STR** (STRENGTH) | BONUS |
| 18 | **INT** (INTELLIGENCE) | +3 BONUS |
| 13 | **WIS** (WISDOM) | +1 BONUS |
| 10 | **DEX** (DEXTERITY) | BONUS |
| 16 | **CON** (CONSTITUTION) | +2 BONUS |
| 13 | **CH** (CHARISMA) | +1 BONUS |

## Resistance

| | |
|---|---|
| S | Poison |
| S | Light |
| S | Paralysis |
| AA | Area Attack |
| S+ | Magic Curse |

## Special Abilities

*Magic Item Creation: Expert*
*Potion Creation: Advanced*
*Construct Monster: Expert*
*Weapon Proficiency (Quarterstaff): Intermediate*

## Equipment

### ORDINARY EQUIPMENT
- canteen
- wine flask
- rations
- utensil set
- sewing set
- chalk
- hand mirror
- portable pen and ink set
- ten pieces of parchment
- flint bag
- hand cloth
- change of clothes
- blanket
- dagger
- three-meter pole

### MAGIC ITEMS
- Staff of Wizardry
- Robe +5
- Protection Ring +5
- Traveling Boots
- Infinity Bag
- Potion Server
- Quarterstaff +5 (light)
- Staff of Undead Control
- Dagger +3 (returning)
- Whip +4
- Cancel Rod
- Medical Ring
- Water Walking Ring
- Resist Fire Ring
- Djinni Ring
- Curse Command Ring
- Telescope Lens
- Protection Circle Chalk
- Pass Wall Glove
- Elven Cape
- Elven Boots
- Enemy Detection Wand
- Dinner Cloth
- ESP Medal
- Anti-ESP Medal
- Mapping Scroll
- Alchemy Tool Set
- Arcane Smithing Tool Set
- Arcane Quill
- Soldiers of Bronze
- Ultimate Coffin
- Skull of Nameless God

## Magic

### RANK 1 SPELLS: 9 CHARGES/DAY
- Charm
- Analyze
- Sprite Porter
- Mana Bolt
- Protection
- Translate
- Spell Copy
- Mana Shield
- Sleep
- Light

### RANK 2 SPELLS: 9 CHARGES /DAY
- Permanent Light
- Detect Enemy
- Detect Invisible
- Telepathy
- Invisibility
- Find Object
- Illusion
- Spider Web
- Wizard Key
- Mirage
- Arcane Postcard

### RANK 3 SPELLS: 9 CHARGES/DAY
- Dispel Magic
- Fireball
- Fly
- Hold
- Infrared Vision
- Lightning
- Protection Circle
- Protection from Arrows
- Water Breathing
- Phantom Horse
- Arcane Rope

### RANK 4 SPELLS: 9 CHARGES/DAY
- Greater Protection Circle
- Control Monster
- Confusion
- Short Warp
- Control Plant
- Illusory Terrain
- Ice Storm
- Ice Wall
- Concealment
- Transform Other
- Wall of Fire
- Curse Break
- Mana Sight

### RANK 5 SPELLS: 9 CHARGES/DAY
- Mana Strike
- Control Undead
- Evil Cloud
- Elemental Control
- Greater Hold

### RANK 6 SPELLS: 9 CHARGES/DAY (continued)
- Mana Pot
- Permeation
- Telekinesis
- Teleport
- Wall of Stone
- Physical Boost
- Enchant

### RANK 6 SPELLS: 9 CHARGES/DAY
- Anti-Magic Barrier
- Death Gaze
- Destruction
- Curse
- Invisible Demon
- Structural Renovation
- Project Illusion
- Petrify
- Wall of Iron
- Weather Control
- Forced March

### RANK 7 SPELLS: 9 CHARGES/DAY
- Create Ogre Platoon
- Sense of the Adept
- Create Monster
- Psychometry
- Dimension Door
- Greater Invisibility
- Mind Crush
- Control Gravity
- Change Statue
- Apport
- Arcane Sword
- Transport

### RANK 8 SPELLS: 9 CHARGES/DAY
- Giga Mana Strike
- Perfect Resistance
- Cloning
- Blast Cloud
- Wall of Force
- Mind Control
- Mind Wall
- Infinity
- Greater Transform Other
- Six Runes
- Create Monster: Special
- Word of Blind

### RANK 9 SPELLS: 9 CHARGES/DAY
- Move Outer Plane
- Emergency
- Create Monster: Any
- Word of Death
- Dimensional Gate
- Complete Recovery
- Invincibility
- Chaotic Wall
- Meteor
- Shapeshift
- Time Stop

## Wallet

| | |
|---|---|
| P P : | 57020 |
| G P : | 3055238 |
| E P : | |
| S P : | 25800 |
| C P : | 580 |
| **Total :** | A lot!! |

## Jewels

15000GPx5

5000GPx58

2000GPx135

1000GPx523

## Experience Points

MAX!!

### Bonus
+10

### EXP to Next Level
Max Level!

# Afterword

**H**ELLO, MY NAME IS Mikawa Souhei. It is a pleasure to meet you.

Thank you for your interest in this book.

*Magic User: Reborn in Another World as a Max Level Wizard* is a story that, in its original form, was uploaded to the novel-sharing site, *Shousetsuka ni Narou*. In English, that'd be something like "Let's Be Novelists." I started posting the story as a serialized web novel on January 28th, 2017. The original title was *Record of a Hesitant Man in His Forties Founding a Nation*. The book you hold in your hands now is an updated and rewritten version of that story.

Readers who are familiar with tabletop RPG tropes will quickly get all the references to real games, I suspect. However, there are many ways in which I have deviated from well-known, official TTRPGs, including the usage of some spells and their effects, in service of the plot. I hope you'll be understanding.

While I think the premise of the novel is summed up in its subtitle, I wrote this story as an answer to the question, "What if an older guy who loved playing tabletop RPGs got transported to another world?"

There are scenes where the main character, a maxed-out magic user, spectacularly defeats his enemies with little effort, and scenes where he is pampered by beautiful women and girls. So, if what you are after is a transported-to-another-world fantasy with cheats and harem mechanics, I believe this story checks all of the important boxes.

On the other hand, it is also the story of an ordinary older guy. Although he is overpowered, he has lots of weak points, and even though he's surrounded by beautiful women, he can't find it in him to take advantage of the situation. He spends a lot of time fretting over how to make his next move. So, in that sense, this is the story of an ordinary old man making tough choices as he tries to start a new life in another world.

If some readers are able to insert themselves into the story and wonder how they might handle the challenges Geo Margilus faces, I think that's great. For that purpose, I've detailed his abilities and circumstances as much as possible.

To be honest, when I first started writing this story and uploading it to *Shousetsuka ni Narou*, I was worried whether there were many people that would want to read a story like this.

Fortunately, enough people supported the web version that publishers took notice, and I was able to have this version of the story published. Of course, I plan to continue updating the web version, so I would be happy if you continued to support me online as well.

There are many people I would like to thank for their support.

First, I would like to thank my first editor, K, for helping me navigate my way through the process, even when I didn't know my right from my left, and my second editor, F. I would also like to thank the illustrator Ryota-H, for creating images that went far above and beyond what I could describe in my writing. Thanks to you all, I believe we were able to make this version of the story a success.

Next, I want to thank my old gaming friends J and Y. The nerdy things I discussed with you over yakiniku became the soul of this book.

Thank you again, everyone who supported me back when this story was in its beginnings as a web novel. It is thanks to your support that I was and am able to continue writing.

Finally, I want to thank you, the reader, for purchasing this book. Thank you very much.

If you thought this story was interesting, nothing could bring me greater joy.